PERSIAN SUNS

A Reflective Novel ✵

✵ The author's rendition of a Reflective Novel is provided on page iii after the author's note.

Author's Books

(As at 2021)*

Non-fiction

The Nature of Love and Relationships **2011, 2016**
Doubts and Decisions for Living:
  Volume I: The Foundation of Human Thoughts **2014**
  Volume II: The Sanctity of Human Spirit **2014**
  Volume III: The Structure of Human Life **2014**
Relationship Facts, Trends, and Choices **2016**
The Mysteries of Life, Love, and Happiness **2016**
Marriage and Divorce Hardships **2016**
Gender Qualities, Quirks, and Quarrels **2016**
Relationship Needs, Framework, and Models **2016**
Being Better Beings **2020**

Fiction

Persian Moons **2007, 2016**
Midnight Gate-opener **2011, 2016**
My Lousy Life Stories **2014**
Persian Suns **2021**

---

* 12 older books are enhanced editions and printed in 2020. They were resubmitted to the Library and Archives Canada Cataloguing as well. If a book's 'print date' on the copyright page is older, the newest version is available at Amazon and bookstores.

A Reflective Novel

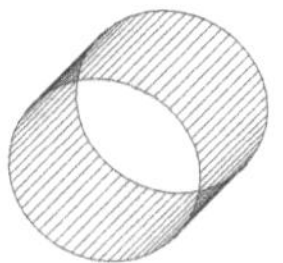

This is a book of fiction. Names, characters, and events are the creation of the author. Any resemblance to persons, living or dead, business establishments, events or places is totally coincidental. Names of the streets, cities, places and shops, when real, are used in line with the general public use of these entities.

Omidi, Tom, 1945—, author
Persian Suns—A Reflective Novel

ISBN: 978-1-988351-15-5 (paperback)

I. Title.

Published by Eros Books,
Vancouver, British Columbia

erosbooks2020@gmail.com

Front Cover: Designed by Tom Omidi

Printed in 2021

Dedicated to fancy Farida,
My missing mysterious beloved.

Table of Contents

Author's Note

Persian Suns is a sequel to *Persian Moons*, though it also stands alone with ample dialogues and reflections to offer all the crucial background smoothly. Then again, reading both novels provides a deeper experience and perspective of its own, even if read in reverse order. Starting with *Persian Suns* would be a more brain teasing adventure, however, in spite of fewer surprises.

Like its forebear, *Persian Suns* is a suspense love saga, while the realism and search for the meanings of life and love in the 21st century are stressed for this work of fiction as well. The romantic revelation at the end of *Persian Moons* develops into a complex conundrum and causes a variety of deep conflicts in *Persian Suns* when powerful people set out to avenge various transgressions and treasons.

While these two novels reveal the depth of the protagonist's dramatic encounters and efforts to find a smart companion for sharing life's challenges together, *Persian Suns* stresses on the ordeals of three heartbroken friends who are the main characters in both novels. In fact, they take turns to express their endeavours and dilemmas in their peculiar ways, as well as their perspectives and preferences for handling the main plots driving the hearts of both novels. They try to bolster their identities and self-images in line with their eccentricities and outlooks, while their reflections augment the story's intricate theme. All along, their precarious fates mingle and stir odd commotions and frictions among them. Still, their friendship gets stronger.

Although intriguing suspense and adventures carry the readers in both novels, my main intention for writing fiction has been to expose people's thoughts and psyches. Especially, in this *reflective novel*, the characters' psychological and philosophical viewpoints demonstrate people's mental efforts and sufferings to cope with their odd dilemmas and duties. Observing humans' varied modes of seeing, thinking, and discussing same topics or events leading to major misgivings and distress is interesting and educational as well. Sadly, our hasty judgments and choices often hinder our communications and cause conflicts and pains in relationships. Accordingly, family relationships have been stressed in these two novels, too, as a general theme for all my writings. Meanwhile, a prolonged pursuit and analyses of these three characters' volatile destinies, as intended in this sequel, add to our understanding of life all by itself. People's coping stories never end, so I may even consider writing the sequel to *Persian Suns* as well, sometime in the future, most likely, if at least a million readers request it!

Yet, *Persian Suns* is not about any of these stories per se, but rather hundreds of precious moments that engage the three main characters in surreal circumstances. Actually, this novel's finest goal has been to display some very special instances of existence carrying one's spirit beyond its common domain. Many people have encountered similar sentiments or have the capacity and need nowadays to relate to these humanly experiences, such as fatherly emotions during dire situations.

Actually, I do not mind divulging my own soppy sentiments when two characters exchange their feelings or thoughts and their delicate dialogues stir anguish, like the one in Chapter Four when Darren's dad answers T.J.'s call and imagines his son is dead. Most fathers relate to these sentiments and episodes more every day, while our culture is damaging the youths' spirits and family relationships callously. Taking in such feelings personally, even when only a character in a novel is experiencing them, is deeply precious. I get carried away in those special moments, feel the depth of characters' tension and emotions, and sometimes even shed tears all over the keyboard when typing some of those sad or romantic dialogues. In fact, another purpose of this Author's Note has been to connect with special readers who appreciate the depth of emotions, expressive notions, or basic vulnerabilities many humans feel naturally when experiencing some divine moments in their lives amidst the normal chaos.

Tom Omidi, Ph.D.
Vancouver, BC, 2021

Author's Rendition of a Reflective Novel

The main intention for calling this novel Reflective and offering an explanation has been to give people a better idea about the nature of the book they would be choosing to read. This fiction is a bit unusual due to its special effects noted below, but satiates some readers' taste, while highlighting contentious social issues.

A Reflective novel emphasizes on characters' deep thoughts, reminiscences, and judgments to show their dilemmas, feelings, and motives behind their words and actions. We think, although mostly rubbish, thousand times more than we act or talk usually robotically. So, capturing even a small portion of those thoughts can enhance the depth of a novel substantially if done effectively.

Sometimes, humans find an incentive or urge to explore their quirks and characters in private or share their hang-ups with their confidants. This is a scarce revelation in our daily encounters and contemporary novels. Yet, such reflections in a novel can provide supplementary information to grasp characters' personalities and roles better, while their mental sufferings, aspirations, and urges hidden in their subconscious and unconscious also become vivid. Without taking away the readers' fun and urge for guessing a character's intentions or missing them fully, getting an impression about the convoluted motives and thoughts behind his/her actions and words raises the effects and fun. Furthermore, showing how we sometimes act or speak contrary to what we think and feel reveals humans' true nature, hypocrisies, quirks, communications, conflicts, and many other complex dimensions. Uncovering these deep contradictions between human thoughts and actions are educational and interesting for people and society in general. Learning the art of reflection is also useful for finding ourselves privately when a person strives to explore his/her identity and self in line with his/her evil urges, self-interests, spiritual drive, and principles. We see, evoke, and maybe even abhor the devil we often feel inside us, but usually only hide and pamper it. We hate to ponder, tame, or discuss this forceful essence of human nature.

People's thoughts also reveal the secrets they like to hide from one another at least out of courtesy or diplomacy. Moreover, some of our thoughts are much profounder, funnier, prettier, or scarier than our actions and words, so delving into them more systematically and consciously could be quite enlightening. Most important of all, so much of our thoughts and sentiments are worth our attention for studying and managing our relationships. In particular, we usually misunderstand and misjudge people hastily in positive or negative ways, since we do not know what they are thinking or feeling, and we refuse to spend more time to listen to their viewpoints at least and maybe learn something, too. We let our predispositions establish our views of people based on some basic words and actions that often do not represent their true personalities. Therefore, we stir conflicts inadvertently, since we usually assume we know what and how others think and feel. Yet, we can always judge and relate to people much better if we take on the hassle of learning about life and people patiently and grasping humans' thoughts that often trigger their vile words and actions. Since this is hard and rarely feasible in reality, maybe we could simulate it in some novels artfully for raising the joy of reading. It also helps us sense, and ponder, the intricacy of human nature and needs. A Reflective novel is for achieving these goals along with lots of dialogues. At the same time, we might develop a deeper sense about the phony world and societies we humans have built around our crooked values and wild imaginations.

In this novel, the three main characters narrate the events and share their stories and sentiments openly. Just try to imagine the variety and delicacy of potential literature evolving when main characters reveal their reflections and self-analyses now and then, despite the added self-pity and stress they endure in the process. Different results and effects erupt when these characters question their beings and personalities regularly or get a chance to express their thoughts, often about the same topics. Of course, including the right amount of characters' reflections and feelings without making the novel boring or confusing is tricky and an art.

Prologue
Mahtab or Erica
(January 1989)

"Why are you living, you wrecked man?" Erica's pesky spirit mocked me again as I stepped into my balcony and looked down at the busy street fifteen floors below me with a sigh.

"Really, Reza...! What're you waiting for?"

This niggling voice had baffled me all day with a mix of fear, indecision, and emptiness, but now it felt urgent to either explain or expire myself. Jumping off the balcony seemed easier, though, since justifying my existence had been gruelling after Erica had dumped me two years ago. Not that I have been weaker or more sentimental than any normal lover, but rather she has had this odd effect on men—something similar to a curse perhaps. Darren had been another victim of hers, enduring a horrible fate and feeling miserable all along after Erica divorced him three years ago when she became my lover. Besides her unwavering spell, her memory has besieged my soul during the last three months after she had apparently thrown herself down Darren's balcony, maybe trying to make a point! Then, today, her spirit has been badgering me tenaciously with lots more energy and a fishy sense of urgency. She had vanished for an hour before calling me again abruptly from the street, "Come on, lazy Reza, you can do it."

"I don't know...," I whispered. "Stop teasing me, Erica..."

"It was easy when I did it," she muttered with her wily charm melting the last grains of my sanity to fly right onto her arms.

I smirked at her with anguish, while leaning over the railing, gazing at the view, and gauging her invitation. In fact, it sounded quite tempting to end my revolving doubts about leading such an aimless destiny. Luckily, the sight of those tiny cars roaring and racing one another helped me keep my senses a bit longer.

"Not today...," I yelled back at her, thinking I could always jump tomorrow! "Stop fooling me again, Erica."

"What're you living for, anyway, Reza?" she asked rudely this time, as if tired of my customary disobedience and hesitation. "What're you trying to prove?"

"My sanity!" I shrieked with rage, yet the irony of my wisdom and serious reply to her mockery amid this hallucination tickled me.

"Do you remember our good times together?" she muttered tenderly now. "Don't you wanna be with me again?"

"I do…But…"

"Jump, then… This is your chance now… Just jump..."

"Are you going to love me again?" I asked like an imbecile.

"For eternity," she replied firmly with her enticing low voice.

"Are you sure this time?" I asked, feeling lousy for softening and trusting her after all the torture she had given me.

"Yes, I promise. Will you jump already!" she snapped with her familiar sneering tone again, rekindling perplexing old memories and her obsession to caress or harass me in rotation.

Her moodiness and gift for manipulation now driving even her ghost felt hilarious, while my romantic brain began reminiscing and dreaming. *Does she possibly love me now at last?*

In the end, the chance of ending my daylong indecision on top of kissing Erica after so long felt too soothing to bypass.

"Okay, my darling, here I come... Catch me softly...," I yelled back at her, while holding on to the railing *carefully* to go over it, stand on the ledge, aim precisely, and throw myself right onto her gorgeous, warm bosom.

Sadly, the sound of phone ringing in the living room startled me and I went back inside to answer it after waving to Erica with a bizarre, incoherent gesture.

"Salam, Reza," Mahtab said on the other side of the line with a jubilant voice.

"Salam to you, my darling sister… It's so good to hear from you at last!" I replied edgily, swiftly enraged about her attitude during the last two months, especially her tenacity to ignore my calls and grim messages.

"Now you must believe in me, Reza," she said with a giggle.

"Why?"

"Because Darren is out of the coma... He didn't die, after all," she replied with pride and a cocky tone of triumph.

"Is that right?" I asked with total disbelief and delight.

"Yes, he's alive and healthy, despite all your pessimism about my travel to Vancouver to look after him."

"Well, that's great... Your mission is accomplished, then...," I said. "So you're coming back home soon, I hope?"

"No… But who is stupid now?" Mahtab asked.

"I'm sorry for saying that," I said tensely for my defeat once more, but also a tiny guilt for not believing in her all along. Then again, coping with my sisters' whims and beliefs all those years had been tough for my family and me. Especially, humouring Mahtab's recent mania to save a dying man would have felt crazy even to a child.

"Are mom and Nazi okay?" she asked half-heartedly.

"In general, yes...! But Darren's recovery is amazing and I'm glad for you getting the rewards of your efforts, plus an excuse to tease me more often now," I said with angst.

"I'd never do that if you just trust me," she replied.

"Everything I say is only for your own good and our family's honour according to my logic."

"Surely, our logics work very differently," she replied coolly.

"The main point is that your adventures worry us because we love you."

"Well, you people will never understand my needs, I guess."

"Anyway, thanks for calling at last and giving me this great news even if it was just for rubbing it on my face," I said wittily in a soft tone, hoping to connect with her now that her presumed mission seemed over and she had kindly given me an audience.

Yet, Mahtab did not waste any time smashing my hopes and making me feel ten times gloomier than I had been earlier in the day and pondering the idea of jumping down the balcony. Besides her news about Darren's miraculous recovery, our conversations were disheartening and cause for more concern and stress. In the end, we merely upset each other all over again. More maddening was the new dilemma she had created for me. That is, while her words and attitude had depressed me vastly with fewer reasons for living, leaving her alone to face the mayhem she was starting seemed reckless to my perturbed conscience.

Suddenly death appeared like the easiest excuse to neglect my obligation particularly towards our sick mother who was already mourning the death of her husband and other daughter, Mahroo. I could not do that to my frail, lonely mom who now needed lots of extra energy just to face Mahtab's tenacity and dangerous games in Vancouver. Instead, I had to plan and pray for the possibility of putting some sense into Mahtab's muddled mind. Now, jumping right in the middle of Mahtab's dreadful plans, instead of Erica's inviting arms, felt imperative. Still, letting my tiny hope to save Mahtab and our mother hinder my own urgent decisions about life and joining Erica's tranquil realm felt pathetic as well.

I returned to the balcony and peered down at the street where Erica still looked confused about my last waving gesture, maybe thinking I had asked her to wait a minute for me to put on my formal suicide attire before showing my eternal love! I waved at her sluggishly this time before turning and going back inside rather rudely. Erica yelled at me from out there, "Why are you choosing your sister over me again, Reza? Not again, you weak man! Just jump…"

Her comment about choosing my sister *again* stirred daunting memories of her jealousy over my love for my sisters. I recalled how my desperate scheme to help my other sister, Mahroo, had angered Erica enough to dump me—merely over a painting I had given to Mahroo instead of her. Sadly, now this time, this other sister, Mahtab, had spoiled my chance of embracing Erica again and basking in the relief she had been promising me all day.

With mixed feelings for disappointing Erica again after her daylong efforts to lure me, I pondered the inevitable hostilities in Tehran because of events in Vancouver and my likely role to stop things from getting fully out of control. My resolve to be the less selfish person again and humour this horrible world merely in hopes of helping my family was a weird irony. This was an unfair duty, especially now that I had acknowledged life's vanity after years of reflections. Only half-hour earlier, I was blessed to be happy and free in heaven with Erica, but now I was back again amongst a bunch of loonies in a fiercer new hell Mahtab was reigniting for us all! *Would I ever learn to live or die for myself?*

Then again, Erica's spell still ruling me felt more embarrassing than the mission of living per se! *Gosh, Erica's memories and living are so irreconcilable…!* At least my last minute sanity to ignore her pleas felt like a big victory after trusting her romantic promises so quickly again today. Luckily, my spirit of living was growing fast, so ironically, all thanks to Mahtab's irksome, timely call *perhaps*—like an omen maybe. At the same time, the notion of owing Mahtab a big apology for several reasons was humiliating and painful, although a right thing to do at least for gaining her trust. I had to make up for my earlier attempts to stop her from going to Vancouver merely based on her juvenile hopes of saving Darren—a presumed dying flesh.

Undecided about visiting my mom and explaining the new developments, fleeing my depressing apartment and thoughts felt imperative. In the elevator, the image of my mom's anguish after hearing more bad news about Mahtab made me wish again, for only a second, I had jumped instead of answering Mahtab's call tonight! Then, I giggled about my erratic mood during the last couple of weeks, got inside my car, and drove away with jubillence. Maybe it was time to sell and move out of both my suites in Tehran and Vancouver that still rekindled so much memories of my intricate love affair with that tricky Erica. Her ghost travelling all the way to Tehran just to bug me or lure me was amazing and another mystery of its own. *How far ghosts can or would normally travel? Did anybody know?* Then again, Erica had always been a special case, anyway, maybe as a travelling, tenacious ghost now as well!

Regardless of my anger with Mahtab and guilt towards Erica, the immense task of animating my mind and spirit, now for some possibly worthy purpose, felt both divine and mandatory, besides the timely reaffirmation of my big love for my sisters, especially now that I had only one left! Accordingly, making her realize the risks and chaos her repulsive romantic adventure could cause appeared like a sacred mission of my own, even more urgent than Mahtab's original mission of saving Darren. I just had to help her at any cost as a token of my appreciation for her call jolting me out of my suicidal mood and Erica's lure. Darren's recovery starting a new chaos already was annoying, yet timely, in itself, for many reasons *perhaps*, including my sense of mission and survival—for better or worse, we just had to wait and see!

Driving leisurely in a splendid mood, I wondered why the women I had loved so passionately had always let me down with their tyrannical behaviour, but also always triumphed over me, anyway! *All four of them...*

PART I

Three Pensive Friends

Chapter One
A New Dawn

Nobody knew the particulars of Darren's mishap and who had shot him in the neck for what. Apparently, the police had no clues, either, but going by his lifestyle and risky relationships with many women, I imagined it had been a case of revenge or rivalry. After visiting him twice at Vancouver's General Hospital, the idea had soon felt pointless with no hope for his recovery, while he had remained attached to some hefty equipments in a coma for the last three months. It had been just too depressing to see such a vibrant young man so listless now with all kinds of tubes and wires sticking out of many parts of his body. We all thought he was a goner.

So, Reza's unexpected call from Tehran with a sombre tone jolted me. "Have you heard about Darren, T.J.?"

My heart thumped fast, imagining the worst: That Darren had passed away at last and I should prepare a urology for such a complex man, even if we ignored his innocent sins. He had no family besides his frail father who lived in Toronto.

"Oh, I'm sorry... I hadn't heard anything," I replied solemnly.

"He's okay, T.J. He's out of the coma."

"Yeah? Really…? When did this happen?"

"Ten days ago apparently, but was discharged just recently."

"That's wonderful," I said. "I'll call him right away to see if he needs any help."

"Yeah, that's a good idea and why I called, but also to ask you do me a favour at the same time."

"What favour?"

"I was hoping you could put some sense into his supposedly working brain."

"You two are at it already?" I asked in bewilderment.

"I'm sorry, T.J., but my life seems to have been jinxed since I met Darren."

"Do you really mean it?" I asked sheepishly, knowing what he meant. Darren has had that effect on everybody, it seemed; for causing squabbles often innocently—though the situations and outcomes have always been much graver in Reza's case.

"You know what I mean!" Reza replied with pain and irony. "He and I getting mixed up in family affairs has been sickening."

"And he's usually the culprit!?" I asked sardonically in return, hinting about his own role in those so-called mix-ups.

"I know, T.J. But this is not the time for counting our faults."

"I'm sorry... What's going on this time?" I asked timidly.

"Well, my sister and he are causing mayhem," Reza replied.

"Your sister...? Didn't she—"

Reza interrupted me, "The one in Vancouver now is Mahtab."

"Is she having an affair with him, too?" I asked jokingly.

"I don't know… But she'll get into trouble or die because of him as well," Reza said with tension.

"Why?" I asked.

"Because she's married…, to a very jealous husband here."

"So, why is she here in the first place?"

"It's a long story. But, basically, Mahtab and Darren might've somehow connected when mourning Mahroo's death and then she's been checking on him in hospital last two months."

"Checking on him…!?" I asked in disbelief.

"She'd mentioned it to me, although she allegedly went to Vancouver to recuperate after Mahroo's death."

"Did she have to come all the way here to recuperate?" I asked with a moronic giggle that I regretted immediately.

"She said she wanted to see Vancouver, too. She's also fed up with life in Iran."

"So what's new?" I asked with more confusion.

"What's new is that she said the other day she's going to tell Bijan, her husband, that she isn't going back anytime soon."

"She probably knows what she's doing... And don't you think Bijan has imagined this likelihood already?"

"No, he'd been quite angry last two months about her travel to Vancouver, but now he sounds like a total maniac," Reza replied. "Gosh, you ask so many questions...!"

"I don't know what to say!" I said.

"Are you sure…? Don't you have any other questions?"

I burst into laughter myself, "No, I can't promise…"

"Bijan has been mad at me all along in particular," he said with angst again.

"Why you?" I asked.

"Mostly for bringing Darren into their lives," Reza replied. "He actually saved his ass last year when he was in jail in Tehran. Is Darren repaying the guy by stealing his wife, instead of kissing his feet for saving his life?"

"Can't you wait even a week or so before jumping the gun?"

"No, Bijan has somehow found out about Darren's recovery and wants me to look into things right away. I wonder if he's had spies in Vancouver all along to monitor Mahtab's movements at least."

"Well, he sounds like another desperate husband gone cuckoo over his wife," I said.

"I've now become his punching bag because he knows how sensitive I am about my mom and sisters."

"You sure sound anxious, so unlike you," I said helplessly.

"Yes, I'm sure Mahtab and others will get hurt if *we* don't do something," he said so matter-of-factly.

"We?" I shrieked with bad feelings already.

"Yes, you and I must do something fast," he replied seriously. "Things can get ugly very quickly."

"Have you called Darren?" I asked desperately, loathing to be dragged into people's love affairs and betrayals again.

"Of course… I can't find him, but you know that confronting him myself won't be useful, anyway, especially on this issue."

"Then, you or your mom must speak with Mahtab logically," I said with growing despair. I was getting exhausted myself from so much effort to find other options for him to spare me!

"No. She's been ignoring me and my calls last few months."

"So, come here and talk to both of them," I said.

"I can't. My mom is ill and I must also try to keep things calm here," he said with a sigh.

"You're in a jam again, it seems..."

"I hate to say this, but Darren's recovery is causing me a lot of hassle," he said solemnly.

"I get it! What do you think I can do?" I asked warily, now really fed up with my failure to dissuade him from involving me. The idea of starting a row with this foolish Casanova, Mr. Darren Durant, just as he has begun living again, also agitated me.

"Just try to get to the bottom of things and see if you can push him let Mahtab return to Iran right away. Go reason with him a little about a very risky situation he might be starting."

"Don't you think he can figure that out himself?"

"I don't know how his brain works these days, but mostly I worry about Mahtab's charm ruining even his basic logic and decency."

"She's that charming, ha?" I asked with a giggle.

"Yes... Most women have immense power over us, anyway, but my sisters have been very persuasive in a hypnotic manner as well," he replied not proudly, but rather desperately.

"And yet you think she needs your protection?" I asked wittily.

"Yes, my sisters are also reckless and adventurous! So, things could get ugly fast, or even fatal, like other incidents Darren has caused before."

"I'm sure you know your sisters best, although I've noticed a few things, too," I said, recalling old events.

"I hate to think that maybe things would've been better if he'd *at least* remained in the coma a few more months."

"At least? You don't mind something even more drastic, then, ha?" I asked with surprise but also for teasing him.

"I feel bad for talking this way, but you know I don't mean it! Or, do I? You're confusing me, T.J., instead of helping."

"Don't worry... His recovery is starting to agitate me, too!" I said for teasing him some more.

"Mahtab was the only person who believed Darren could be saved. Now that she's proven me wrong, she sounds even more confident and obsessed with her mission of taking care of him."

"For how long?"

"God knows… but most likely forever if she can have it her way," Reza said tensely with a titter.

"Why has she been acting like a missionary, anyway?"

"She won't tell me the truth, but hinted twice that Mahroo's spirit has inspired her to help Darren because she couldn't do it herself," Reza replied with frustration. "What a bunch of rubbish, I know... You don't have to tell me."

"She certainly has guts to give such a bizarre excuse! Still, it's innovative and better than none at all, let's admit."

"Yeah, my sisters have also been very creative when they set their minds on doing something, even if it means becoming a romantic missionary," Reza said with a giggle.

"Your tenacity to help them is even more amazing after they refuse to hear your concerns or answer your calls."

"I should for my mom's sake at least, although my meddling also looks silly and often backfires."

"At least you admit..." I said helplessly.

"I do, but I've gone through hell last few months, T.J.; I'm sure you agree."

"I do, especially after Mahroo's incident. Gosh, it all sounds like a soppy opera!"

"I'm desperate, T.J.… I don't wanna bother you more about other issues when the hell breaks loose here in a few days."

"Thanks…," I said teasingly. "I feel your frustration already."

"I also hate to bother you, but I need your help badly."

"Let me see what I can do…"

"So, how's your life and family?" Reza asked.

"Thanks for asking…, at last!" I replied jokingly.

"Sorry… How do you feel?"

"Not so good, Reza. My marriage feels horrible, but can't see myself with another woman, either. I'm in a mess of my own."

"Sorry... Any chance you guys can share a simpler marriage by giving each other more space?"

"I doubt it. We've had a long rough marriage and I've tried all the gimmicks I've been able to think of," I said.

"Let's plan a group suicide, then," Reza said glumly

"Maybe we've got there at last… I'm in…"

"Meanwhile, call me if you need an ear to spill your guts out."

"Thanks, but are we gonna find peace ever without needing each other's ears and advice all the time?"

"I doubt it… At least we have each other, ha?" Reza said.

"But if only you two grow up, my life will be a bit easier."

"Don't count on that, T.J.," Reza replied with a giggle.

"I'm serious… Stop messing up things and making me feel so lousy about my silly advice."

"Don't say that... We like you and rely on your wisdom a lot."

"Wisdom? Don't make me laugh," I said.

"Although you've started whining a lot lately yourself!"

"At least you guys still like me or have use for me! Everyone else now hates me officially, especially my wife…"

"I'm sorry, T.J.…, for dragging you into my problems again. But will you go talk to Darren today to let Mahtab return?"

"I don't seem to have any choice, do I?"

"No, I'm afraid, you don't," Reza replied with a giggle. "The irony is that he doesn't mean to cause problems and often ends up becoming a victim himself."

"A love victim, ha? Bastard Casanova!" I said gaily.

"Yeah... He's usually forced into some odd love and revenge episodes we find in classic novels or operas."

I burst into laughter. "And then drags you with him into all these epic adventures and operas, too?"

"Absolutely... My fate has got mixed up with this joker's life mysteriously since he and I met!" Reza said.

"He's a good clown at least," I said teasingly to lighten him up. "But it's also funny for two grown men who met by accident only a few years ago to brawl over so many love episodes."

"Yeah, it's weird for two idiots from the opposite sides of the planet finding and torturing each other unintentionally mainly over love issues," he said. "It's such a crazy world, T.J."

"Yeah...! Like fate testing our spirit and patience forever," I said rhetorically and helplessly, merely hoping to show empathy.

"It seems like God is playing a game with us for His own fun, that's all!"

"At least it shows too many wild Casanovas live everywhere."

I called Darren right away with no luck. It made perfect sense, of course. After three months of coma, he would surely be galloping around the city with a gorgeous woman equally keen to rejoice his new life together. I left him a cheery message and returned to my boring life, somewhat relieved from the tension of annoying him so fast with my mission, instead of celebrating his return to reality. I would not mind probing him eventually to learn about his likely new adventure with Mahtab, which sounded intriguing as usual already. But doing it as a spy hastily felt at least tacky.

I hoped he would now be a relaxed, positive man after going through such an awful ordeal. Has he been awakened enough to follow a simpler life now, instead of confusing himself quickly again with his customary entanglement in a few tough love affairs at a time and whining about women and life overall? Then again, with Mahtab being so irresistible, according to Reza, poor Darren had his work cut out for him already! *My mushy wishes for his salvation might've been premature!*

I poured myself a cup of coffee, plummeted onto the sofa, and tried to imagine Reza's anguish these days after many shattering incidents around him—his dad's passing, Mahroo's death in a vile accident, Zia's suicide, Erica's mysterious fall from Darren's balcony on the same day Darren had been shot—all within six months. All these nonsensical tragedies had raised my cynicism about people and humanity. The whole world has gone mad, I mused with gloom. I just could not still believe this global havoc also tainting Feri, my darling wife, and our daughters, who were changing so fast—showing their real characters suddenly, while driving me nuts all along. What was Canada doing to my family? What was happening to them, especially Feri, or they hoped to achieve? She was not young or even slightly pretty to hope for a better mate. And I cannot picture a more patient man in the world than me who could bear her nasty personality year after year. *Believe me!*

In return, a grim offshoot of my family's subtle rebellion was my own infantile notion a few times recently about the option of reviving my old adventurous self, at least as an antidote for their apathy. Alas or luckily, my urge for a more passionate mate has always remained merely a dream or manifested through a horrific nightmare when a fairy has lured me to follow her with huge hopes before turning swiftly and showing me her frightening real face—looking exactly like Feri, now with two tiny cute horns!

Just to give you a crash course about my marital state tainting my mood these days, recounting a typical family episode a few months earlier might help.

I took Feri and our three daughters to a fancy restaurant to show my continued support of Feri's *admirable* achievements and celebrate her success in passing the real estate course at UBC and getting such a *prestigious job* as an agent. *I hope I haven't sounded sarcastic!* I was not initially too keen about my wife driving around the city and showing houses to people. I had not favoured the idea of she supporting me financially, especially since she had failed to do so emotionally so tenaciously. Perhaps I still suffered the ancient Iranian mentality. Yet, Feri persisted for two years and I finally gave in. In particular, she kept arguing that if I were not going to work or make more money somehow she would have to take the matter in her own capable hands.

In the restaurant, Feri suddenly expressed the need for driving a fancy car, a Mercedes or BMW. She insisted that her success as a real estate agent depended on it. She announced her demands usually in front of our kids to abuse my reluctance to look cheap or careless about the family's *essential* needs, while her spoiled daughters always saw Feri's demands very urgent no matter how silly they sounded to me. Therefore, bringing up the matter in front of the girls was Feri's plot—as usual—to shut my mouth largely—not totally, clearly! I confess to having a loud mouth of my own, thank god! It had probably been a tiny reason for our quarrels as well, I admit because I am such a fair, liberal person!

"What's wrong with our existing cars?" I pleaded calmly.

"What cars?" Feri shrieked. "Rose needs hers to go to UBC. And I can't count on you not needing a car."

"Count on it... Take it anytime you want," I replied politely.

"It's not gonna work… Besides, it's crucial to make a proper first impression in front of my clients for *my* type of business. Otherwise, I'll never get anywhere. You understand?"

"Honestly, I don't, but—"

"But what? Do you want me feel humiliated before my clients and colleagues for the kind of car you're asking me to drive?"

"Can we discuss this later," I said in hopes of explaining my logic in private. "We're here tonight to celebrate, not argue."

"What's to celebrate or discuss if I can't even have a proper car for my type of job? I just don't understand!" she blurted.

"I don't think this is a good time for this argument," I said as calmly and courteously as I could. "We've come here to relax and have a good family time."

"Don't you want to do even something right for our future?"

"So, what have I been doing all my life so far?" I pleaded.

"Only stopping me from doing what I like to do," Feri yelled with rage, while our daughters glared at me.

"The problem is that you refuse to appreciate what we have and what I've done for my family," I murmured.

"Don't you see that all successful agents drive a luxury car?"

"Don't you think that all those agents bought their luxury cars after they became successful and not in advance," I said with a mix of logic and wit in hopes of making the angry crowd laugh or give me a break.

"No, I don't think so, and it doesn't matter for making a great first impression, anyway," she said seriously, while I grasped her twisted logic, too! My pensive face probably convinced her that her superb logic had worked perfectly, so she continued. "If you were gonna stop me from doing my job, why did you say it was okay to go through all the hassles of taking those tough courses and finding this kind of job? Do you think it was easy? Maybe you should go try it yourself."

I was dying to refute, *so easily in fact,* all her claims about *the difficulty of* those courses and her job's *prestige*. Yet, I simply shut up, since arguing in front of the kids, especially on this supposedly glorious occasion, would only worsen my family's impressions of my fairness and objectivity.

"If you don't want me to work, just say so!" Feri yelled again after gauging my silence for only twenty seconds. She was slyly adamant to seal the deal right there and then.

"No, of course I have no intention to stop you from following your dreams," I replied.

"Then I must buy a Mercedes…"

Still, the four darling women of my life kept glaring at me with disgust in bewilderment, as though encountering a terribly stupid criminal. They were huddled together, three of them in the booth and my eldest daughter on a chair close to them. I was sitting alone somewhat isolated from that cluster of rebellious beloveds. It was just becoming too hard for me to grasp the cause of Feri's growing arrogance by the minute, besides her female friends' influence, of course. She had not even borne me a boy! Instead, she had produced an array of ungrateful girls. They admired their mother's apathy and rudeness towards me, while striving to form their crooked personalities precisely around hers. Sometimes, I wanted to slap them in the face one by one when they smirked at me with conceit. My strenuous efforts to raise them and pay for their comfortable lives and education meant nothing to them, like I had promised to be their obedient servant and nothing more. Feri was their hero and I was only a *halloo*, judging by the way they stared at me in bewilderment about my foolish resistance to buy a new Mercedes for their sophisticated, neglected mom. In return, I was dying to know how my family's brains worked!

So unlike Feri, I did not even know why we needed more money if we only learned to live a simple life without trying to compete with the useless Iranian bourgeoisie in Vancouver. Gosh, we had done enough of that bullshit in Tehran already. In fact, escaping that bizarre, showy environment had been one of my reasons for coming to Canada. I could even bear the new regime in Iran with its radical Islamic ideologies, despite the lower status granted me at work. But, being snubbed by my showy, hypocrite friends abusing even that supposedly religious regime so proudly was driving me nuts.

Then again, I had never imagined the situation in Vancouver could be worse in that regard as well. Especially, Feri's craving for more contacts and excitement in an ostentatious lifestyle seemed untameable. Anytime I asked her why we needed more money or such conceited friends, she only glared at me blankly like I was a total fool. Her astonished eyes and smirk revealed her thoughts and pity for my dire stupidity, *How could a person my age be still incapable of realizing the need for socializing with the highest class in society!*

The rest of the evening, and while lying wide-awake in bed, I considered putting my foot down for once and telling Feri and her daughters to go to hell, since I was not going to buy another car. However, the next morning, I found myself in the Mercedes dealership and signing a four-year lease on a 300 SL model that cost me over $700 a month. Feri sat behind the wheel and left me bemused about my patience. I bet she was in a rush to show off her new toy—the prize of torturing me—to her snotty friends. I drove home in despair and sat behind the computer, hoping to forget the grief I had brought upon myself by coming to Canada —supposedly trying to unfetter my family from the Islamic rules of Iran. I wished I had not been so stupid. During such moments, I really felt that at least my family deserved the type of discipline that Islam forced upon women regardless of its religious value. Some divine authority felt useful to keep them sane and realistic about life and their roles as human beings, rather than losing themselves hypnotically so fast in such preposterous values of the Western culture. *What a culture! What culture?*

When we decided to immigrate to Canada in the early 1985, I transferred about half a million dollars to our bank account here in Vancouver. We still had other properties in Iran to sell in case we needed more money. After many years of struggling and planning, now our finances seemed solid at last and nobody had to work any more. Luckily, I had made a small fortune working for a commercial bank during the Shah's regime. So, it was time to relax and enjoy a quiet life, while I also hoped to do something useful with my life, perhaps even indulging my old passion of becoming a writer, although the idea had sounded bizarre even to my own ears.

The irony was that everybody—especially Feri—had actually pushed all these alluring ideas into my gullible head when we had mysteriously begun contemplating the big plan of emigrating to Canada. They had all insisted we did not need any more money and it was time for me to retire and start doing what I liked. But all those plans and goodwill were seemingly valid only in Iran; no longer now, going by the way they talked to me in Canada—often in English, too, as if already ashamed of Farsi! They had all changed fast, forgetting their pledges and heritage.

Of course, life was getting hard in Iran, anyway. In particular, my daughters abhorred the Islamic *hijab* and similar restrictions. They were just dying to doll themselves with lots of makeup and parade their hairs and skins like their mother. Feri was anxious to join her rotten immigrant friends in Vancouver—to resume her ongoing rivalry with them, I presumed. The idea of immigration had now turned into an obsession and fad for many prospering Iranian population and my spoiled family did not want to stay behind among the leftover losers. They simply could not wait any longer for the chance of getting dissolved in the Western values they had cherished all along. So I agreed to bring them abroad to do all that and more! I rather believed myself we could achieve everything my family was hoping to accomplish abroad easily by investment and interest income—just another great idea, they had all insisted, especially Feri, to pump my poor ego. Then things had changed fast as soon as we had arrived in Vancouver. Maybe something is in the air at Vancouver Airport, because everything started to change right there!

For one thing, we had to buy a house. Renting was beneath us, they proclaimed during the first week. They did not want an ordinary house, either. The four precious women of my life had devoted their entire brains to developing huge tastes and appetites for luxury. The house had to be new, since, they claimed, all the pre-owned houses we had checked smelled of dampness or had major issues with the floor plan! The house must have a good view of the city and ocean, too, as some of our friends had view houses. It must have at least five bedrooms to accommodate the guests who had also kept coming for visits. Anyway, within six months, when we moved to our new home, now furnished by Georgia, a good part of our cash was gone. We had to buy the second car when my eldest daughter started at UBC two years later. Thank God, they had deemed Toyota acceptable! Yet, soon it seemed everybody should have her or his own car, even though I seldom drove a car personally.

So, with our savings depleting fast in the first three years of living in Canada, I could not argue with Feri too much about her ambition to become a spectacular real estate agent and family breadwinner from then on. Surely, I was not about to go do the laborious jobs that Canadians were willing to offer me for such pitiful wages. I had been a bank executive, for God's sake, before coming here. How could I accept the humiliation of driving a cab or becoming a security guard? I disliked the real estate job the most, to be honest without telling Feri, of course. Several times, I tried to convince my family to go back to Iran. I pleaded with them, "Let me work in a bank again, restore my confidence and pride, and make a few more millions for you guys." Yet, they all said no. Once they had tasted the life in Vancouver, not even ten biggest bulldozers could move them an inch back towards their motherland. In their defence, however, they said I could go back alone if I wanted to. Is my family a symbol of liberalism or what? They said it so casually my heart broke into million pieces, as if my presence was now suddenly so inconsequential and perhaps even unnecessary, if not a massive nuisance altogether! But, how could I go live in Tehran without my beloved family?

I had thought giving Feri more space might calm her rooted drive for rebellion. Even better, maybe her allegedly lucrative job could also supplement our income. Most of all, I hoped my dear family would eventually relax and learn to see me as a flexible, fixed member after my lifetime struggles to feed and pamper them—what an optimist fool I have sometimes been, just out of desperation! *I know now!*

Instead, my family's rising apathy towards me had made me more doubtful every day about my likely role in this family. I also began losing interest to work ever again. In fact, I really doubted the chance of accepting any job, not even as the Prime Minister of Canada—not even if the nation begged me for two days!

I kept staring at the computer monitor, but my mind was dull. I could not construct a simple sentence. When I read the earlier pages, they made no sense, either. Instead of helping me focus, reading my past thoughts depressed me regarding the silliness of my efforts to be a writer, especially in a foreign language. Despite studying English at school plus a private tutor, I could feel my limitations for not being born into an English family and country. Then again, I did not like to write in Farsi, besides my seemingly lesser skill in it. My language aptitude was possibly low, yet I could not dismiss my passion to jot down my thoughts in a story or an essay. Actually, I had realized more urgently in Canada that choosing a meaningful hobby, most likely writing, was the only way to alleviate my tension, keep my sanity, and survive in this degrading setting around my weird family in a foreign land.

Of course, I had imagined that writing and research might also cure my curiosity a bit about the oddity of human behaviour. For one thing, I wondered, 'Why people are adamant to behave so idiotically and selfishly mostly against their own welfare!' The psychological forces behind our foolishness were not hard to fathom. Yet, my reflections and failure to find logical answers for humans' inability to get along made me more curious and cynical every day. This mystery, in fact, felt too astronomical to unravel by any kind of science or reflections! It had something major to do with God's original design, I believed!

Luckily, and ironically, Darren's recovery had suddenly boosted my spirit these days somewhat. My sole consolation, after Reza's call, was that at least Darren was alive and I had two confidents again to fall back on at times of distress, like right now. In fact, I must confess that my life had been dull, besides depressing, in recent months after Darren's coma and Reza's long absence in Vancouver.

Naturally, our friendship has stirred its own dilemma! On the one hand, Darren's adventures have often mixed with Reza's fate and caused complex situations and headaches for me, like the one apparently starting again now. On the other hand, their busy lives have kept me amused or involved on the side, while helping me learn a lot about human psychology. Luckily, Darren had always managed to meet me regularly, despite his busy schedule and varied skirmishes with a few lovers at a time. I hoped he would feel healthy soon and find time to see me if his fresh beguiling love affair with Mahtab would leave him enough energy to speak a few words with me as well! Now, finding Darren felt far more important to me for distraction than for fulfilling my promise to Reza, although I was keen to gauge the extent of Mahtab's charm mesmerizing Darren these days as well!

It was amazing how these types of contentious romances have always followed Darren, this time starting just as he had come to. Being shot into a coma because of one women and regaining consciousness with another rebellious woman ready to embrace him was a magical reality I could witness only through these two friends and envy. Women praying for months desperately for him to return to life, so that they could start a scandalous affair with him felt more than exciting or accidental, but rather like some kind of supernatural forcing him into baffling territories for weird outcomes—*mainly for His Almighty's amusement perhaps!* The lucky bastard has always had the oddest fates and challenges with women—usually thrilling until they have gotten nasty or even deadly. He had too many women messing up his mind, and I had too many nightmares managing just one woman, my selfish wife, in a dull and dismal family setting. *His, I'd call a life! Not mine!*

Reminiscing about my odd friendship with two love-stricken young men or struggling anymore with words and sentences felt pointless today. I called Darren again and left another message to call me right away. But then I got out of the house for a long stroll and possibly giving my brain a chance to work a bit better. This was three days after my first call.

Chapter Two

A Place to Recuperate

Horror and confusion besieged me as I opened my eyes amidst hospital equipments and tubes. *Well, who wouldn't be!?* Then, I peered at the two big black eyes that appeared familiar somehow. She looked surprised as well, covering her mouth and howling stealthily, while a nurse and a doctor examined me and asked questions. My name came to me in an hour when the last scene in the coma with Mahroo in a colourful garden turned in my head. She said farewell to me before embarking the Masters' boat, "Farewell, Darren... Go now, my lost lover..." But nothing else was clear about my past or identity, which I was striving to recreate. Especially, I craved to know about that gorgeous woman who stuck around all day, pampered me, and asked questions. I felt shy and hesitant to ask her name, though, sensing her desire to let me rebuild my memory of her on my own rather than prompting me in any way. The game felt fair and amusing to me as well. Meanwhile, the warmth of her touch, when she held my hands and stared into my eyes with passion, made me relax. The blood rushed faster in my body and I got stronger every minute.

She left late in the evening and I fell asleep, still struggling to remember something about my life. I dreamt about the time I had spent in Barcelona, where I had painted the portrait of departed Mahroo with Mahtab's help. That was right before returning to Vancouver and being shot. Mahtab was actually the one who had pushed me to do that painting as a memorabilia—a medium for her family and friends to feel and contact Mahroo's spirit. 'A shrine for all of us to cherish her selfless personality and vivacity despite her gloomy life,' Mahtab had insisted with great passion. The dream reignited my memory. I remembered Mahtab and my life story. Alas, I rather regretted my tenacity to recall that glum reality along with the deemed obligation of facing it all over again!

The police had asked the hospital staff to inform them the minute I came to. However, Detective Stewart showed up on the third day and asked me only some general questions, including my knowledge of Erica falling off the balcony in my suite and dying the same day I was shot. This shocking news caused me a new round of confusion and melancholy, although I was pretty sure I had not pushed her or something. Apparently, Mahtab had hidden this information from me all along to protect me under my frail condition, although I felt she had tried a few times to test my knowledge of Erica's mysterious demise. Noticing my swift distress, the good detective offered to postpone the interview until I felt better. Thrilled with his offer, I promised to call him as soon as I started a normal life again. My reaction to the news most likely convinced him that I had nothing to do with Erica's death, the same way I was *almost* sure about it myself.

At last, I was discharged from the hospital five days later and Mahtab was there to take me home. My motor skills had not fully rebuilt and, in fact, I still felt like a zombie after being a vegetable for three months. However, the lingering confusion was the main hurdle to feel normal again. It was supposedly natural under the circumstances, including the perturbing memory of the shooting incident causing the coma. With a hint about possible depression awhile, the doctor had prescribed some pills. Luckily, though, I had so far relied on Mahtab to get over my melancholy after the initial shock, while she had so kindly been going around making the arrangements for my return to a normal life. Her presence and promise to stick around me *for now* felt like a major blessing and the best remedy for my stress. She vowed to help me face both my present depression and past emotional conundrums before the coma. *Then I would leave,* she had expressed enigmatically, like alluding to a natural ending for her mission of saving me or threatening me wittily to abandon me if I did not behave!

On the way to my apartment, Mahtab insisted on taking me to her place and looking after me awhile at least. As I declined her offer, she noted that she had hired some people to make my suite sparkling clean. Going home, I told her, might best help me recall and regain more of my broken identity, although the notion of returning to the scene of the crime had felt unsettling, including sporadic anxiety attacks about Erica's death at the same time and place. Then again, it also felt necessary for overcoming my fear of living in solitude, which seemed imminent, like a fixed feature of my fate.

Despite the sunshine rushing through the wide, double glass doors and highlighting its cleanliness, my apartment felt haunted. Everything looked as I recalled—the comfortable furniture and ambience that had given me the joy of living a simple bachelor life and painting some worthy art pieces, although they were all gone now. Only the incomplete painting of *Tosca* still hung on the east wall of the suite. I recalled the two special paintings the thugs had ran away with after shooting me. They had always felt like the two most precious pieces about my past life's highlights. So now, both my past and present felt hazy without those two particular paintings I had always insisted on keeping for myself. I wondered where they could be at that moment as I missed them nostalgically. The memory of painting so many canvases in this place also thrilled me, although I felt no urge for painting anytime soon. The Elixir had sold more than six dozens of them when I had been considered a worthy painter—before they had dumped me as well.

The bloodstains in *Tosca* painting around Mario's mutilated body and Floria kneeling by his flesh and screaming her heart out captivated me before an eerie anxiety overwhelmed me. Mario's lifeless flesh reminded me how I might have looked to Erica when she had entered this place and found me dying on the floor. That was how my flesh had looked the last three months as well, laid uselessly on a hospital bed. And kind Mahtab sticking around it and praying for its recovery. Her wish had come true, unlike Floria's. The streak of the blood in *Tosca* guided my eyes down towards the furniture near the painting. The sofa and carpet were spotless with no trace of any blood that my unconscious mind seemed too anxious to find there. Yet, I imagined the entire scene, in particular the blood dripping from my neck, slipping through the corner of the sofa, and spreading on the floor. It was draining my body and sending me into that long coma. I could not believe being alive, standing and staring at *Tosca* again. How could it be true and why did not I believe it? Swiftly, my vague new existence felt surreal with scary challenges ahead, yet again, least of all finishing that huge *Tosca.* What should I do now with my new life? I did not feel ready or eager at all to do any of those presumed duties burdening my brain furtively. The expression on my face must have been quite dreadful from the way Mahtab peered at me with worry!

She rushed over, helped me sit on the sofa, and brought me a glass of cold water from the fridge. After my nerves settled a bit, Mahtab suggested we go on the balcony to get some fresh air. But as we stepped outside, the story that Mahtab and Detective Stewart had briefly recounted to me about Erica rolled in my head. A rush of adrenaline jolted and paralyzed me when I looked down towards the ground where Erica's tiny body must have hit the asphalt. My startle and hypnotic stare also alarmed Mahtab again. She looked tense for bringing me on the balcony. *What a helpless jittery creature I've become,* I mused.

"Let's go back inside," she said quickly. Nothing was wrong with my physical health, as far as the tests had shown. So these lapses were possibly mental, if not a brain damage. Mahtab held my hand, took me back to the sofa, and I rested my head on the cushion.

"Are you convinced now that you should not stay here, for a while at least?" Mahtab asked.

"Maybe I should go to a hotel for now, then," I murmured.

"Why don't you stay in my place? I mean Reza's apartment. He's your friend, after all. You can take the guestroom," she said.

"No, I can't do that."

"Why not?" she asked fretfully.

"It isn't the right thing to do," I said, while recalling a similar episode and exchange with Mahroo in Tehran three years earlier. She had come to the hospital after Iraqi missiles had hit our neighbourhood and I had been injured during a rescue attempt. She had insisted I could not stay in my suite alone with a repaired shoulder and my thumb in a cast. I had accepted her offer at last, which had then led to a big chaos and some people's anguish.

"Reza isn't coming to Vancouver anytime soon," Mahtab said.

"Still… It is not the right thing to do. Many people might get mad at us for no good reason."

"Don't you wanna let me help you?" Mahtab asked tenderly.

"I do. But I'm not sure about putting you in a jam. We must not upset Reza and Bijan."

"Okay, Darren, I don't want to push you."

"Staying together would also confuse us more. We mustn't do anything rash until I have a bit more control of my mind again."

"Actually, you sound quite rational and prudent to me right now," Mahtab said with a giggle.

"That's good news, then...," I replied with delight. "Although I don't feel clear enough about my identity yet."

"Still, you can stay with me a day or so until you're ready to return here or make a different plan. We won't tell anybody and we won't discuss our situation, either."

"Can we avoid talking about our situation and plans if we live together?" I asked with cynicism.

"Why not? We'll wait until you're ready to think about us."

"Let me think for a few minutes," I said.

Mahtab kept staring at me, while I pondered my contentious options. Past the ethics, the bad memories about the unpleasant consequences of staying in Mahroo's house in Iran stirred an alarming fear in my psyche. Then again, Mahtab's gorgeous eyes and silent pleading were too penetrating and luring to resist her generous offer. At last, I packed a small suitcase and she drove us towards her suite.

I mused over my idiocy or desperation goading me make the same mistake twice. The irony of history repeating itself almost to the dot, except with the other sister driving us in a different city, felt more mystical than weird. Even Mahtab's calm, pensive face on the road resembled that of Mahroo's three years earlier with a sense of triumph for convincing me about her wish. These haunting memories were bizarre and also agonizing when they kept rekindling Mahroo's senseless demise and all the pains many people, including me, have endured for losing her precious company, *all for mixing Mahtab's fate with mine perhaps!*

"I like Reza's apartment. How about you?" Mahtab asked.

Her abrupt question startled me. "Umm… I don't know…"

"You've been to his apartment before, right?"

I had to think twenty seconds to remember the answer.

"No, I've never been at his suite before, actually," I replied.

"Didn't he buy this apartment four years ago?" she asked.

"Yes, I guess," I replied.

"So how come you haven't seen it?"

"I don't know…," I replied before spending two minutes to remember why, along with another wave of tension. Obviously, my slow brain after the coma had made me forgetful. More so, however, I reckoned my subconscious' likely attempt to hide an upsetting old story. The reason I had never visited Reza's suite all those years, despite our regular get-togethers, was that Erica had done its interior design. Besides the fact that I had lived three of those years in Iran, I had resented going there and seeing Erica's immaculate taste, mixed with her boiling passion for him at the time, emanating from the décor in every corner of his suite. I had just resented wrestling with the idea of them having spent many hours doing things together and to each other in that suite and so often in the bedroom.

"In fact, I think we'd better go back to my apartment," I said, since even visiting Reza's suite suddenly felt nauseating. Three years of separation from Erica, and not even the sad fact that she had died, so tragically too, did not seem to reduce my rage and apprehension to enter the apartment where she had fooled around with my good friend so casually.

"Why? What happened to you again?" Mahtab asked tensely.

"I just don't think I can be comfortable in Reza's apartment."

"Don't be silly, Darren. We are almost here. Let's give it a try, anyway," Mahtab said. Again, her comment and refusal sounded completely like a repeat of the episode and exact exchange with Mahroo on the day she had picked me up from the hospital. I felt too exhausted to argue with Mahtab, the same way I had stopped arguing with Mahroo in Tehran. We had actually arrived in the building and Mahtab was parking the car. All those years, I had not bothered to find out even about the location of Reza's suite. It happened to be not far away from mine in a luxurious high-rise in downtown Vancouver.

We took the elevator to the 28th floor. As Mahtab opened the door and we entered, the suite's exquisite ambience besieged me with a severe sensation similar to the one I had felt in my own apartment. Not merely the Italian furniture Reza had insisted on, *according to Erica,* but more in terms of harmony and colours showed Erica's meticulous taste and touch. Then, I got angrier when I imagined she had put even more efforts in decorating this place than she had with our house. Every simple object, all those paintings and sculptures, a half dozen Persian rugs, lightings, the silky suede set, the bright metallic coffee and corner tables, they were all elegantly chosen and scattered around his big penthouse, although it had only two bedrooms. Everywhere I looked, I saw Erica, sitting, walking, resting, laughing, kissing, and fucking, but mostly lying about me. Mahtab led me to the guestroom and I put my suitcase in a corner before peering through the glass wall over the cityscape. I was now even jealous about Reza's view of the ocean being so much more expansive than mine.

On the way back to the living area, Mahtab made a point to show me the huge master bedroom as well, as if I had to know where exactly she slumbered during Reza's absence. As I peered inside the room, merely the images of cheerful Reza and Erica naked in the bed rushed to my head, so unlike what Mahtab had probably intended, if anything at all. *Poor woman could've not imagined how my burdened, adventurous mind would react.*

"So you sleep here now?" I asked her like an imbecile just to distract my brain from building further revolting images.

"Yes. It's a waste not to use it when Reza isn't here and I don't think you need to worry about losing your room anytime soon."

We lingered in silence with our private curiosities or dreams. I did not know what we were looking for and why, except for my persistent imaginations of all sorts of repulsive scenes about Erica and Reza. Mahtab, however, mostly peered at the bed with a mysterious grin, as if *perhaps* thinking about seducing me right there and then—or only pitying me if, by any chance, she knew about the love affair between Erica and Reza and envisioned the same pictures I did. After two minutes, I had imagined enough scenes, guessed Mahtab's thoughts, and pained my brain to the brim. I got out tensely and she followed me. I stood at a northerly glass wall and watched a different view of Vancouver downtown with bright buildings and busy streets right below us.

"I'm glad you showed me your nest, anyway," I said at last as a show of my appreciation and she produced a charming grin.

"I'm glad we're neighbours," she muttered.

"Thanks for helping me, especially during the last 7-8 days."

"You're welcome, Darren. Come sit down," she replied.

I took the chair opposite to hers and stared at her, wrestling with many baffling questions.

"You'll feel comfortable here soon, and I'll have someone to talk with after so long, too," she said while pouring us coffee.

"You must've felt lonely last two months away from your family. How is Nazi doing these days?"

"I miss her a lot. Leaving her alone with my mother was a big decision for me. I had been her new mom after Mahroo. Then I deserted her, too."

"Poor Nazi," I said solemnly with guilt.

"Of course, she's happy with her grandma, but my mom is too fragile and depressed to be a good support for Nazi. All of us are lonely somehow these days, just because Mahroo and my father passed away one after the other."

"Still, I bet Bijan is feeling the loneliest after you left."

"I guess," she replied with a sigh. "But I really couldn't live with him or in Iran anymore. After my miscarriage, especially, he was treating me badly as if I'd done it on purpose."

"You're surely the glue that keeps your family together these days. Your mother, Nazi, Bijan, and Reza; they all need you."

"You're probably right…"

"And I hate being responsible for their gloom and missing you so much."

"Are you trying to get rid of me already?" she asked.

"Don't say that, please… But I feel horrible for causing grief for many people and making Bijan crazy most likely, too."

"Didn't you hear me saying I can't live with Bijan or in Iran?"

"Yes, I did. But—"

"I must plan my own life. I have a right to be happy, too?"

"Of course…"

"So, please try to understand my needs and feelings."

"Sorry…," I said.

"You should also support my plans if you care for me."

Surely, my erratic emotions towards her because of our vague situation felt annoying even to me. So, with guilt cluttering my brain, I tried to change the subject hastily. "Did you know Erica and Reza were lovers when she was still married to me?"

She stared at me in shock. "No, I didn't know… Thanks for telling me," she said at last, as though she had also felt my sloppy intention to change the subject.

I was surprised more myself about my slip of the tongue. What had made me spit out such a foolish comment after holding back those depressing old memories almost the whole afternoon? I had not mentioned this matter to anybody else, other than T.J., all those years, either, not even to Mahroo.

"I should've not mentioned this particular secret," I said. "I never ever meant to discuss this matter."

"I'm glad you did, though," she replied.

"I'm not! I can't believe this sentence slipped my big mouth."

"Why not? I think sharing even our hurtful secrets with each other is the best way to reduce our tensions these days."

"Maybe it is, but that was Reza's secret as well. My slippery tongue was possibly another side-effect of the coma," I said.

"The coma is now a convenient excuse for many things you want, or don't want, to say or do, ha?" she asked wittily.

"Of course… But it's probably a real factor for many of my silly talks and behaviour these days as well. So, anything wrong I do or say, only blame the coma for it, not me."

"No, I won't… You must settle your mind soon to help solve our problems… I can't do it alone."

"I'll do my best."

"Why don't you like to share your emotions with me? Aren't we going to be close?" she asked.

"Some information can't help anything."

"But, as I said, I'm glad you mentioned this particular secret."

"Anything special reason?"

"Yes… Now I know Reza's big secret, too, and that he isn't such a saint, after all. I'm tired of his lectures about how to live."

"I bet he's mad at me again for your travel to Vancouver."

"He's angry with both of us, of course," she replied.

"That's terrible after we settled our deep conflicts about Erica and Mahroo finally only six or seven months ago."

"You two had a row over Mahroo, too?" she asked.

"Yes, it related to Mahroo and my painting—the one she gave you and you sent to me at last."

"The poor *Woman in the White Dress*… I miss her," Mahtab said with a sigh.

"God knows where she is now. You know that those stupid thugs shot me because of it."

"Yes… So, did Reza have a long affair with Erica?"

"A year or so. In fact, Erica decorated this place for him. Isn't her taste exquisite?"

"So that's probably how your mind was triggered to share the information about their affair…"

"I guess so… Her efforts look amazing… so passionate and noticeable to me even now, aren't they?" I asked with angst.

"Yes… Is that also why you never came here before?"

"It must've been... You're so perceptive, like Mahroo."

"Was Erica pretty?"

"She sure was!"

"And probably too complex as well?" she asked.

"Why?"

"Just a hunch from all the adventures she created for herself and then even her death is still a mystery," Mahtab said.

"Yes, she was quite complex and mysterious."

"Do you have an idea about what might've happened to her? Could she have committed suicide after seeing you were shot?"

"I can't say, unless she'd felt guilty for something. Maybe she knew more than she told me the night before."

"Are you saying she warned you about those thugs trying to find and harm you?" Mahtab asked.

"Correct... She knew about them, but probably didn't think they'd shoot me. Maybe she got upset about something."

"Yes..., she might've lost it after assuming you were dead or dying," she said pensively.

"Maybe...! God knows..."

"But both warning you in advance and then jumping off the balcony out of love, exactly like Floria in *Tosca,* would be really creepy."

"It'd sure be creepy... Although she kept saying she was back in love with me, and not Reza, and wanted us to reconcile."

"She did? After her long affair and all the pains she'd caused you?" Mahtab asked.

"Yes. But, of course, believing or trusting her was difficult."

"What was this devious plot and shooting all about, anyway?"

"I'd rather not talk about it today. But you'll hear the story if you go with me to see Detective Stewart," I said sluggishly.

At that moment, discussing my past affairs that had agitated Erica and some other people felt like some unnecessary burden for my jumbled spirit. "I'm still too anxious to think or talk about all that craziness," I added.

"I'll go with you anywhere, of course, if you want me to."

I passed out on the sofa from exhaustion, stress, or whatever on the first day out of the hospital. The nap and a long bath revived my spirit a bit—so much so I felt the need for a short walk alone before dinner and told Mahtab so tactfully. She looked surprised and rather hurt for not asking her to come along. She was such a sensitive creature, observing my gestures and moods keenly. She also seemed slightly worried about my solo outing so soon, but probably did not want to treat me like a child, either. She smiled and nodded at last after I swore slyly not to walk too far away—exactly like a naughty boy with no sense of commitment when promising his mom to stick around the house.

"Promise not to run away altogether, either," she said with a grin and I nodded before leaving the suite with mixed feelings about my sudden urge for privacy.

I walked for about forty minutes, sat on a bench at the harbour close to Canada Place, failed to resolve any of many dilemmas muddling my mind, bought a half dozen bottles of gin, whisky, and wine, then strolled back towards the apartment, thrilled that at least someone was waiting for me.

In the apartment, Mahtab delivered a cute smile, as if relieved to see me back safe and sound with a tender grin. I made gin and tonic for us and we relaxed on the sofa as city lights intensified every minute daylight declined. Then, we set out for dinner. We walked two blocks and found a nice, quiet restaurant. I ordered martinis as though my body was trying to catch up for all the time the nurses had deprived it of alcohol. Mahtab and I had been mostly quiet since our somewhat touchy conversations earlier in the afternoon. She probably felt obliged to respect my pensive mood, although her subtle tension showed how my manner was not particularly appealing to her. I wondered myself if anything special made me feel jittery!

"Did the doctor mention anything about drinking alcohol so soon?" she asked.

"Not to me," I replied teasingly.

"You don't seem as thrilled about my presence in Vancouver as I'd thought," she said solemnly along with a sign of relief for getting a big burden off her chest.

"Why do you say that?"

"Our earlier conversations and now your silence."

"Well, I thought you knew that I'm still not quite myself."

"I do. Still I'd like to know what you think about us," she said edgily, as if she had been wrestling with some sore sentiments in my absence and now my silence, as a possible clue about the sad outcome of my solo excursion and contemplation earlier. Most interesting, of course, was her disregard for, or forgetfulness about, her promise just a few hours earlier to do not 'discuss us' if I agreed to stay with her in Reza's place. Then again, I had felt the difficulty of eluding this touchy issue—us—even then.

"I don't know how we should proceed, either," I said at last.

"But I thought you said you loved me, too?" she asked.

"That was probably premature. I'd just come out of the coma and I was so excited seeing you."

"So you don't love me?" she asked wittily, so cutely I could not control myself from bursting into laughter.

"Understanding my feelings is difficult under my condition, I imagine," I replied at last after we both stopped laughing.

"How about everything we felt and said in Barcelona? Were they premature, too?"

"No… I don't know," I said with irritation about my mood. My conscience, logic, or erratic emotions were stopping me—so wisely this time indeed—to make even a basic commitment that she sought.

"Why? Do you have doubts about our plans in Barcelona?"

"To be honest, I don't quite remember those plans and how we'd felt so brave," I replied.

"Don't you want us share our lives and minds?"

"I can't think straight these days, as you can imagine."

"I care a lot about you, Darren."

"I do too. But we must figure out what is right for us to do."

"What we're doing is right if two people truly care about each other. I only hope you believe my feelings and sincerity."

"Of course, I do," I replied. "If you didn't care for me, you would've not wasted so much time on me and taken so much risk only based on a slim hope that I might survive."

"Is something special bothering you, then?"

"Well, both your immense sacrifice and relation to Bijan are tough issues for me to sort out, especially when I recall my mind had been a wreck even before the coma."

"I know and I'm willing to wait and help you recuperate fully and make the right decision for us when you're ready."

"Good… Because making a hasty decision one way or other might make us regret it forever," I said.

"But can you give me at least a small clue," she said.

"You'll laugh if I say I'm waiting for the same thing myself—not about loving you, but the meaning of anything I feel or say these days," I said sincerely.

"No, actually, I appreciate what you're saying so honestly."

"And I appreciate your patience with me," I replied.

"I also think I'd most likely regret it later if I leave only based on your jittery mood nowadays," she said with tears gathering in her eyes. "I'll try not to rush you or myself for a decision."

"So, it seems we agree about our dilemmas at least."

"But I also don't want you feel obligated to me just because I came to Vancouver for you or am staying a bit longer for now."

"No… I cherish your sacrifice, but I don't want to cause you harm as a token of my appreciation."

"Do you think you might eventually love me the same way you loved Mahroo?"

"Yes. That would be easy, I think."

"Then I have a good enough reason to stay for now."

"Still, our troubles won't disappear and circumstances won't change," I said with gloom.

"So we should find a way to change the circumstance to be close. Don't you agree?" she asked so coolly I wondered if she realized the mess she had caused for us by coming to Vancouver.

"I do, but how?" I asked.

"Let's share our feelings and thoughts openly at least, okay?"

"Okay... It makes sense to try it at least," I replied desperately.

"So can I ask you a private question?" she asked.

"Of course."

"Are you still in love with Mahroo or Erica?"

"With two dead women? That's a weird question to ask!"

"Please forgive my bluntness, but you look like still mourning one or both them. They've both died recently, after all."

"No, I don't think I'm in love with ghosts, although mourning or remembering them may be happening subconsciously."

"Sometimes letting go of our deep emotions is hard. The way you mourned Mahroo, especially the incident Reza mentioned in the middle of Tehran streets showed your immense love for her. "

"I'm glad you know about my stories with Mahroo and Erica, especially the incident Reza told the whole family to tease me."

"Was he exaggerating to make us laugh?" Mahtab asked.

"A little... But, that particular day, I was mostly feeling guilty for what happened to her... And now for Erica, too...!"

"You feel responsible for their deaths?" she asked fretfully.

"Yes. In fact..." I paused when another harsh memory crossed my mind swiftly.

Mahtab stared at me in a haze. "In fact, what?"

"I just recalled being blamed for Zia's suicide, too, besides the role I'd supposedly played in causing Mahroo's death."

"Who blamed you for Zia's suicide? Mahroo?"

"She did it a little when she came to Vancouver after Zia died, but mostly Zia's father, Dervish Ali."

"Well, that was not your fault. Zia was a jealous husband and he was hurting Mahroo a lot," Mahtab said.

"He was allegedly my friend, and his impression of Mahroo's affection for me drove him nuts. Even Mahroo said so."

"No, you weren't responsible for his suicide in my book."

"Still, I can't ignore my role in Mahroo's, Zia's, and Erica's deaths somehow, each one differently for a peculiar reason."

"Just stop all these excuses and burdening your brain."

"Let's blame the coma for this, too, then," I said jokingly.

"Yes, that's better," she said. "That way, we can at least hope your mood will improve when the coma symptoms fade away."

"And I'm sure you can help me do this better and faster."

"I hope so," she replied. "I'll always adore Mahroo, but I'm also grateful to her for my present feeling—this special love—for the first time in my life."

"We'll never forget her…"

"She made our love possible, Darren."

"That's true… I think the same way as well," I replied.

"But should I also compete with the memory of Erica?"

"Oh, no, never. I always loved Erica, although she betrayed me. But I never considered going back to her an option for me."

"Never?" she asked as if she knew I was lying. My silence during the day and desire for walking alone could also be taken as clues about my convoluted sentiments about Erica these days!

"Well, to be honest, a couple of times I almost broke under her pressures to reconcile, but luckily fate and circumstances stopped us in time—for good reasons possibly. She'd simply confused me up to the last minute and maybe even now."

"I thought so…! You still seem to miss Erica deeply…, if not being in love with her."

"You think so?"

"Yes, I noticed your reaction to the news about her death, like you were put back into some kind of a coma."

"Maybe you're right. I don't know why she's always had this odd effect on me and perhaps on Reza, too, according to him. Let's hope she won't be haunting me even from eternity," I said rather jokingly, but deep down feared such possibility.

"Let's hope so!" Mahtab said desolately.

"So you have doubts, too?" I asked anxiously.

"Well... Love is often an addiction with bizarre psychological effects, especially if you think Erica has shown her true affection for you, too, during the last days of her life...," she paused with a mix of empathy and jealousy. "...especially if she killed herself after thinking she'd caused your death."

We left the restaurant in a rather great mood and strolled in the quiet streets for half an hour towards Reza's suite.

"I'm sure I'll handle my raw sentiments and Erica's memory better right after talking with Detective Stewart and he sorts out the cause of her death," I said dolefully.

"Yes, knowing what happened to her will help," she replied.

"I really like to move on, too, Mahtab. Erica is gone now."

"I'm glad to hear that. I hope you're right about your feelings about her settling soon, even if it is proven that she committed suicide only for you."

"Erica and Mahroo are not the main issue now," I said warily with fear. "What I'm not sure about is staying in Reza's place."

"I'm sure. You shouldn't live alone and I'm lonely, too."

"Maybe… I must feel somewhat safe and relaxed to put my life back in some order," I blurted sincerely.

"Yes, you now need a place to recuperate."

"And you're an angel helping me get back to normal."

"I'll help you with everything you let me," she said giddily.

"Okay. But don't you wanna tell Reza about me living here?"

"No, not yet," she replied.

"What if he asks you about my whereabouts?"

"I'd probably have to say you went to your place and I have no idea where you might be."

"You're such an adventurous angel!" I said.

At last, we arrived home and settled on the couch again.

"Thanks for being so kind to me, but now we need willpower and some time to think," I said.

"You're right," she replied. "Let's put our heads together and decide how to face the problems."

"Okay then… Let's see if putting our heads together can sort out all these emotional and moral issues," I said with resignation.

"Let's," she murmured, grinned playfully with charm, put her head next to mine, and we pressed our foreheads together very gently.

Thrilled by her subtle sense of humour, I worried about my customary wit that seemed rusty these days after the damn coma —another serious side-effect, I reckoned. I wished I could show my appreciation of her devotion all along, especially the last two months—*maybe in bed?!*

"I guess it is better and safer to put *only* our heads together for the time being?" I said playfully, hoping to be a bit witty at least.

"I guess so… For now!" she replied with a cute chuckle and started walking towards the kitchen.

Chapter Three
A Mad Murderer

In her long, white dress, Mahroo looked very beautiful but sad, ambling curiously with her usual elegance amidst the large crowd in our parents' garden. Filled with nostalgic joy, I watched her furtively, while wondering what we, especially she, were doing there like old times. Still, I hoped to elude her with confusion, as if worrying about the chance of upsetting her. At last, she found me in a corner, mourning our family's fate. When I looked up with a startle, our eyes met and she began sauntering towards me with a glare unfitting her warm character. My urge to escape the sister I had not seen for so long and loved so much bewildered me. Yet, I could not flee, as if chained to my chair. The shock of her incredible, lively presence had apparently paralyzed me.

"Just leave them alone, Reza," she whispered in my ears and disappeared swiftly behind the canopy hanging from the gazebo. I jumped out of my seat and followed her into the gazebo.

"Wait Mahroo, wait please!" I yelled as I reached the other side of the gazebo, which brought me to a dim tunnel with no sound or sight of Mahroo. I flung my arms in the air to find my way around, but suddenly fell into a dark space with a mystifying nature. The crushing pressure of air on my body, as my descent accelerated, was about to explode my head and I trembled with panic about the imminent crash. The pressing compact air filling my wide-open mouth and throat impeded my struggle to scream. About to suffocate, the speedy descent halted swiftly and I floated weightlessly in the air. As I exhaled a sigh of relief, the telephone shriek startled me and I grabbed the receiver with a deep breath, as the sunshine outside the window felt blissful.

"I can't find Darren," T.J. said.

"What do mean, T.J.? Has he escaped the city?"

"Well, I have left him three messages last five days to contact me as soon as possible. This morning I got worried and decided to go to his apartment. I buzzed the caretaker after Darren did not answer. He said, he had not seen him or even knew he had been discharged from the hospital. I asked him to let me in his suite to see if he was okay. I told him I was worried."

"Good show… What happened?" I asked nervously.

"Nobody seems to be living there, Reza. The place is tidied up and six messages on the machine seemed unchecked."

"Where can he be, then? Maybe he is back in the hospital?"

"No, I forgot to mention. I called the hospital last night, too, to find out if he had gone back there," T.J. said.

"I don't like this a bit," I said nervously.

"Maybe he's staying with a friend or one of his girlfriends?"

"Do you know any of them?"

"No. I don't think he has any relatives in Vancouver, either."

"His only relative is his father in Toronto, right?" I asked.

"Yes... Maybe I should call him, then, to see if Darren is there. I guess I have his number," T.J. said.

"It's a long shot… But call him, anyway, please."

"Do you think he has the patience to go to Toronto, especially now that your *charming* sister is here?" T.J. asked teasingly.

"No, I don't think so. But where could he be, then?"

"Unless he is…" T.J. hesitated ruining my day.

"You think so, too?" I asked tensely, although I had suspected this very likely travesty myself already. We can read each other's minds closely even if the matter had not been so predictable in this special case. Still I hated any hint confirming my hunch about Darren's whereabouts and raising the urgency for resolving this daunting scenario somehow.

"Can he be that stupid?" I continued.

"Where else could he be, then?" T.J. asked.

"I'll call Mahtab and leave her a blunt message this time, but it'd be useless," I said with despair. "Can you think of any other way to find him?"

"Not really," T.J. replied giddily, as if relieved a little at least.

"Check other nearby hospitals. Hopefully you'll find him," I said tensely, yet abhorring the evil in my voice and unconscious desire for his return to the hospital, in the same condition perhaps, just to make all our lives easier.

"You rather see him back in a hospital?" T.J. asked wittily.

"Then, we'd at least know where he is when necessary."

"You surely talk like the devil yourself these days."

"I know, but sometimes I have to even act like him to keep my family safe around this reckless Casanova."

"I understand… Bye, Satan," T.J. said teasingly.

"Thanks, deputy devil…! Do your job properly now and call me soon with better news."

Lost in my depressing thoughts about my bizarre role alongside Darren's demonic existence haunting my family's falling fate, the phone rang again. "Hello," I said.

"Can we meet today, Reza?" Bijan sounded quite agitated and his tone was more like an order than a request.

"Sure… When and where?"

"Come here if you can... anytime... I'm not going to work or anywhere else today. We must really talk."

"All right... I'll come by right after breakfast and making a few phone calls," I said.

While preparing and eating my dismal breakfast—only two boiled eggs and a piece of toast—I pondered what Bijan wanted to discuss again. Yet, I could do nothing else about his commands while Darren and Mahtab did not return my various messages in all sorts of tones. Still, I tried to stay calm by inventing some plausible excuses for their apathy. Maybe Darren was travelling or staying with a friend we did not know about. Yet, all logical clues hinted they were just eluding me and getting absorbed deeper in their perversions. I abhorred to entertain such twisted ideas and upset Bijan or myself prematurely, but it felt wiser now to prepare both of us for the worst scenario and get ready to face another mayhem around my jinxed family.

I wondered about my nightmare this morning before T.J.'s call had awakened me. Mahroo had always been in my thoughts since she had left me alone with so much grief—our father's death, our mother's declining health, Nazi's pains to cope with the loss of both her parents one after another, Mahtab's madness and departure, Erica's death all in itself, but also leading to the demise of my business affairs in Vancouver, and on and on. *Oh, my god, are my troubles ever going to end?*

Mahroo had been mostly nice to me in real life and in my dreams after her departure. So, her anger with me about what Bijan was forcing me to do had rattled me. 'Just leave them alone, Reza' she had ordered me briskly and vanished without showing any sympathy about my headaches or helping me when I had gotten stuck in that scary tunnel in my nightmare. In fact, she had possibly pushed me into the tunnel herself, as a warning perhaps, to suffer such a horrific free fall that almost broke all my bones without hitting any object or the ground.

Credulously, we often imagine our dreams and nightmares carry divine clues. Ironically, I had been curious about this likely phenomenon and hoping to gauge its role within my faith. Yet, Mahroo's order sounded fully irrational. How could I leave Mahtab and Darren alone—those silly maniacs? They were not even returning my calls. But if I did not do something fast, the situation could get ugly soon, mostly for them, actually. Those idiots seemed clueless about the mess they were creating. Still, I felt guilty for my intention to ignore Mahroo's wish—merely another burden for me at the time I needed support and solutions instead of blame from my sister's angry ghost as well! I have had enough headaches and confusion with Erica's spirit already and now Mahroo's ghost seemed eager to taunt me, too. In fact, I had enough pains with mortals already without some ghosts rushing to bug me so often as well.

I made some urgent business calls and informed my secretary about going to the office later than usual, if at all. Then, I drove pensively towards Bijan's house in Tehran's chaotic traffic jams for an hour. Tired and tense, I left my car hastily at the entrance of his mansion, which nowadays resembled Count Dracula's cursed, deserted castle. It felt as if blood was sucked out of the few leftover creatures still living there since Mahtab's departure. The sickly Morad, Bijan's butler, whispered anxiously that Bijan awaited me in his study. Then he stood timidly with hesitance in the middle of the foyer as if struggling to gather his courage and ask me a question. In the end, he just kept watching me cross the distance to Bijan's office. The echo of my smooth steps on the soft marble floor in the deafening silence of a once noisy, vibrant atmosphere felt bizarre and horrific.

As I entered Bijan's office, his graver than ever grotesque look, so likely due to sleeplessness, smoking, and agony, shocked me. The wrinkles in his pale face appeared to be spreading in hundred directions so quickly for a man of only thirty-three years old. His normally tidy beard was too long and untrimmed. I had never seen so much anguish so evident in anybody's face ever in my life. And I should confess, I have witnessed my good share of people with immense suffering, especially Dervish Ali who was perishing in Evin—the notorious prison in Tehran. A couple of times, I was allowed to visit poor Dervish Ali—and only because of Bijan's recommendation. The agony I had seen on Dervish's face had depressed me beyond imagination and I had left with tears every time. However, Dervish's anguish now appeared pale compared with the suffering I detected in Bijan upon entering his study. My perception about the possible intensity of a person's misery reached a new height that gloomy day upon visiting Bijan in his haunted mansion.

I stood still, trying to regain my composure and find the right words to conceal my fear of being around him. Thankfully, he turned towards Morad who had apparently been waiting behind me like a zombie all by himself. They were all starting to look spooky, so vacant of soul and hope.

"Do you want tea?" Bijan asked me after I turned around and found Morad at the door.

"Yes, please," I said to Morad who nodded in a haze and left.

"Any luck?" Bijan asked.

"No. I've left a few messages and a friend is looking into this matter as well," I said sheepishly.

"Well this isn't good enough anymore...," Bijan said with rage. "This isn't right at all."

"I know…"

"When was Darren discharged from the hospital?"

"About a week ago, I guess."

"So where the hell they've been all this time? Why aren't they answering their damn phones or returning your messages?"

"I wish I knew," I replied timidly.

"The nerve of these people! How can he already forget he'd be still in Evin, rotting, if I hadn't rescued him?"

"I'm sure he's grateful... Then again, he would've not been shot if he'd remained in jail," I said wittily despite my mood just for teasing him and maybe lightening him up a little as well.

But he only frowned. "You wanna be funny, too?"

"I'm sorry. I hoped you could smile for a second, too. But the point is that we don't know what his state of mind is nowadays after being in a coma for three months. Maybe he's in a different hospital in the coma again or something like that," I said without believing a word of it myself.

"And how about your silly sister? How can she do this to us?"

"She's been angry with me for a few months. It has nothing to do with Darren," I said, believing my words even less this time.

"Is that what you think?" Bijan asked with a glimmer of hope for a moment *maybe*, before regaining his senses and restoring his grotesque grimace.

"Yes…," I replied slyly.

"Are you stupid? Why has she been refusing to talk to me?"

"Why did you let her go, anyway?" I asked calmly, still trying to keep my cool despite his rudeness towards me and my sister. I loathed myself for not putting him in his place just in hopes of preventing the matters getting completely out of hand too fast.

"What other choice I had?" Bijan shrieked with such pity I could almost forgive his non-stop insults, although his extreme efforts all along to watch his language about Mahtab in particular had also been obvious. His reserved hopes and courtesy felt both honourable and pitiable.

"We thought you knew about your marriage's instability and the upshot of giving Mahtab your consent to go abroad alone."

"Is that what you really thought?" he asked.

"Yes… I thought you knew what she was doing and saying and you were okay with it."

"You were wrong, then," Bijan shrieked.

"So, why is she in Vancouver?" I asked.

"She is a liberated woman and I wanted to show I respected and trusted her totally. I assumed she went to Vancouver to relax a bit, think about our marriage, and find a way to make it work."

"Is that what you imagined when she asked for separation?"

"Yes. I wanted to believe her. Temporary separation, she said. I thought she needed some time alone to realize her mistake."

"Then, you were wrong," I replied, happy to return his insult.

"The bottomline was that I had no other option but staying cool and agreeing with her as much as possible, or else get ready for her demand for a divorce."

"So, you realized the gravity of your marriage, ha?" I asked.

"Yes, absolutely… I knew she'd leave me… So I decided to leave everything in God's hand."

"Oh… who? God…? Yes…!"

"Don't be a blasphemer, Reza," Bijan blurted with anger. "That is the last thing I can allow in this already doomed house."

"Sorry," I said like a mouse. "But what this outcome shows?"

"That your sister is a liar!? You know her well!" he blasted.

"But didn't you ask yourself why she went to Vancouver?" I asked slyly to hint about the chance for sinful possibilities, too.

"She said she liked to visit that beautiful city and stay in your empty condo. Was she lying about that, too?"

"Didn't you know that Darren also lived in Vancouver?"

"But you all told me he was dying, didn't you?"

"Yes, that's what we all thought, but she also seemed worried about him and wanted to check on him as well. Maybe she had somehow become obsessed to save his life."

"Worried about him? Save his life?"

"Yes, that was the impression I got… My sisters seem to have turned into missionaries one after another after failing in their lousy marriages."

"So why didn't you open your damn mouth and mention these atrocities to me before she left?" Bijan asked with rage.

"Because I was only guessing myself. But even if I was sure, how could I say anything that could cause more frictions between you two than help the situation? Besides, I really believed Darren was dying, anyway."

"But you knew her real intentions at least, better than I did."

"Even so, she was only trying to help a dying man, a special family friend. She said Mahroo was asking her to help Darren."

"Actually, I guess she made some hints about Mahroo asking her to check on Darren, too," Bijan said with stress and a jolt of confusion. "Did she really believe in this mumbo-jumbo?"

"So why are you upset now so suddenly? Why are you angry with me if she had made a hint about checking on Darren, too?"

"Because Darren is not dying anymore, is he?"

"Apparently not…! He's probably quite well and kicking again," I said slyly to retaliate Bijan's rudeness to me and also do anything possible to prepare him for the worst scenario.

"That's why I'm mad. I don't like this mess a bit."

"Well, I'll try to find them soon and see what's going on," I said desperately.

"That isn't good enough anymore, as I said. I've waited long enough for you to sort out this matter, but we're getting nowhere. I'm going nuts here when I think my wife is out there possibly fooling around with an ungrateful son of a bitch."

"I think you're only imagining these nasty scenarios," I said with compassion and pity, while hating my hypocrisy.

"I hope so, but I doubt it," Bijan shouted.

"So we just have to wait and see if anything has changed now that Darren is apparently not dying."

"But how are you going to find out? When?" Bijan yelled.

"I'm doing my best, Bijan…"

"But you're not getting anywhere... What should I do now, then? I've been ashamed looking into my parents' faces for the last few months and now all this extra chaos. Nobody believes me anymore when I say Mahtab is working on her post-doctorate at a university in Vancouver. I've lost my honour and respect. I can't take it anymore, Reza."

"Worst of all, all this lying will send you directly to hell based on your own religious beliefs. Aren't you afraid?" I said merely for teasing him, despite or because of my mood again.

"Yes, she's even ruined my faith and relationship with God."

"I understand… It is a tough situation," I whispered with fret, staring down at the floor.

"No, you don't seem to understand… And, no, it is not just a tough situation… It's a plain fucking catastrophe. Try to accept it if you really care about your sister!"

I looked at him with both disgust and fear before whispering, "Something terrible must've happened to Darren, since we can't even find him. As I said, maybe he's in a hospital again."

"I don't think so or care. I want you all to know that I won't take this matter lightly anymore. I'm going to handle the situation directly myself," he said with rage, white foam gathering around his fast-moving lips and spattering all over the room as he walked restlessly.

I was terrified looking into his eyes, while the outcome of his wrath looked dire by the way his mind seemed so messy today.

"What do you intend to do?" I asked fretfully.

"First, I must tell you a story," he said with a sly tone.

Morad knocked on the door and entered with tea and sweets. He placed the tray on the table awkwardly like Frankenstein and left quickly. The poor guy seemed even more terrified around Bijan than I had felt myself during that short period.

"What story?" I asked.

"Did Darren tell you why he was arrested at the airport and sent to jail last time he came to Tehran?"

"No. Only once I asked him and he said he wasn't allowed to discuss it according to your instructions."

"Well, at least he's shown some integrity in that regard. Maybe there's still hope for him to survive the mayhem he's causing for all of us, especially himself."

"So you want to tell me the reason yourself?"

"I guess I should, because it relates to what I'm going to do about Darren now."

"Okay…"

"But still we must keep this matter confidential. You shouldn't discuss it with Darren or anybody else. Can you do that?"

"Sure."

"During the last few months he lived in Tehran and worked in your company, he knocked up a girl called Sima who lived in his building. She is the niece of a Cabinet minister I don't want to name. The family decided to keep the matter a secret and raise the child as an adopted war orphan. They were afraid Sima might reveal the secret to Darren out of love or desperation. So they arranged for his arrest at the airport if he ever returned to Tehran.

They hoped he wouldn't come back, but had to take precautions, which proved to be warranted. He was arrested and jailed when he returned after the child was born. When I began checking on his situation in Evin, I was brought into picture at last in absolute confidence by the minister and I was told to make it clear to him that he must leave Iran right away and never reveal the secret or try to see the child. They had decided to tell Darren the truth, anyway, and get his commitment since they were not sure about either Sima or her brother revealing the secret to him someday even if he never came back to Tehran."

"So Sima never found out about Darren's return to Iran?"

"I don't think so… But let me give you the gist of the matter that concerns us now."

"And what is that?"

"Sima's brother. He's a powerful colonel in the Revolutionary Guard and he's been adamant to find Darren and punish him for dishonouring his family and leaving Sima with a fatherless child. He'd never agreed with his family's decision to let Darren off the hook if he promised to never pursue or reveal his son's matter."

"So?"

"He, this Colonel, has talked to me a few times and I've tried to keep him calm. I've somewhat convinced him so far to leave Darren alone. But now I may have to change my mind and in fact help him find Darren sooner than he could do on his own."

"But you know these people kill for reasons much less than family honour. They do it even abroad easily without a trace."

"Yes, I do, very well! That's why I trust them do a good job."

"You want to help them find Darren?"

"What other choice do I have?" Bijan said with satisfaction.

"So basically you don't mind murdering someone to get what you want," I asked.

"To get back what is mine… Although I don't intend to kill anybody myself. All I can't do anymore is protecting a man who is eager to steal my wife. I just don't have any incentive anymore to stop the colonel to do whatever he likes to do to Darren."

Bijan looked like a mad murderer to me at that moment. At the same time, it was perceivable how he might have turned into such a ruthless figure sitting before me. He was just too naïve and madly jealous, offended, humiliated, and desperate. In the end, I somewhat sympathized with him to be so callous when his wife and the man he had saved from possible death in the Iranian jail were betraying him so openly and damaging his honour, too. How many people's lives and honours was this imbecile Darren ruining and hoping to get away with?

"You sound so cruel, Bijan," I said.

"In fact, if this mess is not cleaned up soon, I may even pursue other options, besides helping Colonel find Darren quickly."

"I just can't believe I'm hearing you talk like this, Bijan. Why don't you just divorce Mahtab if you don't trust her anymore?"

"Well, I'll do that if she returns and tells me that's what she wants. But how can I divorce her when she's in Vancouver and leaving me here in limbo?"

"You know there're ways of doing it, mostly on the grounds that she's disobeying you to return to Tehran."

"Yeah, it may be possible. But it'll be harder and take longer. But mainly, I want her to look into my eyes and ask for a divorce, if that's what she wants. I deserve that much, don't you think, especially after destroying my honour?"

"Yes, you deserve that and much more!" I replied.

"I wanna reason with her one last time before letting her go."

"Do you think she'll return to Tehran merely based on your promise to divorce her? Are you that naïve?"

"Well, that's her best option... I want you to know and make her understand that I am very serious."

"What if she doesn't wanna do that and instead asks for her divorce from Vancouver?"

"Then, I can't keep Colonel from doing whatever he's been dreaming to do to Darren. I'm sorry, Reza. I can't do anything else. Mahtab and Darren have hurt me deeply," he said. By now I felt he did not want to reveal the name of the colonel, either.

"But, again, I must say that you'll be a murderer, then."

"Mahtab was the murderer, not me," Bijan replied.

"Why?"

"She murdered our son..., intentionally or with her depression, maybe because of her worries or love for Darren," Bijan stated with angst and anger.

"Well, something has been going wrong for a long time," I said desperately.

"I agree and the only way to sort this out is to let the angry colonel handle Darren at least."

"I don't like the idea of sending some hooligans to confront Mahtab. If my mother finds out, she'll die. Or, actually, she'll kill you herself."

"I don't care about her wrath these days, either. I'm past all these sentimentalities and I've lost my patience."

"Bijan, you're now talking like a maniac. And this guy seems to be crazy, too… What's his damn name?" I asked slyly.

"Who? Colonel Arshadi?" Bijan blurted but realized my trick promptly. "Don't mention his name to anybody for now."

"Okay, but you both sound like murderers and Mahtab will go nuts if I tell her what you're up to," I said.

"I'm only telling you the facts," he replied coolly.

"But taking these kinds of drastic steps would ruin all of us as well as your marriage. Don't provoke Mahtab."

"What do you expect me to do? You've never married and do not understand my agony and disrepute. You don't feel the pain that these sorts of betrayals cause," Bijan said pitifully.

"So that is your position?" I asked with despair.

"Yes… The only other option I can think of is that you go there immediately and report your findings within a week. You'd better go convince Mahtab to return," Bijan said with a serious tone, which I resented very much.

"Me? Why don't you go yourself?"

"First of all, I don't want to face that son-of-a-bitch Darren or fight with Mahtab over there. Second, I need a Canadian visa, which is not quick or easy for government officials, as you know. Nowadays the U.S. and Canada are not letting Iranian officials in their countries mostly out of spite."

"But I have lots of business obligations here," I said testily, witnessing a nasty side of Bijan all of a sudden.

"I don't care…," Bijan replied coolly.

"I don't think I can do much with Mahtab or Darren, anyway. They are as stubborn as you seem to be."

"Well… The choice is yours. But I need your answer by this afternoon, because the colonel wants to see me tonight again and I've agreed. He knows about my mood these days and why."

While pondering Bijan's ridiculous demand, his pitiful eyes and desperation reminded me swiftly of Dervish Ali again whom I had meant to go visit soon.

"Bijan, how are we progressing with Dervish Ali's case? He doesn't have much time left and I was hoping to at least let him die among his family."

"I can't really worry about him. In fact, this matter depends on how you handle things with Mahtab and Darren, too, and how soon my mind is free to focus on other stuff."

"So now Dervish's fate also depends on your mood?" I asked.

"No… His fate depends on Mahtab and Darren," Bijan said matter-of-factly with satisfaction and a vile smirk.

I left Bijan with anger and disgust about Dervish Ali's fate also being in my hand now in line with Bijan's demands. Yet, this situation could drag on for months, while poor Dervish's health and spirits were declining rapidly and he could die away from his family. Then again, I understood Bijan's desperation to resolve this matter by civiler tactics first, including blackmail. If Dervish Ali knew that his fate was now hanging in my, Mahtab's, and Darren's hands, he would get even more depressed.

The idea of traveling to the other side of the world with such urgency only for some news about Darren's whereabouts, to keep Bijan calm, and hope to rescue Mahtab, if at all possible, felt silly.

I was so furious I wished *again* Mahtab had not called me a week earlier, so timely, when dear Erica was also calling and promising me eternal love and happiness in her bosom. Instead, I was now dragged into this new conundrum, while my painful memories of my past futile meddling in my sisters' affairs filled me with guilt and raised my doubt about my right to pry into Mahtab's affairs, *not to mention Mahroo's order to leave them alone!*

After settling my nerves, I began weighing my options to find a simpler solution rather than going to Vancouver. Maybe I could push T.J. further to go to Mahtab's apartment late in the evening when she would most likely be at home. He could use an excuse, such as finding a document for me. If she did not answer, maybe he could even bribe the caretaker of her building, too, to let him check inside her apartment. T.J. was now becoming an expert in handling caretakers and spying on people, thanks to me. Maybe the caretaker had some information; or else, T.J. could hire him or a detective to spy on Mahtab for a couple of days. Still, I did not have the guts to impose such an impertinent chore on T.J. with unpredictable outcome. The chance of angering Mahtab felt too risky as well, though it was merely my suite that she was abusing for sinful activities. Other gimmicks crossing my mind also felt futile and the risks of my plan backfiring and ruining Mahtab's minimal trust in me were high. No, these desperate, last-minute options felt impotent.

So, before reaching my office, I made up my mind to obey Bijan's ridiculous new order and make a plan to go to Vancouver the next day. It was such a tight schedule, but I believed I could manage it since my passport and visa were in place. As I got to my office, I asked my secretary to book my flight to Vancouver for the next day and I called Bijan behind the closed door.

"Okay, I'll fly to Vancouver, tomorrow," I told him.

"Good decision. I'll keep Colonel in check for a week or so," he replied. "Just bring her back with you."

"I'll try."

"You haven't told anybody about your trip, right?" he asked.

"I just told my secretary to make a flight reservation."

"Tell her right away to keep it a secret. Don't tell anybody else, either. Most of all, don't leave a message for Mahtab to run away before you get there."

"Okay, I won't. You don't tell anybody, either," I said. "Not even to your or my family, especially my mom."

"Okay," he said with surprise. "But call me immediately from Vancouver, as soon as you have some information."

"Yes sir!" I blurted with anger.

"Thanks Reza. I appreciate your help to avoid a catastrophe. Trust me, it is the right thing you're doing, for everybody's sake."

I hung up, made a few phone calls, signed a few documents, and asked my secretary to come in to give her some work-related instructions. Then I told her, "Tell everybody, even my mom, if she happens to ask, that I'm in Dubai, but can't be reached for a few days." She nodded with surprise.

Then, I rushed to see my mom and Nazi before my ludicrous departure to Vancouver without telling them where I was going and why. While stuck in heavy traffic, I wondered again how Bijan had found out about Darren's recovery rather quickly. He had just surprised me with the information only four days after Mahtab had told me about this matter in her call from Vancouver. And I had simply confirmed his assertion sheepishly. Did Bijan or Colonel Arshadi have spies in Vancouver checking on Mahtab or maybe Darren all along while he had been in the hospital? That was a worrisome mystery all by itself. But as much as I was keen to know the answer, I hated giving Bijan the satisfaction of lying to me about this matter if I asked him directly. I just had to wait for a chance to drag this information out of him sneakily somehow, too, the way I had done about the colonel's name.

Chapter Four
Forlorn Forgotten Fathers

Quite sceptical about the chance of Darren going to Toronto when Mahtab was in Vancouver, I called his dad twice, anyway, just to humour Reza. My second call was at ten p.m. when Mr. Durant would logically be at home. Still, no body or machine answered. According to Darren, his dad was quite frail, mentally mostly, so hardly ventured out except for grocery shopping or a short visit with his friends. I wondered if the poor man was still alive. What if he had been dead in his cold suite for months and nobody knew? What a dreadful thought and scene, and what a highly likely, sinful scenario.

Most likely Mr. Durant did not even know his son was out of the coma. Had Darren bothered, or even considered, telling him he was awake again? I doubted it with great pain regarding the youths' handling of their parents nowadays. Would he ever grasp his father's depth of anguish? Probably not! Only a father *might* feel the agony those like me endure nowadays, maybe only when mourning their own family's malice! Poor Mr. Durant must now start to suffer all over again from Darren's apathy, too!

The next day, abruptly I recalled Darren's comment about his dad's new habit of not answering the phone. Apparently, some juvenile neighbours made prank calls to him simply for fun or out of spite for his growing crankiness. He had even turned off his answering machine, which would have always been filled with profanities and titters, anyway. Appreciating this poor, old man's excellent excuse for not answering his phone was a relief for me at the time I was getting testy about people's growing arrogance nowadays to not answer their phones or return our calls promptly, if at all. In my case, a big factor had surely been Feri's tenacity to turn everybody against me with endless energy, I imagined!

Luckily, I also recalled Darren's remark about some kind of a private gimmick that his dad had asked him to use when calling him. I had to think for ten minutes to build a vague idea about the weird, cute system Darren had mentioned. Finally, I considered giving it a try. I dialled the number and disconnected as soon as I heard the first ring. Then I repeated the routine immediately. On the third attempt, I let the phone ring.

"Darren?" a quivering voice answered eventually.

"No, Mr. Durant; this is T.J., Darren's friend."

There was a long silence on the phone and I thought I could hear his panting and quiet wailing.

"Are you all right, Mr. Durant?" I asked before realizing the likely cause of his alarm. "No, Mr. Durant..., listen... He's—"

"Has he… has he died?" he asked at last.

"No, Mr. Durant, I have good news... He's out of the coma."

Another long silence with lots more panting and howling. I realized the futility of asking the question I was calling him for.

"He is all right now and resting in a friend's house. I thought I should let you know," I said.

"Isn't he going to his apartment?"

"He will, I guess, as soon as he feels strong to stay alone."

"You are not… lying? What did ye… say your name was?"

"My name is T.J. And no, I'm not lying."

"Can you ask him to call me right away?" he asked.

"Yes, I will. Are you all right?"

"When… when will you be talking… talking to him…?" he asked with difficulty, still panting and trying to talk.

"Soon… But I'm sure he's out of the hospital."

Again a long silence, save for heavy panting and howling.

"Ask him… Ask him to call me… Will you?" he said at last.

"Yes, I will. I promise."

Then I heard him sigh and hang up the phone. I did not think he was rude, but rather as disturbed as Darren had described him a few times. He had hung up most likely to go cry privately and loudly for a long while. The good news had surely shaken him on top of his initial jolt when he had imagined the worst. Still, he had sounded rather intact despite his shattered emotions after my call. To me, even his invention for contacting him, while eluding those appalling neighbours and intruders, felt ingenious indeed.

I wondered why Darren had not called him yet. What a lousy son this Darren was proving more every day to be, really! I felt sick pondering the occasions I'd seen him as my own son—*only sometimes, when I hadn't been so testy about youths these days*!

Why people become so careless about those who love them so deeply? And then waste their entire lives trying to get love from strangers who would only keep disappointing them time and again. Naturally, I was pondering again my daughters' way of treating me. How could they be so reckless about my feelings? Should I fret about their apathy even worsening, maybe turning into hostility? I felt pity for Mr. Durant. Then I recalled I had not called my own father for more than four months myself. He was in his late seventies and quite frail, too. I thought I should call him soon, though he would be surprised. What can I tell him or my mother? Why are we so out of touch and topics to share with our parents? Guilt was clogging both my mind and throat. They had never imagined I would leave them alone at their old age to go live in Canada—on the opposite side of the globe. They were alone there and I was alone here. Their only other son had left Iran to study in the U.S. many years ago, but never returned to

Iran, not even for a visit. Instead, he married an American girl and became totally careless about his parents and brother beyond what we often expect even from the Westerners with their alleged cold attitude. To me, one must be even eviler than devil to be so cruel with one's family.

Feri was on her way out for her weekly women's party, which I believed convened mostly for keeping each other abreast of the most recently tested schemes for torturing their husbands. I could not picture that even the Nazis had so frequent, edifying meetings to conspire or share their new potent tactics. She had put on plenty of makeup, as usual, which made me wonder why these women bothered going through all this hassle when no men were supposedly in those parties. Were they ashamed of showing their real faces even to one another?

"Who were you talking to?" she asked with tension.

"Darren's father," I replied.

"What about?"

"About Darren being out of the coma."

"Can't Darren do that himself?"

"Apparently not… Is it a crime to talk to an old man, too?"

"You care about this Darren, and now his father, more than you care about your family," she yelled testily.

"Because he seems to be the only one noticing my pains."

"Good for you… Have you found him yet?"

"No… Reza and I wondered if his dad knew something."

"He's probably living with one of his girlfriends and not even bothering to let people know where he is. From what I've heard from people, this Darren sounds quite a screwball and selfish."

"See who's talking…!" I said with a tense chuckle.

"What do mean? Say it straight if you dare."

"I don't… Just leave me alone," I said impatiently.

"Last night's leftovers are in the fridge… You and the girls figure out something for your supper," Feri said casually and left.

From the family room window, I watched Feri drive her new Mercedes out of the driveway and turn into the main street. I felt lonely again in this big, soulless house. So I marched towards the study in hopes of forgetting even myself through some writing at least. My sole consolation about spending so much money on a house was the use of the cosy study with a view of Vancouver downtown, the ocean, and the Lions Gate Bridge. Most days, I sat there for hours and tried to write. The breathtaking view made my forced seclusion rather tolerable, while I hid from the callous occupants of the house. They behaved outlandishly aloof these days, like some outer space creatures, anyway, staring at me like I was an alien myself instead of them! Still, hearing their noise and skirmishes around the house usually thrilled me whenever they happened to congregate.

Anytime the phone rang, I jumped, hoping it would be Darren, mainly for forcing him contact his forlorn dad as soon as possible. This mission felt more urgent to me now than fulfilling Reza's request or my personal incentives for finding Darren. Naturally, I was quite keen to hear his voice again along with the percolating tale about his new love victim—Reza's other allegedly charming sister now! But mostly, I needed my confidants urgently as my last refuge when I was feeling helpless in a foreign land alone, unable to do a damn thing about my dwindling fate.

In fact, besides my family's rising animosity making me feel like an orphan rotting in a large city, Darren's coma and Reza's absence in Vancouver during the last three months have been so demoralizing. I have missed our debates and reminisced of those good old times when they had much more than me to nag about life and family! I missed the times when mostly Darren had done the whining about women, while I had offered my two cents with subtle envy. But now it was his turn to listen to my grievances a bit as soon as he had enough strength to bear me, too. Not that I hoped anybody or any wisdom could save me, but just finding a pair of sympathetic ears felt urgent. Most of all, of course, I trusted only them to pour my guts out to without worrying about my words reaching Feri's long ears. Most likely Darren had a lot to talk to me, too, about Mahtab and his new love dilemmas!

Poor guy! *I wondered which one of us was in a bigger mess these days!!*

One *amazing* wisdom I had shared with Darren and he had taken to heart was that, 'One bad decision can change the course of one's life forever and ruin its best parts, too.' It happened to me the day I agreed to wed Feri for silly reasons, I admit bravely like a gentleman! Why did I do it? The more I have pondered it over the years, the more I have believed in my fine theory regarding human genes mapping our destinies sneakily, usually by making a complete fool of us. I married Feri since my conscience dictated it was the right thing to do despite no emotional or logical reason. My silly conscience! It has screwed me really bad a few times! And where did it come from? I would say it was just the product of some naughty genes rushing to map my destiny.

Recounting the story of falling into Feri's trap is humorous in a bizarre way, though painful and pathetic. So maybe it is worth a quick mention for fun and also as a reflection of human psyche's operation in line with older cultures' droll influence! It happened when Iran was in a hurry to modernize and people were dying to liberate themselves by aborting traditions and absorbing all those crooked Western values hastily. Especially, the youths had begun dating behind their parents' backs, while still trying to fake their conventional shy attitude and appearance as well! It was just a big messy revelation—this Cultural Revolution!

After working nine years in hot Abadan in oil industry with huge pay, I returned to my parent's house in Tehran to start my master's degree for a better career. Feri and I started just a simple fling that youths savoured until they found their ideal match. For months, we enjoyed our erotic wrestling in bed *very safely*—all in good faith based on Iranian strict culture those days that ran in our bloods surreptitiously! She seemed keen and capable only for this type of affair! Then one time, she claimed to have lost her virginity after sitting on the top of me firmly.

"Did we do this?" I asked tensely with suspicion regarding her claim, especially since the clue did not look ample in our case.

No shy lad like me could gauge the evidence or the accuracy of allegations most girls made regularly. But she only glared at me with real or phony panic before cringing and crying so loudly my parents would have come to her rescue had they been at home. At least I had been wise enough to bring her around only during my parents' absence.

The taboo of losing one's virginity before marriage attacked mostly Feri, while our limited knowledge of cultural rules raised all sorts of hysterical thoughts for our analysis. I tried to calm her, yet a horrific scene of mob stoning her to death before coming after me haunted me, too. Most likely I deserved some blame as well, since the instrument of her demise belonged to me, although she had abused it. It might have not even mattered how she had brought this *disaster* and disgrace upon herself! I should be the one to be hanged, or possibly *even* forced to marry her, even if I swore until my last breath that she had been the one taking me for a comfortable chair. What an injustice! Being in bed with her was a cultural crime already, never mind ruining her virginity, too!

With a great deal of begging and soothing promises, *except a marriage,* I calmed her down at last and we fled the scene of the crime hastily before my parents returned. In the coffee shop, she nibbled on her sandwich with odd, sneaky tears sluicing down her cheeks. Then, the entire night, I was kept awake by that particular gene that runs our conscience crazy. I tried to defy it—my stupid conscience—with astounding justifications that fully exonerated me from any wrongdoing. Yet, all that perfect logic was going to waste under the pressure of the malicious 'conscience gene.' I felt somewhat in charge of myself again in the morning, I admit. I felt I would die if the gene won, so I strived to prove my youthful resilience and pride. Forget about her, I tried to convince myself —the stupid gene, I mean—while I attended my classes at the university all day with my normal arrogance, as if no international disaster had occurred the day before in my bedroom and the world was not about to come to its end! I met Feri for lunch at the cafeteria, but we did not talk much.

Our relationship remained totally undefined and awkward for a few months. We kept going out and having sex regularly now without raising the topic that had caused her *alleged* disrepute. We just kept enjoying the aftermath of the catastrophe. Now that we had broken the rule once, we might as well smash the records stealthily with great tenacity, while entertaining ourselves with its soothing outcome regularly! Feri's liberalism and sense of quick return to normalcy was most admirable. So stupidly, I felt I could not just break-up with her at this critical point, since at the very least she might make a scene in front of my parents who knew her parents. Besides, not even a naïve, conscientious boy like me could ignore the merits of the status quo rendering tons of sex—such novelty in Iran for unmarried guys—for a year! I thought I must let time cure all wounds and fate does its magic—until she forgot the incident and me, too. Actually, I felt she would soon invent a good excuse for her dire disrespect of our culture, which seemed to be losing its ground fast, anyway, now with too many girls loving the loose Western teachings so much. They just showed an admirable determination to abolish traditional rules, especially those boring sexual ones. A big rebellion was evolving and Feri was one of the flag bearers. Meanwhile, why make a fuss about culture or Feri's claim, I reckoned slyly! *Silly me, really! Such a naïve jerk I've often been, especially during youth!*

Even after I believed I had suppressed that stupid conscience gene, it kept proving its super power through sneaky manoeuvres to lead my life onto a destructive path. I could invent all kinds of fine justifications to comfort myself. I could learn arrogance and apathy abundantly and maybe even abandon her. However, at the end, the gene won. Feri had surely played her hand slyly to help my conscience gene, I should say—to give her all due credits for fooling me more than my conscience could have done it alone. She paraded herself as an angel of mercy, passion, and patience, despite her apparent narcissism and nasty character she strived to conceal in vain. So I kept seeing her, despite my deep reservation for ever marrying such a phony girl, while my casual attitude had possibly been making *the ultra conscious conscience gene* only angrier and more proactive in return to team up with my other vulnerable organs for taming my psyche!

Then, as though all the evidences manifesting so far about the genetic roots of humans' naiveté were not forceful enough, some other sneaky genes also joined in to impregnate her out of spite for all my hard work during our sexual intimacies and *moments of* triumph—bastards! That proved to be the last straw for my exhausted, struggling psyche and an indisputable show of 'genetic intrusion' for setting one's fate through absurd decisions—like the ones besieging and turning me gradually and enigmatically into a soft-hearted imbecile, despite my strict disciplines, alleged intelligence, convictions, and egotism.

At the end, I simply could not bring myself to let Feri abort that tiny, helpless fetus, though she looked open about that option. I felt I should save my first baby—now called Rose—instead of punishing it for our sins during a long baffling sexual adventure mixed with a huge amount of thinking and analyses. Therefore, I married Feri to humour the sneaky gene dogged to contrive my first daughter. And now, her dire apathy, instead of gratitude for marrying her mean mother—solely for saving her—singes my heart deeply. I believe Feri's genes have mutilated the conscience gene I had hoped to gift to Rose, as my reward at least—the gene that had started this whole shenanigan. But no...! I have created her to treat me like an enemy and sometimes like an animal. Or maybe she knows the sad truth and is now mad at me merely for giving her a life, which is possibly full of anguish in her own way, the way living is often shitty for everyone nowadays. A few times, when filled with rage, I have been tempted to strike Rose, with the reality that: More crucial than being her devoted father is the fact that I had prevented a hasty mutilation of her being at the expense of ruining my own existence! Any woman would have also cherished me forever after my divine sacrifice, but not Feri!

The early married years in Iran were not as painful since I was mostly outside making money and Feri was busy spending it. She was also occupied by our three daughters and her part-time job as a nutritionist at Mehr hospital before getting fed up with life in Iran and insisting to emigrate to a modern country. Now here we are in Canada; Feri a novice real estate agent driving a shiny Mercedes, our daughters going to school to learn how to torture their parents, and me just a hopeless self-proclaimed writer!

Feri's real estate license seemed to have become much more than a professional certificate, though! It was serving her in many other ways, including as a licence for 'absenteeism,' especially after the Mercedes! She avoided regular work hours, although she promised to do so. "Do some grocery shopping and make a simple dinner for the kids and yourself," she often said casually on her way out, sometimes in the stairwell going down to the garage. I just had to put the mountain of dishes left in the kitchen sink and around the house in the dishwasher and run it before rushing to prepare the dinner that dirtied the dishes all over. Just because I did not have a real occupation, I had become a slave—a depressed nobody. House cleaners came regularly, thank God. Yet, I had swiftly become responsible for running the household fulltime, while Feri drove in the streets of Vancouver or met her clients or friends for coffee or whatever, with no tangible results so far. This was simply an absurd situation for me after being a successful bank executive for so long and making all the money that those four women of my life were enjoying so lavishly.

Feeling so lonely, just because we had come to Canada, was surely getting unbearable, however it felt too insulting when they told me to go back to Iran alone if I really wanted to! Actually, leaving more household chores for me to do was starting to feel like their sly tactic to push me escape Canada faster. I should have probably done just that right away before things had gotten too confusing and intolerable! My patience had just boosted their persistence apparently.

By the way, I have always believed Feri's senses of liberalism and feminism deserved a big recognition for flourishing Persian's modern culture! She has been a leader in abolishing those boring traditions, after all. The Western values, especially materialism and sexual liberation, would not have engulfed Iran so fast had not been for the efforts of some pioneer sluts like Feri who fought so selflessly to eradicate our trite values! Thanks to her and her keen comrades, now Iranian girls in the middle and upper classes at least have become much more arrogant with no worry about virginity as a traditional bridal virtue. Meanwhile, their modern husbands have become more bewildered and tolerant with no recourse to justice or culture. *Hooray!*

Back to present time hoopla, now Darren's disappearance mostly prickled my curiosity, while finding him felt beyond my means. I wondered if his brain worked properly these days and if he still recalled his past life. I hoped he remembered he had two close friends and a forlorn father eager to talk to him at least! Maybe he was simply lost, wandering in downtown streets like a zombie, while his father cried in Toronto and Reza worried in Tehran. In all, it seemed more likely every day that Reza would be the one giving me the news about Darren's health and hiding place.

Darren has always been hard to find and too complex to figure out, anyway, since Reza introduced him to me. He had returned from Tehran after working three years in Reza's computer firm. Reza hinted that Darren was a heartbroken soul, too, like himself, in spite of his knack for womanizing. To me, however, they both looked like two wrecked Romeos!

Reza's character has also been intriguing me after we met in an Iranian party in 1985 when my family and I had just arrived in Canada. Especially, his limited association with his age group looked weird when so many young girls, including my daughters, chased such a handsome, eligible bachelor in the showy Iranian community of Vancouver. I never grilled him about this matter, while assuming he was simply unlucky with women, like me, or amazingly wise, like a needless guru living in Himalayas. In fact, Darren and Reza were also into spirituality and Reza had studied Sufism with a guru in Iran. They were educated and handsome twenty years my junior. Yet, the age difference had not hindered our connection and consultations rather quickly.

They began confiding in me or confronting each other in front of me with plenty of their juicy secrets soon coming out as well. Especially, Reza's romantic role in Darren's marriage breakdown and the reason Darren had still agreed to go work for him in Iran felt bizarre. Thus, it had probably been natural for our friendship to get messy at times or feel like psychotherapy to resolve mostly their linked family dramas. My role as their mediator has had its fun, too, like a side inclusion in their adventurous love affairs that have often led to intriguing complications and stories, especially since Reza's romantic sisters have kept stirring all sorts of chaos for us three pensive friends. Accordingly, we have grown on each other in a short time and become rather like the three bewildered musketeers in Vancouver.

By the way, explaining the reasons for our intimate friendship in these few paragraphs has been mostly for Feri's benefit and in response to her curiosity and criticism of this pastime of mine as well, like everything else I did. These two young men have been special breeds, rather like old me! Their failure to put their lives together, like me again, felt odd, although I admired their looks, popularity, freedom, and youths with some envy, the way any befuddled, aging man with a nagging wife does, I suppose.

But why should I fuss about their life choices, including me? They sounded like keen scholars to exchange our cynical ideas, mostly about happiness and life—the two crude topics obsessing the sullen public nowadays. Besides, they always brought a joint to smoke when we met, mainly in my house during my family's absence. In particular, I liked Reza for the two new adventures he had introduced to me and gotten me addicted to imprudently—I liked Darren just a bit more than Marijuana, though. Anyway, choosing me as their confidant was also a big compliment and relief for me in itself, since I was running out of friends quickly after arriving in Vancouver and I did not know anybody worth spending my time with. I felt estranged with my haughty old pals, the emerging Iranian aristocrats crowding British Properties and West Vancouver hills. In fact, I abhorred their vile influence over my family, on top of their arrogance, ignorance, and materialism. In return, I was getting cynical and grouchy in seclusion myself, while jotting down plenty of gibberish like a resolute writer pushed by a tough deadline.

Surely, good friends are rare and dear these days, so I have felt lucky in finding Reza and Darren. Our friendship has been both educational and therapeutic for me, despite the agony of being a judge frequently. Accordingly, my family has in fact benefited from this friendship more than me, despite Feri criticism, because it has proven most handy for bearing my family in the new world. Then again, even best friends are pain in the ass regularly. I have wished at times they had not chosen me as their confident and mediator to unload their deepest secrets and betrayal stories on me in their own peculiar versions!

In return, Darren and Reza had probably felt I could help them gauge their shaky convictions about life, as they seemed sceptical about women and modern lifestyles as well, despite their liberal family upbringing. Maybe they thought I knew something about philosophy and psychology, while I dwelled on life's intricacies in modern societies and mentioning my intention of becoming a writer to bear my retirement easier. Still, I wondered if my elderly wisdom has ever been helpful to those two wistful youths, or anybody in fact, especially now that I was drowning in marital life's obscure conflicts myself!

Sometimes, I have wondered if I took them as the sons I never had! In spite of my huge love for my three daughters, playing a fatherly role for Reza and Darren has been soothing, although we three have always viewed our contacts a parallel friendship based on equal wisdom, despite my age seniority and a reserved sense of mental power over them. They sometimes sounded odd, old, and pessimistic for their ages, in their mid-thirties, yet they were also the wisest confused lads around. Ironically, their cynicism and nagging about life have made me like them more! *I also wondered what they have been thinking and saying about me behind my back!*

Curiously, they have liked and respected each other too much all along to let go of their friendship even after major betrayals. They related magically like two old, hurting philosophers making life tough for others and themselves just out of naivety, especially since they have been handsome, bright, and rich. Then again, the youths, including my spoiled daughters, seem to be facing vast dilemmas nowadays!—a sad, novel discovery for me in itself.

Unfortunately, I could not explain these simple facts to Feri, nor would she grasp the meaning of true friendship, the kind Reza and Darren offered me at this depressing stage of my life. She would not grasp my sense of fatherhood towards two strangers when my own kids resented me. Still, in my divinest dreams, I imagined Feri might read this and other facts about her in this book of truths some day, maybe after my death, and feel sorry for both of us sincerely. She might read it at least after her friends and daughters tell her about the great job I have done on exposing her tenacity for malice. It might then help her reflect occasionally and realize, by some miracle, her mostly unique, vile flaws, way beyond humans' general idiosyncrasies, and then plan to redeem herself before dying. This idea—about Feri giving herself a chance for enlightenment—was surely funny and way beyond my divinest dream, though..., maybe even surpassing a wild one!

Yeah… I really had to get hold of Darren as soon as possible. I needed him urgently to hear me even if he was not still quite ready. Listening to his new love story would in itself help me forget my depressing one-dimensional life. I needed a distraction fast before I lost my sanity for so much gibberish and spite piling up in my head. Besides burdening my bored brain cells callously, only so much space I should waste here on paper for whining, instead of letting Darren and Reza do their own bitching in their own chapters. *That's also one way to learn at least a little about what they think and say about me behind my back!*

Chapter Five
Return to the Crime Scene

After our quiet breakfast, I told Mahtab I was going home to check on things, though mainly meaning to spend a few hours alone to reflect, *again*; and to give her a break, too. My silence all morning had alarmed her already about my recurring unintended plunge into the quiet zone this early in the day *again*. Still, she looked hurt and baffled for not asking her *again* to go with me.

"Are you sure you'll be okay going to that apartment again so soon?" she asked like talking about a haunted house.

"Yes, I'm sure," I replied with guilt. "I must try, anyway."

"Okay... Just be careful, Darren," she said anxiously, although her warning might have also been ironical with a personal hint!

Besides her worry about the perceivable risks of visiting the crime scene on my own, my murky mood appeared insulting and mysterious even to myself, let alone her sensitive soul. I worried about her getting fed up with my erratic confusion and aloofness soon and taking my attitude as a sign of my boredom around her. But I stopped fussing after recalling her own mood swings in Barcelona, which I had also learned at last to have been rather justified. She regained her composure soon, too, and offered to give me a ride at least, which I declined with the excuse that the long walk would do me good. I needed the exercise and fresh air, I stressed after kissing both her chicks.

"It seems I haven't still fully recovered," I added solemnly in hopes of justifying my attitude and making her relax. In spite of my muddled mind and mood, keeping her happy felt essential, though tough. "Please forgive my tacky behaviour."

"It'll probably take some time for you to feel normal again," she said graciously with little conviction, like expecting me to know and explain the cause of my recurring urge for solitude. I had some vague ideas about it, yet sharing them with her did not feel wise at this point.

In addition to the effects of being out of this world for so long, my mood swing probably related to the responsibility and pains of getting reacquainted with my life's conundrums and having to make big decisions for myself and others on a regular basis again. With a reserved admiration, I wondered how I had apparently handled such seemingly natural obligations day after day in the past before taking a break for a few months during the coma. My anxiety nowadays about life's extensive demands was most likely related to my bad memories and a subconscious reaction in my psyche about my past failures as well.

Most of all, being responsible for Mahtab's risky decisions in any manner made me anxious. I also had to gauge the situation with my suite and the possibility of returning home in the near future and forgetting the incident during the last minutes of living there. Then, of course, finding a steady source of income, as the biggest condition for living, felt like a huge demand all in itself. Actually, the necessity of earning a living sounded too ludicrous and unfair! These were only a few huge reasons for my pensive silence and desire to be left alone to focus, not to mention the fear of never finding any answer for these primary dilemmas of being. During such brief moments of relapse, striving to fathom the merits of being out of the coma was still an added pain in itself!

Luckily, I always found some rays of resilience in my psyche, loathed my childish negativism and desperation quickly, and felt ecstatic for having a second chance to learn who I was and what life is supposed to be, besides its dubious, laughable challenges. I felt obliged to do it somehow this time around, in spite of my annoying misgivings! *What a messy mood! Does coma replace one's sense of reality with a heftier set of existential dilemmas?*

Ironically, these rather philosophical reflections in line with my erratic mood swings also offered a sad clue about old Darren emerging, as I recalled the pains of my jittery personality all my life, which had probably caused Erica's gradual loss of love for me as well. This was an alarming, timely realization, then, if I intended to keep Mahtab interested in me. I had to find ways of disallowing my old, erratic personality resurface and besiege my psyche and future again, while I also desired to stay honest with both Mahtab and myself about who I was or could be. *Gosh, now this idea of self-cleansing to build a better character sounded like an impossible task and additional burden by itself!*

"I really appreciate your patience with me, Mahtab," I said sincerely. "But I must gradually learn to live like a normal person soon, which doesn't seem straightforward these days."

"I know all that, Darren. But is something also bothering you about our situation?" she asked.

"What situation is that?"

"Me… Am I crowding your life? Because that is how I feel sometimes."

"What nonsense... In fact, it's just the opposite I'm afraid of."

"What is the opposite?"

"I'm afraid of getting used to you around me," I said.

"Is that bad?"

"I don't know… I'd better go now. We'll talk later, okay?"

"Sure…," she replied with scepticism and hurt feeling, though I could also see some tiny rays of optimism in her eyes suddenly after my confession about needing her. "When will you return?"

"Don't know…"

"You want me to pick you up at least?"

"No, I want to walk back, too."

"That would be a lot of walking for one day," she said.

"I feel I need it," I replied.

"I'll cook something for us and wait for you, then?"

I nodded and left, tittering about my cranky mood.

It was chilly in the street, unless my immune system was also out of whack. I pondered going to gym in coming days to rebuild my twenty pounds of muscles lost during my break from reality. I rolled the scarf tighter around my neck and zipped up my jacket to cover my ears and chin. My eyes were watering from the spiky wind that had appeared out of nowhere today. Then, I put on my sunglasses, too, which manifested the cloudy day greyer and peoples' curious stares grimmer. Still, I was adamant to stick to my plan and walk the entire distance rather than taking a cab or going back to ask Mahtab for a ride. My remarkable tenacity, while my eyes got blurrier every city block, felt as funny as my mood, as if my psyche had a special plan for me today. Or maybe I deserved this torture for my sickening gloom!

Halfway through this long, adventurous walk, the scene in the last minutes of my coma began rolling in my head, as Mahroo, Vincent and I argued in the garden at the House in Eternity. I was trying to convince Mahroo to return to life with me, but she kept refusing. At last, Vincent interfered by offering me the option of going with Mahroo or returning to life—just another tough love dilemma embarrassing me right in front of Mahroo in the middle of my near-death experience. I was mad at Vincent for putting me in such an awkward position, while Mahroo's smirk about my hesitance to go with her singed my heart.

Meanwhile, my inability to choose life or love was annoying and excruciating in itself. The hassle of living again, which even Vincent kept reminding me of, versus the ambiguity of love and heaven, especially together, were hard to gauge or compare. At the same time, disappointing Mahroo felt rude, while my normal procrastination and timidity about love felt frustrating to Vincent and me, but funny to Mahroo. Vincent was in fact rude, pushing Mahroo to embark the Masters' boat instead of delaying their departure. At last, Mahroo had made the decision for me by grabbing my arm, leading me towards the House in Eternity, and forcing me to enter. I appreciated her effort to relieve me from my misery—for my indecision to go with her or return to mortal life. That generous gesture of hers alone had deserved my eternal love and immediate departure with her, instead of choosing life. Yet, the spirit of life was calling me vigorously with the excuse that heaven and Mahroo would always be there waiting for me. Thus, with deep shame that had felt irreparable even in the coma I had chosen life over Mahroo.

Mahroo's sad eyes after telling her to go away alone, instead of rushing to embrace her and embark the Masters' boat together, had saddened me. But now, alive in love with someone else, choosing life felt even wiser today than taking the risk of going to some imaginary heaven with Mahroo only for a promise of love. In that moment, during my near-death-experience, life had felt dearer than love and it did even more today! In fact, this timely reminiscence felt quite relevant these days when now loving Mahtab could put me face to face with death again.

"Thanks Mahroo," I had murmured to her sheepishly at last, while leaning and kissing her goodbye. Then, I had gone back inside the mansion, ecstatic, basking in the luxury of existence, with a sigh of relief that merely showed *again* a good level of my hypocrisy about both love and my presumed indifference about existence. I had just watched Mahroo go away with the Masters.

I laughed in the streets like a lunatic about the amount of logic and analyses I had apparently applied so admirably during my near-death-experience to choose between life or love. Now, all that reflection and ensuing decision felt quite glorious and divine, as I basked shamelessly in the luxury of my rebirth blissfully with amazement. Now alive and happy, I needed even more wisdom and analyses to handle a similar situation with Mahtab in the real world this time, I reckoned, as I strolled towards my suite and ruminated that ironic hallucination right before exiting the coma. It was indeed weird to be placed in such love-life dilemmas time and again, and more ironically with two sisters.

I wondered about sharing this story and my selfish decision of choosing life over Mahroo with Mahtab playfully, too, so that she fathomed the nature of the man she was dying to love forever. Maybe she must know how cruelly I had humiliated her beloved sister, our precious Mahroo, right in front of Vincent's mocking, arrogant smirk.

At this point, I just burst into a hysterical laughter that I was sure pedestrians took as my lunacy. Luckily, I realized promptly that I should never tell Mahtab this ironical episode that could abolish her view of my character and our chance for romance. How foolish she would feel for her efforts to raise my passion if I told her my story of abandoning Mahroo near the heaven's gate! *She'd laugh at my logic that made perfect sense to me even now.*

Still, I cherished that love episode with charitable Mahroo at the end of my coma, despite its embarrassing finale and the thrill and torture today again, this minute, with a new decision at hand regarding the risks and privileges of having Mahtab around me. She was hoping and expecting, like Mahroo again, that I choose love despite all the death threats. But, even if I promised to love her, how long could I keep her here or she would stay? I had no trust in good things happening to me or lasting a minute longer as soon as I trusted the stability of love and the chance of a blissful fate replacing my chronic glum and misfortunes. In fact, loving her or even giving her any hope could cause her demise, too, like Mahroo's case again.

On the other hand, my playful, mysterious sixth sense goaded me to believe in my chance to embrace the miracle of life during some magical moments like the one filling me right this minute along with an opportunity for a budding future. Being alive and walking freely in the streets felt too precious and sufficient all in itself even without love! *What an amazing, erratic mood, really,* I reckoned again giddily. *And what a big effect just some strolling in the cold air seems to have on our spirits!* Now I was thrilled also about my decision to flee Reza's place and reject Mahtab's offer for a ride as well. I was a blessed human, after all, at least for all the love offered to me so kindly.

Immersed in my fantastic dreams, I realized my approach to my building when I saw petite Mrs. Stanley and tiny Fluffy in her leash coming towards me. We chatted briefly after she expressed her delight to see me alive again. Still, she could not give us a break from her routine probing habit.

"People who shot you... were they the same guys I'd told you about? Those foreign lads with glasses asking for you?" she asked.

"Yes, Mrs. Stanley… They were the same people you had kindly mentioned to me."

"I knew they didn't look like descent people, but you would've not believed me if I'd told you they were trouble."

"I would've believed you," I said teasingly. "You should've told me."

"You would?"

"Of course…"

"I knew they were up to no good! But you said they probably wanted to buy your paintings. I knew you were wrong and I should've insisted more. I should—"

"Why didn't you?" I asked with a superficial grimace.

"I… I really didn't—"

"You should've insisted, Mrs. Stanley…," I stressed with a deeper grimace, but almost ready to burst into laughter. "You could've prevented the whole thing, and what if I'd died? Who would've been really responsible?"

"I'm sorry, but I really thought you wouldn't believe m—"

"Thanks, anyway, Mrs. Stanley… I know you always look out for me. You should've insisted, but I'm in a rush now," I said and left after patting her on the shoulder. "I'll talk to you later."

As I walked away, I wondered if I had been rude to her again, not only for teasing her, but also for cutting her short. Yes, I had been, I thought, so almost turned back to go apologize or at least chat with her for ten minutes to make her feel better after loading her old soul with so much guilt. Instead, I just kept walking and agreeing with my tired legs voting against any non-urgent chore today. Next time, I promised my conscience! No, not next time… but soon, since the next time would most likely be in an hour or so when I return to the street. She was always wandering in the lobby or around the building as if eluding her home or loneliness. My legs and conscience apparently do not like each other, either.

The scene of the crime was extremely cold. I turned on the heater and the electric kettle in the kitchen to make tea. I plummeted onto the sofa facing the half-finished *Tosca* I had been working on passionately the day the thugs had shot me. All that blood in the painting reminded me of my nausea here a few days earlier. So, I got up and went to the balcony for fresh air, but again peered down at the front of the building where Erica's body had smashed, as if still denying Erica's demise or hoping for some evidence to disprove this malicious claim. Still, only some horrid images of her bloodstains down there kept flashing before my eyes. Those dreadful marks would probably never be erased from the asphalt. I felt sick again like the first time, too, but kept staring hypnotically. Tears gathered in my eyes, recalling her beautiful face when she had asked me to love her again in our meeting the night before the fatal incident. I had told her I must think still some more, but never got a chance to do so.

I had been the lucky one, given a second chance. How about her, then? Did she jump herself or someone pushed her? Could by any chance I had done it and now my sly psyche denied it like many other realities I could not, or loathed, to grasp about my past? Maybe that was why I kept returning to the scene of my crime, looking at the spot poor Erica had left me alone at last, and sobbing as though I still loved her like the old times. I wished somebody, maybe the police, could clarify these matters, even if it only established my guilt. I wished they or some other authority could also tell me if I still loved Erica in a mystical realm or I was now safe to move on! *Why can't they figure out what happened to dear Erica? Why wasn't I sure about my innocence or feelings for her? Was my heart still under her spell? Was Mahtab right about this possibility as well?*

I went back inside and listened to my phone messages listlessly —eleven of them. I put the big load of mail piled up on the table, mostly bills, in my small, leather briefcase to read later. I sat on the sofa with the second cup of tea and peered at *Tosca* again in the hope of mustering my thoughts and courage to begin working on it soon and finishing it. I liked the way I had handled it so far. Near completion, it was turning into a nice work. *I am not a bad painter, after all, eh?* I thought with pride, thrilled for having many things to do if only I regained my guts and returned to my suite. I grinned and gauged my mood to start painting right away. Why not? But my loathing for any routine needing diligence and focus took over quickly. Many unsettled dilemmas cluttered my mind to allow any inspirational venture. The main one crippling me nowadays was Mahtab, of course. I just had to decide fast one way or another. Was I—or both of us—ready for the imminent, immense risks and guilt of being together? Many people would not let us live in peace, if at all! Was I ready to love her forever and tell her so with plenty of genuine words? *Gosh, I was killing my spirit with too many tough questions these days!*

My memories from my trip to Barcelona with Mahtab and her parents around four months earlier felt both vague and disturbing. I recalled Mahtab and I exchanging some romantic moments and phrases. Still, weirdly enough, we had implied a possible union, while I had struggled with the crazy idea of marrying someone else's wife, whom I had met only two months earlier, known so little, and had not even kissed. My consent in Barcelona to marry her now felt like another one of my impulsive reactions during a moment of emotional breakdown, most likely due to Mahroo's demise and my soulless existence in Vancouver without Erica. Mahtab looking and behaving exactly like Mahroo, the women I had felt special about in a short time before her sudden death, had probably confused me, too. Nevertheless, my main responsibility now was to resolve this paradox about Mahtab quickly.

Mahtab and I had shared tough times and discussed modern life during my stay in their villa near Barcelona for a week, while I had painted Mahroo's portrait. These two sisters have led awful fates and then dragged me into their intricate lives as well so casually, if not selfishly. While they have been the real victims of their odd destinies, I have been entangled with those tragedies all the same. Could, or should, I try to elude the risks of Mahtab's fate painting mine with dark colours, too. All I had to do was to tell her to go away. I just had to stop being too concerned about ignoring her feelings or her sacrifice to abandon her husband and come so far to Vancouver merely to watch over me with so much, rather foolish, hope for my recovery. It had all been her decision, after all. Had not she dumped me herself once in Barcelona after making me promise to marry her already? I could express my sincere gratitude, but then tell her I did not wish to be a part of the rest of her adventurous destiny—just to put it mildly. I just did not want to die because of a contentious love affair. More ironically, though, choosing life over love would be the same selfish decision I had once made, for a good reason, during the last minutes of my coma when abandoning Mahroo so coolly. *Should, or could, I do it again ? Hadn't I just come out of a coma after being shot due to a similar case of jealousy related to another woman? Hadn't I still learned a lesson?* T.J.'s corny advice about one bad decision ruining one's life forever haunted me as well.

On the other hand, I also sensed the enormity of making such an insensitive, reckless announcement and causing havoc at least in Mahtab's heart. Still, I might indeed be doing her a big favour by rejecting her and preventing a looming catastrophe around us. All these predictable hassles felt not worth the possible love that God knew how long would last, anyway. Our love was not meant to be, I could tell her bluntly, even if love could ever be a reliable factor for building a good relationship in the first place. 'Thanks, but no thanks,' I could tell her with gratitude. Alas, I seemed to be in love with her, too, very much. How much longer, and why, should I just let the mere fear of death prevent my chance for real love that was evolving magically around me? Then again, was I ready to change course totally and choose love over life this time? Oh, gosh, how should I handle all these fear, confusion, and agony? No wonder my mood has been so messy!

My decision felt tough and delicate, while I wondered wittily if lovers analysed their feelings and choices to death the way I had been these day! One thing was clear like the blue sky in spring, though: I had no right to keep Mahtab in suspense much longer, especially with all the daily developments around us and people calling to know what was going on here. I had to talk with her soon, maybe that same evening, about the way I saw our situation and how I liked it to proceed.

I felt proud and happy to think straight amidst the emotional hurricane blasting my brain. Occasionally, some mysterious hints of sanity triggered some precious thoughts and doubts in my head: Was I really in love with Mahtab or only needed her compassion at this trying time? But was the difference essential or clear in the final analysis, I wondered the next moment? I really wanted her, needed her, loved her. That was all that mattered now and I might as well stop beating around the bushes trying to fool myself or anybody else. I must face all the potential risks of loving her and fight for her like a devoted mate if my feelings for her were true. Was not taking risks like this a main purpose of living—to love and fight for it with others as well as with our own doubtful self? Love felt like a straightforward, sane option to choose instead of depressing Mahtab further and letting her go back empty-handed again—like the first time in Barcelona when I had just remained passive, even though she had made the final decision to leave me and go back to Bijan. I did not fight for keeping her then and a third chance would most likely not arise. So, it was time to make her realize I was a reliable man and her sacrifice had not been in vain, a horrible waste. Then again, if this romantic paradox had any rational justification, why was I still sitting there, two hours later, so lost and depressed like a moron? How could I be logical? *Isn't love the toughest dilemma god has confused us with?*

I laid back and closed my eyes to rest awhile before heading back home. But, swiftly, the memory of Erica jumped in my head about the day she came to see me right here a month before I had taken my second trip to Iran just for seeing Mahroo and testing the meaning of my last-minute, magical attraction to her. Erica's scent and perfume possibly seeping from the sofa, where we had had sex for the last time, might have triggered my subconscious. I reminisced about how hard it had been that day for me to resist Erica's charm and decline her plea for us to reconcile. She had called me and pretended she was coming over merely to wait for Elizabeth and convince her to return to Jeff—all as Erica's plot, I had imagined, to exploit my loneliness without Elizabeth around. At the time, Elizabeth was shacking up with me in my suite after we had started some type of an affair. Yet, the relevant points today were that I had melted under Erica's charm that day and that I might be letting it happen again with Mahtab now! Had not Mahroo also lured me so fast enigmatically? *Maybe I am merely a weak or sentimental man!*

My hunch about Erica's sly intention felt warranted when she arrived giddily only half-hour after her call and kissed my lips firmly as I opened the door. We had not seen each other for over three years since our separation. My heart had begun pounding from the minute she had asked to come for a visit. Then, seeing her next to me just kept pumping blood into my veins vigorously. She looked even prettier than before, yet I was amazed of my swift eroticism after all the agony she had given me. I had always assumed I would at least spit in her face the next time I saw her. Now, my sentiments were weirdly tender instead of antagonistic. I was only angry and amazed of my impotent spite, unless lust had crippled all my senses temporarily. Excruciatingly, I strived to control myself and maintain my pride by showing a serious face and acting totally businesslike. Yet, I believed, Erica, like most women, could detect even the slightest emotion or twitch in my face. She looked thrilled for the chance of seeing and seducing me in the shortest time in our history. She did not even bother hiding her zeal to succeed. Instead, she even exaggerated her charm to draw my attention to her as quickly as possible, as though she were in a hurry to get to the point about the purpose of her rather rash visit before Elizabeth arrived.

Recalling that historical, odd afternoon with Erica had stirred my emotions again today. I rose, somewhat enigmatically indeed, went to the balcony, and stared down again at the spot she had died. I wondered when I might stop repeating this bizarre act. This time, my lingering stare felt soothing, while I mused over the gist of our bizarre conversation that afternoon, surprised about my fine recollection of her words, despite my usual short memory even before the coma.

"You're getting more handsome with age, Darren," she said.

"Thanks. You look great too," I replied, while pouring coffee.

"Are you really glad to see me?" she asked.

"Yeah… It's been a long time. Especially, I'm glad you're so concerned about Elizabeth now," I said wittily with sarcasm.

"You lovebirds better be careful with whatever you're getting yourselves into. She belongs to a very jealous man. And you…," she paused abruptly, apparently struggling to stop her mouth.

"What about me?" I asked.

"By the way, I want to thank you for painting me so elegantly, according to Reza's opinion. I'm thrilled about getting it soon."

"Oh? You want this painting, too?"

"Shouldn't I?"

"Why should you?"

"Well, apparently you'd painted it as a token of our *eternal* love," she said so matter-of-factly I burst into laughter, which she reciprocated with a grin before continuing, "He also said you like this painting more than all your other works."

"It's true that I've considered it as one of my best works."

"When he showed me its picture I felt in love with you again."

"You did?" I asked in shock, wondering humorously about the curse in that painting possibly travelling through pictures, too!

"Yes, and even more when he mentioned your feelings for me. I've been excited about my role in inspiring you and hoping to have this memento of our love. In fact, I hope you still love me like the time you painted me, if not more," Erica said casually.

Again, I was stunned by her copious expressions of love after everything we had gone through. How could she be so unaffected? Did she still really love me? I was speechless, pondering all those bizarre bursts of emotions in only a few minutes.

"Well…? Don't you still love me like before? Don't you think that our love is eternal and we can be happy only together?"

"No, but I'm surprised at myself for still feeling attracted to you, despite all the agony you've given me," I said with confusion about my own feelings that seemed too disorderly, like hers, after our long ordeals and separation.

Erica got closer to me on the sofa, realizing my vulnerability. She tried to embrace and kiss me, but I resisted with the excuse about Elizabeth arriving any second. Of course, I also doubted the wisdom of intimacy or even a simple friendship with Erica.

"Don't worry about Elizabeth. She already knows about our situation," Erica said.

"What situation?"

"That we are still married."

I was startled hearing the news. She said she had refused to sign the final divorce documents and convinced her lawyers to wait for a while. I had given her lawyers the power of attorney to sign on my behalf since I was going to Iran. So we were legally still married, she stressed again with triumph. I was flabbergasted and angry with both of us for not pursuing this divorce project actively. I was mad at Elizabeth, too, for not telling me she knew I was still married to Erica when we had started our own affair. The nature and meaning of Elizabeth and Erica's friendship all those years since high school boggled my brain as well.

The long story short, Erica lured me into having sex together and also agreeing to consider the option of reconciling with her and returning to her house, all in a matter of one hour. My shock and confusion about my feelings for Erica and Elizabeth, and women in general, reached its height that day. But the irony was that I was really tempted to go with Erica and love her again. At least that was how I had felt tentatively that afternoon and the same thought occurred to me occasionally later, too. It seemed I could never stop loving Erica even after knowing her capacity to hurt me emotionally time and again, and despite a few other love episodes in my life at the time. Erica had brought me the kind of passion that only some blessed people experience, and thus suffer because of it forever, too. As if God has contrived a cunning scheme within humans' DNA: the stronger the love, the more psychotic and hurtful it would always end up to be! A big price must always be paid for love, He says. The choice is yours, if you let yourself go!

Even the fact that Erica was dead and would never be a part of my life again did not seem to stop me from loving her despite my words to Mahtab to the contrary. Her death had possibly even revived my dormant feelings for her, which I had supposedly tried to bury for many years merely for protecting myself against her charm. Now, I no longer feared her charm harming me again! But I could never forget the pleasure of making love to her on the sofa that afternoon, after three years of separation, with a mixed feeling of anger and passion, after she told me she was still my wife. We did not even care if Elizabeth opened the door abruptly and witnessed the intensity of two estranged spouses entangled in passionate, wild mating. We both were determined to continue even if Elizabeth arrived and stood there watching us finish our vulgar erotic show.

In the end, I had luckily gathered enough willpower to resist Erica's offer to reconcile immediately, because I did not trust her words, although I believed our love for each other seemed intact. My bad experiences with other women after Erica had confirmed my cynicism about love as well, while I also loathed my naïve impression of passion when Erica and I had felt inseparable since high school. Alas, trusting love and women's sloppy expressions of it had felt foolish in line with so many different meanings we give to love for various purposes. Now, today, all these varied sentiments were also convoluting my impression of Mahtab, while crippling me to decide about a future with her. I recalled my promise to Mahtab merely a few days earlier about lacking any leftover emotions towards that dead woman, Erica, but it seemed I had lied to her! I seemed to be still in love with Erica in a special way, even now that she was not around to love and loathe me in rotation. So ironically, she had often hurt me even while demanding to love her. I could still feel her warmth and scent on this very same sofa I was sitting this minute, where we had made such a passionate, rough love for the last time.

My memories with Erica would always remain too rooted and precious to let go. This stern reality was becoming clearer even to my stubborn subconscious, even if I developed the willpower to erase that old chapter of my life. Instead, I was quite afraid that the emptiness in my heart after Erica's death would never be filled. I was also afraid of hurting anybody else whom I might try to love, or feel in love with, especially if I was still under Erica's spell.

I wished at least I had the *Woman in the White Dress* after all my trouble of getting it back from Reza and Mahtab. I had painted it with a humongous longing for Erica guiding every single brush stroke, while my tears had dropped and mixed up with the paint I had put on that canvas. I believed half of the medium used to paint that love tableau had been my tears! This had been four years earlier at the shores of the Caspian Sea when I had also sensed Vincent's spooky presence in the room for the first time. Ironically, the thugs had shot me only for stealing that painting, too. Right away, as I sat alone in my suite, stared at *Tosca*, and mourned Erica, I decided swiftly that finding the *Woman in the White Dress* must be one of my priorities for the coming months and years if necessary. I must help the police and pressure Jeff to find the thugs—not just for revenge, but mainly for getting the painting—the dear Erica's memorabilia—back.

Only people who have experienced a coma might know the ensuing mixed senses of rebirth and numbing confusion for weeks and months. Still, in spite of the grim tragedies, especially Erica's death, clouding my mind, eluding the facts, especially Mahtab's needs, felt reckless. My deep daylong contemplations had helped me see my future in a much clearer perspective. I merely had to defeat whatever the heck was holding me back from returning to my own place. Starting to paint and living like before felt urgent to rebuild my identity. This suite was the only thing keeping me connected to my past, other than the *Tosca* and Mahtab maybe. At this point, I seemed to need something or someone to remind me of my past just to keep my slippery self intact. I also needed time alone with my thoughts—no matter how stressful—to defeat the lingering symptoms of the coma. In all, eluding or selling my suite in fear of events that happened here four months earlier was neither practical nor wise. Erica's memories or her death should not hinder my return to this place, either. At last, the only logical factor hindering my immediate homecoming was the possibility of the thugs returning to kill me, this time merely for stopping me from identifying them to the police. So, I decided to stay with Mahtab a bit longer until I discussed the matter with the police and sought their advice.

I heard the phone ringing while opening the door on my way out, but I merely left without answering it or even waiting for the message. Most likely it was Mahtab, I reckoned, maybe worrying about me, but even if it was somebody else, I just had to rush back home before she got mad at me for abandoning her the whole day. Besides, I had no patience or stomach for another plea from Reza to call him or hear any other troubling news that the caller would most likely dump on me.

It was colder than this morning out in the street as the dim sun had set and the wind blew harder. I considered taking a cab to go home—home! Mahtab was my new home for now. In the last minute, the long stroll towards home felt helpful for finalizing my thoughts. I needed this last chance to consider making any kind of commitment to Mahtab. Unless I still had any doubts by the time I arrived HOME, I had to express my position to Mahtab right away, hopefully tonight, if I was really ready to fight for her like a man and willing to love her the way I felt this minute. *Or choose life again!*

I ambled in the noisy downtown streets during the rush-hour commotion. After another hour of reflection in the cold winter with watery eyes and burning ears, a timely sign confirmed my final position about Mahtab in the very last minute, just before entering her building. I went inside the flower shop with a sudden impulse to buy two dozens red and pink roses. The next minute, I was in front of the building and buzzing the intercom. No answer. I kept doing it another half an hour in case Mahtab had been in the washroom or something and not heard the buzzer. I should have listened to her and taken the spare keys she had left for me on the counter. Now, I did not remember why I had not taken them or maybe I had simply forgotten.

I wondered where she could have gone since she had insisted in the morning about having dinner together. Many silly thoughts about her whereabouts crossed my mind, but none was as vile as the slight chance of her abandoning me due to my attitude and lacklustre show of affection. *Maybe she had made a decision and was already at, or on her way to, the airport!* It was a chilling thought and feeling during those few minutes of hallucination. I was suffocating suddenly, as though my intestines were being knotted together in hundred places. I could not bear the idea of her departure, exactly the way I had felt on the day Mahroo met me before leaving Vancouver. That was the last time I had seen her.

I rang the buzzer again and again, wondering if somebody had kidnapped or killed Mahtab. All along, I held the bouquet of flowers like a delicate baby in both my hands with my small briefcase also dangling from one of them. Still no answer, while my heart pounded faster and faster.

Chapter Six
Tangled Minds and Destinies

I bought another doll for Nazi and went to my mom's house to see them before my secret trip to Vancouver the next day.

"I'll be in Dubai for a week or so," I lied to my mom, ashamed of hiding my chance of seeing her rebellious daughter that she missed so much, yet refused to even mention after her departure against our mom's pleas. Her attitude had saddened our mom as much as it had maddened Bijan. I wished I could ask her if she had any message for Mahtab, but confessing why I had to drop in on Mahtab secretly, mostly because she refused to return my calls and Bijan ordered me around was humiliating. My mom nodded sadly, but grinned as Nazi ran towards me with her doll.

"Thank you, Uncle Reza. She looks like my mom and Auntie Mahtab..., so pretty," she said, while my mom hid her nostalgia.

"Let me see her again?" I asked and stared at the doll with surprise and admiration for Nazi's accurate view of the doll's resemblance to my sisters. "You're right. She looks like them."

"When is Auntie Mahtab coming back, Uncle Reza?"

"I don't know, honey. Soon, I hope," I replied.

“May I call her now and tell her to come home?” Nazi asked with tears in her eyes. “I wanna tell her that I really wanna see her and show her all these new dolls that you’ve bought for me.”

“I don’t think she’s home now to answer the phone,” I said with gloom for lying to her, too, and felt miserable when peering at my mom who looked quite shaken by Nazi’s request.

“Can we call her to see if she’s home?” she asked.

“Okay, honey,” I replied, staring at my mom’s pensive face. Even if my mom agreed to call Mahtab for Nazi’s sake, it would be useless, as Mahtab would not answer. Briefly, I played with the idea of Nazi leaving a mushy message to melt Mahtab’s heart and call back. I could then grab the phone and talk to her, too, thus avoid a tiring trip to Vancouver. But the chance of Mahtab talking to me even if she called back and I happened to be around would be slim. Only Nazi’s heart would break if Mahtab did not return Nazi’s call, which was quite likely and risky for Nazi’s emotions. At last, I made the call and passed on the receiver to Nazi in case Mahtab answered. Nazi watched me anxiously with a cute grimace before returning the receiver with the answering machine blabbering. I did not even bother leaving a message.

Without Mahtab around and my mother’s illness, watching over Nazi had found a top priority for me, although a maid took care of them as well. Nazi could have stayed with me if I had a normal life without so much travelling, maybe with a wife and children, too. Both our lives would have been easier if at least I could grasp women’s minds just a bit or choose a mate, anyway, and hope for the best! The only hurdle was that I never built the huge nerve needed nowadays to bear marital headaches. Mahroo and Mahtab had already given me bad impressions with their idiotic infatuations for a particular, peculiar man at the cost of torturing their poor husbands and me. Especially, witnessing my brother-in-laws’ anguish for years had demolished my last bits of confidence and courage for marriage. Then, T.J.’s and Darren’s marital failures had further tainted my impression of marriage in modern culture. In return, my cynicism and criticism have turned my sisters and Erica against me. Ironically, these three women could have been perfect wives for any mature man. Yet, they had been unlucky and misguided when choosing a husband and then going nuts over this one man I had befriended allegedly for his high qualities—this Darren. He has caused mayhem all along, including the need for this absurd trip to Canada merely in hopes of putting some sense into his numb head. Damn you, Darren! Ironically, he has always ended up getting hurt a lot himself.

At home, I strived to invent a last minute excuse to ignore Bijan's order and cancel this trip, but a mixed sense of guilt and duty goaded me to honour my goal of bringing Mahtab back to Iran. I simply had to stop her from causing the last blow to our family's honour and welfare. In fact, my success to make Mahtab more realistic about her marriage felt like a chance to redeem myself and maybe *even* learn to indulge women for a higher cause: To choose a spouse to raise Nazi together. Like my sisters, now I believed to be on a holy mission of my own: to save Mahtab, my mom, Nazi, and maybe even that idiot, Darren, too. Oh, I forgot Dervish Ali… His life also depended on my success to bring Mahtab home. *Sadly, I owed everybody the pain of travelling to Vancouver to prevent more disasters for all of us! Bon voyage…*

I tried to get some sleep at least, but my brain was restless, as I mostly worried about my frail mother's health. I have always loved her with respect for her liberalism, although she never let me feel close to her, somewhat like my sisters! Now that she had time and special needs, we were disappointing and hurting her with our apathy, recklessness, and work in my case. Her growing illness after Mahroo's and her husband's deaths had also reduced her enthusiasm for socializing with people. I dreaded her looming death, too, and the prospect of being stuck with Mahtab and Nazi all on my own. This poor child has hardly had any luck in her life, with both her parents dying at such young ages. Now, she only had us to rely on after Mahtab had also left us. How could she bear her grandma's death, too? How could I take care of this little angel alone, especially when I had to travel for business so much and now maybe for intruding in Mahtab's conflicts as well? A barrage of sore memories raised my sense of guilt as well, as I questioned the wisdom and value of meddling in Mahtab's life, my chance of helping her and the rest the family, and the strategy most likely useful for achieving my goal.

Trying in vain in the last ten years to mend people's marital conundrums or love messes, including my sisters', my parents', Erica's, Zia's, Darren's, Bijan's, and even T.J.'s, has surely been bizarre, if not a dire psychotic ailment. Letting myself being dragged into these humiliating episodes has been ridiculous for a supposedly sane, professional man. In fact, jumping into people's emotional lives or hoping to advise Mahtab to curb my mom's pains felt too pathetic for a man who has had difficulty finding himself a mate. In this new case, especially, confronting Mahtab and Darren felt hypocritical, too, as I had been justifying my own sinful love affair with Erica even after our immense passion had failed to flourish! What is love, anyway?

We imagine our love is true and eternal. But how realistic is this hope? I just could not stop being on the safe side and pamper my cynicism about love for facing up to Mahtab and Darren. My father's words about luck being the only factor for finding and keeping our soul mates also seemed to hold water, while luck itself was not even something to hope for seriously. Still, all these facts and factors about love were not *quite* helping me tonight to build a firm stance against Mahtab's and Darren's actions.

At least I had proven my father wrong about Ms. Perfection's existence, albeit at the expense of making her husband mad and handy for my sisters' adventures in return. He had sensed my difficulty accepting people, in particular women. "Reza, stop looking for perfection… You'll never find it," he had warned me. Yet I had found it in Erica, and thus fallen in love with her even though she had been my friend's wife. I did not care what Darren said about Erica's malice. To me, she was quite compassionate indeed, if one knew how to treat her. So, perfection was possible, though I had found it only after braving and breaking all the rules of decency to taste the ecstasy of courting an exquisite woman. More importantly, I also believed now, rather sadly with shame, that such fleeting experiences, like Erica for me, were worth our utmost sacrifices and patience to seek and explore, even at the cost of sabotaging our principles and pride. Ironically, not even my failure to relate to Erica fully at the end had curbed my desire and search for perfection. I still dreamed romantically about that mysterious goddess deserving my passion, at least as a sacred ambition rather than a practical endeavour. Sorry Dad!

This sleepless night's reminiscing of the heat of my passion for Erica and my sorrow for losing her had reminded me that her general resemblance to my sisters and mother had most likely drawn me to her. Accordingly, I knew now, more than ever, that my compassion towards my family was too rooted to bypass. These sentimental thoughts had ironically offered another major clue about the sanctity of my mission to rescue Mahtab, mitigate my mom's worries, and save Nazi, all by butting in Mahtab's life as my natural duty. But how? Besides finding a practical tactic to convince her, my goal and the topic of love itself were too vague to plan for. *Oh, gosh, my spirit is so burdened!*

Recalling my anguish after losing Erica also raised a crucial dilemma regarding Bijan's actions and glum these days, although Erica and I had at least separated on a friendly term. Darren has also suffered this suffocating feeling once at least when Erica had dumped him. Still, as much as I felt for both Bijan and Darren now, I could help only one of them at the cost of hurting the other. Could or should I choose, then? How?

It was two in the morning with many daunting dilemmas and memories still bombarding my brain way worse than most other nights, as if my baffled brain mocked the urgency of some sleep before my trip to Vancouver in five hours with no idea of what I was supposed to tell Mahtab. *Dad, please help!*

Many years ago, I realized my weakness as a man and feared my soul's vulnerability. Luckily, I met Dervish Ali, Zia's uncle, and tried to rebuild my confidence and spirit through meditation and learning mysticism. That was around the time I had begun my affair with Erica, basking in the joy of finding the *perfect* woman of my dreams, and loathing my duplicity around Darren as confidants. I had always believed in my power to keep my integrity under tough circumstances, but then lust and love had wiped out my conviction in a matter of seconds. Therefore, I strived to find refuge in Dervish Ali and hoped he could show me a way to deal with my burdened conscience and messy lifestyle when my dad could not be privy to my sins.

A year later, when Erica and I separated, I needed Dervish Ali even more to bear my lovesickness and hiding everything from Darren still, while he worked for my company in Tehran and our friendship grew stronger. Dervish Ali took me to their rituals a few times, but just as an observer sitting in a corner and a promise to be admitted to their circle of divinity once I matured. Despite my doubts about my ability to thrive, the mere access to Dervish Ali's personal wisdom kept me content and sane.

Ironically, I had introduced Darren to Dervish as well to get advice about his sullen spirit after Erica had left him. He was hurt emotionally and professionally, in spite of his efforts to impress Erica and save their marriage. He had even abandoned his artistic dreams to work in Erica's company in hopes of making her see him as a practical, real man. He whined to me sometimes, 'What am I doing in Iran working as a network technician and fooling around with women as if I was taking revenge on love?'

I had hoped Dervish could help him build his self-image to find a mate and follow his passion for painting regardless of its rewards. Apparently, my scheme worked perfectly, as his artistic genius evolved and his trust in love was restored thru my sisters along with lots of headaches and shame for me, especially when his actions hurt Dervish Ali inadvertently as well.

Ironically again, and maybe also hypocritically, I had tried to console Darren myself, too, after seducing his wife, but at least had convinced him to come work for my company in Iran, which

I always believed had been a good refuge for him. Even more ironical, Erica left me after only one year, mainly because she was still in love with Darren. Yet, most ironical, her love going in circle between Darren and me had raised my naive *hope* all along —another contentious topic—about the chance of Erica returning to love me again soon with a stronger faith in me this time. *She had done so, in fact, except in spirit!*

Now, after years of efforts and triumph through Dervish Ali, even my bare sense of spiritualism was fading fast along with my spirit due to life setbacks and family duties. Dervish Ali has had a terrible fate himself, despite his strong beliefs that are supposed to shield a man of divine convictions. He has always had family troubles of his own, mainly with his nephew, Zia, even though he had raised him and his siblings after Zia's parents had perished in an earthquake in Kashan. Zia had become an atheist and detested Dervish Ali and his convictions. Many factors had already ruined Zia's mind, so he went berserk when he learned about Mahroo, his beloved wife, having nursed Darren after his release from the hospital due to his injuries during an Iraqi missile attack. But that was my fault, too, again. Since Zia worked in Shiraz and I was going to Dubai, I had asked Mahroo to go pick up Darren from the hospital and look after him for a few days until my return. Me and my big mouth! My lingering sense of guilt towards Darren—simply because I had stolen his wife, rather inadvertently—had made me feel indebted to him forever like a lifelong slave!

It seems my brain is dogged to keep me awake tonight to count my mistakes and suffer my guilt.

Then, Zia lost it when his suspicions about Mahroo's deep feelings for Darren escalated. His growing anger and eccentricity affected Dervish as well. Zia had stopped visiting him and his family for sometime. So, I was the only link for keeping Dervish abreast of Zia's general condition, although we knew nothing at the time about Mahroo's infatuation for Darren or the cause of Zia's mushrooming madness. Meanwhile, Zia's treatment of Mahroo increased her depression and attraction towards Darren who displayed a calm personality, so contrary to Zia's. So, now, everybody's rising depressions and madness was linking oddly and spreading fast, including Dervish Ali's and mine. Amidst all these perplexing mayhem and depressions with unclear sources, I felt stuck and sad. I could not explain the situation to Dervish or even raise my old dilemmas about Erica and Darren to alleviate my conscience, especially because his imprisonment and Zia's behaviour had sucked life out of him. In the end, we were killing one another's spirits inadvertently during a torturous two-year period. We all behaved like a bunch of deceitful, lost souls trying in vain to make sense of our lives, while hoping in vain to help those we cared for deeply. I bet we all also wondered why God has created us so cruel and helpless at the same time.

Dervish Ali was struck with more grief after Zia's brother—a crippled war veteran—and then Zia committed suicide within a short period. These events broke even a guru's alleged stability and spiritual mental power. Later, Dervish was officially accused of anti-Islamic propagandas and thrown in jail. Things just kept going wrong for him at so many levels even in the Evin prison, especially after he found out inadvertently that Zia's madness had been partly the result of his jealousy about Mahroo's infatuation for Darren. He felt sorry for his efforts to help Darren before and in the prison, but was infuriated also by the possibility of having played an indirect role in the demise of his beloved nephew, Zia —probably by helping Darren restore his self-image and believe in love again, too. Becoming cellmates and Darren making touchy confessions to Dervish could be seen as karma all in itself!

Darren was actually the one telling me initially about Dervish Ali's imprisonment and poor health in Evin's tough condition. He pushed me to find a way to get Dervish out of Evin before it was too late—maybe hoping to curb his guilt for hurting Dervish and Zia inadvertently. I asked Bijan to help Dervish Ali fast—the same way he and his father's official status in the new regime had secured Darren's temporary release from Evin and then got him out of Iran safely. After two weeks, Bijan got me a special pass to meet Dervish, who was no longer the man I had known for years. The officials had been torturing and pushing him to renounce his beliefs. He looked frail and frightened, maybe not only of death, but for dying alone in prison with his convictions and family striped from him during the last years of his life.

Oh, gosh, my insomnia tonight is rekindling so many horrific memories and stirring so much soul-searching! Or vice versa?!

Bijan's father had never seemed eager to resolve Dervish's touchy situation related to both politics and religion. But now, Dervish Ali was dying fast in the prison, while Bijan stressed that his father's revulsion about Mahtab's attitude around their family could not be remedied until her return to Tehran. Meanwhile, I could not tell Dervish that his fate was linked to the events in Vancouver, too. Darren had already caused him enough grief in relation to Zia's death, but now hindering Dervish's own freedom felt even beyond karma. This situation and my inability to at least explain the snag behind his freedom made me feel sick and guilty, while those two selfish lovers, Darren and Mahtab, had refused to answer the phone or return my calls.

Now, introducing Darren to Dervish felt like a bigger mistake than I had imagined before! Promising Dervish in prison about help being around the corner also felt like another stupid thing I had done to him, while I had not even dared to go see him and receive the kind of moral support I needed these day the way he had offered me in the past. He was going to die in prison soon, and I had no guru to guide me, unless I could get through to Mahtab, while she ignored me so adamantly and made me feel helpless. *No..., counting my big mistakes will never end!*

Witnessing many people's destinies intermingling around me towards such fateful outcomes during the last few years has been painful, especially when feeling my big share of responsibility regarding my sisters' adventurous infatuations for a forlorn man, whose dear wife I had seduced inadvertently, who had in return been beguiled by my heartbroken sisters one by one somewhat innocently without anybody's intention to hurt anybody. Despite the ambiguity of people's roles and guilt, my conscience insisted I had played a big part in derailing my sisters' and Erica's lives and maybe even Darren's. Were Erica's, Mahroo's, and maybe even Zia's, deaths also my fault, at least partially? Then again, you might agree that Erica herself had started this whole chain of mixed-up destinies when you learn later how our love had begun!

Nonetheless, my sense of guilt for hurting many people I have tried to help, would hopefully be useful now that I was going to Vancouver in hopes of helping Mahtab and Darren this time. This was a good knowledge and reminder for my looming encounters.

Why did I let Bijan push me into this awful mission? How totally different our brains worked, Bijan's and mine! For one thing, I have come to believe in an unorthodox perspective of man free from hope and religions, so unlike Bijan. It just felt too naïve to me to fuss over these illusions and live based on such foolish cognition of the universe. Still, in my subconscious, 'hope' has apparently driven my existence all these years; otherwise why have I let social conditioning and family obligations hinder my resolve to honour my radical beliefs about existence, including the illusive, yet imperative, role of 'hope,' along with many other arbitrary notions and ambitions I have seemingly developed, too, just to indulge my soul and reach a relative sense of serenity.

In particular, letting Bijan push me into this vague, degrading mission, in spite of my wisdom, presumed convictions, and high self-image, felt too pathetic. Ironically, just a hunch along with my knowledge of Darren's and Mahtab's characters had made me jump the gun and assume some passion percolating behind the scene between Darren and Mahtab—most likely even going back to the week they had been in Barcelona with our mom. Then again, a similar clue was messing up Bijan's brain, too, so much so that he had to send me all this way for an investigation.

I had not imagined taking another boring, long trip anytime soon, but here I was fretting over the one in five hours, fighting insomnia and painful memories in my haunted bedroom.

Chapter Seven
Meeting an Old Beloved

Ten days since I had left my sentimental third message on Darren's answering machine, hoping to pick his sense of irony at least, to no avail. "This is your old pal, T.J., just in case you don't remember my voice any longer. I also have an urgent message from your dad."

But no response… Darren was missing seriously. Was it wise or time to call the police now, and whose job was it?

Luckily, Reza had not called me again from Iran to enquire about Darren or give me more instructions. Maybe he was pissed off after I had shrugged off his latest request to visit his building, too, and talk with the caretaker or Mahtab about their knowledge of Darren. Today, however, I pondered exploring this idea alone or with the aid of the police as a final resort, mostly for personal reasons, though!

Surely, Darren's mysterious disappearance from the face of the earth was both worrying and intriguing. Strangely, however, Feri's growing atrocities made the matter of finding him so much more urgent for pouring my guts out to a confidant as soon as possible before I did something crazy out of despair, like killing Feri—maybe tonight, instead of going to a party with her in an hour. Alas, my other confidant, Reza, had not come to Vancouver in recent months, either, and already had enough worries of his own, anyway. Even my sudden zeal all day to fathom a way of finding Darren had been helpful by itself in distracting my mind away from Feri and the awful idea of going to a big-shot friend's house. Then again, Darren—or the senseless challenge of finding him—being my last resort to keep my sanity felt pitiful.

I attended these parties mostly for Feri's sake, although I did not mind doing it to inject some variety in my boring life as well. However, it was getting harder for me every day to justify my association with this smug group. I was sure they despised me equally, if not more! Actually, I believed we would not be invited to these parties any more if Feri stopped her dire coxing routines and daily phone calls to them and volunteering to help for any particular chore. I was astonished by her resilience and energy to spend so much time on the phone talking and sucking up to those morons, especially now after becoming an agent and hoping to list their houses for sale someday. If she was not cajoling a client about real estate, she was wheedling her snooty friends for higher stakes. She did not get discouraged even when they ignored her or her messages more often than not. Anyway, I was happy about Feri's coaxing aptitude satisfying my family's thirst for swanky socializing with a bunch of vile idiots. In a bizarre way, I actually admired her knack to absorb people's pomposity so casually—the gift I lacked deeply. Alas, *or luckily,* I just had no patience and personality required for such a demanding and demeaning flair—systematic cajoling.

I called Darren again hopelessly, anyway, with no luck. Then I wondered if his father had heard from him yet. Therefore, after going through the absurd, *allegedly* secretive, calling scheme, finally Mr. Durant answered the phone.

"Darren?" Mr. Durant asked with excitement, sounding ready to weep already. Poor man!

"No, Mr. Durant. It's me again, T.J.," I said.

"Who?"

"T.J… I'm Darren's friend who called you ten days ago, too."

"Oh, do you have any news?" he asked with a sigh.

"No, I was wondering if you have heard from him, because I've left him a few messages to call you, too."

"No, he hasn't called… Are you sure he is alive?"

"Yes, but now we can't find him," I said.

"I've left him a couple of messages myself," he said sadly.

"You have?"

"Yes… Now, he probably has more excuses to mention for forgetting all about me," he uttered with great disappointment.

"Sorry to bother you, Mr. Durant. As soon as I find him, I'll make him to call you," I said sheepishly.

"Thank you," he said and hung up a bit less curtly this time.

Judging by the way Darren had been ignoring even his father, my curiosity about his affair with Reza's sister was also starting to surpass my worries about his health and whereabouts. Something quite serious, or seriously romantic, was going on, then, when he seemed so nonchalant even about his dad's messages.

Gosh, I wished he would at least let his poor father know he was alive, since Mr. Durant did not seem to believe me, as if too many prank callers had ruined his sense of trust as well. Anyway, after chickening out about the idea of dropping on Mahtab, no other venues occurred to me for finding Darren and fulfilling my obligation towards his dad at least. Then, swiftly, not finding him felt like a blessing when I imagined the instant hassles of probing or spying on him for the touchy, private information Reza wanted me to drag out of him. I felt happy, *for only two minutes,* while laughing about my tricky brain's effort to invent these ludicrous justifications just for humouring itself now that it had failed to fathom a means of finding Darren!

Swimming numbly in my bewildering thoughts, Feri came to my study and yelled at me about my procrastination to get ready. *She had a point this time!*

While getting dressed hastily, I pondered my admirable sense of obligation to accompany Feri and bear her apathy all evening among some vulgar people, although those parties' conflicting effects on my marital life were also analysable: On the one hand, Feri's joy for associating with *those people* reduced my burdens of living with her a bit. At least they kept her busy. On the other hand, witnessing her zeal to cajole such lowlifes, while ignoring or humiliating me throughout the party, was torturous. In fact, I believed her arrogance and hostility towards me grew just to make up for the humility she bore for being included in such a crooked circle and striving to befriend those conceited women. Only torturing me seemed to relieve her inferiority pains around those sluts! She certainly also blamed only me for her lower status among that lot due to my dogged reluctance to even try making more money, on top of not being rich enough already.

Besides obliging Feri and eluding my computer occasionally, the chance to explore the minds of the rich, so engulfed in vanity and seemingly enjoying the social chaos, reduced my reasons for self-loathing a lot as well. Then I thanked God for not being rich enough, even at the cost of Feri's rising apathy towards me, if shallowness was so akin to wealth. Luckily, those parties kept me amused within a bizarre setting I had now become so keen to fathom and study, maybe like a bitter bankrupt. Socializing with varied personalities and social classes had felt imperative to me for my writing purposes as well, along with daily affirmations of human nature's wickedness. The more I observed and suffered those charades, the more I grasped the ominous reality I strived to digest and explain in my writings like a crude vengeance.

Some surprising encounters or conversations often amused me during or after those parties, too, beyond the pervading themes of vanity. They also evoked some pale nostalgia along with pleasant memories of yesteryears when I had enjoyed pedestrian ambitions and the hoopla our youthful gatherings had offered to the point of even bearing my snooty friends' idiotic mentality with admirable patience. Yet, I could have never imagined my luck that evening bringing me face-to-face with such a beautiful ex-lover from the old era. *Wow…!*

An aura of maturity and elegance now augmented her pride, which she had always emanated unpretentiously and never for teasing a man—oh, so much unlike Feri again! Her name was Homa. The way I recalled her, she was a person most akin to her nature, as if social fads could never corrupt her being. Whatever she had said I had believed unequivocally. I had even believed her when she had told me she loved me as much as she already knew I loved her. Then, I was quite immature, however, to cherish that divine blessing despite my undeserving character. I was honest enough myself, a bit like Homa, to realize what a jerk I could be around girls, abusing their interest in my youthful charm. I was distracted by juvenile joys and the idea of commitment to another girl, even Homa, scared me; although, I realized my foolishness a few years later; only after we had separated and she had left with her parents to start a new life in London. Too late…

Lurking amidst the crowd like a cagey tiger, I peered at Homa from a safe distance. At last, a twitch in her eye hinted that she recognized me, too, maybe due to my timid stares. Then, she turned her head towards the woman next to her and laughed. In those large parties, guests either knew each other or somebody introduced them during the party if necessary or by accident. So I had no idea who Homa's husband or escort was, or whether she was there alone in case God still meant to show me His merciful hand, while reminding me of my lifelong stupidities. Instead, many fantastic ideas about rediscovering her flashed in my naive mind, while I kept my fingers crossed in my pocket. I did not want to make the first move and approach her, since, not only marriage had turned me into such a coy man, but also I had a slight doubt about my imagination of who she was. More than thirty years had lapsed so fast since I had last seen her. Besides, I realized my life condition these days—the seclusion and all—had blurred my judgment, not to mention the chance of hallucination in line with my psyche's desperate search for a quick refuge.

After some hesitation, at last I walked closer to her vicinity near the bar, asked for another shot of whisky, and went outside on the large patio when she appeared so amused by her friend. A dozen guests had adventured the cold to smoke. They chatted vigorously or swam in their thoughts alone. As a non-smoker, I felt estranged among that particular group of addicts. Besides their embarrassing habit, the added humiliation of standing in the cold to satiate it looked pathetic. Their grimaces showed their subtle irritation for being politely exiled to the cold patio despite all their monies and arrogance. This new smoking etiquette certainly felt rude and unfair to them. In return, they peered at me with even more pity, probably assuming I was not only a forsaken smoker, but also cheap, *or bankrupt,* to buy my own cigarettes. They soon eluded my keen stares to prevent my likely approach and request for a cigarette. At last, a man who probably wanted to flaunt his generosity approached me with a grin and offered me a cigarette. When I proudly said, "Thanks, I don't smoke," his kind grin turned into a subtle glare with disgust, gazed around at spectators in total confusion, then rushed away like I was a total jackass. Some bystanders monitoring his show of generosity furtively, rather disapprovingly, now also looked even more dumbfounded and spiteful for my suspicious intrusion and attitude.

I almost proved their suspicion of my idiocy with my laughter when I felt obliged to explain my vividly purposeless presence on the patio, unless as a spy or a critic. Then I thought it would have certainly sounded even funnier if I had told them the truth: That I needed some cold air just to get over the sudden nostalgia filling me after Homa had stirred my forgotten sense of romanticism and imagining *what my life could have been.* Even if the woman was not Homa, still the memories of my youth with Homa and a few other lovers made me feel old, cold, and useless. My nerves were entangled and if those people were not around on the patio, I would have probably not been able to hold back my urge to cry —not for Homa or my past, but merely out of pure desperation about my present. The air kept getting chillier, still I felt timid going back inside, plus a sense of needing a good punishment for the kind of person I had turned into—so lost and lonely—now standing aimlessly like a loony amongst a lot of pathetic smokers on this freezing patio.

After taking enough punishment, I returned inside and looked around for Homa anxiously like a lost child. However, the crowd had gotten thicker and scattered onto the adjacent foyer and the recreation facility next to the indoor pool. I strolled all over those areas and inspected the crowd furtively until I found her in a dark corner chatting with a tall, handsome man in a fine suit and tie!

Gauging the guy stealthily stirred my insecurity regarding my appearance along with my paltry grudge against suit and tie. The wisdom of looking uptight in a suit and tie in those supposedly informal gatherings had boggled my cynical mind recently along with an ironical fear of missing a crucial point myself. Surely, my curiosity felt sillier to me than the custom itself, yet seeing Iranian men in their jackets even for visiting a grocery store on a hot day tickled my nosy brain, as if they loved their suits too much to be swayed by commonsense or heat. Still, I never got the nerve to probe and satiate my curiosity, except for surmising that the less affluent were probably trying to economize by sticking to one or a pair of suits and look tidy, too. But what was the riches excuse? Personally, I eluded suits unless for attending a wedding or funeral —even then, only out of fear of Feri.

Tonight, however—at this particularly historical moment—I wondered and worried about Homa's impression of my beard and casual attire, perhaps even feeling embarrassed to introduce me to her well-dressed husband merely on account of my shoddy appearance! Had she changed as well and become showy now to keep up with social norms, or for her husband's liking alone?

I admit again, I must have surely been getting too bored with my life or losing my faculty, wasting so much brain energy on such silly stuff. Just another clue about my growing senility... *perhaps!* Blame it on Feri, though! The reason is that my hang-up about suit and tie might be partly the outcome of Feri's nagging about my refusal to dress up as another means of insulting her and the host, in line with our growing dislikes of each other's tastes and priorities in life. Maybe my aversion had a deeper root in my distrust of our crude civilization or for feeling obliged to wear suit and tie for twenty years as a boisterous banker. Maybe it revealed my rebellion against humanity! Yet, Feri assumed I did it *only* out of spite for her and our snotty friends, though I had explained my reasons to her twice. She had also found it vital to tell everybody, that my childish 'dress code resistance,' on top of my recent habit to grow a beard, was another clear clue about my dwindling hygiene. In fact, my beard had now turned into another contentious issue for Feri to nag. Personally, growing a beard had initially felt necessary to me for irritating Feri before laziness had also barged in. Yet, I believed beard also gave me a better chance of becoming—and resembling—a full-fledged, renowned writer much easier and faster! Anyway, my attire and beard had grown into new causes for Feri's embarrassment and whining when we went to these exhausting parties, yet I did not care, or maybe even enjoyed her frustration—*like a silly, sick man, perhaps!*

The casual manner the handsome man in his impeccable suit and tie treated Homa made me angry, but also more certain about being her husband. His bushy hair alone, instead of a big beard, had intimidated me already and mitigated my zeal to meet Homa and her presumed husband. So, I turned to go hide somewhere, besides the cold patio this time, to let my nerves settle. However, I realized my glass of whisky was empty and had no choice but to saunter to the bar for a refill. While waiting for my turn at the bar, I peeped in her direction furtively, but only once she peered back at me with accent. At last, I started my excursion towards an unknown destination, all along conscious about the possibility of Homa watching my back or even following me. So, filled with wishful imaginations, I felt obliged to walk on a straight line within her visual perspective, instead of turning around a corner and going to the billiard room as I had initially planned. I had to keep her interested in the game I was playing and make her job of chasing me easy. However, crossing the length of the rooms on a straight line diligently did not offer a spot to linger logistically—no chair to occupy or a familiar person to engage. I cursed my bad luck as I got closer and closer to the wall in the drawing room. How embarrassing my abrupt stop or turn would look like, unless I went towards the fireplace and pretended to be warming my hands or enjoying the soothing sight of the burning lumber. Thank God, I heard somebody calling my name.

I turned and found Mr. Ghadir with a haughty grin. He was an elderly man who tried to get advice from everybody even about simple matters, usually with no intention of using it. My take of his weird approach was that he had made a radical decision about something already and discussed it with others only to brag about his projects, while hoping to find any information or person that supported his normally risky decisions. Sharing his thoughts and decisions also seemed like a clever or desperate scheme he used to prove his modesty and friendliness. He explained his points diligently and persistently, as if obliged to convince others about his decisions. He was quite a character, rather keen to pretend his knack to gel with everybody nicely, despite his enormous ego and wealth according to rumours and Feri. He used me casually any chance he got mostly about Canadian taxation and why or how his income in Iran should be declared here. However, he had not yet invited me to his mansion, despite his embellished respect for me on top of his knack for picking my brain so liberally. Hopefully the only reason was that his wife disliked Feri!

We shook hands and he started a story, which gave me a good chance to linger and peer at Homa from the long distance I had put between us now so stupidly. I noticed she peeped at me more often now, while continuing her conversation with the smart man in suit and tie, which by the way I could not stop admiring. I never felt anything wrong about some men's effort to look their best or spending time to shop around for those kinds of clothing and fussing over a matching tie. Maybe if Feri was around and noticed my praise for that handsome man's knack for fashion, she would have mocked my jealously and idiocy. "You see how nice it looks?"

As much energy Mr. Ghadir was extending to enlighten me, I did not grasp a word he said. My mind and eyes were distracted by that special lady who now stood near the bar. In my deprived, drunk head, she still looked like the time we had dated and she had made my heart pound with excitement for years when we had been together or I had thought about her. The super power enabling a confused lover boy walk away from her, then—even after his dad's seeming words of wisdom regarding the risks of marriage at young age—felt amazing!

The man in suit and tie was interrupted by an ancient friend, apparently, by the way they got too excited, hugged, and planted three kisses on each other's cheeks, before repelling me with their energetic, phony laughter and chattering. That was exactly what I felt Homa and I must be doing, too, as a reward for finding each other after such a long time. As the two men got engaged in their warm conversation and Homa's deemed husband ignored her further, she nodded to them softly and began sauntering elegantly towards my vicinity. I decided to test the opportunity of speaking with her just in case she got close enough to me. When she peeped at me stealthily, I told Mr. Ghadir I would catch him later. Without waiting for his consent, I left him with his jaws open in disbelief and rushed to meet Homa half way.

"I can't believe my eyes," I said as I stood next to her.

"I wasn't sure about you at first, either," Homa replied.

"I look very different, I'm sure."

"We've gotten thirty years older, of course."

"You don't look it at all. You still look young and beautiful," I uttered tensely, mesmerized by her presence, before blurting like a drunken idiot, "You must tell me your secret."

"Well. It's all a matter of proper diet and a simple life without children," she replied generously to humour me.

"So, you are not married?" I asked with hope.

"Oh, yes. For twenty-five years, but have no children."

"It's better this way perhaps, I promise privately."

"Maybe... Jian and I can spend more time together, anyway."

"Instead of spoiling a few naughty kids...," I said ludicrously.

"It seems you have some children you've enjoyed spoiling."

"My wife has monopolized all the spoiling responsibility. But, yes, I have three daughters."

"Children are fun for most people, I guess," she said timidly.

"For a short while usually, I believe."

"You sure sound like a testy expert!" she said with a grin.

"True, you've learned a lot about me already," I said glumly.

"Still, I wonder how my life would've been with a few kids," she said with a subtle air of lost opportunity.

"And I wonder how my life would've been without them," I replied with a hint of likely lost opportunities of my own.

"It would be a different lifestyle and experience altogether."

"In what way?" I asked keenly.

"It gave Jian and me a chance to focus on life itself and learn something about ourselves. We didn't have to fuss about parental duties in vain or hoping to teach anything to some lost souls."

"Is lucky Jian the man you were talking with?"

"Yes, he is."

"It's stupid to say the other thing I'm wondering about, but I hope you forgive me for saying it, because it is the truth," I said.

She kept peering at me with a stiff grin, or a subtle rude smirk if she had already guessed the childish idea rolling in my drunken head. I even tried controlling my big mouth, but failed. I simply had to expose my sullen subconscious in that second. In fact, her smirk, or grin, encouraged me to do just that, nonetheless. So, either she or alcohol made me talk like an imbecile.

"Many times I've wondered how things might've been if we hadn't separated. Then, seeing you tonight with Jian, I imagined being in his place. Forgive my frankness, but I know you enough to state my feelings without fearing the chance of being ridiculed. We probably won't meet again, so I spoke my mind openly."

"Have you been carrying all that weight for thirty-five years?"

"Somewhere in my subconscious, I guess, maybe waiting for a moment like this to make a fool of myself."

"Are you happy in your marriage, too?"

"So so! But it's not what I'd imagined."

"And you said you have only three daughters?"

"Only…? That feels plenty already when I hardly know them despite my efforts and desire."

She chuckled. "Sorry to hear this. It's perhaps harder for men to understand their daughters. Maybe it would've been easier for you if you had a son, too."

"I guess... You should've not abandoned me to go to London," I said rather rudely and tensely, as if finally finding an excuse or opportunity to blame somebody for not having a son on top of all the tortures Feri had been giving me. How I had made a total fool of myself in front of her amazed me more than it had probably upset her. Alcohol alone could have not stirred so much idiocy!

"Oh...? I thought it was a mutual decision. You didn't want to promise me anything."

"How could I? I was only twenty years old."

"I understand. It was not in our destinies."

"At least you were dealt a good hand," I said sloppily again, rather sarcastically, while realizing my impertinence and lunacy all along in hopes of learning more about her marriage.

"Yes, I am happy. But let's look at everything positively. We might've not lasted long if we'd married at our ages then."

"That's true. That's how I felt, too, after talking to my father."

"You talked about us with your father?" she asked in shock.

"Yes, I did, and he succeeded in washing my brain."

"So, you're saying it was all your father's fault?"

"Yes, I definitely think so. But don't worry, I made up for it."

"You did?" she asked with a cute grin and curiosity.

"I disappointed my parents badly with my choice of a spouse in return! But first, I went to work in hot Abadan for nine years to elude my family and our memories in Tehran. So, my parents and I got our good shares of torture after your departure."

"At least you were smart, then, controlling your feelings."

"I thought I was, ha?" I asked. "And still failed in life."

"Perhaps you were smart or not! I let you keep wondering!"

"Thanks… Do you live in Vancouver?"

"No, in San Francisco. We're visiting one of Jian's friends."

"Jian… It's a nice name. The handsome man in suit and tie."

"Anything wrong with a man in suit and tie?" she asked with surprise, gauging my attire and beard with pity—possibly even judging my hygiene as well—the way Feri often did. Her subtle grimace made me wonder again if she had changed, too!

"Of course not," I replied.

"For a second, I thought you were mocking my husband," she said, while her grimace deepened.

"Sorry, it's just that I have become an even more of a casual dresser since I've arrived in Canada."

"That is fine too, if you prefer it that way," she said with pity. "Anyway, it was nice talking with you and good luck."

"Good luck with what?" I asked.

"Just in general… Maybe your daughters," she replied with her smart charm that further reignited my past memories with her endless magic around me when we had felt much more natural towards each other than we had been able to manage even for ten minutes tonight. As much as I, and perhaps she too, had tried to talk naturally tonight, we had failed miserably, especially me.

"So, good luck to you in general, too," I said childishly again as though I had lost my brain altogether after seeing her.

"Thanks," she said and walked away, probably with a sigh of relief for her luck to dump me just in time thirty-five years ago.

I watched her saunter towards Mr. Jian, who suddenly looked interested in her and the bald man she had talked with for a few minutes. He sure looked like a big show-off, too, with his suit and all... *Besides, what was the point of having so much hair? Who cares, anyway?*

Feri popped up in front of me like a jinn. "Who is she?"

"She lived in our neighbourhood," I replied with a smirk.

"You still remembered her from a thousand years ago?"

Her jealousy over the attractive woman speaking with me was thrilling. But she mostly despised my brief joy or even fantasy by chatting with a pretty woman who was kind enough to humour me. So, I was ecstatic mostly for her suffering from my happiness even for a few minutes. What a bizarre relationship!

"Why didn't you introduce me to her, then?" she asked. "You saw me coming and standing around you."

"No, I didn't..., and honestly wasn't thinking, anyway."

"Does she live in Vancouver now?"

"I don't know," I lied slyly, hoping that tonight's episode, plus her imagination of Homa living in Vancouver and meeting me sneakily sometimes, would give her a lasting pain for years to come. "What is the matter with you? Are you jealous?"

"Don't be silly. I just don't want you to think I'm stupid."

"Stupid about what?" I said, knowing exactly what she meant.

She vanished like a jinn again without answering me. Losing her chance to grill and turn Homa against me quickly had most likely hurt Feri more than jealousy. I wondered if Feri's spooky appearance and our spiteful, childish chitchat had been merely my imagination, but the burning scent of her normally excessive perfume convinced me otherwise. I thought she wore so much perfume to overpower other women's scent when she entered a circle of friends. 'I am here, hey everybody.'

I wondered if Homa still had any feelings for me, but hidden it as masterfully as she had apparently concealed herself from me for the rest of the evening. Still, this episode at least proved how foolishly we think and express eternal love so confidently when we are young, the way Homa had claimed. I also wondered if even having Homa in my life would have made me happy, even if she had loved me eternally! *Was I only dreaming again?*

We left the party sooner than usual, anyway. Feri claimed she had a headache and wanted to go home. I bet she merely hated the chance of me chatting with Homa a few more minutes and tasting the joy of a civil conversation ever in my life again with a female whose brain Feri had not yet washed against me totally! I wished Homa lived in Vancouver at least, so that I could dream of the chance of bumping into her again sometimes. Then again, if she did, I would be wasting my life in malls all over the city every day in hopes of making that dream come true, instead of writing so many masterpieces! Still, maybe I should start going out every day for hours, anyway, just in hopes of irritating Feri with the idea of seeing Homa behind her back!

The fluke encounter with Homa had reopened a can of worms for my already tired brain. I was quite depressed for a few weeks, ruminating my life when I had been a handsome, young man and girls looked at me more favourably. What happened to my youth and how fast this annihilation had occurred? We never understand when people say life is too short. More importantly, however, now I realized, our useful years are much much shorter than we can imagine, because we are intoxicated by the events during those fun years, and then poof, it is all over and we are married and old and abandoned and desolate. I used to be somebody in the past, played a big role at work, had lots of silky hair, said no to so many girls, and now… Now, I could not get even a simple 'maybe' from a pretty woman. Another reason I liked Darren and Reza was probably because they rekindled my thrilling, youthful memories subconsciously. They revived my 'being' indirectly at the time I was sinking fast in a deep abyss. Of course, we three also thought and talked the same way—cynically—and felt each other's anguish naturally, despite our wide differences in age and life priorities. All along, I had envied them, Darren a bit more, for their adventurous lives, like the way I had at least tried to live in my ancient history. Where was Darren nowadays and how deeply had he succumbed to Reza's irresistible sister? *Lucky bastard!*

My old, profound wisdom, *one wrong turn often derails one's entire life journey,* has kept banging my brain more often after that brief encounter with Homa. 'Hey, young people, be careful!' Marrying the wrong person, in particular, turns into the biggest mistake anybody can make when often we get stuck with a crazy spouse and a bunch of kids created with equally crooked genes as exact replicas of him or her as younger lunatics.

Even worse, marrying just for integrity or saving a fetus, like I had, has felt a much stupider and shallower gesture after meeting Homa. How foolishly I had let my playful conscience inflict me with a horrific destiny I could not do a damn thing about or even learn anything from to help myself now or ever. Integrity—what nonsense, especially in retrospect!

As I sulked over my lost life, my radical scepticism about the value of integrity now posed a bizarre dilemma of its own and caused me fresh confusion. Now, integrity felt like an overrated concept people apply selectively to humour their conscience or boost their spirits in a chaotic world driven by humans' idiocy and duplicity! Can we at least manage to do it rather consistently, or simply forget about it?

Accordingly, I began wondering if my aristocratic friends' general lack of integrity might be also justified, including their knack for patronizing and bribing the corrupt officials in Iran to get filthy rich. Their chronic duplicity and vanity was not a crime anymore, then, the way I had often imagined in the past!

Furthermore, did my new stance oblige me to make amends with my old friends and Feri, embrace and admire their lifestyle, and make substantial mental adjustments? Maybe I should in fact go apologize to many people for my bad behaviour in recent years? Maybe Homa would like me better that way, too, without a beard in a fancy suit and tie. Still better, maybe it was time to go find and dust off my impressive CGA certificate to hang in my new tax consulting office, at last, hire a gorgeous secretary to drive Feri nuts, and begin ripping my rich friends off with my fat invoices just for showing my sincerity? Feri had loathed that darn CGA diploma for its sneaky hints, while it hung in my study a few months, yet she still gloated about her Real Estate Certificate hanging in the foyer, like parading a Ph.D. in Space Physics!

Chapter Eight
Good Questions

Mahtab's reminder, 'Don't forget to take the keys, Darren,' rang in my slow brain as I waited twenty minutes in front of her building, still clutching the bouquet of roses with both hands like a baby or a box of pizza. Maybe I feared dangling it would ruin its freshness or importance, while wondering why I was so silly. Passersby probably thought I was stood up by my callous lover in the way they peered at me and the flowers with pity. In return, their smirks tickled my wit with the idea of returning the roses to the florist and asking for a refund or at least keeping them fresh in water for me until I found someone to give them to! A few people got in and out of the building and I finally braved to sneak in fast after holding the door for an older lady coming out. She smiled and thanked me before I got inside, took the ride to the 28th floor, and knocked on Mahtab's door on and off. No answer.

The smell of Persian food seeping from her apartment stirred the memories of my times in Tehran, while my paranoia grew. Had she left me already or was not opening the door for a reason? Was she playing some kind of a game with me to retaliate for my cold attitude that morning, excluding her from my plans all day, and returning home late—after eight hours without even calling her, instead of 2-3 hours I had promised her? My paranoia was not fully baseless, either. Erica's elaborate games and retaliations yesteryear had made me quite cynical. *Did passion or frustration make Mahtab commit suicide already, too, like Erica maybe!*

Nah..., I tried to disallow Erica and my imaginations ruin my lovely impression of Mahtab. She was beyond playing games with me, not even for drawing my attention to my procrastination about our love affair—which, if true, it showed something very important: That I had a lot of trust in her, which can only be the result of my deep appreciation of her. It meant I believed to know Mahtab much more than I had considered all day in my suite. Now, in just a few minutes, I had felt something very crucial I had failed to do during my daylong deep reflection! This level of trust in another woman, which I had realized only now, was a major consideration and a blessing for my inevitable discussions with Mahtab about our plans. The next minute, I wondered if this sentimental conclusion merely reflected my vulnerability, naiveté, or desperation. I knocked on the door firmer again, pondering the idea of getting a cab and returning to my own apartment, after all, regardless of the likely hazards of living there. The hell with it all. The only question keeping me around a few more seconds like an aggravated idiot was whether to leave the flowers behind the door for her or take them all the way home with me to remind me of another failure today! Whether she still deserved the flowers surely depended on her reasons for keeping me in suspense for ten minutes in the middle of hallway after all that waiting in the street! Accordingly, making a decision felt so cumbersome. This timely dilemma convoluting my mind for a minute saved me a lot of hassle and misunderstanding about a flourishing love affair. As I turned to leave *with the flowers*, the elevator bell rang and Mahtab stepped out with a lovely grin.

"Didn't you take the keys?" she asked, noticing my agitation.

"No, I forgot," I replied.

"Here, come help me with this bag," she said before noticing the flowers and the briefcase in my hands. She put the bag down and opened the door. "Have you been waiting for long?"

"About half an hour."

"I had to go buy some grocery and wine. I needed some fresh air, too. I was beginning to feel depressed alone in this place."

"Sorry for taking longer than I'd promised," I said.

"Dinner is ready unless you rather have wine first."

"Wine first... I need it," I said, dropping my briefcase, kissing her cheek, and giving her the flowers. "These are for you."

It was a sweet kiss but still not on her lips. I needed it more than wine and she deserved it. She smiled and took the flowers. She smelled the roses and clutched them near her chest, then leaned and kissed me on the cheek, too.

"Thanks, Darren. They're nice."

The flowers' good ending was also encouraging!

I examined the wine bottles in the brown bag and chose a merlot, while Mahtab put the flowers in a large crystal vase and placed it in the middle of the coffee table. I poured us wine and we sat on the same sofa near her. We clanked our glasses and sipped our wines.

"Did you enjoy your long walk?" she asked wittily.

"Very much…"

"Was everything okay at the apartment, too?"

"Yeah, I guess…"

"How did you feel there this time?"

"It still felt a bit sad and awkward at the beginning, but I could relax and think better gradually. I even thought about painting, but couldn't."

"You'll feel normal soon again," she said with a cute smile.

"I hope so… I like to start painting and go to my place more often after seeing Detective Stewart who's also left a message."

"Yes, let's go see him if you're ready."

"Maybe tomorrow... I must also decide soon about the other messages and maybe return the calls."

"What kind of a decision?" she asked.

"About my whereabouts, in particular," I replied. "I don't like to lie too much if we ever start answering our phones."

"Has Reza left you a message, too?"

"Yes, more than one. Also T.J. has called a lot with urgent or suspicious messages, but I didn't call anybody today."

I did not mention Elizabeth's curious message that possibly showed her knowledge of Jeff's involvement with the thugs who had shot me.

"Reza has left a few messages for me as well," Mahtab said.

"It's obvious what he wants to talk to us about."

"Of course."

"He has probably asked T.J. to spy on us, too," I said.

"Would T.J. do that?"

"No. I mean just finding out where I am and what we're up to and reporting to Reza. I can't call either of them until I know what to say."

"Me neither...," she replied.

"But, first, we must decide soon what we want to do."

"And when we do, it'll either hurt some people badly or kill me at least," she said rather romantically.

"That particular option would most likely kill me as well," I replied wittily with a chuckle.

"Most likely, ha...?" she asked with a giggle.

"Okay, it'd definitely kill me, too," I replied and kissed her cheek before adding, "...eventually."

"Then let's not choose that awful option that will kill me for sure with a slight chance of killing you eventually as well."

"Yes, unless it is the right choice to make!" I replied with a presumed deeper wit and wisdom.

Mahtab burst into laughter and punched me lightly. "So, we must ignore people's calls for now."

"But how much longer?" I asked.

"As long as necessary. Forever if you want."

I swallowed a big gulp of wine pensively, stared into her eyes passionately, and realized she meant it.

"But how? They'll find us sooner or later," I said.

"Let's go hide in the U.S. or another place, although we need money. I should've sent more money before leaving Tehran. But I was in such a rush my mind couldn't think this far in advance."

"Or…, maybe even you couldn't imagine I'll last this long?"

"True… Maybe deep down even my own psyche doubted my dream about your recovery!"

"Anyway, I don't think running away can help."

"It might, until something happens to make it easier to explain things to others," she said.

"Not even a miracle can ever make explaining easy," I said.

"Do you want me to go back to Iran, then?" she asked.

"Only if you think it's the right thing for you to do."

"No, Darren. I don't think leaving you or living in Iran is the right thing for me."

"So what should we do?" I asked. "I can sell my apartment to flee to the US, but don't think it'll work."

"I guess… But first you must know how you feel about us."

"I think I'm getting brave enough to fall in love again."

"Oh…?" Mahtab uttered with a pleasant surprise.

"Maybe you've eased my fear of attachment after Erica or are the right person to do that gradually."

"I'm flattered, but how have I achieved such a big honour?" she asked with a grin spread all over her beautiful face.

"I feel I can trust your emotions and words. I hope I'm right."

"Thanks. Everybody has some paranoia about love, especially after making mistakes. But maybe we have been lucky to find each other in such a hectic circumstance," she said.

"I'd reached the same conclusion in Barcelona and now after everything you've done for me, and the way I've known you. But love can't solve our problems, can it?" I asked.

"I don't know, but hope it does eventually," Mahtab replied.

"Is by any chance your Ph.D. in psychology?" I asked.

"No, in economics..., both Bijan and I. Why?"

"Because of the way you see things and talk... But I also just realized I didn't know this important info."

"And it's a pity that neither Bijan or I have had a chance to use our knowledge properly yet. What a waste of life!"

"I hate to lose you, too… You're a wonderful woman and I feel thrilled about our romance, although we haven't still kissed."

Mahtab peered into my eyes passionately: "Do you wish to kiss me right now, then?"

"Yes, I like that very much."

We stared at each other tenderly for a few seconds, pensive and excited about the risky adventure we had eluded for such a long time rather wisely. Then, we both leaned and kissed a quick one on the mouth. Next, I embraced her tightly and planted a much firmer kiss all over her lips. We hugged for a long time. When we separated at last, she cringed to hide her wet eyes and quickly excused herself to go check on the dinner.

"Are you ready for dinner yet?" she asked from the kitchen at last, apparently after sobbing a bit in private, maybe fearful about the prospect and risks of what we had subtly meant to begin.

"Yes, sure."

We chatted and laughed giddily all evening, thanks to all the wine we drank to forget our fears for a few hours—like some kind of subtle resignation. Still we discussed our options, too. For one thing, we reaffirmed our pact to ignore Reza's and T.J.'s calls for now, while laughing a lot about lacking a long-term plan for the outcome of our delaying tactic amidst varied threats. All we felt genuinely was love and no more hesitation to express it over and over openly. We kissed all along during the evening and I stroked her smooth long hair slithering over her bare shoulders, which I caressed and kissed as well. She smiled and touched my face and hair pensively with subtle tension in her eyes similar to the one she could probably see in mine. We sensed the mixed sanctity and insanity of our romance—such a sinful adventure—though our hearts were filled with defiance like two naughty kids.

We realized the stronger our love grew, the harder handling it would get, yet naively believed to be capable of overcoming all the hurdles, even if necessary to elope to some foreign lands as our last resort. *Oh, how love ruins our senses…! Right before lust also rushes in to mess up us totally.*

Later in the evening, we kissed again before going to our own bedrooms and closing the doors behind us like two bashful lovers unclear about their next prudent move beyond kissing. Our stern gestures of closing our bedroom doors felt so meaningful, but not rude, with many psychological interpretations if I cared to ponder for amusement. I stood behind the door wondering if I must go knock on her door to break the last barrier of decency. I wondered if she expected me to do just that. Most of all, I was quite horny after nearly five months of sexless life. This was a record for me in recent years, even considering the three months I had been in the coma. I giggled when movie scenes of lovers' attack to rip each other's clothes and get naked rolled in my head. It made me laugh aloud, thinking that my gibberish thoughts and hysterical laughter were most likely related to my rational fear of Mahtab's fanatical husband, Bijan. If Mahtab had heard me, she might have thought I was a lunatic laughing aloud alone instead of going over to boost our romance to its apex!

Knowing Mahtab, neither of us found sex an urgent issue—except for the inevitable taboo we both wished to avoid as long as possible. We could have it with joy, or ignore it with pride for now, since our selfless, spiritual love did not need sex to validate itself. *That, or I was inventing so much nonsense to fool myself!* Very deep in our hearts, maybe we felt a miracle would happen overnight and we would be much wiser the next day to elude all the traps our emotions were pressing on us and before a sexual relationship closed that door. More crucial than my conscience and *midnight philosophy* was to decide in advance about what could or should come after sex. How could we sleep separately again once we embraced each other's naked bodies and let the magic of love merge all our cells together? Were we ready for that kind of reckless life filled with fear and ecstasy? Did our situation, even after our open expressions of love, warrant such a big commitment and sin? Regardless of our apparent passion, both Mahtab and I needed still more time and assurance about our love before we mixed our bodies, too, and indulged ourselves with incredible sex night after night, convinced of the validity of our deed only based on an expression of eternal love. We must be ready to die the way it happens in operas or mushy love stories. Except that, our sin was real with a huge risk of leading to many people's anguish and revenge, while both lovers of this dramatic opera could get murdered because of a contentious decision that Mahtab and I had to make soon. But not tonight, thank God.

The old analytical Darren was back, I reckoned giddily, as I pulled the blanket over myself in the bed at last. The poor guy had been super active all day, trying to rationalize every step for rebuilding his life, even forgoing sex so admirably despite his horny mood. Yet, he had figured out nothing besides condoning sex as a necessary, automatic routine the way it occurs in modern movies. Instead, that wild, passionate image had only triggered the scene of meeting Bijan outside the Evin prison for the first time. He had come with Reza and my release papers, to save my life possibly. Haunting, embarrassing thoughts made me tremble with a tense giggle and shaky conscience.

The exhausted analytical Darren must have dosed off at last with no clue about his wisest or most practical course of action in coming days!

The next day, I made an appointment with Detective Stewart, but fretted over the task of explaining my view of Jeff's involvement before talking with Elizabeth, who had also sounded eager to find me. However, contacting her before knowing how to grill her for handling Jeff for my needs felt unwise. Besides, I did not mind letting her fret awhile for the way she had simply dumped me right after I had returned from Iran, a day before I was shot! The chance she could, or would, tell me anything against Jeff was low

—even less than the chance of she having already dumped Jeff, too, maybe after realizing his involvement with the shooting. Many things could have happened to their relationship during the last three months, after all. Maybe she was hoping to resume our old affair! Anyway, despite her zeal to see me, and my curiosity about her motive, I chose not to call her today, either, mostly due to the limited time left before meeting Detective Stewart! Many people I dodged these days for a variety of weird reasons.

"You look quite healthy today, Mr. Durant," Detective Stewart said seriously after a quick peek at me, while searching his desk for a binder apparently about my case.

I smirked, as Mahtab and I took our chairs. "Thanks... I hope my mind is working well, too," I said with grief for abandoning my chance to expand on his serious diagnosis of my health, as if he were also a physician. Both his comment and my thoughts were funny to share at least with Mahtab later, although I feared my juvenile humour only raising her suspicion about my sanity and health. *Sadly, not enough people have yet appreciated my ironic sense of humour the way Elizabeth did! I'd loved her for it!*

"Let's check your mind, too, then," he said with a silly giggle, as if reading my mind and enjoying his nerve to keep teasing me.

"All right… *Let's check it!*" I said tensely, winking at Mahtab and thinking that this Detective Stewart was really asking for trouble today. "What do you want to know?"

"Why don't you tell me everything you know?"

I had mixed feeling about letting in Mahtab on my past affairs and damaging her impression of me, but she was bound to find out sooner or later, anyway. Detective Stewart glanced at Mahtab curiously, as if he had *detected* my dilemma about talking in front of her while choosing to bring her along. He also looked eager to know about our relationship, although I had introduced her as a family friend. I just hoped he would not pry into this matter.

"I met Erica at the Kegg's the night before the incident," I said.

"The Kegg's in downtown?"

"Yes... The one in Dunsmuir Street," I replied, pondering the importance of the location and his seeming diligence.

"Okay, please continue."

"She said some guys may confront me in the street or another place. A common friend of ours had apparently hired them after going berserk, because his girlfriend had moved in with me at the time. But the girlfriend—"

"What are the names of this friend and his brave girlfriend?" he asked, rather intrigued by the promising juicy story. Mahtab also seemed alarmed slightly as I peeped at her furtively.

"Jeff Wright and Elizabeth Conner."

"Okay, please continue," he said after jotting down the names.

"Anyway, Elizabeth reconciled with Jeff and moved out of my suite when I returned from Tehran. Jeff had apparently tried to find the thugs and cancel the contract for confronting me, but failed. So, he'd asked Erica to give me a heads-up and tell me to humour the thugs, so that they'd go away. That's basically all Erica told me at the Kegg's in downtown," I said giddily, as if asking for trouble myself by stressing on the location!

"Okay, then what happened the next day? Erica came to see you in your apartment again?"

"No, I didn't see her that day. But she was supposed to come by to pick up a painting from my apartment."

"So how'd she end up falling from your balcony, you think?"

"I have no idea… I didn't let her in my apartment that day."

"Okay, so tell me what happened that afternoon?"

"I let in the FedEx to deliver a painting to my apartment around 3:30. After he left, I turned to close the door behind him when suddenly these two Oriental guys appeared at the door and pushed their ways into my apartment. They closed the door and began threatening me. I told them Elizabeth had already moved out and that Jeff wanted me to cancel their contract myself. They looked furious when I asked them to call Jeff for confirmation. They pushed me around and said they would take two of my paintings for their efforts more than one month to find me and now the chance of not even getting the money Jeff owed them. I tried to stop them and that was when one of them shot me. That's all I remember."

"Are you sure you have no idea when Erica arrived and what happened to her?"

"Yes, I'm sure, as I said before," I stressed slyly. Yet, swiftly I panicked again from the chance of having pushed Erica off the balcony if my wicked subconscious has been blocking this truth. Or maybe I did not recall it due to the injury and the coma.

Luckily, Stewart's next question stopped my suspicious mind. "Do you know how I can find Jeff and Elizabeth?"

I gave him their phone number and answered his questions about my stolen paintings and the thugs' appearance.

"What's the best way to contact you?" he asked.

"Call me at home but I can give you another number, too, if only answering machine comes on and you need to talk with me immediately," I replied, peering at Mahtab for consent.

As she nodded, I passed on her phone number to Detective Stewart. He said he would contact me soon after speaking with Elizabeth and Jeff. Just as we turned to leave, I thought I should ask him a smart question myself, though mostly for kidding him.

"Excuse me, Detective. Do you think it is prudent for me to live in my apartment?" I asked.

He looked perplexed for ten seconds before getting my drift.

"Actually that is a good question. No. I think it's better to live somewhere else awhile until we can investigate and discuss this matter again. Can you manage to stay with a friend or in a hotel?" he asked while peeping at Mahtab stealthily.

"I'll try. But…" I paused in time before letting out a sarcastic remark just dying to jump out and humiliate him outright.

"But what, Mr. Durant?" Detective Stewart asked.

"Oh, nothing, never mind. Thanks."

As we left the police station, I noticed Mahtab's curiosity to know more about the incident and related issues, especially my affair with Elizabeth. Was it really over? I did not have to be a psychic to read her mind about many plausible concerns she might have grown suddenly. Meanwhile, I thought about calling Elizabeth out of courtesy and curiosity and giving her a heads-up about Detective Steward's imminent contact with her.

"Did you mean to ask him another question before changing your mind?" Mahtab asked.

"Actually, I had a few sarcastic questions, but I'm glad I stopped myself in time. I shouldn't upset him with me."

"Has he done something wrong?"

"Well… For one thing, his indifference or incompetence felt annoying."

"What do you mean?"

"Don't you think he should've thought about the risk of living in my place? He's a goddamn detective supposedly, eh? What if I hadn't asked him the question?"

"You're right."

"He hadn't considered warning me or just didn't give a damn about it," I said, thinking that the uptight, analytical Darren was really back!

"But even you wanted to live there before I pushed you to stay with me."

"But I'm not a detective… It is his job to stop me," I said.

"At least now we have this great excuse, too, in case someone finds out about you living in my apartment," she said.

"What do you mean?" I asked.

"We can always say that Detective Stewart forced you to stay with a friend and he ordered us not to answer our phones or let anybody, even family members, know where you were living."

"Wow… That's a great idea," I replied with delight.

"Didn't I tell you yesterday that something might change to make it easier to justify our actions?" she asked playfully.

"Yes, you sure did, Einstein!" I replied giddily. "Although we might still sound like big lying idiots."

"It's still better than having no excuse," she said with a giggle.

"Yeah, they should all go blame this Detective Stewart for our actions and secrecy if they want to," I said with a chuckle.

"Absolutely," she replied with loud laughter. "It's also okay to sound like idiots, just for obeying him unconditionally."

"I'd better call Elizabeth right away and give her a heads-up about Detective Stewart at least," I told Mahtab after our long idiotic laughers and jokes, while we strolled towards her car.

"Okay, let's find a public phone," she suggested.

After I left a message on Elizabeth's answering machine, we went to a café to relax and plan for the rest of the evening, which was again full of laughter, romance, and serious conversations. Then, I also had another long, frustrating debate about sex with my analytical self after we shut our bedroom doors sternly, but playfully, again. *He* insisted again that our love was too fragile to consummate before ascertaining its long-term viability and while our minds were besieged by personal issues and analyses about our options. As a most solid rationale, my playful spirit insisted that Mahtab and I were playing in a sacred epic opera, not a sexy cheap movie! This precious milestone should not be spoiled by a rash sexual episode now that we both felt the need for a rational plan to support our emotions.

Most likely, Mahtab also preferred a practical plan first before complicating each other's lives with some hasty decisions. She preferred to wait until we understood, and stood ready to fight for, the consequences of our deeds. We surely needed a miracle or superpower to contain those ferocious people who abhorred even a simple friendship between Mahtab and me, let alone a mushy love affair. We might as well pray the thugs finished us first before those vengeful, mad people found us. Then again, maybe I was only fooling myself by these logical thoughts or my imagination of what Mahtab preferred! What if I was wrong?!

Despite all these beautiful and humorous thoughts to distract the devil, I was still very horny! I wanted to strangle that snotty, analytical angel inventing all these silly excuses so fast to stop this suddenly numb, patient devil from doing his regular job and starting all those fun things he would have usually done by now in similar circumstances. Worst of all, putting so much thoughts and analyses into this normally pedestrian topic—sex—felt too shameful and beneath any intelligent person's dignity!

"Okay, okay…, I got it, you told me all these stuff last night already," the devil yelled rudely at that petite, wise angel. "Let me get some sleep at least!"

No such luck…

Instead, the image of many parts of Mahtab's beautiful, soft body lying uselessly in bed perturbed my conscience about the chance of Mahtab missing me right that minutes and preferring something totally different from what I liked to imagine. She was most likely feeling lonely and horny, too, while wrestling with similar dilemmas about love versus decency. Maybe she had made a braver decision already, unlike my suddenly angelic self, and wished I were in her bed, while I merely tried to imagine her thoughts on top of humouring my own newborn virtuous mind? —*maybe all this nonsense boggling my brain about decency was just another side-effect of my coma!* I prayed to God that coma had not annihilated that cute devil inside me that has been both handy and humorous all my life!

Thank God, this gibberish made me doze off at last without a sensible idea about the prospect of my vague relationship with Mahtab giving me some comfort or assurance. The matter was now getting too complex, as the angel and devil seemed adamant to fight in my head, only God knew for how many more nights! I simply could not fathom a way out of this sexual bottleneck on top of so much emotional burdens already killing our spirits these days.

Chapter Nine
Saving My Beloveds

No man has probably adored and admired his sisters like me with awe—a stressful mix of wonder and fear. Accordingly, my failure to alleviate their pains and desperation during some crises has dispirited me. Worse, the likelihood of my deeds causing their distress—by introducing two oddballs, Zia and Darren, to them—has disturbed me, so much as crippling my own life quite a bit.

When I was a teenager and things had not gotten so out of hand, my father had also noticed my likely paranoia goading me to butt in my sisters' lives more often than not.

"Listen, Reza," he said. "Women do what they like no matter how much advice we give them. I know you love your sisters. But try not to meddle in their lives. It'd be useless and only make them hate you and possibly get even wilder."

"But you know how reckless your naughty daughters get sometimes, don't you?" I asked.

"Yes, they're your mother's daughters, after all. But there's not much we can do about this matter."

"You probably weren't strict enough when raising them."

"I did my best, Reza," he said with gloom. "Your mother let me do only certain things. I had to accept the upshot of marrying an educated and liberal woman like your mother. She wanted to raise her daughters as independent and progressive as possible."

"And you let her, ha?" I asked slyly. "You didn't discipline them like other fathers of your generation."

"I had no choice," he replied

"And this is the outcome now," I snapped rather rudely.

"To tell you the truth, I wasn't in favour of sending them to Switzerland to finish their high-school and then go to Paris to university. I was against letting them grow on their own, sort of, at such early ages, despite living in a dormitory."

Finding my father so helpless to control his daughters and wife had made my job more urgent; to at least observe my sisters closer, especially when our parents became frail and our father passed away. I have felt pressed and possibly possessed to defuse my sisters' tenacity to mess up our lives somehow year after year. Not enough space is here to go over their earlier idiocies and my pains prior to their marriages. I just wonder amusingly how many young men have fallen victims to their playful charm!

I watched from a distance or missed Mahroo and Mahtab, in particular when they schooled in Europe and turned into such gorgeous, liberal ladies. Their girlish games and juvenile secrets felt cute to me, although their seamless bonding made me feel envious and dejected. Still, like a proud big brother, I guess, I just wanted to keep an eye on them in case they ever showed mercy on me and decided to seek my help and advice. Most likely, my protective sentiment towards them had something to do with our Bakhtiary pride genes, too, and our strong culture to beware of and ward off the devil luring mostly women. Meanwhile, my scrutiny seemed to raise their tenacity to shrug off my empathy, exclude me from their lives further, and yet keep playing their sneaky games to tease me with more joy. Ironically and pitifully, I found even their sneaky games cute and a partial inclusion. In return, I got keener to perfect my own means of protecting them against many evils goading girls even before turning into reckless teenagers, especially my sisters' kinds: so beautiful, adventurous, naïve, and romantic—such a fatal mix.

As an ironical, added source of frustration, I had sometimes questioned, and tried to contain, my possible paranoia about the necessity of keeping an eye on my sisters. Now, however, my wisdom all along has been proven unequivocally, *at least to me!* My predictions and fuss about my sisters' knack for sabotaging their lives has been rational indeed, like I had been a psychic. Yet I had never imagined deserving lots of blame myself for their misfortunes, mostly for bringing Darren to Tehran. In particular, my sense of guilt has risen and hurt me a lot after Mahroo passed away despite my efforts to help her and I could not stop Mahtab from following Mahroo's footstep and ruining her life for Darren, too. My inability to get through Mahtab, while we might still have a chance for redemption, has been excruciating during the last two months.

My father's frailty around women has possibly also made me cynical about women these days and keen to find justice for him—for so much pain our three beloveds had inflicted upon my lonely, confused father. Poor man had to endure a lousy life in quiet with many unsettled questions in his tormented mind. I had noticed his suffering in his kind, patient demeanour, while my paranoia and personality had evolved amidst a bunch of rebels supposedly behaving as modern parents and siblings.

The misty clouds dancing near the tiny window on the flight to Vancouver kept me amused. The worst part of long flights for me has been the boring, forced containment in my seat for hours. It is like being put in a tight spot cunningly by a mystical force to dwell on and suffer my family dilemmas and sore memories, while hoping to grasp the roots of my growing confusion in line with my keener belief about life's vanity. The matter felt graver on this flight, though, as many aspects of my peculiar destiny seemed to demand serious rethinking and finer planning urgently.

When Mahroo married my friend, Zia Taymori, I hoped he could satiate her sensitive soul with his immense passion and sense of humour. Now, one less headache for me, I imagined naively! In fact, I felt proud for indirectly making my first sister happy and settled. Yet, it worked for only a few years—until Zia's hidden quirks began irritating Mahroo. She looked sad and cynical about marrying him, despite his rather good looks and bright future as an engineer working on major projects. I got disheartened myself witnessing Mahroo's stress around an overly jealous husband and a newly born daughter, Nazi.

Actually, Mahroo's dying spirit raising her impatience around Nazi was one of the major symptoms worrying the whole family and making me feel guiltier every day for introducing Zia to her. I began blaming myself even about Nazi's looming fate already. Still, I strived to keep my mouth shut about Mahroo's marriage, since I had no opinion for the first time, anyway, which caused a lot of extra pressure on my nerves in itself. Later, however, with her and Nazi's moods failing fast, I tried to alarm her subtly about the risk of bearing an unsettled marriage with so much gloom. I did it by giving her the *Woman in the White Dress,* Darren's new painting, in hopes of helping her through its subtle messages. Sadly, however, my indirect intrusion backfired inadvertently in the end without us realizing the extent of mayhem my brotherly intention had been causing behind the scene.

Ironically, this event was itself the offshoot of my goodwill to hire Darren for my firm in Iran, as a favour to get him out of his slump in Vancouver. It proved to have been a catastrophically bad timing in itself, which caused only more headaches for my family and me—simply for bringing the second evil man into Mahroo's life and heart.

Despite Zia's hints a couple of times, I could not imagine that Mahroo's accidental, private infatuation for Darren had depressed her even more, while Zia's suspicions had raised his jealousy to the roof—maybe parallel to Othello's. Darren's vague words to Mahroo about the sad woman in his painting had also given her a wrong impression regarding his private feelings for her in return. So, for three years, things had been going wrong in many ways behind the scene. Without knowing the cause of Zia's bizarre behaviour and pressures on Mahroo, I had attributed the whole situation merely to Zia's innate madness. So, saving my beloved Mahroo had felt quite urgent.

After Darren's departure to Vancouver and Zia's death in a seemingly suicidal car crash, Mahroo went to Vancouver to test Darren's level of interest in her. Instead, she received the biggest shock of her life after realizing her misunderstanding and bearing the added pains of her big disappointment, though later Darren found himself mysteriously attracted to Mahroo, too. This time, he chased her to Iran, was jailed for twelve days, and released on the day poor Mahroo was stabbed at work by a distressed war veteran inadvertently and died. All these demonic deaths were driving me crazy, like watching a foolish cheap movie. Yet, this is the true tale of my darling sister who got merely a glimpse of a promising romance. Such a short and sad life she had.

While still suffering the loss of Mahroo, my faith in God was shaken altogether when the turmoil around Mahtab's marriage soon turned into a new nightmare for my family and me.

Mahtab had chosen the man of her dreams—*without my help, thank god!*—while studying at a university in Los Angeles. She claimed she had never anticipated the extent of Bijan's radicalism and adaptability to the new socio-political life in Iran. As a son of a chief government official, he had suddenly become an Islamic fanatic in a rather high official post with deep devotion to the new government's ideologies and policies. So, Mahtab began losing interest in him. Most people would probably think that my sisters sound too fussy and I agree with them, which in return justifies my chronic concern about their behaviour and welfare! Now, at last, you probably get my drift!

When mourning Mahroo, Mahtab apparently finds Darren the only person feeling the depth of her grief for the loss of Mahroo truly. After all, they were the two people who had loved Mahroo in a spiritual manner—as an intimate sister and a *heart-broken* man in love again after so long. Mahtab savours the opportunity of mourning Mahroo so lovingly mostly with Darren, who had seemingly appreciated Mahtab's passionate character, wisdom, and friendship in return.

Then, Mahtab had probably found Darren also closer to her impression of an ideal man, the same way Mahroo had three years earlier. Nevertheless, leaving her family and husband to go to Vancouver to nurse Darren had felt like absolute madness, while I was starting to think that maybe he deserved being shot for whatever reason, after all. He had it coming at least for his dreadful effect on my sisters and many other women, in spite of a dire fate tormenting him the most amidst endless chaos. *He was jinxed or Devil had taken his soul;* that was the kindest I could say about him these days on this tiring, long trip to Vancouver.

Ironically, my friendship with this devil has gotten closer, but also messier all along, while bizarre, accidental love stories have stirred mysterious mix-ups amongst some colleagues and friends, all thanks to my sisters' and Erica's knack for romanticism.

Still, the biggest factor behind these fatal romances had been my submission to Erica's allure that had led to bringing Darren to Iran and starting different mayhems when we all, including Erica, Mahroo, Darren, and Mahtab had felt lonely and vulnerable. My role has been more ruinous in this case than introducing Zia to my family, and thus a bigger source of my growing sense of guilt. In the end, Erica introducing Darren to me, when my association with SDI for software development began, should be considered a malicious coincidence leading to so much agony.

Especially, when she decided to fall in love with me as well!

I have hinted about my passion for Erica sloppily, while moaning so much about other people's lives and loves. So, now, it is time to explain and rebuke my own sinful attraction to Erica, my sole beloved—besides my mom and sisters—who has spoiled my life and sanity, too! In fact, I was probably drawn to her since her personality and beauty paralleled the other three's. I never meant to surpass decency or derail her marriage as we worked on our companies' shared projects, although my fast attraction to her felt bizarre—a first for me. Still, I had no reason or right to even think about her. In fact, soon my initial sexual draw towards her turned into the familiar urge of protecting her against the world's evils she also seemed eager to embrace—like my sisters again! I just do not know why or how this sacred notion felt stronger and more natural as I learned more about Erica. *Isn't human psyche and psychology dictating our fates so closely and oddly?*

Nobody would probably grasp or believe my confession here. It might sound merely like an effort to justify my evil, I admit. In particular, my peculiar excuses for being lured into a *seemingly* sinful trap, right after scorning Darren's and my sisters' shocking infatuations, would surely sound hypocritical. However, I believe some affairs are not just a straightforward sin, but rather a slow spiritual growth beyond a normal person's realm of sanity and control. Ours was something of that nature—a divine experiment, unless this sounds like another desperate BS! Yet, personally, I thought ours was the former, at least until close to its end when our egos surpassed even such a spiritual revelation. At any rate, my sincere confession about *the nature of my love* for Erica might at least help me curb my burden of guilt for innocently causing my beloved women's grief and cleanse my conscience a little. *Then you judge me, too!*

Dear God... My inability to take even a nap on the plane when others do it so easily and making me jealous is bizarre. Instead, I must wrestle with so much sour thoughts during these darn flights from Tehran and Vancouver—and not even for business this time!

Erica was bright and mature, too, like my sisters and mother again—a trait I had missed in other girls so far. People, especially my mom, have kept criticizing me all along for being too picky about a mate and bypassing many qualified girls who had shown interest in me. But Erica was the only women who had satisfied my thirst for meaningful, calm conversations. This quality had felt like an icing on the cake after my endless failures to relate to my intelligent sisters and mom. Especially my mom seemed keen to talk only in a sardonic tone, which I had subsequently detected and resented in other women as well, while feeling for my dad! So, Erica emerged as a perfect woman that my father had warned me not to expect to find!

Soon she felt comfortable with me as we trusted each other and shared our family dramas and dilemmas—maybe she had found me perfect, too!! She said she had missed open communication with Darren. Thus, our friendship grew in a way most people dream. All along, the success of our joint projects made us feel closer and more dependent on each other, especially since her partner, Cameron, could not offer much technically.

Then one day Erica told me she was sceptical about her future with Darren. I was taken aback by her zeal to share her private thoughts so liberally out of the blue. His personality and artistic setbacks had seemingly eroded their marriage with a big blow to their psyches as they had assumed their love imperishable during the twelve years of initial dating and subsequent union. From that point on, we discussed her marital situation as though she sought refuge in me to relieve her tension, which was affecting her work performance as well. And I did not mind showing my support. It felt so natural and delightful, as I had always craved doing just that for my sisters; and since they had resisted my interventions, unlike Erica whose demand for more of my advice and empathy thrilled my psyche. The satisfaction of consulting and consoling an intelligent woman just for mental support felt sacred. I could not imagine I was walking on thin ice; until it was too late. In six months, I had also told Erica a lot about my family conundrums, especially Mahroo's troubles with Zia and her melancholy. Then one day Erica said time had come for her to do something about Darren. I assumed she meant his mood and professional life.

"Why don't you hire him in SDI?" I suggested. "Help him build his confidence, which would then help your marriage, too."

"You think so? As an office boy or a secretary?" Erica asked.

"No... Send him for training as internet technician or a graphic designer. SDI can use his artistic talent for these jobs."

"You really mean it?"

"Of course… He'll be ready in six months. Besides, the point is to get him out of the house and rebuild his confidence. Maybe marriage counselling helps as well after he starts working."

"Thanks for being here for me, Reza."

"I wished my sisters appreciated my advice, like you. I've been worried about Mahroo, but now I'm worried about you, too."

"Thanks again... You're so kind," Erica said with charm.

"You can always count on me as your friend," I said.

"I know, Reza. I really like you."

Erica leaned over and kissed me on the cheek. We were in her office, sitting at the table we used to work together. Sometimes, Cameron joined us, too, but usually let us do the real work. Erica's regular enthusiasm about my suggestions, while disregarding Cameron's odd ideas rather bluntly disturbed him slightly. They were often silly and reflected his ineptitude in the field he was supposedly an equal partner with Erica. She said a few times that she put up with him only because his father apparently brought them many sub-contracts and new clients.

I saw more of Darren in the office, while he did his training and working at SDI. He had looked friendly and charming when I had first met him in Erica's house-warming party. I imagined he was smart and easygoing if Erica had married him. I hoped we could be friends, too, the way Erica's friendship felt dear already. Yet, he started looking uptight and reserved at least around me without me knowing why.

A few months later, Erica told me that her relationship with Darren was not improving in spite of their efforts and marriage counselling. She was quite upset and burst into tears abruptly. I tried to console her by a simple touch on her shoulder. But, she just jumped into my arms, put her head on my shoulder, and kept bawling. From that day on, she was overly nice to me, while I still tried not to read too much into her expressions of loneliness and desperation. *Then again, now I believe Erica cast her spell over me that day, forever maybe!*

She also encouraged me to buy a condominium in Vancouver since my new projects with SDI kept me there a lot now. Maybe I did it impulsively to please Erica, although paying a lot to hotels felt senseless when I kept substantial cash in Canada. Real estate was booming in this city, too. I guess I did not know what I was being dragged into, while she looked thrilled about her growing influence over me during a short time and seeing me spread my roots in Vancouver. She volunteered quickly to decorate my suite as a friendly gesture or due to my regular praise of her creativity. Her exquisite taste was clear if you ever visited her house or saw her way of designing computer systems.

I appreciated her offer as well as her attention and affection during this rather long, boring task of decoration. Meanwhile, I loathed the way Darren glared at me in the office and parties with suspicion. Ironically, this happened at the time Zia's jealousy was hurting Mahroo and our family. Watching Zia and Darren suffer from love and jealousy felt odd and annoying to me for different reasons, maybe because I had never gotten too attached to any woman myself to taste this powerful human urge. I hated their attitudes hurting the two women I was adamant to protect and whose stress and fatigue were affecting our moods. In Erica's case, her temper and preoccupation influenced our work as well. Her creativity and span of attention were fading drastically, while Darren's rising jealously baffled me the most. Apparently, he saw my sacred intentions to help them with their marital problems negatively. *Oh, god, this is such a long flight…*

Darren and I kept our distance at the level he was comfortable with. Still, his mood and behaviour around me looked so weird I would have laughed my heart out if someone predicted we would become confidants eventually. Yet, it happened and progressed on a mysteriously wobbly path along with numerous incidents and betrayals sabotaging the chances of our friendship. We have so far defeated the devil that is dying to ruin our friendship

I told Erica a couple of times about Darren's seeming dislike of our working so close all day long in her huge office not too far away from his tiny cubical. I bet he wished we worked in not only separate offices but different cities. I suggested to Erica to at least invite Cameron to sit with us, too, to reduce Darren's rising suspicion. I said we could be a bit more empathetic towards his mood until he built up his confidence. She merely shrugged and insinuated we could not and should not change our work routines just because Darren was such a weak person. Arguing with her about the issue felt unwise, too, as she seemed determined to handle the situation head on. She insisted, in fact, he should come to his senses and grasp her difficult position at work, as well as her emotional needs, and respond to them, or they must go their separate ways. She looked like she had a plan, again the same way my sisters often looked during their own sly contemplations. She also appeared fed up with Darren's general negativity during those trying years. She said life was too short to haggle with him for the rest of her life. *I was learning a lot about women, too, way beyond my other beloveds' teachings so far!*

I had felt particularly vulnerable and lonely during those early months of arriving in Vancouver and working with Erica, mainly since Mahroo had seemed gloomier every time I had returned to Tehran, which had made me feel guiltier and sadder for bringing Zia into her life. The only person I could discuss my sentiments with was Erica, which might have then made her feel closer to me, too. I bet if I had met T.J. only a few months earlier, Erica's charm or spell would have probably not abolished my integrity and well-persevered innocence rather fast.

Well…, that's how we fell in love and cherished each other for a year. Ironically, regardless of Erica's ridiculous reason for leaving me and never trying to reconcile with me, *at least when still alive*, the pain of losing her did not seem to subside. I never grew any grudges against her, either, and, in fact, I simply loved her more every day in her absence. So, my devastation when both she and Mahroo died within a month is fathomable. The agony of never seeing my two beloveds was augmented by the torturous truth that both of them had stopped their passion for me in their own ways because of Darren, just to love him instead, although I surely adored them more than Darren ever did or could. This hurtful belief alone would always burden my spirit, while striving to disallow it taint my friendship with Darren.

I hope my long blabbering about the roots of my affair with Erica has by now convinced you of the legitimacy of my *alleged* sin. Even Darren has agreed a few times that Erica had been the main culprit and forgiven me generously—until reminding us of my sin again and again. Anyway, if you still do not believe in my innocence, I think you are an unromantic person, or maybe even heartless! Most of all, I hope you do not take all these sentimental details as pure self-serving BS!

Gosh, my sore spirit flies all over the map, especially on planes!

This romantic reminiscing reminds me of something interesting T.J. once said when Darren and I were bitching about each other at his house. "You two are the weirdest friends I have ever had and yet the most rational ones!" he said with laughter.

"Why?" I asked with surprise.

"Because any two people who've had so much conflicts and likely betrayals between them would've at least stopped seeing or talking to each other ages ago, if not killing one another already. But you two just seem to feel closer to each other, while whining more every day as well," T.J. said and we burst into laughter. He was right, after all, about the way we three felt about each other, despite all the troubles we have caused one another regularly.

"Well, if we hadn't found you in time we would've surely killed each other by now," I replied sincerely.

"So, I've saved at least one of you!"

Meeting T.J. has actually been a blessing for me, while our friendship has grown fast naturally despite our tense debates. He had just arrived in Vancouver and anxious to adapt to Canadian life. That was three months after Erica and Darren had separated and Darren had just started working for my company in Tehran, while I galloped freely in Vancouver with his estranged wife. It was a critical time in my life, as I felt a bit guilty for my possible role in Erica's view of Darren leading to their separation as well. I did not tell T.J. anything about my affair with Erica for a long time, although I told him plenty about Darren's fine character and marriage breakdown—the topic that began our ongoing analyses of marital issues and relationships' intricacy in modern societies.

T.J. also reminded me of Dervish Ali, my mentor in Tehran, who taught me Sufism those days. With his radical ideologies and grey beard, he complemented Dervish Ali's traditional, rigid beliefs. As my love mayhem with Erica started to take hold of my life, I hoped to draw on T.J.'s experiences to face a variety of dilemmas complicating my life since arriving in Vancouver and meeting Erica. Many revelations were charging and changing my life, which I tried artfully to hide from the rest of the world.

T.J.'s sincerity and zeal to play a fatherly role towards me has also been a novel experience for me, since my relationships with family and friends have felt awkward all my life, especially with my father as much as I loved and respected him. This makes me sad, wondering sometimes whether something is seriously wrong with people or me, while I hope and pray the former is truer!

Anyway, T.J. became my overseas guru, when I was away from Dervish Ali so much those days. Eventually, I felt Darren might also benefit from T.J.'s old-age wisdom. So I told him to check T.J. out when he returned to Canada. My close knowledge of Darren during those early years of our friendship indicated to me that he probably needed T.J. more than I did. The peculiar ways our conflicts about women intermingled often in bizarre ways needed concrete resolutions, while we strived to maintain a close friendship as well. So, we sort of trained T.J. to become a catalyst for mediating and keeping us in check and together. We have been using him, like Dervish Ali, to listen to our personal grief as well as our accusations about each other's betrayals. T.J.'s marital life and random nagging about his wife also felt quite educational and timely to us, especially when I was about to boost my affair with Erica to the next level—just before Erica's tenacity regarding Darren's infamous painting ruined our thriving relationship prematurely, for better or worse, but at least ended our rising arguments. That damn painting has hurt many people, including Mahroo, Erica, and me.

Sadly, within a year or so, T.J. himself started nagging about modern lifestyles screwing women's minds without getting into his private family life. Only recently, he has suddenly grown the loudest voice about women's cruelty, while insisting on being trapped more than Darren and me. At least we had no wife and kids to worry about or bear their non-stop nagging. Thank God! Accordingly, our rivalry to fathom and compare the big messes the three of us are in, in our own unique, bizarre manners is cute and curious all in itself. What a bunch of hopeful romantics we three pensive friends have turned into! This is all simply a very big irony!

Nevertheless, T.J.'s fresh experiences and complaints have most likely raised our paranoia and confusion about marriage, too, but we have found good reasons to humour him. Ironically, our incessant nagging about our empty lives and affairs with women has heightened our friendship, while we have possibly ruined one another's psyche, too. Accordingly, our efforts and hopes to help one another resolve our unique psychological and social conundrums just by using our busted brains feel absurd!

The pilot announced we should fasten our seatbelt for landing. Thank God, I could now *hopefully* stop my gibberish reflections. Thank God, our thoughts are not loud to make people laugh their hearts out... Most of all, I could now look forward to a deep sleep in my own cosy bed very soon... I really needed it after almost forty hours of insomnia!

Chapter Ten
My Snobbish Old Friends

NOW what? Now, what was I supposed to do with the rest of my years besides this reclusive writing? How was I going to bear an evil family, a lot of snobbish old friends, a lousy humanity, and a horrified brain sensing so little prospect?

Once I asked these questions from Reza rather rhetorically to relieve my tension and maybe draw his empathy as my confidant.

"You're asking the wrong person, T.J. In fact, I believe there is no hope for your corny idealism."

"You think I'm too idealistic?" I asked in disbelief.

"Yes, we both are! We should forget about people's mentality ever making sense or improving even slightly."

"But how can we live without hope? It'd be too depressing," I said against my own rising cynicism about hope, while *hoping* to tease him with my nagging that he had been criticizing recently.

"Well, it's hard but wise… For one thing, T.J., why don't you leave Feri if your marriage has gotten so unbearable you want to become a writer with so much efforts merely to live another day? We may get a break from your whining, too!"

"That's a great question... I wonder sometimes myself."

"Still, you must have a reason?" he asked.

"Yes… Living alone is difficult after raising a family. Finding a new mate or peace in another marriage is also hard."

"I don't even trust or like people much these days," Reza said.

"At least you don't hate humanity altogether like me..."

"Actually, I think I'm getting there fast," Reza replied. "Still, I hate myself the most quite often."

"That's odd for a young man who's not been married or had many relationships."

"Well, my dealings with women and in business have been quite informative, not to mention listening to you and Darren."

"Sorry for explaining our marital headaches and ideas."

"Too late... You two have ruined my life, too," he said wittily.

"Yet, I bet you think about a companion regularly."

"Of course... And, ironically, in hopes of finding peace and stability, if not for love as well."

"Isn't it weird we imagine a mate can help us feel and manage life better?" I asked.

"It sure is."

"It also reflects the greatest human irony, in my opinion."

"What irony?" Reza asked.

"Humans' natural inability to find peace either personally or by relating better to one another," I replied.

"Because we're too pompous despite our huge stupidity."

"And we've also grown too many superficial needs. We just can't run a simple life and learn humility."

"So marriage usually gets painful, too, right?" Reza asked

"Yes, keeping even basic peace is hard nowadays, especially since we're impatient, don't know how to relate, and can't keep our expectations low... Darren and I haven't been lying to you too much."

"No, you haven't," Reza replied solemnly. "Still, lust and love make us look for a mate forever, don't they?"

"Yes..., and do you know what the worst is?" I asked.

"No… What's the worst?"

"That we humans would probably never get smart enough to admit these basic facts and invent better ways of living in peace."

"That's bizarre for sure; especially since most of us realize that love and peace in relationships are fantasy nowadays."

"So we're doomed... We must simply jump into a relationship and hope for the best if we're desperate and brave."

"Or try to do what you're apparently doing," I said wittily.

"And what's that?" Reza asked.

"Trying to live and find peace alone."

"Which I've failed so far to do after all these years...," he said. "But choosing solitude in hopes of finding peace also feels silly."

"That's right, although I seem to have no other choice."

We had this depressing chitchat ten weeks ago when Darren was in the coma and we felt our vulnerability more than usual. At this point, we delved into some kind of forced meditation for a long time, but I mostly pondered his profound question about my desperate tenacity to become a writer just to bear Feri another day.

Feeling the futility of my efforts to indulge Feri had been a source of torture all along in the last twenty years, not a new revelation. My patience and knack to humour her realistically without killing my logic and pride altogether had failed terribly. Even worse, my inability to make my evil family appreciate my love for them or at least learn myself to face my gloomy fate alone had been too disheartening. Especially, my daughters' resistance towards my desperate efforts to get close to them or share even their basic thoughts and plans with me brought tears to my eyes regularly. Instead, they had gotten wilder and put more demands on me, while sinking deeper in their juvenile vanities toward foreseeable failures. Their evil mother ensured they ignored their father easily and rudely, all in hopes of maximizing her influence over them. So, I was stuck in a sticky situation with plenty of time to muse over my looming lousy future. On a positive note, though, Feri's tyranny, perfected diligently in Canada, had begun manifesting as a blessing—for forcing me into seclusion with a divine urge to learn more about myself in the new world. These self-cleansing efforts felt even actualizing besides keeping me alive, while my writings also improved and progressed nicely—all thanks to Feri!

This sacred resignation, in fact, affirmed my premonition five years earlier to take on writing, while I wondered if this sudden passion had been an accident or a divine revelation in itself. Most likely the latter, I believed deeper with more delight as time went by. I sensed and embraced the value of my faith in a mysterious hand supporting my fate behind the scene despite my misfortunes along the way, especially a broken family now pushing me deep into spirituality inadvertently! Besides rendering a refuge to bear the growing tensions at home, my new hobby helped me create smart characters to make up for my family's ignorance and lack of character. Facing real people's demands and idiocy was tough! Instead, my truthful, imaginary characters had real needs, genuine causes for suffering, and ways of expressing their anguish clearly at least, rather than merely dreaming and nagging like my family. Those thoughtful characters made me laugh, cry, think, feel, and learn much more and better than my family and friends or any book or teacher had ever done for me. They grew on me so quickly I feared the possibility of respecting and loving them soon more than I was allowed to cherish and respect my family naturally. Then I got attached to this fantasy world as it helped me elude Feri and her crooked reality. It also helped me bear this idiotic world we humans have created for ourselves.

Still, writing itself sometimes felt just like another worthless obsession to devote myself to, similar to the one I had wasted on my cruel family for many years before realizing my stupidity. So, as my passion for writing grew, it also felt confusing like a freaky parallel to my marriage, while handling either of them effectively appeared tough. Ironically, hiding in my study last few years and writing fervently to forget Feri and her malice had turned writing itself into a new 'Feri' with its own torments. Yet, I persevered on both grounds out of necessity. I loved all those characters now, including the ones in my novels! I felt even for the evil characters whose actions were triggered mostly by potent natural urges, such as jealousy or love.

Writing proved tricky as well, both technically and tactically, in a house where arguments and nagging hardly stopped. Then, it caused me even more headaches when some wicked characters kept emerging unexpectedly, but naturally, and forcing me build and follow nasty plots that hurt the protagonist and other kind characters I had created with so much efforts. Still, I could not prevent these devils' intrusions. They had a right to exist, which made me wonder if my family had a right to be evil, too!

My new writing routine and the characters' skirmishes in fact affirmed another big irony: That I was addicted to my marital life and its burdens as much as I was suddenly attached to writing, despite its own headaches. Even more bizarre, I often thought that perhaps I was also addicted to Feri's nagging just for getting my *deserved* punishment for marrying her—just a daily reminder of my life's biggest mistake. That was another crucial discovery that stressed two conflicting facts: First, I could not dismiss my family readily, despite their zeal to ignore me. Second, my two addictions felt incompatible. I could never be a good writer if I stayed married to Feri. Must one of them go, then, and if yes, which one? I could never be a good husband, anyway, judging by 20 years of failure! Reading about reputable artists and writers had also revealed that most of them had had major issues with companionship and bore loneliness routinely. So, perhaps I was on the right track to become a reflective, honest writer simply because my marriage had hurt so much! Anyhow, the next phase of my life had begun shaping when I decided to be a great writer and ready to pay the price of nurturing another stupid addiction in my already burdened life. Finally, I knew what to do with the rest of my life! And if I must divorce Feri to do so, so be it!

This conclusion was still another perplexing revelation, since the option of leaving Feri had never occurred to me before my addiction to writing—like a fanatic catholic perhaps! Maybe my traditional sense of integrity or laziness had been the reason. Yet, even if I could ignore the sanctity of our twenty-year marriage, my three wacky daughters had always felt like good reasons to stay near my family in Vancouver at least, hopefully in the same house. Otherwise, I would have returned to Tehran long ago as my family had suggested to me so casually a few times. Now, however, things felt differently and divorce did not feel a taboo!

Ironically, my writing passion had opened yet another freaking can of worms about my chance of finding a more suitable partner eventually, even if it meant quitting my writing addiction to focus on her—and if so, was that a wise choice? Actually, this idea had manifested like an awakening—a bizarre revelation—all in itself along with a bunch of pertinent questions! Did this possibility exist for me at my age, especially in Canada—a nation with its own mixed-up culture in terms of relationships? Forget about finding a soul mate, I told myself. But maybe I could at least find my soul and a casual mate, if I looked for them separately. Or, alternatively, I could focus on saving my self and soul by learning to live alone without a mate's hassles. Anyhow, I was dogged to resolve my two new dilemmas now about my marriage and 'who I was' together. They seemed to be highly related. At least I had to establish, *who I was or could ever be in this marriage, or with a different mate.* Later, in fact, these new thoughts, especially the necessity of a divorce, felt like two other divine inspirations on top of the writing urge itself. None of these revelations could have happened just by a fluke, I reckoned with awe, but most likely through some kind of supernatural intervention that also satiated my faith. *Wow…! Was I entering a new realm of existence now?*

Meanwhile, my sudden passion for writing, after being such a serious banker for so long, had baffled my family and friends. My decision to stop making more money in order to waste my time putting the strings of words together had felt like the most outlandish rebellion against social norms to them, while I had felt finally blessed with a blissful mental maturity. What had all my previous struggles gotten me so far? Not even a family!

My attitude seemed particularly silly to people—even myself sometimes—after spending two years with great efforts to get the official designation for practising accounting and taxation services in Canada. I had even framed the large, impressive certificate and hung it in my study a few months just to show off my incredible achievement! Here, see it for yourselves, assholes: I am a CGA—a Certified General Account. Yet, I never grew the motivation to use my knowledge or the damn degree! I put the certificate away, too, after enough people glared at it and me with pity and envy. Ironically, taking it down proved an even more crucial point to those morons, I imagined, though it had not been my intention! I was merely sick of looking at it when I was writing my novels and even the characters laughed at me for wasting my money, time, and mental energy to obtain such a useless piece of paper.

To be fair, I must acknowledge my concerned friends did not merely ridicule me. They also tried a few times to put some sense into my silly head in hopes of stopping my rising senility. They pushed me to open an office and offer my financial services to the public. They promised that managing their investment and tax matters alone would bring me a lot of money. Thus, I must now waste the next few pages to explain why I felt less interested in them and their patronage every day even if I ever regained any incentive to work or gather more wealth.

On the one hand, sometimes I wondered if they envied me for finally convincing myself that more money could not make me happier or better. Their guts and conceit, pretending to be worried about me while snubbing me, upset me immensely as well.

On the other hand, I realized their dilemma about me. They now had major difficulty fitting me and my family within their aristocratic mentality and lifestyle if I kept insisting to be such an idiot with inadequate appreciation for wealth, let alone my rising distaste for capitalism in itself. Even amongst themselves, the level of respect they extended to one another was at the exact proportion to their wealth and their thirst for more. Especially, the latter, greed, was a vital attribute that its absence barred a person promptly! At least they were not prejudice towards me due to any discriminatory criterion they would not apply to themselves as diligently, anyway. In a weird way, that was a big consolation for me. Of course, some pretended to be wealthier and greedier than they were by extravagance and bragging in hopes of attaining a higher status, all in vain, of course. The rivalry amongst them, in line with their showy attitude and conceit, was stiff and funny. Their scrupulous methods of establishing a rather accurate view of other people's real worth—in strict correlation to their wealth, of course—was also comical and depressing. Most of those filthy affluent old friends of mine had invested heavily in Vancouver's real estate and caused artificial inflation in housing market. They still kept their lucrative businesses in Iran, too, of course.

In return, my friends' dilemma about handling me had turned into a big headache for Feri and a laughing matter for me. How could they keep humouring her if I refused to do something about my failing faculty, and more crucially, how could they explain my conceit and character deficiency amongst them, especially if my wealth was not growing fast enough for their liking, either? They were willing to help me catch up to an acceptable standing according to their friendship criterion, but first I had to show my appreciation of their values, generosity, and patience with me. Meanwhile, with my refusal to adapt, my whole family's status in that setting had declined fast, while Feri's flattery was going to waste more every day. This outrageous outcome of my attitude was infuriating Feri the most and raising her hostility towards me; although she was happy about my CGA degree off the wall now!

To tell the truth and be fair to my friends again, I must confess that they had snubbed us from the beginning, anyway. At least I was used to it, although its degree had heightened noticeably in Vancouver, maybe due to their novel sense of importance in Canada, their wealth growth, or my declining status. Probably a mix of them. Thank God, their snobbery towards us had not been solely for my new attitude, I consoled myself. I also believed and mentioned to Feri a few times in vain that a main source of their snobbery towards us related to the fact that our modest house was in North, instead of West, Vancouver, although ours had a great view of the city as well. They had built their castles on lavish lots with wide views of the city and ocean with too many bedrooms and bathrooms for a family of four or five. When they had kindly accepted our invitation and honoured us in our humble house with their pompous presence, they had been restless all evening, as though this particular association might inflict them with a fatal plague or a kind of irreversible disrepute. They simply could not hide their sacrifice for being at our *North Vancouver* house for a few hours, mostly out of pity for Feri. The amount of favours they were rendering us by their scarce visits, after Feri's repeated invitations, appeared insurmountable and irredeemable in their minds, even if I ever cared to grasp the enormity of their sacrifice the way a petite bourgeoisie, like me, should. How could they rectify the situation? Unless... Unless, by some miracle, I became at least as greedy, if not wealthy, as they were, which would be merely a comical dream in all our minds!

Anyway, they were always anxious to get their visit done and over with, and escape our *North Vancouver* house, right after overindulging themselves with lots of liquor and tasty food. They raced among themselves for leaving the fastest without appearing too rude about Feri's hospitality at least. That was just another comical game to witness, pity, and humour all in itself: The later they arrived and sooner they left, the more prestige they allegedly hoped to preserve! *Supposedly!* Their rivalry to do both without appearing too rude or abnormal was quite challenging and stiff! At the same time, they paraded their presence at our house, to us and each other, as a clear proof of their generosity and humility! Their excuses for late arrival and early departure killed me the most, as I laughed, often in front of them, about their stupidity to imagine any idiot, besides Feri maybe, bought their silly excuses, let alone a cynical wiseass like me. The upshot of the first early departure on other guests was also immediate and deep. They got tense about being outdone and anxious to leave, too. So, parties in our house usually ended much sooner than it did in my friends' houses. Explaining the absurdity of the atmosphere, contents and interactions in those parties needs a few books in itself, though Feri cherished every minute of them with no sense of pride, while refuting my claims about our friends' low regard for us. Her total loyalty to them was more annoying than my friends' conceit and betrayal. Two more books must explain her mannerism around that phony group. Her defence of their tyranny both in Iran and Canada tormented me to my bones. Many times she yelled at me merely for my apathy towards people she adored vehemently.

"You're jealous they found ways to get this rich. All you could do was to run away and hide in Canada," Feri said a few times.

"All that hypocrisy and corruption wasn't something to envy. I couldn't work in that environment in Iran anymore," I replied.

"Now see what has become of you," she said with contempt.

"What has become of me *now*, explain?"

"I don't know… Just sitting in a room and writing nonsense."

"Didn't we come to Canada to give our kids a chance for a better future? Don't we have enough money already if we just stop competing with a bunch of pretentious lowlifes?"

"Now you call them 'lowlifes' and you are Mr. Perfect? Maybe I should tell them what you call them?"

"I know you'll tell them, anyway, but I don't give a damn… Go tell the whole world how I think about all of you. I'll write about them, anyway..., buying a good part of Vancouver and all."

"I'll tell them that, too. But I still say you had no guts to stick it out a bit longer. We could've come here a few years later, too. They're here now, too, aren't they? Their kids will have thousand times more money than our kids and I would ever have."

"Nobody can get this rich without being in cahoots with dirty officials. And I can't respect or flatter them the way they expect."

"None of these things is a crime… You're only jealous."

"No, it's only amazing you don't see them as traitors who've sold their integrity for money. Besides, you guys were the ones pushing me so much to move to Canada."

"We didn't. You forced us to come here."

"You are just the biggest liar God has created. He has surely intended to test how much malice He could inject in one person, and now He's either astonished about creating you or proud how closely you resemble the devil. I'm certain He's now laughing about His games and creations driving me nuts."

"You're the liar! God made you the most selfish asshole."

"What did I lie to you about?"

"You promised me so many things before we got married."

"I promised you nothing, but you guys don't even appreciate the comfortable life you're now enjoying, anyway."

"You call this a life? It is hell living with you and it is hell not living like all the other people in the main circle," she shrieked.

"The main circle? What the heck that means?" I yelled back.

The haunting images of some other friends who worked like slaves in Vancouver and still could not afford even a basic life marched before my eyes. They had high educations and positions during the Shah's regime and now drove cabs or delivered pizza to feed their families. Whenever they visited us, their praise of our house and envy—how luxurious and huge it looked to them—depressed and confused me, as I recalled our aristocrat friends' low opinion of the same house. These new immigrants suffered all kinds of financial and emotional problems regularly since they had no wealth to bring with them.

Of course, we socialized much less with the labouring friends due to Feri's zeal to expand her allegiance with the aristocrats as much as possible, while also looking down rather openly on those who had seemingly failed to prove themselves to her liking. She hid her random association with this lower class from her favourite category as well. Still, both groups loved and respected Feri ten times more than they cared for me, despite my efforts to respect and help the labouring friends fifty times more than Feri did. Even more ironic, this group of friends were as much pain in the ass as the aristocrats. Their drive for snobbery, rivalry, greed, and hypocrisy often exceeded those of the billionaires', which perfectly proved human nature's 'equal opportunity' privilege for devilry and idiocy! A big contrast, however, was that this lower class always arrived quite early to our parties and left as late as they could—only when Feri's quiet and yawning alarmed them. I guess they tried to prove, show off, or establish their affinity with us. Still, as much as this group sucked up to Feri, especially, she just preferred and enjoyed sucking up to the other group herself.

Nonetheless, caught in the middle of these ridiculous humans with their confusing social values and worries, facing Feri's sad eyes and selfish inquisition now and then was most annoying: Why was not I as rich as my billionaire friends were? Her belief and question felt just too ridiculous to justify even a response.

"All I can say is that you must go look at other people's lives and thank God for the chance we've got for living here," I said. "You've just gone nuts competing with those crazy bitches."

"You'd never understand… Just leave me alone," Feri cried.

"Just look around and see how normal people live and suffer."

"But I always had more aspirations. I could've married much richer guys if you hadn't fooled me with so many promises."

How vastly her claim contradicted the facts crushed my brain. I wished I were rude, like normal people, to throw the truth right at her face, perhaps even in front of our kids or friends: *I married you mostly to save Rose, and also out of pity, as I swear nobody else would've indulged such an evil, ugly girl.* Ironically, I could swear she knew all these facts perfectly, yet insisted on denying them, even to her own psyche. Instead, I said, "I promised you nothing! You're just the biggest liar born and even you know it."

"As usual, you are talking nonsense. Is that the kind of bullshit you also write in your books?" Feri asked.

"I write about social issues and my experiences. That's all," I replied timidly, while leaving the room to put an end to this silly conversation with no perceivable benefit to anybody.

"Are you writing about me, too?" she asked with rage.

"About you? Who gave you such an absurd idea? You think I have nothing more sensible to write about?" I lied with a giggle.

Her plausible intuition about being the root of my interest in writing, mostly for badmouthing her, felt amusing. Yet, she surely could not imagine how whining and writing about her evil and sadistic nagging have been fun and liberating as well.

"Anyway, don't lie about me in your book, which nobody is gonna read, anyway."

"How do you know nobody is gonna read it?" I asked with an odd curiosity more than being insulted.

"Because, it's all bullshit... I'm sure you're writing all these nonsense only to badmouth me, I know you are."

"Rest assured, I have much better things to do or write about."

"So, why? Why do you waste so much time writing instead of thinking about your family?" she yelled. I just left the room without answering her, because it would have been a futile effort.

Another big irony was that Feri got keener to suck up to our aristocrat friends the more my comments about them upset her. Then I suffered even more when I witnessed how callously they humoured her or talked down to her regardless of her dire zeal to flatter them and her embarrassing efforts to act and talk like them. Despite our fights and open animosity, I still abhorred the notion of anybody, especially such illiterate women, treating my wife with lesser dignity than they extended to their own kinds. Still, she loved them more, the more I loathed those sick women. *The amount of life ironies is just endless and amazing!*

At the same time, I felt those rich women's concern about the slightest chance of their devoted husbands catching my weird disease and curbing their obsession for making more money, too. Maybe those poor men could try the option of enjoying the rest of their lives in a meaningful manner or maybe even finding new spouses or mistresses instead of sucking up to their wives forever. Once when I had been drunk or trying to be funny, the gang had heard me saying that we had reached that special stage of our lives where we needed new wives since our spouses seemed too impatient with us. Maybe we had to find younger girls with more patience and appreciation of who we were and the money we could spend on them. *Me and my big mouth, as usual!* The next day, when sober, I *rather* regretted my blunder for making silly jokes that agitated those obnoxious women in a major way. *My stupid sense of humour!* Another big excuse for Feri to despise and scold me, above usual, for a few weeks.

It was funny how fast people took my humorous comments to heart seriously with spite and loud objections, but ignored my vital complaints so casually. Then again, I thought my jokes must have reflected enough reality to make so many people edgy. Any truthful point is bound to make people nervous no matter how hard you try to make it sound innocent or funny. People prefer to avoid truths and touchy stuff, nowadays, as if hiding diligently from life's realities or their despicable secrets. So, what was my boastful friends' lives all about now? How much longer were they going to only discuss the hassles of exploiting the financial chaos in Iran, their projects' difficulties, and their new ingenious plans to accumulate more wealth? The way they mixed their bragging and nagging drove me nuts, I tell you!

I asked them why they bothered with all those humiliating hassles, then. 'Why do you spend half of your lives travelling back and forth to Iran in order to make more money when even your great-great-grandchildren could bask happily in your present wealth without doing a single day of work?' They merely stared at me with pity, like witnessing a lunatic with no clue about the meaning of his words or the game they have been playing so faithfully. No wonder my lifelong friends just kept getting more impatient with me than they had been even two or three years earlier. I recalled my own impatience and pity for them all along at high school and university. Those times, they liked me only for our youthful games, while I enjoyed my mischief and bullying; but now they had no use for me! Well, that is life...! Of course, they apparently also assumed they had earned a special right to be haughty, simply due to their success in exploiting the situation in Iran and its poor people who suffered under such awful economic condition. How could I connect with people so reluctant to slow down their tyranny or at least stop bragging about their genius to push their endless atrocities? They have surely contributed to the corruption in Iran to become multi-billionaires and come here to snob the rest of us. In the end, I just could not bear them anymore even if they liked me again by a miracle. Instead, I only sought salvation—maybe by even a bigger miracle—perhaps by sewing the strings of words to appease my own absurd dreams.

After reading the last few pages, most likely many people have by now taken side with my snotty friends and believe I am a fool thinking and talking so childishly. However, my job as an honest writer is only to reflect my feelings regardless of people's impression of my sanity or the validity of my observations. I'm merely striving to be a sensible, open-minded writer! That's all!

Fortunately, and most ironical, my efforts to learn not to care about what people think about me, as long as I have a plausible faith in myself, seems to be working! I have also admitted now that—like any addiction, including a nagging pressure to give up writing—my obsession would remain painful with no guarantee about my efforts ever making me a renowned writer eventually, *for the right reasons only*, not to mention the stress of justifying it to myself and others every day.

By now, Reza and I had been meditating for an hour during his last trip to Vancouver when Darren was still in a coma, Mahroo and Erica had died recently, and we felt the vanity of existence deeper. These tragedies stirring a murky mood had also helped me affirm a few things in my edgy head that day. Still, our long, private reflections had probably felt depressing to Reza as well.

At last Reza broke the sacred silence with a giggle. "The more I think, T.J., the more I believe you and Darren have killed the last ounce of faith I had in humanity and relationships."

"It took you an hour to realize this?" I asked with a chuckle.

"No, but my cynicism now also makes me wonder who I am."

"Now that's really bizarre," I said with surprise.

"Why…?" he asked, looking bewildered and forlorn.

"Because I've been feeling the same way for years, but more so in recent months, especially during the last hour," I replied.

"You have..., ha? I guess this modern world and relationships destroy both our identities and spirits, so we wonder who we are."

"Especially nowadays, with Darren in a coma and my family problems growing, the question, 'Who am I?' rolls at least in our subconscious more often," I replied.

"Then, I doubt the point of working and travelling so much to grow my business when I can't find good reasons even for living," Reza said with a sigh. "Even pleasure feels hollow to me now."

"Yeah, we just live in delusion among arrogant, phony people and repeat the same hollow routines like robots," I said giddily for another chance to reiterate my own life's vanity.

"You've become a philosopher, too, T.J., besides a writer."

"Like yourself, yet these philosophies can't help us, either!"

"True… I'm not surprised if Dervish Ali has turned me and maybe also Darren into such cynical, testy philosophers," he said.

"So, what's really the point of travelling so much between Tehran and Vancouver, Reza?" I asked for teasing him, as I did with my aristocrat friends in Vancouver for driving them nuts.

"Didn't I just whine about the same thing?" he asked testily, which was just contrary to my old friends' reaction. It showed his objectivity, philosophical mind, and pains.

"Except for the pleasure of seeing Darren and me more often, of course," I said teasingly. "And learning more marital lessons."

"Of course," Reza said. "Dervish Ali discussed relationships as well when Darren and I visited him, all in vain it feels now."

"Let's hope Darren can soon join us in these childish chitchats again. I miss him," I replied solemnly.

"Me too. Our meetings aren't fun without him..., although he may start new headaches for us right away," he said giddily.

"Still you hope he recovers, right?" I asked jokingly in return.

"I guess so! No, definitely, I'm just kidding... I'm drunk. But do you think he'll come out of the coma?"

"Let's pray and stay positive, but it seems unlikely," I replied.

After Reza left that historic night of reflection and philosophy, along with our prayers for Darren's recovery, I mulled over our conversations and wondered if we three pensive, lonely friends had helped or hurt one another with our stories and philosophies, especially since they had a long life ahead of them! The way we had influenced each other's outlook in spite of our own peculiar lives and minds felt odd sometimes. We had become too cynical too, as if reflection raised scepticism, or vice versa! The youths seemed to be hurting as much as I was, in spite of their freedom, untainted minds, so much partying and pleasures, and no family obligations. Who was happy then, I wondered? Personally, I only wished to regain my spirit to bear my family and loneliness and maybe write a book or two about life, too. That seemed to be the best I could hope for, if anything at all.

Sometimes, I wondered whether my failures in both marriage and life were indeed my own faults, due to not only my mistakes, but mostly my crude personality. The answer to 'Who I was?' was right there in front of me if I looked into the mirror longer, stopped nurturing self-pity, and assessed my needs critically—including my addictions to writing and Feri. Maybe Feri was in fact innocent and her views of life were closer to reality and more plausible than my idealistic views about the world? Maybe I was too eccentric or a lunatic, after all, as Feri claimed and asked me to admit, too, so that we could live happily ever after, while she controlled my decisions and destiny? Her tenacity and frustration to make me at least accept and act on this simple demand of hers had made her lose faith in me and our marriage altogether!

Reza's profound comment about my sense of obligation to write to elude the pains of living with Feri, instead of leaving her, resonated in my head over and over. I felt he had a good point worth my deeper thoughts perhaps, yet I still could not imagine living without my family, including that tyrant Feri, so I just had to keep on writing. *This vicious cycle seemed irresolvable!*

Reza's other remark about my writing obsession turning me also into a grouchy philosopher sounded flattering and truthful by the way I had been analysing facts in hopes of resetting my life's path properly. For instance, one reason for my painful hesitation to leave Feri had been my conclusion about humans' inherent entrapment in their beings per se, thus their failure to make valid decisions. Especially, we have now reached a global stalemate in terms of humans' disability to relate to one another practically in any form and capacity—personally, socially, and universally.

Another big irony was that I wanted to learn and write about love and life, while nobody, not even Shakespeare or Rumi, had been quite successful to grasp and resolve these primary human dilemmas despite their zeal to do just that. Yet, our search and obsession to answer, 'Who am I?'—with or without love—goes on, actively by some curious souls and subtly by others, because we all need a remedy for our loneliness and aching hearts.

Surely, these observations also showed that I had let self-pity taint my self-esteem and self-image. My sole consolation was that Feri was also going nuts due to my resistance to accept her ruling about my lunacy. Instead, I kept telling her myself that, in fact, she was an absolute loony herself! *Naturally, the answer to 'Who I was,' 'Who Feri was,' or 'Who was crazier' remained excruciatingly unsettled all along in this daunting circumstance overwhelming two deeply arrogant, deranged partners!*

Anyway, I decided to stay focused and persevere to sort out my dilemmas, mostly about my family versus writing addictions. Writing provided my only hope for being, in line with a chance for salvation, as long as I preferred to stick around Feri and my snotty daughters. That was my only *hope* to bear the humiliation of living with people who abhorred me with such oddly spiteful tenacity of their own. Then again, suicide sometimes felt like a more honourable option than living with no pride day after day. Naturally, I also felt obliged to assert my existence merely out of vendetta for Feri and my aristocrat friends who loathed my guts for writing about them rather than reconsidering my sad being or at least making more money. Carrying the burden of living for idiotic goals is just too humiliating! Such is life!

PART II

Two Bitter Enemies

Chapter Eleven
A Mesmeric Moment

The subtle rattle in the kitchen awakened me with a surge of serenity as I pictured Mahtab out there making breakfast for us. We still slept separately in our bedrooms. *We chicken, silly lovers!* Still, her presence around me was a blessing not only to avoid mornings' deadly silence, but also for having a jobless partner to make leisurely plans for an entirely idle day. She had brought me soulful joy, the kind I had missed since my early years with Erica. The prospect of having a soul mate again was also riveting. This lovely idea incited my dozy brain to let me go kiss her as soon as possible. And that was exactly what I did finally after ten minutes —a tremendous record for a bum like me these days.

"Did you sleep well, Darren?" she asked after we exchanged two genuine grins and a small kiss.

"I did, but I felt a bit lonely," I replied teasingly.

"Only a little?" Mahtab asked with a smile. "It is better for our souls, though... Maybe..."

"In that case, I have the healthiest soul in the country now."

Mahtab only smiled while pouring coffee for us.

"Spring is coming soon," she said.

I realized the poignancy of her remark—the approach of the Iranian New Year on the first day of spring. However, I wondered if this information had any specific purpose for my benefit.

"Do you like to be with your family for Norooz festivities?" I asked tenderly, wondering how she felt being stuck here with me, instead of enjoying her large family who celebrated Norooz with joy and plenty of social gatherings during the first two weeks of spring. She would probably feel homesick away from his family, country, and the New Year's traditional commotion.

"No festivities this year in my family because of Mahroo."

"Oh, I forgot. She'll be missed even more during such times."

"So, I do and don't want to be there, but I can't, anyway…"

"Do you like to go for a long ride to Horse Shoe Bay?"

"Yes, it'd be nice to spend the whole day together somewhere in nature," she replied excitedly.

"It seems like a sunny, gorgeous day. Some trees already look like getting ready to blossom."

"Yes, nature looks wonderful here even in winter."

"You haven't seen much of our city yet, though, after all this time you've been here, ha?" I asked.

"Now you have lots of time to show me everything."

For every true love, I presume, a divine sensation and natural connection binds the lovers together in a mesmeric moment. Our plans prior to that moment dissolve into abyss and future appears nonexistent or irrelevant. The tortuous games lovers had played all along to impress each other are thrown out the window and instead they embrace the looming torture of passion, selflessness, and devotion. Lovers often feel these sensations simultaneously, as if a match was struck in front of their eyes to ignite their hearts. Or as though they swiftly realized their match had been made in heavens, as the old saying goes.

This was exactly what I believed happened between Mahtab and me in that fateful moment at breakfast. We had exchanged some affection in Barcelona and more in recent weeks after my release from the hospital. But this was the first time this celestial sensation besieged us entirely without either of us uttering a single word. I felt it from a matching flicker in her eyes and a twinge in my heart, but also from my belief that Mahtab had similarly seen the same subtle flicker in my eyes and had felt a similar aching sweetness in her own heart. We both seemed to have sensed each other's joint realization—that the final clue about our inescapable bond had just manifested. This was the moment we both had felt committed to the imminent unbearable condition of our passion whether we liked it or not. We faced and felt our own and each other's sad vulnerability. At that moment, we accepted to pay any price for the aftermath of this particular love affair with all kinds of its obvious obstacles. Our last twelve days of contemplation had not offered such a definite belief, maybe even in anticipation of this blessed revelation! This mesmeric sentiment was so unlike the love I had felt for Erica. Its unique dimension was infinitely obscure, but contained a certain mystical potency I could not have imagined possible for any infatuation. Probably Mahtab had not experienced this blissful marvel before today, either, if my sense of her sweet confusion in that moment was also real. I thought I should try soon to compare this romantic revelation with the love I had borne for Erica for so many years and assumed it had been true as well. What is this then, and what was that? Maybe only different but love nonetheless! Was it only Mahtab's novelty making this moment manifest so spectacular, out of this world's realms? Was it an upshot of my love deprivation, loneliness, and cynicism for many years maybe? Or just another weird symptom of my long coma? Had it been merely the effect of our idiotic, diligent efforts all along to deprive ourselves of sensual desires we had imagined might ruin the spirit of our infatuation? *Well... whatever it was, it'd felt real and sensational.*

Yet, Mahtab and I did not say or do anything about this weird love attack other than holding hands and staring into each other's eyes right there in the middle of breakfast, most likely wondering if the other person had felt exactly the same sensation at the same intensity. Tears had gathered in her eyes and I felt like crying as well. At last, we managed to finish our breakfast calmly without falling apart under the pressure of our speedy heartbeats and short breaths. Most amazingly, *of course,* even that magical experience rousing such explicit love manifestation had not induced the need to rush and rip each other's clothes to make love on the breakfast table. In spite of my wit trying to ruin the mood, it was merely a mesmeric moment! And it was only a private sentiment for now, although discussing the experience with Mahtab at an appropriate time felt inevitable. At last, we retreated to our rooms serenely in solemn bewilderment, dressed up alone quickly, and left the suite hand in hand—like a wise, bemused couple!

In the elevator, Mahtab passed on the car keys to me and asked if I could drive. Maybe she feared ruining her romantic mood or meant to test my driving aptitude after the long coma. Grabbing the keys, I mulled over my friendship with Reza—living in his luxurious apartment, having an affair with his lovely sister, and now driving his fancy Jaguar, too. All behind his back!

I wondered if my own rusty car would start after sitting idle nearly four months, but there was no point checking it while I was stuck in Reza's suite and had no place to park it around this building. I missed it, while planning to at least ensure it was still there, in my building's garage. *It wouldn't hurt to say hi to it!*

After crossing the Lions Gate Bridge, I took the Marine Drive route to Horse Shoe Bay instead of racing through the highway. My goal was to give Mahtab a good tour of the country-ish part of the city, while the slow ride would be a good mood-sustaining means after this morning's revelation. The scenery surrounding the winding road would be blissful to relax and keep basking in the aftermath of the sacred sensation befallen upon us magically. Our long pensive silence was surely a symptom of our jubilant, divinely besieged souls. In fact, a personal reflection felt vital to absorb the meaning of that magical moment bestowed upon us by higher powers, although we still had to be the ones in charge of quieting our minds to gauge the core and implications of our volcanic emotions as well. First, we had to internalize our grasp of the incident before celebrating its splendour alone or together. Besides, no word or gesture could add any value to the naturally imposed solemn mood still lingering after that peculiar spark so early in the morning. Most amazingly again, I felt Mahtab was entertaining the exact sentiments and need for reflection herself. This tender belief in itself goaded my resolve to stay quiet. Now, finally, my mysterious silence around Mahtab felt romantic and tactful, instead of irritable, as she also seemed to prefer it that way herself this time. We were literally tongue-tied blissfully.

Most paradoxical, for me at least, was my inability to stop doubting our entitlement to feel so blessed right now or even try to digest or discuss the ecstasy of that enigmatic experience. Was this joy justified even in our inebriated minds, let alone by hurt, humiliated people who would kill us swiftly upon discovering the state of affairs between us? So, we both kept our thoughts private rather sacredly with joy and an urge to avoid ruining the mood or questioning its rationality for a few hours at least. My old idiotic dream about the 200th forbidden love when I had started my affair with Elizabeth at Jeff's expense singed my brain momentarily, though, and I shuddered from guilt. Immediately, I pushed my curious subconscious and nosy conscience to their separate, quiet corners in my heaving head. *Let us be, for a few hours at least...*

I drove on the snaky road for thirty minutes before we arrived at the Whytecliff Park right past the last mountain bend. I parked the car with pride for my driving diligence after months of no practice and an odd fear of steering a car again. We strolled hand in hand toward the edge of the cliff where the large round gazebo stood. Only a few people walked around the vast grass area away from us. Only the sporadic shrieks of seagulls and the distant sound of surfs crashing the mountain base at the shore invaded the quiet in the park. It felt mysteriously secluded and romantic with tall pine trees rising high to point out the blue sky and spread smooth shadows on the lustrous green grass. It seemed people had stayed away deliberately that day just to let Mahtab and I have the place to ourselves—to celebrate our ultimate discovery and reward in total privacy—to scream from joy, if we desired or dared. Only a dozen kids were also playing in the playground with their mothers or nannies watching their commotion from a distance.

As we stepped up into the gazebo, Mahtab stood awe-stricken by the view of the Howe Sound stretched majestically in front of her eyes for the first time. The cobalt waters of the Pacific Ocean surrounded the stretch of mountain formation in the horizon. A ferry was breaking the shallow ripples towards the Bowen Island where some colourful dwellings were visible from the distance. I knew that facing such scenery for the first time would take any visitor's breath away. That was precisely why I had brought her there. Yet, she was simply swept away beyond my expectation, with tears gathering in her pretty eyes again. Five sailing boats were also slacking on the calm surface of the Pacific Ocean. At last, we sat on the bench overlooking the scenery and held hands again. Mahtab leaned towards me and placed her head on my shoulder. I pulled my hand out of hers gently to caress her hair before placing it over her shoulder and embracing her tightly. We kissed fervently as our short breaths and pounding hearts told the intensity of our joy surging our volatile sentiments.

"Darren, did you feel something special this morning, too?" Mahtab murmured.

"Yes, and I felt it happened to both of us simultaneously," I replied tenderly.

"What was it?"

"Well… Isn't our silence all along a sign of our inability to explain it?" I asked.

"You're right…"

"But now I feel even more confused about our situation and future," I said with gloom.

"Me too... I feel both happy and nostalgic."

Silence lingered for a couple of minutes as we only stared into the horizon in a trance.

"Had you felt this way before, maybe with Erica or Mahroo?" she asked softly.

"No, I don't think so. You?"

"Unfortunately, Bijan was the closest I got to a man, but I do not think I was ever in love with him properly."

"But still married him?"

"I liked his intelligence and compassion, which were ruined later when he began serving his father and similar people."

"Something I can't still decide after all these years," I said.

"What is that?"

"Is life easier and wiser with or without love?" I asked.

"Most likely without love, I'd say."

"So why are we making it difficult for ourselves and letting the situation get out of hand?"

"Because not everybody can bear a simple life. Not me…"

"Maybe we should force ourselves a bit more," I said.

"What're we supposed to do, then? Simply ignore our feelings again and again?" Mahtab asked.

"Maybe we should... Especially in our risky and complicated situation," I replied with angst.

"Darren, I'll get my divorce somehow, I promise."

"And until then?"

"It is up to you… Can you take me as a single woman with no other commitment or desire, but to love you?" she asked, staring into my eyes with a soothing charm.

"Can we do that realistically?" I asked with confusion and a sense of helplessness.

"I told you already… How about you? Can you do it for me?"

"Honestly, I don't know how, although I must do something about my present feelings for you."

"Then tell me…," she said.

"I want to tell you, but it's difficult," I said with guilt for both options of saying or eluding what she had been expecting to hear from me for so long patiently and kindly.

"It is?" she asked. "After everything we've been through?"

"Yes, especially since I know your culture and men's extreme pride and possessiveness," I replied. "I'm actually amazed how relaxed you seem to be about this matter!"

"I understand, but I guess Mahroo and I lost our cultural sense after our mother kept us abroad most of our lives."

"Still, you've been somewhat conflicted, too, and that's why we've been extra-cautious so far," I said.

"So, it's still hard for you to share your feelings with me?"

"Yes, I feel guilty, especially since I told Bijan in his face that I owed him my life… You were present when I said it!"

"I know all this too, but things change... None of us could've foreseen this situation... So, maybe it's time to move on."

"I don't dare. How can we let love alone change things so fast and drastically?" I asked sluggishly, admiring her courage.

"Dare! Just tell me," she demanded this time. She stared right into my eyes so passionately I felt speechless before a swift blow of fatalistic bravery overwhelmed me.

"Okay, Mahy... I'll love and cherish you," I said with awe for my likely foolishness, while also thinking I could not remain a conscientious or coward lover forever if I wanted to keep her.

"Oh, Darren, thanks. I love you too," she said with a chuckle.

"The way I said it sounded funny, ha?" I asked timidly.

"No, calling me Mahy was! Mahy means fish in Persian."

"Oh, I'm sorry, I didn't know," I replied with a grin.

"I realize how hard it must've been for you to finally express love to someone again," Mahtab said.

"I'm surprised too. Did you hypnotize me with your charm?"

"What if I did?" she asked giddily.

"I'm glad, anyway... I feel relieved in a way at last, like I'd been Erica's prisoner for a century."

"Then I'm glad for rescuing you," she said with a giggle.

"Maybe it's the effect of what happened to us this morning."

"Maybe... Maybe god got tired of waiting for you to decide!"

"Don't blame god! I know you did it and that's fine, although I still feel trapped by other sentiments."

"You feel trapped already?" Mahtab asked teasingly.

"Well, love is confusing enough already even without the complications in our case."

"So, are we going to move on or not?" she asked dolefully.

"I guess it's time, because I love you," I said and kissed her.

"I'm so glad to hear you talk openly at last, Darren."

"Sorry for keeping you in limbo. Thanks for being patient."

"Okay, I forgive you if you say it again."

"Okay, I tell you again and again, I love you … I love you… I love you…," I said before bursting into loud laughter.

"Is loving me funny, too?" Mahtab asked with a grin.

"Yes, the way I said it this time, like a juvenile."

"No, it was romantic... Although love usually sounds funny, especially in our case, right?"

"Yes... We sound like clowns since we can already imagine the chaos we're starting," I said fretfully. "Still I'm glad I got it out of my chest today."

"Didn't you even say it to Mahroo?"

"No, we never reached that point, but I think she knew at the end that I loved her in a special way."

"So you tortured my darling sister, too, ha?" she asked.

"Not intentionally. She was adamant to drag it out of me, too, like you. But only you succeeded, I hope for a good reason."

"It's been for a divine reason and now we must prove it."

"In fact, the way I'd been so serious about avoiding this word now feels strange," I said.

"Was it because you'd said it to Erica a million times?"

"Possibly... That corny word 'love' had felt like a symbol of betrayal more than anything else for so long."

"I hope you won't start using it all over the town on women now that you feel silly for avoiding it four years?"

"Well, I hope it won't be necessary," I said and we laughed.

"I bet I've acted silly today myself!" she said giddily.

"For making me so brave after hypnotizing me this morning?"

"Yes, I had to do it, since you'd been so careful."

"But our deep affection has felt real for a long time already, anyway, hasn't it?" I asked.

"Yes, I think so too. And I'm glad you've been so stingy all along for using the word love even for Mahroo."

Mahtab and I embraced and kissed for about ten minutes since nobody was around to witness our juvenile display of affection, like two teenagers showing off their devotion during their first romance. We hugged tighter and closer to a point where finally Mahtab was sitting in my lap and our legs, hands, and the rest of our body parts were intertwined like two cobras getting ready for mating. Smartly, however, we contained our passion to a bearable level and retreated to our partially civilized positions. We only sat tightly next to each other, held hands, and kissed sporadically. We alternated gazing at the Howe Sound and each other's eyes, as though mixing and matching the power of our passion with the glory of the universe. Breathing the fresh air and taking in the beauty of nature seemed to be our last desperate means of relying solely on our own instincts to validate our sinful love.

"This scenery reminds me of your painting," Mahtab said.

"The *Woman in the White Dress*?"

"Yes. I hope they catch the thieves and find *our* painting."

"I miss it too," I said. "I'd promised it to Erica and she was supposed to come pick it up the same day she fell off the balcony. She died in vain because of my timing or that painting's curse."

"Or merely a coincidence," Mahtab said.

"I don't think so…," I said dolefully.

"Paint it again, but this time let me be the woman in the white dress or maybe a pink one this time. How about that?"

I laughed and kissed her again.

"Actually, it is not a bad idea if I ever get in the mood to paint, but why not do a new painting about you altogether?" I said.

"Well, you could. But since all of us, including Mahroo, have had a special connection to this particular scene and mood, you should do it again if the original is not found."

"Maybe...! Only for my Mahy, although I usually don't like to paint the same theme twice."

"I felt so lonely after I gave it back to you. It was a steep price for getting Mahroo's portrait from you."

"It was your idea… Why were you drawn to this painting?"

"Its mood, of course. But now, in the hindsight, I guess I was already falling for its painter unconsciously… And then…"

"Then, what?" I asked.

"Missing the painting actually made me miss you more, too, and come to Vancouver."

"So, it happened to be a blessed exchange for many reasons, including my recovery... Thanks for coming to Vancouver..."

"This painting has moved many people, both emotionally and literally," she said delicately.

"Your phrase is so poetic and true."

"Of course… Just see how much Mahroo, you, and I have travelled because of this painting. Then, its movements among us have affected Erica, Reza, Zia, Bijan, and others emotionally, too."

"Alas, it also seems to be cursed. Even your confessions about how it'd affected you may be a clue," I said.

"Still, we should find it and maybe even find a way to release the soul trapped in it, too, at last."

"Maybe it's released already!" I said pensively.

"You think so?"

"Well, if it belonged to Erica or Mahroo, maybe it's free now."

"So, maybe it isn't cursed any more, either," she said.

"Maybe…"

"I recall your story about Vincent Van Gogh helping you do this painting and borrowing a woman's soul for it, too. Were you pulling my leg?"

"No. I sensed his presence in the room when I was painting it. Then, during my coma, he also confirmed his role in creating this painting and all the rest of it. It was all his fault," I said teasingly.

"Did he say whose soul he'd borrowed?" she asked wittily.

"No... I even asked him but he was so cranky. Actually...," I paused with a sudden thought.

"What?" Mahtab asked.

"I think I somehow found out myself during my coma whose soul it was, but now I don't remember again."

"And you sound so cute when you talk like this and believe in these stuff," she said.

"Didn't you say that the woman put you in a special mood, like she was alive and talking to you. I felt it as well and so did Mahroo. Maybe others have also felt it, including Erica."

"I don't know what to say now, but it made me dream a lot."

"These types of magical sentiments are likely if we believe in love and supernatural that may be connected as well."

"I agree," she said. "I thought I was she and I had to escape—from whom and what was obvious in my case, anyway. So, she felt more real to me every day."

"Well, you finally escaped and are here now. Is all this chaos really worth whatever you've been after, you silly woman?"

"It is. It is... I cherish our love. We must be together forever."

"I do too."

"Do you know what love is, anyway, Darren?"

"No. I'd tried to find its meaning and role in relationships to save my marriage and then for finding a reliable mate without making too much fuss about love."

"And you couldn't, ha?"

"No, it's just gotten more confusing... I studied and discussed it with my guru in Iran and then my friends in Vancouver, too."

"With Mahroo, too?"

"Yes, but we seemed to look at the matter differently. At the end, however, she proved to be standing on firmer ground with her simple theories."

"How did she do that?"

"Just the way I fell for her, anyway, despite my rigid rules for avoiding love. So I returned to Tehran only for her. And then… And then…," I paused.

"And then, what?"

"And then, you tainted even more of my beliefs about love and relationships in Barcelona with your astonishing request to marry me. You two sisters have simply been peculiar when it comes to love and you two have ruined both my willpower and beliefs to stay practical," I replied.

"Good…!"

"I drove so many women and my friends crazy with my love theories and discussing it so much, all in vain it seems now!"

"So, where do you stand now?"

"In what respect? Love in general or our special case?"

"Both… Tell me both," she asked.

"Well, I still believe love is merely a myth that gives us some relief from reality temporarily. Then, our childish or exaggerated impressions of love also hinder our chances for building practical relationships."

"Exactly like us right now, ha?" she asked dolefully.

"I guess...! Most of us know that love alone can't make any marriage successful, but often ignore this fact, instead of learning about practical factors," I said.

"So, loving me is against your beliefs?" Mahtab asked.

"Yes, it is. For sticking to my pledge, I must stop both of us from making fools of ourselves."

"So, should I start packing?" she asked wittily.

"Not yet. I feel powerless to do the right thing suddenly. I've let myself fall in love after all the sensations we've shared. I'm as silly today as you've been all along?"

"I'm so glad you feel this way, exactly like me. I want love in my life, even if we're making fools of ourselves," she said.

"Look at us now... back to square one... still clueless about the meaning of love... and in love! ...after trying for years to make sense of it, all in vain," I said pensively.

"It wasn't in vain. You were waiting for me," she said giddily.

"You're right, I hope. It seems most of us are too romantic to stay practical and avoid love even in foolish cases like ours."

"Especially when a mesmeric moment makes us feel so close."

"Still, this particular love, filled with treason and threats, feels much sillier after avoiding even a simple love for four years."

"I should be much prouder of myself, then, for making you break your love strike for such a risky one finally," she said gaily.

"I'm sure you are! You won't stop until we're dead, ha?"

"I'd missed love all my life, and now that I've tasted it, you say it may not be the whole truth, right?" she asked.

"Yes, let's hope its hassles don't hurt us too much or ruin the whole thing," I said dolefully.

"So, we probably have different senses for love right now."

"In what way?"

"Well..., mine is rather virgin without the cynicism and sore memories that you seem unable to shake off," she said.

"Yes, yours is surely dreamier," I replied.

"Don't worry too much, anyway... Let's be happy..."

"Well, let's hope there's an omen behind this infatuation even if we die for it," I said happily. "At least we might meet Mahroo in heaven!"

"Yes... That's all that matters now. Like a child that you said I've been all along, I'm just gonna trust love and jump into its risky adventures," Mahtab said coolly.

"Okay... Let's be childish intentionally, then," I said foolishly, as if today's peculiar mood and sensations had wiped out the last grains of my sanity.

I embraced Mahtab tighter again and then leaned and kissed her lips and cheeks and neck. We cuddled awhile in the gazebo, then strolled down the hill towards the beach. Two dozen boats in bright colours, mostly glossy blues and reds, were lingering in the bay and bobbing along with the rhythm of ripples reaching them. Seagulls flew in all directions and some merely sauntered close to us leisurely on the sands, as though we were only genial ghosts. We crossed the deck and stopped at its edge to look into the deep clear water for any fish and crab that often swims around those shallower parts of the bay. Then, we rambled towards Reza's car as the cooler air started to roll in with darker clouds thickening and spreading from the horizon, nearly covering the bay by the time we reached the car. I drove to Horse Shoe Bay, only five minutes away from the park, went to a restaurant in the main street near the ferry terminal, and ordered a bottle of wine and shrimps first. We stayed around two hours, had a fiesta leisurely, and watched the boats and ferries trafficking in the bay. It was dark when we started towards home, this time driving on the highway zigzagging at the upper levels near the interlaced hills and mountains. I was becoming a rather good, careless driver again, going fast towards home with some fantastic dreams.

We were ecstatically exhausted and romantically spirited after our daylong reflective expedition. So, we plummeted onto the couch and stretched side by side, with Mahtab's head on my chest. The soothing effect of wine was still in our bodies and most likely responsible for the nap we took calmly in each other's arms for about thirty minutes. We elongated our evening drinking some brown Persian tea that Mahtab brewed. Then, she said she wanted to soak in the tub for a while before going to bed. I said I would do the same.

When I got out of the shower, Mahtab was still in the tub or her room. So I poured myself a shot of cognac and turned on the music. As Rachmaninoff's Piano Concerto resonated, I stretched on the couch in my robe quite leisurely. Some fifteen minutes or so later Mahtab showed up in her robe, too.

"You're still not tired enough to go to bed?" she asked.

"Oh, yes, I am. I'm going soon," I replied.

"You don't have to feel lonely in your bed again tonight."

I sat up and looked into her eyes for the hundredth time today. I finished the last drops of the cognac fast, placed the glass on the coffee table, and moved towards her. I could no longer see any reason to reject her generous offer and deprive myself of one of the most gratifying pleasures of life any longer merely for the sake of some traditional principles.

When the second movement of the piano concerto began, Mahtab and I were out of our robes and rolling in the middle of her large bed. Like two hungry tigers, we roared and rolled around each other's bodies as if looking for the right place to bite and finish our slippery prey after so much anticipation to catch it cautiously at last in a joyous mood of self-sacrifice and salvation. Eventually we calmed down in the latter part of our pleasant toil with a tight squeeze at the highest point of ecstasy, just as the third movement of the concerto finished. I rolled over and lay beside Mahtab and she stretched across my chest and put her head on my pillow near my shoulder. I embraced her waist tight, caressed her buttocks, and let my fingers slide up and down the soft, exquisite valley along her spine. The touch of her body was smoother than silk and her round breasts looked gorgeous as I kept patting and admiring them. She asked if she should turn off the light and I agreed. She pulled the blanket over our bodies and we refitted ourselves into a cosy cuddle, then we fell asleep at last after a daylong drama filled with daring dreams.

Now, we had really done it this time!

It must have been one or two hours later when I thought I heard some noise at the door. Yet I was too tired to move and so decided it had come from the outside, or it had only been my imagination. I dozed off again immediately. The next thing, I opened my eyes with a startle to witness Reza standing in awe, staring at Mahtab and me with a mix of horror and anger in the lit bedroom.

Chapter Twelve
The Big Surprise

Etiquette had been my *very* least concern on top of the risk of a heads-up sabotaging the purpose of my trip to Vancouver if Mahtab went hid somewhere. In fact, she deserved any likely consequence of my surprise arrival after ignoring my calls and messages in the last two months. Besides, I was simply returning to my own apartment and used my key to get in.

I sauntered silently to the kitchen first and drank a glass of water. The apartment was dark and quiet as I went towards my bedroom and turned on the light, not expecting to see even Mahtab in my bed, let alone such a shameful sight in the first minutes of my arrival. There they were, casually entangled in my bed in deep sleep—my sinful sister and my shameless friend. Speechless, I merely kept looking at the lovers furiously, unable to make a decision. At last, Darren rolled over and opened his eyes. Listless in shock, he kept gazing at me, too, like witnessing a ghost. Then, swiftly, Mahtab also woke up with a startle, as if Darren had pinched her under the blanket. She sat up and peered at me with fury, while pulling the bedcover over her naked body.

"What're you doing here, Reza?" Mahtab shrieked.

"I live here… Do you remember?" I replied with agitation.

"Thanks for reminding me... But what're you doing here now at this hour so unexpectedly?"

"If you'd showed the decency of answering my calls, I didn't have to come all the way here just to talk to you," I cried.

"I have nothing to talk to you about," she yelled back.

The scene was just too disgusting to bear for another second. So I turned and left to find some liquor. I poured myself whisky and plummeted onto the sofa with rage and revolt. A long silence in the bedroom was broken by some murmuring, before a loud burst of laughter echoed in the suite. I was startled and amazed, while anger and humiliation overwhelmed me. Were those two morons amused by the situation and mocking me or had simply lost their brains? I was dying to know what they were telling each other and laughing a few rounds at my expense!

At last, Darren appeared fully clad. He kept exchanging shy glances with me while punching the numbers on the telephone. It took him a few minutes to get through and ask for a cab, while he now tried to avoid my probing eyes and rage.

"Sorry Reza, I'd better go now but we'll talk later," he said while opening the door to leave.

I only stared at him, not knowing how to respond. I could not even bring myself to tell him that I was happy to see him alive out of the coma. I just nodded, which was more than what I felt he deserved under the circumstance. Mahtab stormed out of the bedroom, too, all dressed up and carrying a small bag.

"Wait Darren… I'll go with you, too," she said.

"I'm going to my apartment," he replied.

"That's fine. I'll go with you."

"Why are you making things worse than they are already?"

Mahtab did not answer me. She just went to Darren, grabbed his arm, and they left after he peered at me briefly. I went to the other bedroom and noticed that someone had been sleeping in that bed as well. I changed the sheets with tension and exhaustion in hopes of getting some sleep after twenty hours of traveling so earnestly to arrive just in time for witnessing such a vulgar scene, this display of... I could not think of a name for it, nor could I sleep. I tossed and turned and tussled with many new questions for another hour before deciding that lying in bed was pointless as long as my sullied eyes saw only that ghastly love scene inside the spooky darkness. The mix of jetlag and jittery nerves simply hindered my attempt to relax. Instead, my fantasy on the plane to get plenty of sleep in my cosy bed had turned into a horrendous nightmare. I lurched to the living room and poured another glass of whisky.

Despite our suspicions about this likely scenario, new emotions and pressures now singed my brain after ten hours of torturous reflections on the plane already. I felt defeated in the first minute, while also imagining Mahtab's resistance in coming days even if I could manage to receive her majesties audience. What a mess.

Should or could I still play a role here in this private affair soon turning into an appalling public turmoil? Whom should I remain loyal to, Bijan or devil, about the sinful scene I had seen? This marital betrayal appeared beyond my jurisdiction now that our hunches had proven correct and the matter had gotten out of control already. Ironically, however, washing off my hands and going away felt impossible. In fact, my role seemed even more crucial now, starting with the task of keeping Bijan in the dark for now at least! What a messy situation, really! Why had I let Bijan force me come so far just to witness this atrocity? How could Darren behave so foolishly? Had he now lost the rest of his senses during the coma? What was to be done, anyway?

I returned to the master bedroom and retrieved the suitcase in the corner of the walking closet and its key and took them to the living room. I had always kept that big, suspicious-looking case locked and hidden its key in a secret place to prevent Mahtab, or anybody else, checking out its contents. In fact, I had not opened it myself for almost a year after I had put all of Erica's belongings in it and locked it. She had left behind a few sandals, nightgowns, shoes, dresses, books and papers, and a bunch of other stuff that I had eventually dumped into the suitcase to keep out of my sight. I had endured enough torture seeing them around my suite and missing Erica. Still, I was glad she had never come to get them. I had felt unable to throw or give them away, too, even after she had passed away.

My sudden urge to excavate Erica's belongings that instant, in the middle of the night, was most likely triggered by the sight I had seen earlier in the bedroom. It had rekindled my memory with Erica in the same passionate position on the same bed many nights for almost one year. Like those two lovebirds tonight, we had embraced each other all night and held each other's hands sometimes, too, even in deep sleep. *Had Darren imagined some of those scenarios while sleeping in that bed? Good!*

Suddenly, I missed those magical old times with his beautiful wife. And now he was reciprocating casually with my reckless married sister. How could world's ironies be any more bizarre? How would I have reacted if the situation had been reverse—Darren catching Erica and me naked together? I wondered if he understood my brotherly feelings. *I wished he had a sister I could seduce as well for revenge at least*, I mused wittily with tension for a possible distraction.

The scene tonight had been appalling, however the depth of romance those two imbeciles had manifested, in the way they had clutched each other so snugly in their sleep, had felt genuine and hard to ignore. How could I stop them or convince her when she seemed so idiotically, yet believably, in love? How could I now be responsible for sending my poor sister into the grips of a mad husband who was becoming so arrogant and more out of touch with humanity every day? But how could I not do all those things? That was exactly what I had come here to do with superb reasons, while Bijan had kept threatening all of us.

I felt stuck! The more I stared at, touched, and kissed Erica's belongings, the lousier my job of convincing Mahtab to return to her husband felt. Why was I in the middle of this crazy situation, facing two equally insane options and forced to choose? Why was I playing with Erica's stuff like a lunatic at this hour? I smelled Erica's negligee again and felt gloomy by her scent still lingering around to torture me forever.

I was glad Darren and Mahtab had fled before I had found a chance to tell them anything that I might have regretted later. I liked them dearly and loathed annoying them. However, if I did not do my job, even at the cost of making them also mad at me, Bijan would surely hurt them—or even kill them. I knew all these facts when I had started my trip to Vancouver. The only thing I had not anticipated was my vulnerability in terms of facing love. I had not imagined witnessing their passion would make my job ten times harder, if I still meant to stick to my initial intention of separating them and sending Mahtab home. Yet, a fast decision was needed whether I liked it or not. Craziest thing of all was the way I had arrived so quickly at such a radical conclusion: That the scene I had seen in my bed had been a true love story, rather than merely a naïve infatuation or even lust! Was it only because it had reminded me of Erica?

I kept drinking whisky and pondering love, loyalty, treason, duty, and many other tortuous human impulses that combined collectively to convolute the purpose of my travel to Vancouver. Was this humiliating situation a part of my karma for my affair with Erica? For the tenth time in the last 24 hours, I wondered why was I prying in or worrying over other people's lives rather than having a life of my own, maybe with a wife or a mate, and perhaps a bunch of naughty kids to drive me nuts, too? Now, even Darren seemed over Erica, so why had not I found a woman of my own to replace Erica as well.

At the end, now fully exhausted, I realized the difficulty of my mission. So I postponed making any decision until the next day when my mind might possibly be a bit more relaxed and I was not so affected by jetlag, the scene, and so much alcohol I had been drinking all along while playing with Erica's belongings. To rejoice my wise brain—for delaying my verdict about Darren and

Mahtab until the next day at least—I poured myself another big shot of whisky, while promising my spirit that it would be the last one for tonight. I smelled and kissed Erica's negligee once more and put it back in the suitcase along with all the other items I had spread around me like a treasure. I locked the case, hid it in the walking closet carefully, and put its key back in its secret place. Then, I took my whisky to the bedroom, lay on the bed, and took a couple of aspirins to curb my pounding headache. I shut my eyes, hoping to stop thinking anymore tonight—near dawn.

Near noon, I woke up with a headache and hangover, pleasantly surprised for having slept seven hours. The intense sun shined out there when I opened the drapes slightly and closed them quickly before my eyes burst out of their sockets or my head exploded. Wisely, I took two aspirins with water only after a long hesitation about applying more whisky to remedy my hangover,

NOW, more than ever in my life, I needed a head empty of alcohol and false emotions to think clearly about a vastly intricate issue and do the right thing—the right thing for Mahtab, not me or Bijan! A promise to my psyche to stay sober for a week at least felt like a good start for a wise man.

During a light breakfast, I wondered if some hope still existed for salvaging the damage. The matter had felt so clear when I had left Tehran and even now considering Bijan's ultimatum. Yet, my niggling doubts had now crippled me after the sight of those two idiots in my bed last night had reignited my mixed-up senses of romance and betrayal. Why had I lost my resolve so abruptly? The ricochet of Mahroo's order in my dream, "Just leave them alone, Reza," was not helping, either. I wondered about the kind of rational that might work in these circumstances, how to elude my personal emotions, and the way to defeat my indecision for encountering Mahtab.

After wrestling with many conflicting thoughts and no logical answer, I left home in hopes of gauging my options better outside in fresh air. I meandered along the Granville Street towards the

Burrard Inlet, while my headache and hangover subsided largely, too. The North Shore Mountains stretched in the horizon and the Seabus blew its horn as it began its short crossing of the inlet to the north shore. I kept strolling towards Coal Harbour, stopped at Canada Place and sat on a bench on the quiet deck with a wide view of mountains, ocean, the Lions Gate Bridge, and a few large ships in the harbour.

Without Erica around, it had not made sense for me to work with SDI or travel to Vancouver. Yet, here I was… watching the harbour view hypnotically or wandering in the streets aimlessly, while ignoring my business obligations in Iran and Dubai. I had told Cameron not to count on me doing new projects with SDI and had been thinking about selling my suite in Vancouver, too, right before Mahtab had asked to use it.

For an hour, I tried to focus and analyse my dilemma from various angles. Still, no viable conclusion rendered itself. But at least I decided that if I had to get really tough with Mahtab to put some sense into her inebriated head, so be it, even if I would have to con her. And if I should let her be, then I had nothing else to do here in Vancouver. I had come all this way only to realize I had no right to deprive Mahtab of making her decisions at whatever cost to all of us, even if I could entertain the chance of she even listening to my pleas in the first place, let alone conning her. If so, I just had to take the next plane back. Or stay a few weeks and keep feeding Bijan with all sorts of lies about Mahtab and Darren playfully and happily. How about that? But in that case, he would immediately activate his horrible plans and unleash his wild dogs to find Darren at least. I moseyed to Gas Town and had my late lunch in a cafe before walking back to my apartment, exhausted and desperate.

I spent the rest of the day and evening in search of a solution, to no avail. At ten pm, I decided that I had done enough thinking soberly for too long with no sign of value for a clear head. So I poured myself a glass of whisky and returned to the couch. Still bemused by my resolve in the morning to stay sober for *an entire week* at least, my mission felt even more complex and risky by the minute along with lots of whisky. Trying to convince Mahtab to return to Iran or merely let her be and hope she could survive Bijan's wrath felt like two toughest alternatives to compare with no third option in sight. At least the first gulp of whisky made me realize that this matter was too emotional for me to sort out alone. The only thing I had settled after a daylong contemplation was that both options sucked and I was in no position to choose or even make any judgment in this regard!

Still, this realization felt essential like a huge accomplishment all in itself, which made me proud of myself—simply because it showed my guts and objectivity to avoid doggedness or a hasty decision. Most admirable was my ability to resist even the natural spite that influences any person who is mocked and laughed at so loudly the way those two morons had done to me the previous night after I had caught them in bed. Surely, ignoring their idiocy and insult was a sign of my growing, divine wisdom as well, rather than indecisiveness.

Defeated and helpless, at last I came up with the most brilliant idea I had had all day: To call T.J. and at least share my dilemma with him in hopes of exploring new ideas or a third option. The notion appeared so promising I called him right away. A woman answered the phone and paused after hearing my polite request to speak with T.J. Finally, she asked my name rudely, as if I had awakened her or at least my intrusion so late was unappreciated. After I introduced myself eagerly, she did not even bother to say hi. Instead, she told me to wait in an even rougher tone after a short pause. I heard her calling aloud for T.J., who was seemingly in another part of their big house. Her tone and arrogance alone —despite my late call—made me feel eternal empathy and pity for T.J. Now I promised myself to bear happily as much bitching that poor man would decide to torture me with in the future.

After the customary greetings and T.J.'s surprise about my presence in Vancouver, I said I wished to pick his brain about a very important matter as soon as possible.

"Have you found that devil Darren and *charming* Mahtab?" T.J. asked wittily, as he had apparently guessed the topic of our looming consultation.

"Yes. And they're the topic I'd like to discuss with you again in more detail perhaps," I said before taking another big gulp of my whisky and fighting my urge to mention the condition I had found them in.

"Okay, sure," T.J. said with scepticism. "Is Darren okay?"

"Oh, he looks quite all right. Much better than you and I could imagine for a person coming out of a coma after three months," I said, hoping that my sarcasm had not sounded rude. T.J. laughed.

"When do you wanna meet… Not tonight, I hope?"

"Oh, no, sorry… Tomorrow is fine," I replied.

"Where?"

"Anywhere. But if you wish to come downtown, we can have lunch and go to my place for tea and private conversation," I said, wondering how private this matter would stay if I should discuss it with a few people, including Mahtab and Darren soon.

Suddenly, the seemingly *brilliant* idea of consulting T.J., after my useless analysis so far, worried me, too, and consumed more whisky after we hung up. The secrets Bijan had shared with me along with his threats were necessary information for drawing a full picture regarding the severity of the situation and the likely consequences of any wrong decision. Yet, doing so might raise havoc. Apparently, Darren had been loyal about the contentious secrets he had promised Bijan to keep, since he had not revealed them even to me and possibly T.J.

In the end, getting Darren's and Bijan's permissions appeared prudent before screwing up matters further, although the notion of calling Bijan and calming him with some lies for now agitated me. He was surely restless to hear about my discoveries so far, so I decided to stay diplomatic and humour him, despite my earlier urge to let him sweat a few more days.

I called Bijan the next day around noon, Tehran's time, suddenly hoping he would not answer and I leave him only a message.

"Why didn't you call sooner?" Bijan asked nervously. "I've been waiting for the last forty hours."

"I arrived just two nights ago with the jetlag and all," I replied, surprised that he was apparently not going to work these days.

"I tried to call you earlier myself, but either your phone was busy or nobody answered," he yelled with agitation.

"There's nothing to discuss, anyway. I haven't had a chance to talk with Mahtab yet," I said.

"Why not?"

"Because I'm waiting to catch her in a right mood."

"That may take a year or forever. Don't count on that."

"I know what I'm doing, Bijan." That was the biggest lie so far, of course.

"Is she in the apartment?" he asked nervously.

"Not right now. She's probably gone shopping or something."

"Does she live there?"

"Yes, of course."

"So why hasn't she been answering the phone?"

"I haven't asked her that, either, Bijan," I replied, flustered.

"Can you make her talk to me when she returns home?"

"I don't know, Bijan. But that is not the right thing to do now. Let me talk with her first and see how things are before you two start fighting and messing up the chance for reconciliation. Can you wait a few days, please? You must trust me and let me do my job properly."

"How long that would take, you think?"

"A week…, to make sure I don't screw up everything from the beginning," I said.

"A week…?" he asked with irritation.

"At least… I need time to do this job the right way. Do you still want me to do this or just get out of the picture," I said, deep down hoping he would fire me from such humiliating, torturous duty with no foreseeable good ending. Although my involvement could possibly help my sister and friend, maybe letting a natural course prevail was smarter. My intrusion and naïve assumption about the chance of helping people, in particular two stubborn individuals like Mahtab and Darren felt ridiculous often. How had I even imagined being smart enough to advise anybody?

"Yes… I want you to do your best, because if the matter gets out of hand neither of us can control the outcome," Bijan said. "Do you see what I'm talking about?"

"Yes, Bijan, I hear you loud and clear. But if you push me too much I can't do anything and I might actually resign from this horrible project."

"Just do your darn best to make her understand the situation."

"I will. But I might've to reveal some of the secrets you told me about Sima's brother and other related issues to Darren and others. Is this okay?"

There was a long silence on the phone.

"Bijan? Are you there?"

"Yes, I'm thinking..." He remained quiet for another twenty seconds before talking. "I guess there is no way around this if you must convince them about the risks of making a wrong decision, but do it only if necessary and in private."

Bijan's attitude reaffirmed his efforts to remain loyal to other parties involved and the severity of the secret. It was good to have his blessing now, too, for discussing these matters if necessary.

"Let's see what I can do," I said.

"When're you gonna call me?"

"I'd say in a week or so. As I said, if this thing is gonna work, I must approach Mahtab step by step diplomatically after I gain her trust first and let her relax around me. Otherwise, she'd stop talking to me altogether and maybe even move out, too. You know how stubborn she is, don't you?" I said.

"Of course, I do... Okay, do as you see fit, but call me at least every other day to tell me how it's going, okay?"

"Okay, I'll try, Bijan," I said, ready to hang up.

"Umm…," Bijan murmured with a sigh, as if unsure about something important to share with me.

"Is there anything else?" I asked with stress.

"Not now… Let's wait a few days, then!"

"So, goodbye… You'd better go get some sleep at least if you're not going to work," I said sarcastically.

"Sleep…? Are you crazy?"

"It may help you relax... Anyway, leave everything to me or at least to God," I said wittily.

"Listen, Reza… I'm just hoping that everything you're telling me is god's honest truth. Right?"

"Of course. Why do you say this?" I asked with tension, sort of feeling his suspicions about my words and intentions, or maybe even imagining the bedroom scene I had seen.

"Well, I just wanted you to remember that I won't forget or forgive people who lie to me or betray me. Right?"

"Sure… Can't you see I'm trying so hard to bring peace back into this family," I replied timidly with frustration.

"I hope so, for your own sake… Do it in 2-3 days."

"I'll try, Bijan," I replied. "I hope you realize that I'm in a rush myself to go back to Tehran for my mom and work."

"Yes, hurry up…, and goodnight," he said.

The receiver dangled in my shaking hand from both fear and anger. As much as I was proud of my lies to keep Bijan calm, I knew that outsmarting him would be impossible for much longer. He was a terribly intelligent man with a Ph.D. from a prominent university in the United States, after all, despite his preference to be a religious fanatic as well. How can a person be so intelligent, yet influenced by such outlandish religious beliefs, I had always wondered.

Chapter Thirteen
A Definition for Heaven

Here we go again! Agreeing to listen to Reza about another dramatic love story irked my mind with mixed feelings. He and Darren—the odd couple—were at it again by the way Reza had sounded on the phone with hints about Darren and Mahtab hitting it off *so nicely!* Had not I listened to Reza and Darren and tried to help them in vain once already in relation to the other sister?!

I wished a time would come in my own pathetic life when I would struggle with a love saga of my own—maybe with Homa behind Feri's back—instead of witnessing so many of others' and envying even those allegedly *tangled* mayhem around them, which would still look pale compared to daily tortures Feri gave me so generously! I wished I could *at least imagine* a day others would discuss my love-ridden commotions and pains with envy.

During the breakfast, the next morning, I asked Feri if she had any appointments in the morning and she said no cautiously after thinking with confusion about the purpose of my bizarre inquiry and sudden interest in her. So, after feeling ecstatic for having cornered her, I asked her to give me a ride to downtown. She said no immediately with the excuse of suddenly remembering she must go to the office, after all, and take care of some paperwork.

"It'll take only thirty minutes to give me a ride and return."

"Take the bus. I have nothing to do in downtown," she said.

"I know that… I only asked you for a ride."

"Why are you meeting Reza today, anyway?"

"We just like to meet after so long. Is there something wrong also with meeting my friends?"

"Friends?" she shrieked. "He's a bachelor half your age. What kind of friendship is that?"

"I'm just amazed. What does age or marital status have to do with friendship? Do I nag about the kind of friends you keep?"

"What's wrong with my friends?"

"Hmm...! Do you even have to ask?"

"Don't you dare insulting my friends again, you understand?"

"What if I do?" I asked wittily and bravely, I assumed.

"I'll slap your foul mouth silly… That's what I'll do…," she said with so much arrogance I could strangle her on the spot.

"You'll slap me silly now, too, ha?" I shrieked sternly.

She froze with a startle and her eyes twitched from absolute hatred of my guts. Swiftly, however, she decided to recover and show off her nerve. "You'd better believe it," she yelled back.

"Just forget it," I said with angst, "I'll just keep paying for the Mercedes every month and when I ask for a lousy ride I have to face all these ridiculous conversations."

"Go to hell," Feri yelled at me as I walked towards my study.

"I hope so," I yelled back and banged the door with rage. "It's probably more peaceful in hell than the life I have with you."

"The whole neighbourhood thinks you're a crazy old man," Feri shouted outside the study. I almost burst into laughter for her spite and tenacity to run so fast to the study just to insult me.

"Not the whole neighbourhood… only the bitches like you think that way," I replied after opening the door and sticking my head out. Then I slammed the door hard again. *Wow, my tenacity and spite* ***almost*** *paralleled hers!*

Feri's refusal to even give me a ride felt too humiliating, not to mention her sneaky excuses to never let me drive her new car. Anytime I had set out to see how driving a Mercedes felt, she had recalled she must go somewhere right away. Only the outrageous lease payments belonged to me. I pondered the point of arguing with her about anything the way logic had eluded our marriage from the start—twenty years ago. I pondered the point of walking around and thinking every day until our brain cells blasted from so much humiliation and worries we must endure all our lives, especially in relationships nowadays. What if we did not have to do all these foolish stuff daily for nothing? Would that be the real meaning for heaven? I tried to build an image for Heaven:

It is probably a place we do not have to argue, reason, think, feel, or worry, while we already know nobody has to work there! Right...? In fact, some religions suggest lots of houries are also awaiting our arrival to entertain us till eternity! I just hoped we do not get bored to death in that lazy-land Heaven, though! Still, living away from Feri felt like a big incentive to go meet God right away—and maybe whine to Him a bit as well, about His deliberate design of such a demented human nature screwing up our chance for interactions and causing all these pains!

Feri's mocking remark about a man of my background and age befriending two reckless young men rekindled my insecurity and doubts about this issue again, like I had to justify it with more clues even to myself every time she nagged about it. Luckily, I promptly realized again that Reza's and Darren's authenticities and grasp of social dilemmas, especially relationships, had been most handy for me to bear my vile family and aristocrat friends. Besides helping each other intelligently, discussing the absurdity of social life nowadays ironically had helped us learn to cope with life easier. They also had more time for me, contrary to my family and old friends who hardly spent any time with me to talk about anything. So, even the likely hassles of being dragged into Reza's new emotionally tangled conflict with Darren were worth their honest friendship. I wished I could tell Feri that mostly her escalating malice had made me so needy for Darren's and Reza's wisdom. I owed them big for keeping me sane!

Even the odd couples' squabbles have always distracted my mind nicely for a few hours, although a loser like me giving them advice on emotional matters felt absurd, especially nowadays with my messy mood about relationships and all. So I planned to warn Reza, although he probably had a special agenda or use for me.

Watching Feri pull out of the garage and speed away without me tore my spirit too much to focus or write. I pondered calling and asking Reza to meet me sooner and closer to my house, but then decided to take the bus downtown—as Feri had ordered!—walk around awhile before lunch with Reza, and then stay in his place as long as possible. I needed some change of scenery and plenty of time away from this madhouse and neighbourhood.

The plan indeed proved refreshing. Besides the joy of seeing Reza after three months, the secrets he shared with me were both intriguing and worrying. Especially, Darren's Persian lovechild being connected to several threats and people's collaboration to find and punish Darren and Mahtab, *merely for family honours,* rattled me. Still, listening to the story made me forgot my family's tyranny towards me, exactly as I had hoped! Thank god, at least I had no family honour to be threatened or fuss about!

"And you believe these threats are serious?" I asked Reza.

"Yes... These people can be ruthless," he replied.

"Did you hear the story of Fereydoon Farokhzad?" I asked.

"Yes, I heard they simply decapitated him in his apartment in Germany and vanished just because he'd criticized the regime."

"In fact, I met him in a party in Vancouver just a few weeks before he returned home and got slaughtered," I replied.

"There're many similar stories and I think those dishonoured people after Darren and Mahtab aren't bluffing."

"I know... And they seem so casual about it."

"That's amazing... murdering people all over the world and the police can't catch those mad dogs," Reza said.

"You must somehow push Mahtab to go back, then, Reza, for now at least," I said, fretting about the new pressures on Darren's broken psyche as soon as Reza brings him into picture. *Besides, I really needed Darren alive to mitigate my anxieties! Selfish me!*

"But it's not easy," Reza replied.

"I can imagine… But you must find a way."

"That's why I wanted to discuss it with you, too."

"To me, the only logical thing is to make Mahtab realize the danger and go handle her husband first."

"I'd felt the same way before arriving in Vancouver."

"And now you've changed your mind?" I asked with surprise.

"Not totally, but feel guilty after seeing them in bed together."

"You caught them in action?" I asked teasingly.

He nodded with a sigh.

"So why do *you* feel guilty instead of them?" I continued.

"Well… I got upset initially, of course," he replied. "But then later, I questioned my right to stop their affair and send Mahtab back to Bijan's grip in such a cruel environment. She must live her life the best she can, instead of suffocating in a marriage she abhors, and maybe even perishing unexpectedly like Mahroo."

"So, you're considering defecting and taking their side now?"

"I might…! But I'm not sure."

"Well, you're very kind to them after seeing their vulgarity on top of ignoring your phone calls for weeks."

"Even worse!" Reza said.

"Something even worse happened?" I asked with surprise.

"Well, I think they laughed at me after I barked at them and left that awful sight," he said with angst.

"They laughed at you?" I asked with still bigger surprise.

"Yes, that's how it sounded to me, like they were mocking me and enjoying themselves…"

"That's horrible…," I said with sympathy, not wishing to be in his place. Even advising him felt much trickier now that the matter seemed so personal and sensitive to him.

"On the other hand, I must be mature and realistic," he said.

"You're a wonderful brother... And such a good friend."

"I must help her even if they mocked me like lunatics."

"What're they thinking? Hide and deny everything forever?"

"I wish I knew... But my mom will die if something happens to Mahtab, too. She's still mourning my dad and Mahroo."

"I'm surprised Mahtab doesn't feel the same way," I said.

"What should I do, T.J.?"

"Do exactly what you did with me today."

"What's that?" Reza asked.

"Tell'em all these facts. Mahtab knows about Bijan's wrath, so your points won't sound crazy. Darren has learned some good lessons in Iran, too, especially from his time in prison. Tell'em your job is much tougher now, since you value their love. Make them trust you and tell'em you'd respect their decision."

"You think any fact-checking will move them if romance has crippled their brains, which seems to be the case."

"If you help them see the whole picture and your sincerity, you've done your job and your conscience should be clear."

"No, I must also consider other options, such as threatening, scaring, or lying to them, if I decide to push Mahtab to go back."

"Still, trying logic and facts is the best strategy to start with," I said confidently and proudly.

"I'm not sure, T.J… Sorry… Logic might not do the trick in this special situation," Reza said.

"Why not?" I asked timidly, feeling useless and offended.

"What if it doesn't work? Changing my strategy will be much less effective later, if at all."

"Maybe…!" I said defiantly.

"Nobody can feel Bijan's wrath and his allies' determination these days, especially these two lovebirds."

"You probably know more about infatuation ruining lovers' senses," I said wittily with envy and a sigh.

"Yes, I could do all sorts of foolish things recklessly just for keeping Erica near me this minute. I wasn't even afraid of death."

"You loved her that much, ha?" I asked with astonishment.

"Yes... In fact, I almost jumped off my balcony in Tehran two weeks ago when her ghost was calling me to join her?"

"Oh, my god... She's still haunting you?" I asked.

"It seems like it, but please don't mention this to anyone."

"So, you're worried about Mahtab's sensibility these days?"

"Plus Darren's state of mind after three months of coma."

"Yes, these are additional causes for concern, not to mention Mahtab's magical charm that you've been worried about all this time!" I replied wittily.

"Especially that!," Reza said sluggishly. "So I must convince her somehow to return to Iran before something terrible happens."

"Then, not even a trick might hclp if their brains are busted."

"Still some kind of a trick or lie might have a better chance of giving them a shock or something to think a little."

We drank our teas, while I gauged his valid points about love making us lose ourselves. I felt stupid for not seeing the fuller picture along with his finer logic. Reza had apparently pondered this operatic situation much deeper and my primitive solution had surely occurred to him in his own first round of analysis.

"Maybe you can also mention your concerns to them," I said.

"About the chance of being carried away by love?"

"Kind of… Maybe a bit more tenderly…"

"Do you think lovers can set aside their emotions to think?"

"You're right," I replied with angst about my slow brain.

"The toughest love ordeal is lovers' inability to know if it's real or just an infatuation unless it lasts forever, which is rare."

"That's right! Even the truest love won't last long nowadays."

"You'd expect people realize these facts," Reza said.

"No, we hate to doubt our rationality and emotions even when we aren't lost in love," I said.

"We wouldn't have these discussions today if I didn't doubt Mahtab's sanity these days. Things she seems willing to do for love, maybe even more than Mahroo, is just amazing or crazy."

"I see your point, but can't think of anything, besides letting them make a decision themselves."

"I disagree… I think I must make one for them before fooling them or whatever necessary," Reza said so matter-of-factly.

"You really mean it?" I asked in bewilderment.

"Yes. I used logic with Erica, especially for sharing my worries about Mahroo, and still she left me out of jealousy or pride."

"So that's another Erica episode goading your mind now."

"Yes, T.J., I'm really worried about Mahtab. She's the only family near my age and I can't just sit idly by and let her destroy her life for what, I don't know!?"

"So, you must be sure about your wisdom to decide for them plus your power to fool them?"

"Yes, I hope so," Reza replied with a giggle.

"You think you can do both?"

"All I know is that I'll be devastated if something goes wrong and I believe I could've prevented it. I must try at least… right?"

"I guess so…"

"Yes, I should try hard… Otherwise, it'd be a kind of coping out at the time my sister refuses to see the big picture."

"You sound so wise and determined today!"

"I'm glad my resolve is clear, for my mom's and Nazi's sakes at least. And relying on facts alone would not cut it in this case."

"Your astonishing grudge against honesty today is funny and educational," I said out of despair and we laughed.

"Has your logic and honesty ever worked with Feri and your daughters?" he asked wittily with a chuckle.

"No, never…," I replied timidly.

"Yeah! It is not time to be liberal and logical," he said sternly.

I was again impressed by the level of thoughts he had put into this matter before coming to me, which surely showed the depth of both his worries and love for Mahtab. My ideas today sounded impotent and advising him seemed impossible, while I realized his fine point about the necessity of a radical approach. He was ten times smarter than me today. Now I felt useless and pathetic even more than how I had felt like a loser this morning when watching Feri drive away without me.

"Didn't you say their love felt real after you saw them so cosy in bed?" I asked desperately.

"Well, I could've been affected by the scene in two ways."

"In what ways?"

"Can you keep another secret; a sad confession in fact?"

"Yes, go ahead," I replied.

"The scene reminded me of Erica and I on the same bed and how we'd struggled with a mix of love and confusion one whole year before a small incident shattered our hopes for emotional stability and we separated."

"So you worry about being either too sentimental or cynical about love based on your own affair with Erica, right?"

"Yes, those lovebirds remind me of many side-effects of love, besides its likely sad ending. I might be affected by my unsettling love memories one way or another!"

"Both fun and failure parts. I guess I get your intricate point."

"Even if they're in love, what could it do for them if they're dead? Or what if it doesn't last at all?"

"Your sisters' and Darren's marital failures are good examples. My naggings might've affected you now as well," I said sadly, as Feri's attitude and words this morning aggravated me, especially when she had said, *Take the bus.*

"Maybe. But Mahtab and Darren look crazy, anyway."

"Then again, you said you also felt guilty about the possibility of ruining a true love," I said.

"That's why it's been hard for me to decide, T.J."

"Honestly, Reza, I don't understand why you even considered consulting me. I'm flattered you're sharing your dilemmas with me, not to mention Darren's top secrets, but how did you imagine I could add anything to your perfect analysis?"

"That is not why I asked you to help me, T.J.," Reza said.

"Oh...? What'd you need me for, then?" I asked with absolute embarrassment and a final blow to my pride.

"I just hoped you could tell me if my analyses and options made sense to you, too, and that they weren't rash or emotional."

"No, they sound perfect to me," I replied hastily, if not testily.

"But most importantly, I want you to be my ally and possibly talk to Darren privately, too, to push the same points. My chance of success rises if he hears the same ideas from both of us without even knowing that we have collaborated."

"You tricky bastard...," I shrieked.

"I know... Sorry. I might need your help even more if we have to resort to some kind of a trick that I must work out."

"Wouldn't Darren get mad at you for sharing his secrets with me or playing tricks on him?"

"Honestly, T.J., I can't fuss about Darren's reaction anymore. I must only focus on Mahtab and my family…"

"You're right again."

"Besides, I don't think he minds if his lovechild or even love affair with Mahtab was discussed among us at least."

"How you wanna put sense into his head, then?"

"Poor Darren. He's been pressured at so many fronts already. Even worse, we, and even he, don't know much about the effect of the coma on his state of mind these days."

"Yeah, I don't know whether to cry for him or laugh about his luck with women?" I said teasingly.

"Are you jealous about his luck?" Reza asked with a chuckle.

"Well, he was shot because of a love affair, comes out of the coma to find a new lover awaiting him, while the secret about his lovechild with yet another woman is causing another commotion for him and his friends already."

"I think we should cry for him more than laughing at his crazy lifestyle and spooky luck."

"All right, then. How should we proceed?" I asked. "As much as I like to linger and discuss Darren's endless love and revenge sagas, I'd better go home before midnight."

"Can you do a recap before going?" he asked, as if giving me a final chance to redeem myself after proving my idiocy all night.

"A recap?" I asked tensely, uncertain about his request after humiliating me all along inadvertently.

"Yeah, just a summary of my ideas plus any other solution that also makes sense to you now."

"Okay, let me think a second. Can you refill my whisky?" I asked, feeling obliged to reciprocate his generosity to humour me all evening, while knocking down my petty suggestions all along.

"Do you mind if I record it just to remember our talk tonight?"

"So that you can blame me later for everything that might go wrong?" I asked wittily.

"No, I won't...," he replied giddily. "If you like, you can say at the beginning that you're only repeating my words."

"What's the point?" I said with a chuckle. "You can always take out my disclaimer even if I said it ten times."

"Oh, boy… You're as paranoid as Darren and I… I love it."

Reza poured us two large shots of whisky and turned off the radio playing pop music. It was now past midnight and I was getting anxious to go home before Feri started to worry about me and called the police!! Holding myself from a blast of hysterical laughter after this silly thought was tough. However, I managed it somehow to avoid giving Reza an impression of laughing at him and his hilarious mission. I sipped my drink, while contemplating and failing to find any new solution for Reza. So, I tried to sum up his options based on his own seemingly sound analysis.

Clearly, Reza's fear of his raw logic or memory of love affair with Erica misleading him showed his wisdom and worry at the same time. He seemed both confused about, and obsessed with, love, very much like Darren himself. No wonder they were good friends! Meanwhile, I could also both sympathize with Mahtab and imagine the high likelihood of her recklessness these days due to her special life circumstances, since I knew firsthand about the tough situation in Iran, especially for women.

"Okay, I'm ready," I said. Reza pressed the recorder's button on the coffee table and I continued.

"Do you have any reason to doubt their love's authenticity regardless of its chance to last or not?"

"No… I can't say that. Why?" Reza replied.

"Because if you have a reasonable doubt, the matter is easy. Take Mahtab back to Iran, for now at least, even if you must drag her or lie about her mother or Nazi being too sick or something."

"No, I can't judge their love's nature," Reza replied. "But I've thought about using Nazi and my mom to soften Mahtab…"

"In that case what I've suggested all night becomes a bit more viable."

"Which is?"

"Talking to them sincerely. Explain the risks of Mahtab not going back to Iran. Mention the high chance of their infatuation impairing their judgment these days, maybe even offer examples of likely scenarios in all love affairs, especially for this special case. You may even boldly explain your feelings for Erica, its effect on making personal mistakes, and your love's insufferable aftermath. Then tell them you'd respect their decision and might actually help them in anyway you can."

"Yeah, these are my two options, but I still don't know which one is better," Reza said as he turned off the tape recorder.

"Turn it on again." Reza did and I continued, "Stress you'd most likely get killed if you fail in your mission of convincing them to do the right thing. Raise their burden of guilt for you, your mom and Nazi as well, if something happens to you."

"See...? You could offer good ideas, after all," he said giddily.

"After making me believe lying is more potent than logic."

"Yeah. I think our meeting today was very useful. Now I can prepare myself perfectly to drive their conscience nuts if they see me at least," he said with a giggle and turned off the recorder. "I'll mix lies and facts for the optimal effect."

"Still even your facts are merely your views of things."

"That's true... The whole thing would be a sham, but it's all in good faith for a hopefully good ending...," Reza said. "Thanks a lot for helping me tonight, T.J."

"You're welcome. I must talk to you guys soon about my life and Feri, too. But now it's getting late and I'm afraid my family is sick with worries about me!" I said and we laughed. "But let me ask you one question before I go."

"I'm always glad to hear your love stories, too. Go ahead…"

"Do you think I'm crazy a little or a lot?"

"That's a weird question! Why do you ask this silly thing?"

"I don't know… I just wonder sometimes…"

"You think Darren and I would've consulted you all the time if we thought you were crazy?"

"I guess not. But it's hard to know who's sane these days."

"Unless…!" Reza uttered with a hint of revelation.

"Unless what?"

"Unless Darren and I are also lunatics…!"

"Oh, don't worry, I guarantee you two are not crazy, either," I said very seriously before we laughed again.

"Why do you even think this way suddenly?" Reza asked.

"Well, last night Feri told me that the whole neighbourhood thinks I am a crazy old man. My aristocrat friends also think I am crazy because I do not wanna work anymore. What's the point if you have no incentive for making money, are 55 years old, and your family has turned against you?" I replied.

"Yeah, I'm aware of those people's stupidity. I'm supposedly friend with many of those assholes myself."

"You do, I guess… They've also mentioned you sometimes."

"I don't even wanna know what they think about me, but I'm sure it's probably not flattering."

"In fact, at least one of them hinted that you were weird or a screwball as well," I replied.

"Didn't I say I don't wanna know what they say about me?"

"You and I have surely made quite a reputation in this city!"

"I know… But what's the neighbours' beef with you?"

"Well… I think the whole thing relates to one incident."

"What incident?" Reza asked.

"I've gone for a walk around the neighbourhood for years. People in a house on my route have a tiny dog that's usually hanging around, barking, and attacking people. I'd complained to people living there about their mad dog. Besides the fear of biting my leg, its barks and growling rattled my nerves every time I walked around that haunted house. Sometimes, it hid in a corner and then leaped at me and shattered my guts when I was lost in my thoughts.

"Anyway, one day the dog was coming along with a woman and started running towards me and barking like hell. When I felt it might bite my leg, I kicked its jaw. It wailed, sat, and stared at me with surprise and pain possibly. The woman also kept staring at me.

'How many times should we tell you stupid people to get hold of your dog?' I yelled at her.

"She didn't peep and went away with the dog. The following day, I saw a different young woman in the street approaching me with fury and the crazy dog in her arm.

'Are you the guy who kicked my dog yesterday?'

'I guess!'

'See what you've done to its jaw…'

'I've told you people a million times to keep your dog on the leash, instead of letting it roam around the neighbourhood and attack everybody with its deafening barks.'

'It doesn't bite,' she yelled, which made me giggle furtively, as it reminded me of Inspector Clouseau in *Pink Panther*.

'How do you expect people to know that or take all this abuse even if it doesn't bite? All this attacking and barking is driving us crazy, you selfish woman,' I yelled back at her

'The next time you come close to my dog, I'll report you.'

'Stupid woman, it's your dog that comes close to me and not the other way around,' I replied.

'Just don't kick it, I'm telling you,' she shouted.

'I promise I'll kick your dog again if it attacks me.'

'Then I'll take care of you myself, you moron,' she yelled.

'Are you gonna bite me now, too, you bitch?'

'I'll show you, you stupid psycho.'

'Just keep your dog and yourself on a joint leash, bitch,' I shouted, while a few neighbours had gathered by now to watch us amusingly.

'You're the one who must be chained in a madhouse.'

'You're stupider than your dog, you know? This poor animal is doing this silly thing because of your inability to train it, but you're thinking that everything it does to people is alright since it's your dog. You're a selfish imbecile.'

'Crazy old man,' she said, showing me her middle finger and walking away. I wondered what she meant by that gesture!

'Bitch…,' I yelled back and hoped the whole neighbourhood, besides the ones already present, heard me and felt as good as I had by telling her what she was..." I paused and stared at Reza.

"It was funny. What happened next?" Reza asked.

"Nothing… I changed my route after that day. I'm taking a less appealing walk near the high traffic these days just to avoid that whore and her dog."

"So she won?"

"I just didn't see any point escalating this conflict. I couldn't avoid kicking the dog if it attacked me again, which was quite likely. I might've killed an innocent dog because of its master's stupidity."

"You see, your decision to avoid more confrontations shows all by itself that you're sane."

"Of course, another factor was that I noticed her following me that day to learn my address. So, I went around the block a few times to drive her nuts before finally going home when I couldn't see her anymore. Still she might've found out about my address somehow, anyway. She looked like a real bitch and I'm afraid of her now, too," I said and Reza burst into laughter.

"So, now you think this dog incident has made neighbours say you're crazy?" Reza asked.

"Only some bitches and Feri think that way. Some neighbours have actually told me in private that I was a hero for kicking the dog and calling its nasty owner a bitch. I have some supporters, although they all think I'm different, anyway—brave, psycho, weird, or whatever," I said with a chuckle.

"Good for you…"

"I heard that a neighbour had said I was an alien."

"By alien, you mean a foreigner?"

"I think they meant I did not belong to this planet altogether."

"That may be a big compliment indeed," Reza said giddily.

"Maybe. At least you think I'm not crazy," I said. "I needed a confirmation *today* in particular after my big argument with Feri before coming to see you!"

"Then again, it seems we humans are all loonies for a good bunch of reasons or another," he said.

"I agree. At least that's how people see and judge one another. Especially, odd people like us look even crazier than usual."

"I think around 50% of people are about 200% crazier and stupider than the rest," Reza said. "Not us, of course."

"Wow… It's 1:30…"

"We sure tackled a lot of urgent issues tonight, especially about your sanity," Reza said with a chuckle.

"We sure did. I'd better go fight with my loony family, then, if I'm not crazy," I said and rose. "They'd swear I'm a lunatic, anyway, even if the neighbours changed their minds. Tonight, especially, they may think I've lost my way home, too, as another symptom of my senility."

When I arrived home exhausted, everybody was sound asleep with no sign of anybody fussing about my extraordinary absence for so many hours this late at night. The deadly silence in the house, save for Feri's loud snore in the master bedroom, singed my sensitive soul, especially after imagining all along on the way home that everybody was wide awake, worried sick with a bunch of policemen standing in front of our door and working diligently over a possible catastrophe and my whereabouts.

Chapter Fourteen
Back to Reality

It was high time to stop goofing around, I mused the night Mahtab and I escaped Reza's apartment. We chatted sluggishly in my suite, mainly lingering on the sofa and hoping daylight could abate our trauma from Reza's inconsiderate intrusion and finding us exposed in his bed, not to mention shattering our deep sleep—imbecile. At last, we dozed off for two hours before going to a coffee shop and mulling tensely over the likely purpose of Reza's rash travel to Vancouver. Still, we felt somewhat relieved from the agony of eluding Reza forever with no plan.

"Kay sera, sera...," Mahtab said at last cutely with a shrug as our *best perceivable plan* and we laughed superficially.

Still, living in my suite felt risky, while my conscience nagged again about the urgency of returning to reality—to gauge my shaky career, the threats lurking around us, and the wisdom of dragging Mahtab along my foggy future. Meanwhile, performing some obligatory duties as a human seemed ironically both natural and weird after having relaxed in such a soothing, long coma. Thinking straight to restart my life felt surrealistic, while too many absurd demands for coping augmented my mental and physical indolence. Then again, postponing the seemingly urgent chores only burdened my confused psyche further. *Humans' psyche and brain often have too many conflicts between them to sort out!*

At last, I decided to attend to simpler daily routines to curb my anxiety and build up my confidence for tougher so-called life responsibilities. I scanned and sorted the mail, including a letter from Erica's lawyers asking, *so considerately*, to contact them *at my convenience* to discuss some outstanding issues. What issues? Poor Erica was dead now, I mused, with distress. Those lawyers had betrayed my trust in them to finalize my divorce from Erica, so let them fret awhile until I felt ready to discuss any outstanding issue, probably a bill. No longer did I need them for a divorce, thank God, despite the sadness of the circumstance taking care of this one difficult task at least.

I peeped at Mahtab's pensive face with a mix of joy and guilt, while calling my mechanic to send someone for recharging my car's dead battery and other stuff now that we no longer had the luxury of using Reza's car, either. *At least, I still had his sister right there peeping at me curiously!* Accordingly, the tough chore of returning people's calls was postponed again as she looked bored and hungry. We went to McDonald's again for lunch, while I felt embarrassed for not only economizing at coffee shops, but also letting Mahtab pay the bills often when we went out. The situation reminded me of the time Elizabeth was living with me before I went to Iran. My self-image had been shattering for too long, while I had grown a habit of abusing my lovers' generosity. That was depressing and another immediate concern beyond my financial distress. I had to restore my pride somehow soon, too, I reckoned, in addition to so many other parts of my seemingly odd character! Gosh, living imposed too many demands, while my psyche was starting to believe that laziness has also been in my nature—yet another worrisome character flaw, instead of another effect of the coma that I had been waiting patiently to disappear on its own soon! *I must've been a dreamer, too!*

To disprove this silly idea of being a bum by nature, I set out to return the pending calls as soon as we got home. Especially, my dad's and T.J.'s messages to call my dad needed attention. So I rang him according to his elaborate scheme, while reminiscing his last, depressing call when I had been shot and bleeding on the floor, and yet getting sadder by his whining on the phone about his nutty neighbour, too. At last, he answered.

"Darren?"

"Hi, Dad."

"Oh, Darren, I'm so glad you're back with us."

"Thanks Dad. How're you?"

"I'm fine, sort of… Struggling as usual."

"Does your annoying young neighbour still bother you?"

"Yes, the nasty piglet. He's a real jackass," he replied.

"I heard your long horrific message about his new tricks, the cockroaches and all, when I was just shot and fainting."

"So you feel fine now?" he asked tenderly.

"Yes, dad. I'm feeling normal now," I replied.

"That's great... Will you come to Toronto, then, to see me and maybe even move here for good?"

"No, Dad, sorry. I have many new problems here that I should handle immediately."

"Will you come afterwards? How long before you're ready?"

"Dad, I really don't want to go live in Toronto. My apartment and friends are here."

"How about me? Don't you wanna help me even just a little? After everything I always did for you and your mother?"

"I'm stuck with big problems and don't feel too great, either."

"Didn't you just say that you felt normal now?"

"But not mentally yet," I replied, admiring his memory and continued knack for catching my blunders.

"I see…!" he said tensely.

"But I'll try to come for a visit to catch up."

"Okay, I get it. You don't give a shit," he said and hung up.

"Dad…? Dad…?"

Well, everything had sounded normal with him, including the usual hanging up at the end. So, he was fine probably!

Mahtab was busy in the kitchen, apparently unable to sleep or feeling *lonely* in the bedroom. Hopefully, she was planning for supper at home, instead of dining at a coffee shop again. She had heard some of my conversation with my dad, too.

"What happened?" she asked, entering the living room and seeing me in a haze with the receiver dangling in my hand.

"He hung up on me like usual," I said with anguish.

"Why?"

"He's been asking me to go live in Toronto. Anytime I say I prefer to stay in Vancouver he hangs up."

"He surely misses you and needs your compassion at least, if not other kinds of help," Mahtab said.

"I suppose, but I don't like to live in Toronto. Besides, he's a difficult guy to get along with."

"It's hard to humour old people, anyway. I've had similar headaches with my own parents sometimes. But we have a duty to bear them, even if we don't love them naturally."

"I agree, but don't know how, especially these days."

"What's his main shortfall, if you don't mind my asking?"

"Nothing drastic besides senility maybe. He's now suddenly religious with weird ideas and hallucinations that are hard to bear too long and he doesn't like to live in a retirement home, either."

"Maybe you should go visit him or ask him over for a week."

"Not now. You and I don't have a safe place to stay ourselves and I don't want to confuse him even more with my problems."

"Then, do something for him once things get normal here... Maybe ask him to come live in Vancouver in his own place."

"Maybe… when the dust settles around here…, if it does."

"Tell him something positive for now, just to give him hope, like going for a visit or something."

"A short visit may actually help both my dad and me."

"I think so too," she said. "Although I hate being alone even for a week. It's getting harder to be separate."

"Then, I won't go, if you'd suffer *so much*," I said childishly.

"Now you have another excuse to ignore that poor man, but let's hope we'll find a way to help him, too."

"Now you sound like T.J.—" The phone rang and I answered.

"Why did you hang up, Darren?" my dad asked.

"I didn't hang up… I thought you did," I said.

"No, you always do it when I ask you to come to Toronto. If you don't wanna come, just say so. Don't hang up or get angry."

"Dad, I have a few issues to solve and help the police with the thugs who shot me. As soon as I'm free, I'll go there and we'll discuss our options. Maybe you can come live in Vancouver or something that works for both of us. How about that?"

After a long pause, he finally talked. "Okay, Darren... I like that idea. I like to see you enough before I die one of these days. But at least call me more regularly until you come to Toronto."

"Okay, dad. You call too, if you feel like talking to someone."

This time nobody hang up as we said goodbyes civilly.

"So, at this point, we don't know who is hanging up and why, right?" Mahtab asked with a cute chuckle.

"Right… The jury is still out on this one, although we know it's related to my refusal to go live in Toronto!"

"Do you think he's lying, confused, or hoping to trick you?" she asked with a giggle, pumped up to fool around with me for a while. I was feeling much lighter and giddier swiftly, too, merely due to this simple, funny reconciliation with my dad.

"Maybe a mix of them," I replied and we laughed again. "I'll let you solve this puzzle. I have many other mysteries to tackle."

"What other mysteries?" Mahtab asked seriously.

"The mystery of life most of all... Why living feels so difficult and absurd to me these days?"

"Oh, that mystery...! Anyway, I like your dad," she said with a giggle. "He sounds tricky like you."

My dad's mental condition and calculated communication made us laugh a lot, not maliciously but caringly, until we at last decided he just had the guts to make such an outlandish claim confidently and believing to get away with it easily, too. At least he had succeeded in confusing us enough!

Although calling my dad had satiated my conscience for now, witnessing his despair and gradual demise always put plenty of pressure on me. *Sometimes,* it has felt hurtful even when I had been a stronger man with a normal life. Still, I worried about his remaining years, while I had to wrestle with so many urgent stuff for a long time and nobody else was around to help him, either. My failure—most likely a genetic flaw—to empathize with his problems wholeheartedly, the way he expected, was unsettling at least. Whether my genes were guilty, and regardless of my dire mental state nowadays, my seeming inability or unwillingness to deal with this matter without depressing myself even more was deplorable. *I was more selfish than I loved him!* I surmised with angst at last. Meanwhile, I strived to convince my sad psyche in vain that *I was not the only evil person in this world!*

Then, I started dialling T.J.'s number.

"I just fulfilled your order to call my dad *immediately,*" I said.

"After two weeks…!?" he replied wittily.

T.J. expressed his genuine sentiments for my recovery. First, he scorned my negativism and jittery mood when I said, rather jokingly, that being in a coma had felt easier and wiser, not to mention our obligation for making a living just for surviving in such a phony society. Weirdly enough, however, he changed his tune fast and agreed with my points after I asked him about his life. Swiftly, he became the one depressing me with a few hints about his wife and daughters driving him nuts.

"We're doomed, still you're luckier as usual," he said.

I sighed, hating his habit of repeating the same old gibberish anytime I had whined about *anything* and he had *still* confessed to be envious of my casual love affairs.

"Should we finally escape to a remote island, then?" I asked.

"It sounds wiser every day. We're running out of options."

"Should we ask Reza, too, if he likes to tag along?" I asked slyly to gauge T.J.'s knowledge of Reza's mood and plans.

"Yes, he's also in a mess. Just trying to find you last ten days has made him crazy," he replied.

"He found me... He's in Vancouver now, just for confronting Mahtab and me, I believe," I whispered, although the bedroom door was closed.

"I know… I saw him the other day… I guess he got tired of waiting for your call or hearing me say I couldn't find you."

"Well, sadly I had to hide and delay returning people's calls."

"You're back to normal now?" T.J. asked.

"Yes, I guess," I replied cautiously, hoping that he was not tricking me with his question, too, like my dad!

"What's going on, Darren? Are you out of your freaking mind again? Already!?" T.J. asked.

"That's exactly what I've been wondering about myself."

"Didn't you cause enough hassles for him and yourself over his first sister? What're you thinking?"

"I just don't know, T.J., but all these revelations have been beyond my control. Believe me…"

"Everything has always been beyond your control, hasn't it?"

"This is a long story, T.J. But you seem not in control of your life, either, after twenty years of trying to sort out your marriage."

"That's true. I've lost control of my wife and life, too. Now, I'm probably in a bigger mess than you are."

"So, it seems you're not an expert on these matters, after all, ha?" I said with presumed humour.

"I guess not… You'd better find yourselves a new guru."

"Listen T.J., I like to chat and we must meet soon to catch up. But I must make a few urgent calls before losing my energy."

"Sure, Darren, call me as soon as you have time for me. I'm really glad you're back with us."

"That's what everybody, including my dad, says…"

"Because we all love you."

"But I expected at least you understood my point about the value or vanity of facing this shitty reality again."

"I do, believe me. Feri reminds me every minute," T.J. said.

Finally, I gathered my strength to make another tough call.

"Oh, Darren, I'm glad hearing your voice and you're okay," Elizabeth said. "What happened to you and Erica was horrible."

"And I hope you know Jeff is responsible for everything?"

"What're you talking about?"

"I'm talking about your stupid fiancé causing this mayhem."

"How?" she cried with frustration.

"Hasn't Detective Stewart talked to him and you yet?"

"Not to me? But Jeff looks upset the last few days."

"Then perhaps they've talked."

"About what?"

"His crimes," I said with a mix of crude vengeance and wit.

"What's going on, Darren?"

"Jeff had hired the thugs who shot me and maybe threw Erica over the balcony, too?"

"I can't believe my ears… Are you sure?"

"Yes, I am. I have firsthand information I'll share with you later. For now, you'd better go check things with Jeff directly and see how clean he comes about this matter."

"Can you please give me some more details?"

"No, I'm tired and very busy now, but also really surprised he hasn't told you anything during the last three months about his role," I said tensely and said goodbye to her quickly as I noticed Mahtab coming out of the bedroom and staring at me curiously. Was Elizabeth truly unaware of Jeff's role or only testing me?

Mahtab and I decided to go for a short walk at the edge of False Creek near my building, do some grocery shopping, and have a cosy dinner at home. Outside, Mrs. Stanley was strolling with Fluffy, her cocker spaniel, as usual. As she charged towards us with excitement, I recalled the pledge to myself a week earlier to be courteous and talk to her for at least ten minutes to make up for my rudeness in our last meeting. Yet, immediately, I felt today was surely not the right time for me to be nice to anybody, either. Soon… *I'll do it soon.*

"It's good to see you again with your girlfriends like good old times. Everybody was worried and kept asking me about you."

Her genuine tone of voice broke my heart, although her naive comment about my 'girlfriends' could taint my image in front of Mahtab; unless she had done it slyly for reprisal! I also wondered why people had kept asking *her* about me, before recalling her self-appointment as our building's Sheriff!

"Thanks, Mrs. Stanley. I'm happy to see you, too. Thanks also for holding the floor in my absence," I said, baffled about my rising impatience towards elderly.

"You're welcome…," she said to me before turning towards Mahtab. "I see you've returned to Vancouver, too."

Mahtab looked puzzled and I realized Mrs. Stanley's mistake.

"She's not who you think," I said hastily, while both women peered at me with confusion. "She's her sister."

"You're Mahroo's sister?" Mrs. Stanley asked.

Both Mahtab and I nodded with melancholy.

"You look so like her. Is she here too?"

"No, she's not, I'm afraid," I said.

"She's a really nice girl… How's she these days?"

I noticed tears gathering in Mahtab's eyes.

"She had an accident and passed away a few months ago," I said with gloom and grabbed Mahtab's arm to start our stroll.

"I'm so sorry… She was an angel already!" Mrs. Stanley said with a genuine tone and sad eyes. "She gave me a nice present, too, before returning to Iran. I liked her a lot…"

"Even strangers loved her," I told Mahtab as we ambled with our eyes filled with tears and our throats clogged from emotions. Mahtab started crying openly as I held her tight in my arms in the same spot and manner I had held and kissed the sobbing Mahroo a couple of days before her departure to Tehran.

We walked only a short distance, sat on a bench, and watched the Creek and the boats sailing smoothly in the distance. We held hands and kissed occasionally, but mostly talked about Mahroo. I showed Mahtab the Aquabus (or the gondola in my mind) that carries people between the two banks of the False Creek. Then, I told her about the times Mahroo and I had taken the gondola to Granville Island on the other side and engaged in very heated and often controversial arguments. I told her how good Mahroo had been in making sound arguments, especially about love, so deep sometimes I had felt totally stupid a few times. My account of Mahroo's words, arguments, and habits made Mahtab relax and feel good and happy. She chuckled a few times when I recounted Mahroo's tough stands against my silly opinions. So, I mentioned more of my memories with her and she did the same, as if that particular evening belonged only to Mahroo and her connection to us and nothing else. We had suddenly forgotten our worries and plans, until we started feeling cold and hungry. At last, we went for a quick grocery shopping before returning home in a splendid mood.

Mahtab's delicious spaghetti with meatballs again reminded me of Mahroo often cooking the same dish as tastefully during the few months she and her parents lived in this building. We drank wine and discussed our situation with stress and frustration about so many people's tenacity to spoil our love affair. *How dare they?* I thought wittily before trying to make Mahtab laugh, too.

"How dare these people butt in our lives?" I asked seriously before laughing. When she only smirked, I tried to restore the pensive mood she seemed to prefer at that moment, "I'm sorry we can't dine out often until I find some money."

"Don't worry about these things. I like cooking," she replied.

"Are you sure…?" I asked for teasing her.

"Yes, I'm sure," she replied.

"Otherwise, I must start looking for work or a gallery to sell my paintings, although I don't even have any painting."

"I should find a job, too," she replied with a soft chuckle. "My late father left us plenty of money and I'm glad I refused Bijan's request to mix our assets even after he got nasty and persistent."

"You've been smart. That's the right way nowadays."

"Now the problem is that I can't go to Iran to send money here. Reza and my mom might stop doing it, too."

"Would they do that?"

"It's possible. Everybody is mad at me for coming here and ignoring Bijan. Even my family seems to take his side instead of understanding my gloom for living with him and in Iran."

"Even I think you've been brave and taken a big risk," I said.

"My family thinks I came here only for a silly infatuation I've grown for you, the way Mahroo had."

"I thought the same thing myself," I said, hoping to be witty.

"What do you mean?"

"I also thought you left Bijan and Iran only for me?"

She smiled and kissed me. "No, it is also for myself... It's not only for you, my darling."

"Great…," I exclaimed with a fake sigh of relief to tease her more. "Then I should feel less guilty now!"

"And also less self-satisfied, maybe!" she said with a chuckle.

"Well... That'd be tough for anybody in my position," I said.

She laughed again. "You mean for anybody who can steal married women's hearts so easily?"

"Exactly," I replied, enjoying her growing sense of humour.

"But then if I get a bit poorer, I'll have to go back..."

"Don't worry. I'll make money somehow," I replied after a pause with deep doubts about my ability to keep my promise. "Although it seems more likely that I must sell my condo."

"So you'll be homeless soon, too, like me," she said jokingly.

"At least we still have each other, right?" I asked either wittily or desperately if my subconscious was already anticipating the chance and pain of losing her.

"For now at least...," she said and burst into laughter.

"I can't live alone here or in the streets if we are homeless."

"But I can't promise anything about living in the streets," she said giddily. "I'd probably have to go back to Iran in that case!"

"You're really cruel with me tonight, but also cute," I replied playfully. "Did you put pot in our dinner?"

"No, but you can't have the right for all the teasing."

"That was a good wine, anyway, and we drunk a lot, I guess."

"Yes, I liked it too," she said, staring at me with passion. "But can I stay with you while you still have this condo?"

"Of course... As long as you realize the danger of living here, especially if the thugs come back to finish me."

"I'll have to take the risk mostly since I have no other place to go, but also for being with you…, while you have this place!"

"You're not only homeless, but also a little heartless today for not loving me totally," I said.

"Maybe tomorrow… Today we'll only whine about money."

"Don't fret. We'll be okay, like it happens in mushy movies or operas," I said.

"Yes, we'll both be rich again soon, too!" she said giddily.

"Do you recall any movie or novel in which lovers fuss over money or discuss it so seriously like us ?" I asked with a giggle.

"No, not until they're finally married," she said.

"Yeah, it's like they own a restaurant or never get hungry."

"It's just another known side-effect of love," I said pensively. "Lovers lose their sleep and appetite and then their brains."

"But not us. We're regaining some of our senses."

"And you're already planning to leave me if we're homeless," I said jokingly. "But, seriously, the way lovers seem adamant to only live together or die with love sounds crazy to me!"

"No, it's not... Let's do the same," she said half-teasingly.

"In our case, we're lucky to have enough enemies to kill us before we suffer hunger and die in the streets," I said giddily.

"Are you going to start painting soon?" she asked anxiously, as if all these talks about destitute and homelessness had finally worried her after restoring her senses.

"Yes, I promise," I said hastily before she started packing.

"That's a good idea," she replied with a *furtive* sigh of relief in a mysterious tone. *She was most likely joking, too! Yet, I wasn't sure.*

"Actually, I feel an urge recently to finish that one at least," I replied, pointing to the incomplete painting on the wall.

She stared at the painting awhile. "This is a powerful scene from *Tosca* for painting."

"Yes. Finishing it might be the best way to get back to my normal routines and have something to show to galleries."

"Don't you work with a particular gallery?" she asked.

"I did until six months ago before we had a situation and now I must try all over to find another gallery if I do some paintings."

"I think you should also consider painting my portrait as soon as possible before hunger and worries make me thin and ugly."

"In that case, I'd better start tomorrow…," I replied with both wit and worry. "But I thought you weren't interested in doing your portrait to avoid competing with Mahroo's!"

"I know… I've had my doubts. Looking so alike has caused odd situations and decisions sometimes."

"That's how I've also felt about doing your portrait, although it'd be a good challenge to distinguish and display those few tiny personality differences that appear in your faces subtly, too."

"I also feel jealous now about you having painted only her."

"I couldn't imagine you'd ever be jealous of Mahroo," I said.

"Only in a loving manner... Although...," she paused, looking pensive and distressed.

"Although what?" I asked at last with curiosity and worry.

"A few times in fact I had stupidly felt jealous of her," she said in a dramatic tone. "But I don't wanna talk about it."

"Are you okay?" I asked as tears sluiced down her cheeks.

"Yes... You just live and paint like I'm not around," she said hastily and seriously to change the subject, as though her swift reminder of her past jealousy towards Mahroo had revolted her.

"Oh, don't talk so formal. I loved your wit and teasing me all day. Let's be like that forever," I asked Mahtab with love.

"Sure. But let's also get serious about a plan to handle Reza."

Our whining tonight, especially about destitute, would certainly sound silly for novels or movies! I cursed my brain for analysing, instead of forgetting, life's basic realities that all humans embrace obediently without dwelling on them like me. Still, many bits and pieces of the reality I was expected to understand and indulge felt strenuous and irrational, let alone thrilling, aside from the fact that Mahtab was in it to stir some mesmeric moments. Especially, any presumed duty towards some precious people—mostly Mahtab and my dad—or even being fully connected and accountable to them amidst many other emotional pressures mostly reignited my two recent doubts about the value of my being and the validity of my character.

Adopting some illusive ideals with hopes for happiness and relief *supposedly* reflected the meaning and nature of life and I was now expected to rebuild my senses and future like others, at least for Mahtab's sake. Maybe she had been a sacred cause, after all—even a divine intervention maybe—to stop my inkling for the option of inexistence, I mused. Still, being a reliable lover and provider or a decent son, at least by engaging in short chitchats with my dad, felt tougher and stupider than jumping off a cliff. During these moments of truth, regaining the urge and energy to face life's hassles and duties did not feel straight forward enough for my liking at the present time at least.

These erratic emotions and reflections also made me wonder if reality had felt this illogical before my coma! This proved to be a great question that made me reflect and recall another fact about my curious personality: My mood had always been jittery, while I had strived for years to cure myself in vain. *Why wasn't even the power of love healing at least my chronic pessimism, then?* I mused playfully while watching Mahtab go back to the bedroom.

Chapter Fifteen
The Dying Spot

My indecision, after all the pains of my rushed, long travel to Vancouver with so much reminiscing and planning, felt quite embarrassing, while Darren and Mahtab did not answer my polite phone messages and pleading at least. I also went to his building a couple of times, rang his suite's buzzer awhile uselessly, and left in rage. Their apathy was humiliating, but fathomable for two rebellious romantics shacking up casually and assuming people would stop looking for them or cannot find them if they merely refused to answer the phone or the building's buzzer. Idiots! I was merely amazed of Mahtab's nonchalant disregard for such a fanatic husband and playing with fire like a maniac. At last, I left a threatening message for the lovebirds. "Avoiding me wouldn't solve your problems. Bijan is now totally out of control and we'd better work together to find a solution before he does something crazy that would hurt all of us."

It worked. Darren called me with distress and we agreed to meet at the coffee shop near his building.

"I'm speechless," I said to him after we settled at a table.

"Let's go back home, then," Darren replied mockingly.

"Can't you leave her alone even a few minutes," I said. "Must my sisters' lives be at your mercy forever?"

"Listen, Reza, I've never forced your sisters to be kind to me. They're nice by nature and we happen to share similar thoughts."

"But you seem to have some special effect on women to drive them away from their husbands and families."

"I wonder if I can say the same thing about you?" he replied mockingly with sarcasm.

"No you can't, if you're referring to Erica again. But even if I was guilty, too, it doesn't wash your guilt or effect on women."

"In this case, I was even in a coma when Mahtab came over."

"But both Bijan and I now believe you must've done or said something to her when you were in Barcelona."

"I promise, I never asked her to do anything for me or leave Bijan for any reason, especially me."

"So how all these things happened? Why are we in the middle of this big mess, then?"

"What mess are you talking about first of all?" Darren asked.

"Are you kidding me or only stupid? I really do not have time for playing games with you two."

"We're not in the mood to play games, either," he replied.

"What're you two planning to do, then?"

"Nothing special. We're just attracted to each other and wish to spend some time together, if possible."

"But it's impossible! She's still married to a very angry man."

"We can imagine that, too," Darren replied with angst.

"So, what? Are you numb about the consequence of your silly infatuation, then?"

"What do you expect me to do, Reza? Just tell me and I'll do my best to fulfil your request."

"Just let Mahtab go back to Iran," I replied.

"I'm not stopping her, but you must respect her choices, too."

"The thing is that she, and most likely you too, are probably lost in your delusions about love and happiness together."

"I don't think Mahtab is a child to get delusional. She seems to have been making all the right decisions, except perhaps for marrying a fanatic like Bijan. Everybody can make mistakes once in a while."

"And now her infatuation with you might be her second big mistake and cause a great deal of bloodshed."

"Bloodshed?"

"Yes, bloodshed... Don't be naïve, Darren… You guys should not underestimate Bijan and his affiliates," I said.

"But we can't understand or overrule Mahtab's feelings about living in Iran with Bijan, can we?"

"But she might think better if she's not so attached to you. Now, her brain might not be working full speed."

"Staying around me is her decision, too, not mine," he replied.

"Darren, I have not come here to argue about things, but only explain what will happen if she doesn't go back to at least get her divorce."

"She says she'll do that, too," he said casually like a fool.

"But she must do that first, instead of causing a scandal."

"Okay then. Explain what could happen now," Darren said.

"Bijan has sent me to state his ultimatum to you in particular. He wants to give you just one last chance."

"Or else?"

"He would let Colonel Arshadi loose to do whatever he likes with you at least."

"Who the hell is Colonel Arshadi now?"

"Your son's angry uncle," I replied.

"Yeah, I recall the famous colonel. Bijan told me about him."

"He wants you to know how tricky the situation could get if he no longer keeps the colonel in check."

"So he's told you the secret he'd forced me to keep forever?"

"Yes, he had to, I guess..., just to make the gravity of the situation clear to both of us."

"Who else knows about this supposed secret?"

"I've mentioned it only to T.J."

"T.J.? Does this means that we can now share it with people"

"I don't know. I said it only to T.J. to help me find a solution."

"Did Bijan also tell you that my imprisonment was only for making me agree to keep everything to myself?"

"Yes."

"Does Sima's family know about Bijan's sudden madness and revealing their secret so casually?"

"Probably not. The thing is that not even Bijan knows what he's doing these days. He's just gone nuts, I tell you."

"You'd better find out and let me know, too," Darren said.

"Find out what?"

"That he no longer cares about me revealing the secret about my son. If he can do it, I must be allowed to do it, too."

"I'll ask him," I replied. "But I don't think that can help."

"Tell him I've kept my mouth shut all along only for his sake. I didn't mention it even to you."

"The way he talked, it also sounded serious to me," I said.

"Actually, he insisted or exaggerated that there'll be a civil war in Iran if Bijan's father or Sima's uncle betray each other's goodwill and let this secret out. He forced me to promise on my honour."

"On your what…? Honour…?"

"I had some at least then!" he replied wittily.

"So, why so many people are now lining up to at least kill you for dishonouring them?" I asked tensely. "They're all probably also thinking that your son is better off with you dead."

"So, they want to kill me at least, ha?"

"Yes, you'd better think about Bijan's ultimatum."

"I will, but you also ask him if he no longer cares about me sharing the information about my son with others... I should let a few people and maybe the police know all these facts right away before anybody kills me," Darren said with an idiotic giggle.

"It's now certain that coma has ruined your brain altogether."

"Just ask Bijan my question, anyway."

"Okay, but he doesn't seem to care about anything, not even his father's promises to Sima's uncle, their honours, or even a civil war in Iran. He's just gone crazy, I'm telling you."

"Then, tell him that besides talking about my son to people, I may even hire some lawyers here to assess my chance of getting a visiting right if I gather the courage to go back to Iran. Maybe I can at least now contact Sima to discuss or see my son."

"Ok, I'll ask him your questions and tell him not to count on you honour any more, either. But you're playing with an angry lion's tail."

"Why do we men lose our minds when we get obsessed about a particular woman?" Darren asked with despair.

"Have you asked yourself that question first?"

"Yes, and still have no definite answer. What do you think?"

"It's because we're such insecure, weak creatures, way more than women are apparently," I replied.

"You think this Colonel Arshadi or others can find and harm me here in Vancouver?" Darren asked with some air of concern showing in his eyes for the first time all afternoon.

"Yes. They have thugs around the world, but in this special case, the colonel might take the trouble of traveling here himself to teach you a lesson personally."

"Everybody is trying to teach me a lesson these days," Darren said, probably hinting about the reason for him being shot and put in a coma.

"So you'd better start acting a bit more wisely before getting killed this time."

"I don't wanna fight with anybody. I just wanna get back on my feet now and learn to live again. But I can't force Mahtab."

"But you must convince her to forget about you or at least get out of Vancouver. You two not living in the same city might put Bijan's mind at ease a little for now, until she decides what to do. I bet she'll return to Tehran if you're out of her life."

"I don't think so," he replied. "But is it fair or right for her or me if I do that? Forcing her out of my life is as much of a crime as pushing her to stay here with me if she wasn't totally sure. I only want her to be happy. Don't you?"

"That's my biggest desire. Can't you two see that?"

"Then, we must let her make her decisions."

"But Bijan wants her to go back and get her divorce civilly. His pride is extremely bruised and he blames you mostly for his honour being shattered in front of his family and friends."

"And he expects Mahtab to trust his promise?" Darren asked.

"Yes, that's what he wants."

"I don't think she's that naive. How can she believe him when he's already ignoring his earlier agreement to live separately and divorce her if she asked for it at the end? He's already reneged on his previous promise to her."

"I don't think they've had that kind of agreement. But Mahtab has been provoking his already messed-up mind by refusing to even speak with him on the phone for two minutes," I said.

"Maybe...! She's actually been playing with this angry lion's manhood besides its tail," he said with another silly, tense giggle.

"Can you at least convince her to see me and listen to all these points directly instead of you and me speaking for her?"

"I'll try, but don't hold your breath," Darren said.

"Is she in your apartment right now?" I asked.

"She was when I left to come here," he replied.

I sipped my coffee, replaced the cup, and rose. "Let's go to your apartment right now and talk with her."

"No, this is not a good idea. She'll not talk to you and get mad at me, too."

"We must take the risk. I don't have much time to sort out this matter and report to Bijan," I said and stormed out of the café.

"Wait, Reza. This isn't the right way to handle Mahtab. Don't you still know your sisters?" he yelled while following me.

"There's never been any right way to deal with my sisters. They've always been so difficult and selfish. Let's go confront her," I yelled back at Darren.

"No, I can't partake in this plot or let you in my building."

"I'll go upstairs somehow."

"She won't open the door, I'm sure. Don't cause any more problems for both of us. Let's handle this diplomatically."

"How? Do you have a better suggestion," I said as I opened my car's doors for us to get in.

"At least let me go ask her first if she's in the mood to see you right now," Darren suggested.

"Okay, okay. Close the door," I said and started the car.

I parked near Darren's building and we walked towards it fast.

"You wait here until I come back, promise me," Darren said as we got close to the building entrance.

"Okay, I promise," I said.

"By the way, this is the exact spot Erica hit the asphalt when she fell from my balcony."

We both looked up at Darren's balcony; then he shook his head and walked towards the entrance. I lingered in awe, startled by the idea of standing on Erica's dying spot. I imagined her tiny body shattered into pieces four months earlier and her blood flowing everywhere. Swiftly, I felt terribly sad and missed her so much, much more than ever. I cursed my stupidity to let her leave me merely out of our seemingly justified tenacities at the time.

I had been missing Erica a lot all along, but now standing at this daunting spot was causing big havoc in my heart and head. I regretted our arguments about the *Woman in the White Dress*—for giving it to Mahroo instead of Erica. I had been only hoping to help Mahroo reassess her situation and regain her confidence through that symbolic painting. Yet, I had failed on that ground as well. The painting had caused only more headaches and her ultimate demise after making her love Darren—again for all the wrong reasons and romantic imaginations.

The idea of a cursed painting making Mahroo fall in love with Darren and Erica fall out of love for me after falling in love with Darren again before falling down his balcony—the four horrible falls related to Darren and leading to the deaths of my two most precious beloveds—was bizarre and upsetting. The way these odd love episodes had caused so many deaths, with the chance of more bloodshed looming, was driving me nuts. However, it also seemed that anybody loving Darren had endured a daunting fate and even sudden death judging by Mahroo's and Erica's endings. That was why I had no wife to soothe my spirit and had lost one sister that could console and help the other married sister think straight at such a critical time. Yes, this painter appeared to be a bigger curse himself, after all, than that particular painting of his.

How horrifically our decisions and fates had mixed and led to catastrophes one after another! Mahtab's actions in recent months showed that she had been also affected by that cursed painting when Mahroo had mysteriously given it to Mahtab just a few weeks before dying! Gosh, if only I had given it to Erica in the first place, instead of Mahroo, they both would be alive right now and happy in their simpler worlds. Erica and I would have most likely been married, too. What I had done—just out of love and worries for Mahroo—was unforgivable. I deserved a punishment for meddling in Mahroo's life and ruining many lives, including my own. And now, I was doing a similar thing to Mahtab. Now, lingering with remorse at Erica's dying spot and sobbing subtly, I prayed Darren could get me an audience with my other equally sentimental sister. *In fact, maybe I've been the curse, not Darren or his painting, after all! Why can't I forgive myself? Should I leave Mahtab alone?*

Still, not all these regrets and lessons felt like good reasons to sit idly by and let Mahtab also make the mistake of loving Darren. Instead, the most relevant point today, like a divine reminder, was that as much as I had loved Erica, I had adored Mahroo even more at the cost of losing Erica and the chance of enjoying our few naughty kids together these days. So, letting only my love for Mahtab and our mom dictate my decisions now made complete sense. My mission now felt even more sacred, too, merely for making Mahtab grasp the risks of her actions and the curse of loving Darren—this doomed painter who was angry with me merely for telling him to get out of our lives.

Lost in a cloud of rueful and romantic reflections, Darren emerged out of his building with a long face.

"Did you mourn Erica enough while I was gone?" he asked with his annoying sarcasm.

"Yes, thanks for showing me the spot we lost our love idol," I replied with a grimace.

"You're welcome. So, do you remember now what being in love means? Maybe now you realize what Mahtab and I might be going through?"

"Actually, I just realized something even more miraculous and maybe romantic as well," I said.

"What is that?"

"Although we still don't know if Erica jumped herself, maybe out of love for you, she surely saved your life, anyway."

"What do you mean?" Darren asked with surprise.

"Well, if Erica had not fallen off your balcony right after you were shot or if those thugs had shot her, too, the police and the paramedic would've not come and found your body in time. You would've bled to death before your corpse was discovered or somebody could help you."

"Wow… You're right… My corpse would've rotten in the apartment for sure, because hardly nobody checks on me."

"I'm surprised you hadn't thought about this before," I said.

"I haven't had a chance to think much about anything yet. I haven't yet even figured out how to pay my bills."

"Because you've been busy with Mahtab every minute since you've come out of the coma, ha?"

"Of course… But I'm glad you figured out this Erica's thing. Maybe that was the whole purpose of bringing you here to this spot myself."

"It probably was, and you're welcome," I replied.

"Now I must show lots more gratitude towards Erica and feel more guilt for what happened to her," he said with a sigh. "Let's walk away from this sacred spot."

"Walk away? Go get a permit from the city to build a small garden and maybe put a statue of her to show your appreciation."

"Of course… I'll think about it if you pay for the project."

"I'll be happy to do it. I owe her a lot, too, for other reasons."

"Okay, let's do this joint project for our shared beloved."

"So what'd Mahtab say? Can I speak with her?" I asked.

"No, she doesn't wanna talk with you," Darren replied.

"Why?"

"She knows what you wanna say and she's not interested."

"Do you know why she's so angry with me?"

"Besides meddling in her life?"

"Yes…"

"She's angry about your previous arguments with her about coming to Vancouver in the first place. She believes she's played a major role in saving my life, which would've been impossible had she listened to you."

"You can see that she's gone cuckoo, right?"

"No, actually, I appreciate everything she's done to save my life, thanks to her stubbornness to ignore your advice. I would've most likely died if you had it your way."

"Thank God… Your death would've been my fault, too, if she'd listened to me," I said. "I'm responsible for many already."

"Yeah… The kind of friend you've turned out to be!"

"Well, okay… Maybe I was wrong about Dr. Mahtab's knack for healing you… Now what?"

"Now, I must build another garden somewhere with Mahtab's statue, too, as a token of my appreciation for her saving my life again after Erica had done it first."

"Yes, you're right… Two women have saved your life one after another—the life of a man who's caused the deaths of Erica and Mahroo himself."

"You must pay for the costs of building this second garden, too," Darren said.

"I'll pay, since I've felt guilty for these deaths as well."

"Now I belong to Mahtab, then, at least for saving my life. In fact, you just made me love her and feel indebted to her even more, didn't you?"

"Yes, you owe every single day you live to Erica and Mahtab now," Reza said. "Are you such a lucky man or what?!"

"Now, it is my turn to protect and respect Mahtab's desires, then. I must be her slave forever."

"I don't know what to do anymore, Darren. Please help…"

"Neither do I! I'm in a haze myself these days," Darren said.

"At least you have her ears… Please do your best to make her understand the gravity of our situation if you really love her."

"Do you think Bijan might hurt Mahtab and you as well?"

"Don't you worry about getting killed yourself?" I asked.

"I'm still undecided, but often don't mind dying," he replied.

"I don't know how far Bijan might go. But he just doesn't act normal these days after he heard she'd been nursing you during the coma and now guessing that she's still here because of you."

"Well, if he kills me, I guess Mahtab would go after him and he'll be forced to hurt her and you as well," Darren said.

"Now, finally, you seem to get the picture! We'll all get hurt merely because he is mad about his wife," I replied.

"I hope he doesn't know where she's living these days?" he asked fretfully.

"I hope so, too, but we can't hide from him much longer. In fact, I often think he may already have spies watching all of us."

"Why do you think that?"

"Well, for one thing, I still don't know how he'd found out about your recovery so fast," I replied.

"Maybe you're right... Maybe that's how he even knew about Mahtab visiting me during the coma?"

"It's very likely... We must be really careful, Darren."

"I wish I knew how... But do you think he'd been suspecting something happening between Mahtab and me even before my coma?" Darren asked.

"Yes, I believe so…," I replied.

"Why? How?"

"It is not hard to guess these things. Especially, since he knew about your affair with Mahroo, he imagines, correctly mind you, that Mahtab has become Mahroo's replacement in your broken heart and mind."

"It sounds like a logical conclusion, I'd say," Darren said.

"It is easy for people to draw these conclusions," I said. "You don't have to be a genius or psychiatrist to guess."

"And oddly enough, it may actually be true, too, without me or Mahtab realizing it, either," he said.

"That's exactly what I'm also worried about. You both might realize soon that you've been affected by Mahroo's death and all the sentiments surrounding it," I said sternly with stress.

"You might also be right… I'm confused myself and maybe Mahtab is under some kind of spell, too."

"Most likely she is… Maybe it's also related to the curse of your damn painting again… That's why we should do something before it is too late."

"I can't think of anything I could or should do at this point," Darren replied with gloom.

"You can talk to her if you really want to help."

"I don't think so… She'll only get angry with me."

"So, you're not willing to promise anything today, are you?" I asked with desperation.

"Listen Reza, I can only promise to talk to Mahtab about your concerns and push her a little to see you and listen to your pleas."

"That's all I want, but please push her a lot," I said and Darren nodded.

"There's something else I would like to ask you, Reza."

"What?" I asked.

"The situation with my paintings in Iran. Are they sold now?"

"Oh, yes, they are."

"How should I contact the gallery to send me my money?"

"We've already got the money, which is around $28,000."

"Have you brought it with you?"

"No… That's another condition Bijan has imposed on me."

"What do you mean?"

"He doesn't want me to release the money, until this situation is settled and she's at least away from Vancouver and you."

"Why do you listen to him, Reza? I'm really short of cash these days."

"I must obey him because I want to keep some kind of leash on Bijan and stop him from hurting my sister or me. He can do it in so many ways you'd never imagine."

"This is getting really out of control!"

"This is just only the beginning, I promise, my friend."

"Why don't you give me my money, anyway? I won't tell him or anybody else."

"I'll think about it, but I'm afraid to take any risk and act against Bijan's orders."

"Are you also afraid of him?"

"Yes, I am, sort of. You'd be, too, if you knew him and his friends, including this Colonel Arshadi. Besides, I'm also upset about the situation here. I'm still your friend, but feel unhappy about our friendship these days after your behaviour, especially not returning my calls."

"I couldn't call, and I hope you'll forgive me," he said.

"I'll try, if you don't push me and your luck too much."

"I've been trying to do my best, believe me," he replied.

"We should repair our friendship again soon as well, I hope—this time over my second sister you've spoiled!"

"Then lend me some money first. Do you want us lovers die of hunger?" Darren said with a charming plea.

I laughed loudly and replied, "Well, that'd be a great solution for everything and make Bijan completely happy, too."

"Then you guys don't have to wait much longer… We are destitute. Your sister hasn't had a decent meal for a week now and she's getting too skinny already! She doesn't have energy to talk or listen to you, either."

"Listen, Darren, I'll give you your money privately, behind Bijan's back, if you can convince Mahtab to see me for an hour and listen to my concerns. She might change her mind if you go back and spend enough time and energy to tell her everything I've said about the situation and Bijan's wicked plans. Will you do that," I begged him.

"I'll do my best, I promise," he said.

"Do you want hundred bucks for your dinner tonight?"

"No, but thanks for the offer," Darren said giddily and left.

I stood next to my car and peeped at him stagger towards his building pensively. He stopped at the spot I had mourned Erica myself a few minutes earlier, looked up at his balcony, shook his head, and resumed walking. I wondered how often he did this ritual nowadays and how much longer he might keep doing it in the future if he stayed in this building. His mourning and gloom at Erica's dying spot would probably even heighten now after realizing that only her timely arrival and fall had saved his life. He turned and peered at me, as if he had heard my thoughts, then waved before disappearing inside the lobby. The manner we both seemed haunted, perhaps forever, with our romantic memories of Erica—such a selfish, eccentric woman—felt surreal.

Chapter Sixteen
Moving Out

My corny habit of comparing the messes we haunted friends —Darren, Reza, and I—were in at any point felt unseemly. Yet, our sardonic analyses of our moods and conundrums for fighting the evilest people on earth, especially my cruel family, had been amusing as well! To me, their current snags and fights with some vengeful people felt rather transitory relative to my terminal stance with a broken family after two decades of honest efforts to prevent this exact situation. They still had some hope and time to change course and redeem themselves eventually if they just made a few decisions properly. I, however, could not even hope about my future getting at least bearable again at my age after the ugliest fight with Feri and my daughters. I wished they had time and patience to hear about my dwindling life and I had the nerve to rub the new developments all over their already frantic faces. Now, communicating with, and salvaging, my family appeared impossible, as they had ganged up and humiliated me fiercer in recent months, while I had tried harder to explain my concerns to these selfish, illogical women as politely as possible. Suddenly, my stay in that big house—my home—was stressful amongst a mob of ungrateful beloveds who saw me as a misplaced alien and their biggest enemy. Worst of all, my lifetime diligent planning and efforts to support and cherish a selfish family felt absolutely ridiculous. I simply had to go live somewhere more civilized where my presence was not so openly resented. But where could I possibly go? At last, I decided to ask Darren about the chance of staying with him for a week or so until I could put a longer-term plan together. My brain was so tired I had forgotten all about Mahtab possibly living with him these days.

I left Darren a message, pondering people's new habit of not answering their phones or returning my calls more civilly; or else I was getting too picky about these simple matters as well. *I am the only person left on this planet with traditional principles and mannerism,* I mused sombrely, while imagining the chance of my family resenting me for the same thing. Luckily, the phone rang to stop my sense of self-pity carrying me to even sadder realms.

"Thanks for calling back quickly," I said teasingly, yet loathed my cheeky mouth exposing my cranky mood, despite my recent pledge to myself to act a bit more diplomatically around people.

"Sorry for my tardiness and not getting together. But we'll do it soon now that Reza is also here," Darren replied.

"I hope so, too, while we're still sane and have some energy."

"Are you okay, T.J.?" he asked.

"No, I'm not. My life is just getting odder and sadder."

"Let me guess…; your wife again, eh?"

"Of course… Nobody else is eager to torture me this much."

"I thought you've realized that having a family takes lots of patience and sacrifice. We're all stuck in this social mandate."

"I hope you and Reza remember this wisdom, especially you in your current situation."

"You mean, before falling in love again?" he asked.

"Exactly... Remember my agony and naggings, too."

"How can we forget?" Darren asked with a chuckle. "Your endless stories have killed even the tiniest faith we used to have about this matter after our own sour experiences. You've ruined our perceptions of marriage forever. Now you remember this...!"

"That's exactly what Reza said a few months ago about you and I ruining his brain."

"He's right. We've damaged Reza the most, haven't we?" he asked wittily and we laughed.

"Yes, I guess we have with our marital stories, especially, but for the better," I replied.

"How can you damage someone for the better?"

"He's smarter now, and maybe happier more often as well, despite his loneliness."

"Still, all we can do now is to just sit back and make the best of all the nonsense around us," Darren said.

"I just can't do that anymore," I replied with angst seriously.

"What do you mean? Getting ready for suicide at last?"

"No, I'm just gonna escape for now. I need a break at least."

"Escape where?" Darren asked.

"I don't know yet."

"Staying away from Feri awhile may help. Let's find time to also meet after so long if you're still in town."

"Maybe your chance to indulge me for a couple of weeks has come up, you lucky man," I said with a chuckle.

"What do you mean?"

"I was wondering if I could stay with you for a week or two until I sort out what I should do. We can also catch up a little."

"Oh, T.J., Mahtab is living here these days, too?"

"Oh, I didn't know," I said, while suddenly Reza's hint about Mahtab running after Darren rolled in my head.

"One or two nights would be okay, but Mahtab and I are in a tough situation and must sort out many private stuff."

"I understand, sorry... But she's got nerve shacking up with you. I mean for a woman married to an angry, fanatical husband the way Reza explains him."

"We're aware of the situation, but thanks for the notice. I'm also gonna tell her what you said about her nerve."

"Oh, no. Please don't… I hope she isn't around to hear you."

"No, she's taking a shower," Darren replied.

"Good... But she's really brave."

"There's a kind of recklessness or perhaps even lunacy in this family. We've talked about it before and you actually witnessed a big instance with Mahroo yourself. Do you remember?"

"I do. But you act equally reckless yourself, if I may say so."

"I agree, but I'm stuck again, believe me," Darren replied.

"I know… You always get trapped in tough love episodes. I'm crying for you every night, too."

"That's my fate and I'm tired of fighting it!" he said. "I don't even have some extra tears to lend you at least, now that I can't give you a room."

"That's fine… Anyway, good luck fighting your tricky fate."

"So, what're you gonna do?" Darren asked.

"I don't know… Maybe go live in a motel or something."

"Why don't you call Reza? He has an extra bedroom now."

"I don't know… Mahtab may wanna go back there soon…"

"Maybe... Sorry for not showing enthusiasm myself," he said.

"Don't worry. I just remembered it's dangerous to be around you lovers these days, anyway, from what I hear."

"That's true too," Darren said.

"I still prefer a natural death," I said rhetorically, but didn't mind a quick end, instead of becoming a familyless, homeless, hopeless, and helpless man after a lifetime of mindless struggles. In fact, I envied Darren even for having so many enemies who may come any minute to relieve his burdens of living and loving. I wished I could at least stop loving my kids—one less burden—now that God was adamant to keep them so vulgar and silly!

"Go make up with Feri and bear her silliness if possible at all," Darren said childishly, although I appreciated his good intentions.

"Despite your sad experiences, you're still naive about family pains and humiliation these days, especially during old age."

"You're right again… I'm such a forgetful man!"

"That's worrisome now…; when your new love story needs both fast and long-term risky decisions," I said matter-of-factly.

"I know… I'm worried a lot about that myself, too, T.J.," he replied solemnly. "Who's gonna help us now that we three are lost in our deep messes at the same time?"

"God knows... But I must insist again that my situation is much graver than yours and Reza's."

"I disagree! I'm not trying to compete with anybody, T.J., but only to give you some hope. Go reconcile with Feri."

I felt so wise after deciding not to even respond to his idea.

I called Reza, anyway, and he agreed graciously to let me stay with him, as I promised to move out if Mahtab decided to return home after coming to her senses by a miracle, which sounded like a funny dream! I was surely safe in Reza's place with no worry about homelessness at least! Obviously, Reza was curious about my rebellion at home and leaving when I arrived with my small suitcase and sad face. So, I felt both obliged and eager to whine as a price for his hospitality.

"Basically, they've all ganged up against me now and hate my guts to be alive or live in my own house," I said in the end.

"Did something special happen recently?"

"Well, I did an odd thing last week," I said with a tense giggle.

"What'd you do this time?" Reza asked with a chuckle.

"Well, this time my youngest daughter caught me right in the middle of counting their shoes."

"Counting their shoes?" Reza shrieked with loud laughter.

"Yes. I'd been wondering for a long time about the number of shoes Feri and our three daughters had altogether. So, a few days ago, when I was alone and bored to my bones, I decided to satisfy my curiosity. I counted Feri's and my elder daughters' shoes in forty minutes. I was almost done with my youngest daughter's shoes, too, when she sneaked upon me and made a big fuss about being in her room. My damned usual bad luck!

'What're you looking for?' she asked with fury.

'I was counting your shoes,' I replied jokingly, hoping to turn this catastrophe into a laughing matter. Stupidly, I thought telling the truth was better than an excuse that raised more suspicions."

"Oh, gosh… You've really done it this time," Reza said after laughing loudly awhile.

"Anyway, she made a big scene and reported my tyranny to everybody. The whole night they yelled at me and made me feel terrible about myself, but more so for creating and feeding them."

Reza laughed louder and longer. "So, how many shoes did they have?" he asked at last.

"I couldn't count the last pile, but there were over 338 pairs of shoes between the four of them. They donate a bunch of shoes and clothing to charities every few months as well."

"Wow…! Just multiply that by the average price of a pair of shoes and that's a lot of money," he said.

"Not to mention the amount of time and energy wasted on shopping around, buying, exchanging them, etc."

"Did you tell'em your reason for doing it and the final tally?"

"Yes. I thought I was making an important point with humour, while justifying my intrusion of their privacy, too."

"What did they say?" Reza asked with a chuckle

"My reasoning and explanations only made the matter worse. The more logic I presented, the angrier they got."

"Did they give any explanations of their own at least?" Reza asked to prod me for more laughing matters. My story seemed to have given him a chance to forget his problems awhile and laugh heartily after so long—at my expense, mind you! I was already paying him back big for his hospitality by so much hilarity in the first hour of my arrival. His energetic laughter also made me wonder why my family resisted so adamantly to even smile when I told the funniest stories to amuse them! Even if the entire world laughed at my jokes, my family would only frown.

"Their justifications were even more infuriating, especially my youngest daughter's was really funny," I replied.

"What'd she say?"

"'They're not all shoes…!' she said with absolute disbelief about my stupidly.

'So what're they?' I asked her in total confusion myself.

'They're sneakers, jogging shoes, long boots, half boots, dress shoes, and regular ones with low heels, etc. They're all different.'

'You forgot colour...!" I said sarcastically. "They're different colours and models, too, of course.'

'Of course...! They are all *so* different,' she said with a sigh of relief to see a tiny sign of sanity in their father occasionally.

'Still, they're all shoes,' I said like an imbecile and dashed my family's momentary hope. *Silly me!*

'No, they aren't,' Feri yelled at me, as if I were a total fool and to end my arguments."

"That's a funny story," Reza said. "Tell it to Darren, too, to make him laugh a bit as well."

"Oh, there's another factor to consider as well."

"What's that?" Reza asked.

"They have the same shoe size and constantly search each other's closets to borrow shoes, too. So, they have practically 350 pairs of shoes at any point and still keep nagging around me and each other about needing new ones."

"This damn consumerism has ruined our senses and culture."

"In fact, I told them that their fights over borrowing each other's shoes without permission or damaging them had mostly pushed me to count their shoes. So they were in fault, not me."

"What did they say?" Reza asked giddily

"They only insisted that I go straight to hell right away."

"It's probably easier to live in hell than among four females."

"You won't believe my torture over the topic of shoes alone. But that night, about a week ago, it was just a horrific scene."

"Your story reminds me of TV clips showing poor refugees in many parts of the world walking barefoot on cold or hot rough terrains for days and weeks."

"Send one of those clips to my family if you dare."

"No, I don't wanna die, but don't they see them themselves?"

"Don't know! I'm quite worried about my daughters' brains shaping around so much superficiality in society."

"Family stories are endless, but making yourself homeless over shoes takes the prize," Reza said with a giggle.

"I'm glad my family's idiocy entertains you so much," I said with mixed feelings about my pathetic life stories making my buddies laugh so much when they were stressed out.

"It's the way you say it, besides causing your exile."

"Shoe obsession is, of course, only a clue about the money they waste on clothing and other stuff. The amount of energy and time they spend on shopping is just maddening."

"You always make me cherish my lonely life more!" he said with a sigh that ironically showed his dilemma about not having a mate, while Darren and I fed him awful clues about the perils of family. Poor Reza was totally confused now.

"It's hard to say which option is wiser," I said with a positive tone, hoping to curb the damage my life story has made on poor Reza. "But facing our family's tyranny at my age is horrible, let me tell you."

"Don't you and Feri consult about your kids?" Reza asked.

"Are you kidding me?" I asked.

"Isn't she worried about her daughters suffering later?"

"She's worse than all of them."

"Is she?" Reza asked so naively I felt he must never marry.

"Absolutely. She acts like a spoiled child herself. She imitates her daughters and behaves like a teenager nowadays," I said.

"The situation must be especially tough for a traditional man like you, eh?"

"They hate me just for daring to remind them sometimes of their shallow values and addiction to this shitty Western culture."

"You rescued them from one extreme of human folly and now should face this other extreme of human lunacy."

"Exactly! That's another matter bugging me when I sometimes wonder about the wisdom of coming to Canada and witnessing their speedy transformation into such arrogant, useless beings."

"Although people everywhere have become too materialistic and only trying to have more fun."

"I go nuts when they look at me like I was the biggest idiot for not understanding their precious values," I said with a sigh.

"Don't worry… Most women think that way about men."

"But much more about their husbands," I added.

"You and Darren know that better... What does Feri want?"

"They just don't want me around to see their silliness or nag accidentally. I get a feeling sometimes they hope I go live in Iran alone, so they don't feel obliged to act even a tiny bit *normal*."

"Apparently, the new 'normal' is how people behave in this supposedly modern culture," Reza said.

"I know… You and I are totally abnormal now. But how my family behaves these days is just too darn frustrating."

"Feri looked wise and calm to me when you'd just arrived in Vancouver," Reza said.

"She's always been a master in hiding her malice and looking innocent. But she's a full-fledged slut now, I promise."

"Oh, come on, T.J. You're probably too sensitive these days."

"She also feels much more important suddenly after getting her real estate licence and working."

"Well, she's the breadwinner now," Reza said with a giggle.

"And quite liberated, more than ever."

"How?"

"She's always flirted with men, but now does it casually with her daughters' boyfriends, too, like hoping to revive her youthful memories."

"It's probably mid-life crisis."

"She's dying to enjoy life to its fullest. I married a slut, Reza, and then we created three more heartless sluts, too."

"You sure sound more pissed off than ever," he said.

"I'm not exaggerating. I've been running a slut factory. That's what Feri and I have achieved together as soul mates."

"You'd expect people get wiser and humbler with age and also more realistic, instead of getting shallower."

"In Feri's case, the situation seems even weirder."

"How?"

"She's getting also more malicious every week, as if devil is possessing her soul a bit more every day."

"Just find a way to relax somehow, for your own sake."

"Yes. Especially now I must keep myself busy away from her to avoid overreacting. I must ponder my next move rationally."

"That's wise… You might even miss Feri and feel you still love her," Reza said with humour, but also sounding like Darren earlier today for giving me the same optimistic advice.

"Don't be silly. We've passed that stage, my friend," I replied.

"You never know... Even she might realize she loves you!"

"Now, you're pushing your imagination wild," I said.

"No, I'm serious… Maybe only your recent experiences have messed up your moods and feelings for each other."

"Surely stress has made me testier these days. Then again, lots of hostility has been piling up in both of us for years."

"Today was your turn to whine, anyway," Reza said.

"Actually, my main goal was to raise your pity for a homeless man and let him stay here a while. Staying alone in a motel might've killed me."

"You did a great job. I admit you. Don't worry about whining as much as you like, either. I'm in the same boat and know how much whining helps."

"Your sisters' wandering around the world so casually has sure been hard on you."

"Exactly! I still don't even know what I'm supposed to do here in Vancouver. Bijan's threats feel serious, but Darren and Mahtab also make me angry."

"What're they thinking? What're they up to?" I asked.

"I haven't the slightest clue."

"Let's go find out," I said to unwind him a little. As he stared at me blankly, I continued, "Let's walk to Darren's place and maybe convince him to go for dinner with us. Maybe we can get him drunk and test his sanity and health in general."

"I don't know if that's a good idea. But let's get out of here, anyway," Reza replied.

We walked towards Darren's place in a sombre mood, although Reza looked uneasy about being around Darren tonight. He had even stopped me from calling and asking him to join us. Near his building, he pushed me to a corner abruptly to hide ourselves.

"There they are, the idiots," Reza exclaimed, pointing towards two figures I could hardly detect in the shadows. We watched the couple stroll hand in hand romantically towards the Aquabus.

"They're going for dinner or something. I hope they didn't see us," Reza said with rage.

We watched them from a safe distance kissing and cuddling, as if showing off or taunting us. The more we followed them, the more confused Reza seemed to get, as though he did not really know if he should be happy about his sister's joy and chance for happiness or feel disgusted by her total disregard for decency and tradition right in the middle of crowded streets.

"Don't you wanna go talk to Mahtab before they get on the boat?" I asked. "This may be a good chance and luck."

"No, it won't work this way...," Reza replied.

"They look so relaxed," I blurted before realizing my silliness to upset Reza further with my innocent observation.

"Yeah… Just look at them," Reza said with fury.

"They're probably really in love, then," I said with a giggle so imprudently and idiotically.

"They appear like fools, don't they—holding hands, laughing and kissing so casually in the public!" he replied. "Then again, only these moments of love and carelessness make our existence and struggles worthwhile."

"That's true, although I've almost never felt these types of sentiments about another person besides a few early infatuations. That's probably the privilege that both Feri and I have missed in our lives," I said, dying to tell him about meeting my old beloved,

Homa, in a party recently and how I had felt. I was still basking in those old memories as my only source of basic joy and being.

"Maybe that's why Feri acts silly and is spiteful towards you."

"It's possible…," I replied.

"She's probably been missing this kind of soppy feelings, too," he said, pointing to Darren and Mahtab still kissing and giggling in the distance even sillier.

"Yeah... Most likely love mirage and deprivation have now made both of us restless and caused this marital chaos," I said, pondering my darling Homa all along.

"Then, all you must do now is to rush back home and express eternal love to her. Problem solved!" he replied and we laughed.

"The problem is that her lying and hypocrisy have always stopped me from getting close to her or building a relationship."

"Yet you guys haven't missed much, after all, going by all the love hassles, especially the kinds Darren and my sisters cause," he said, probably hoping to curb my self-pity the way it must have been apparent on my face, while Homa's image had kept dancing in my head.

"I guess you know better, especially witnessing your sisters' fun with that guy," I said with a chuckle, pointing to Darren and Mahtab who were boarding the Aquabus now.

"Ironically, I enjoyed similar sentiments with that guy's wife when we enjoyed love awhile. I still taste and miss those special moments that no other woman has ever been able to give me."

"Then maybe you must leave Darren and Mahtab alone."

"No, because I've also suffered the most from that love affair. Love isn't a valid excuse even if Bijan wasn't so dangerous in this case. I rather believe that everybody, especially Mahtab and Darren now, takes all these risks and hassles for nothing."

"Again, you probably know better than me."

"I do. Love adventures have severe drawbacks and miseries, I promise you," Reza said with gloom.

"But didn't you just say that only these moments make living worthwhile."

"I've been trying hard to remember and reconcile these facts. That's why I recount these pros and cons to myself and others."

"Has anybody tried to make Bijan realize the stupidity of his vendetta—maybe you or his parents?" I asked.

"Not me, but some men like Bijan just can't bear losing their beloveds or forgive their betrayals. Ironically, his rather normal behaviour looks wild and stands out when I recall how generously and civilly Darren had let me love Erica," Reza said.

"Tell that to Bijan," I said wittily and we burst into laughter.

"He's ashamed around his family, but mostly maddened by Darren's ultimate betrayal after rescuing him from the prison and possibly saving his life from the grips of some vengeful people."

"So, he's madder at Darren than Mahtab?" I asked.

"Yes. He may even forgive Mahtab, but will kill Darren out of pride and for the sake of principles," Reza said.

"Then, you should convince Bijan that your sisters have been too charming to resist and Darren is only a naïve romantic caught up in the wrong circumstances," I said mainly for teasing him.

"He doesn't understand these kinds of logic," Reza replied.

"I see your point and maybe Bijan's points, too. I'm sorry for my advice being so useless this year."

"Having you around fulltime now is a blessing these days."

"Thanks for saying this, but I really needed your generosity to stay away from my family for a while at least."

"Let's go back to a restaurant closer to my place," Reza said.

On the way back, we remained mainly silent, while I thought about my family and their likely reaction to my sudden decision to abandon them. I had only left them a note about staying with Reza awhile. In my deep, naïve subconscious, however, I hoped they would rush over and beg me to return home. What a fool I have always been!

"The sad thing is that I feel sorry for Feri, too, for being so easily brainwashed by her friends and even her daughters, not to mention all these symbols of Western civilization," I said to Reza to break our silence.

"She probably knows what is good for her, don't you think?"

"No... My comment may sound selfish, but she doesn't know what's good for her and our daughters in the end."

"Nobody seems to know that," Reza replied.

"Because we're too conceited to get along in a simpler life, and because we stress only on our short-term needs and fun."

"Yeah… Modern social norms have ruined our senses and culture."

"Still, it's weird that I feel sorry and worry for Feri, too—such a wicked person who has destroyed my life," I said solemnly.

"Because you still love her..., that's why," Reza said giddily. "Just go home and tell her."

"I'm starting to think that you're now just trying to get rid of me… Is that it?"

"No, you can stay. But didn't you guys ever love each other?"

"No! But, most of all, I've been surprised about the way her brain works against her own and our kids' welfare."

"She certainly doesn't think so," Reza said.

"Of course… Nobody likes to even consider the possibility of thinking and seeing things from a different perspective."

"So why are you surprised of her tenacity?" Reza asked.

"You're right! I must be only amazed of my own stupidities."

"Which ones?" Reza asked wittily.

"Well, my two biggest mistakes in life have been marrying an evil in the first place and then bringing her to Canada to become even more demanding and selfish."

"Don't blame yourself too much, my friend," Reza said. "We all must be ready to pay a big price nowadays if we decide to marry, no matter where we live."

"I know…"

"Why did you guys marry if you never loved each other?"

"Well, that's a funny, horrific story I might tell you someday."

"Both funny and horrific…?" Reza asked.

"Yeah...! But I'm too tired to whine any more tonight."

Chapter Seventeen
Sister and Brother Reconciliation

Mahtab did not notice Reza and T.J. lurking around my building, possibly spying on us. I did not mention them to her, either, to avoid spoiling her mood or tainting her feelings towards Reza further. Actually, taking her to a restaurant tonight—a big investment for a penniless person—was my brilliant scheme to soften Mahtab a bit in the hope of bringing some peace between the brother and sister, which could lead to the release of my small assets that Reza and Bijan had confiscated. So, I distracted her on our way to the gondola platform, while also watching my silly pals hid in a corner first before following us.

To fool around with Reza in particular, I hugged and kissed Mahtab repeatedly, while checking my friends from the corner of my eye, giggling, and wishing I could read their minds. Most likely, the scene made Reza furious and T.J. jealous. They sure deserved it, I reckoned and chuckled. Mahtab was surprised by my sudden surge of affection in the street with all that kissing and giggling, but did not object or comment. She only grinned with grace, maybe thinking I was a cuckoo, after all.

Surely, I worried about my theatrics in the public provoking Reza enough to confront us and ruin Mahtab's mood and the chance of getting my money. Still, I took the risk and kissed Mahtab more, as teasing Reza felt so much fun to bypass. Like any naughty kid, now my immediate joy superseded the fear of retribution. Then again, my behaviour also showed my childish obsession for horseplaying even at high risks to myself.

"You'd better talk to Reza when you're ready," I told Mahtab in the restaurant after we ordered food and sipped our wines.

"I don't know when I'll feel ready… Maybe next year!"

"He's only trying to help us. Why are you holding a grudge?"

"The *same reason* I had when he tried to convince me not to come to Vancouver in the first place." she replied.

"Do you enjoy testing me with your riddles?" I asked with a chuckle to tease her.

Mahtab giggled too and replied, "Yes, I do."

"Well, I don't want to hazard a guess. So you'd better say it clearly to prevent any misunderstanding!" I asked playfully.

"Do you enjoy making me repeat it was because of you? That I loved you, then, and even more now?" Mahtab asked.

"Of course, I do… I love you more now, too."

"Reza doesn't understand this," she said with angst.

"But even then, Reza had tried to make you be realistic about the tiny chance of saving my life even if you were a physician."

"When you care about someone you don't think about these things; or you may rely on the miracle of passion and prayer."

"Still, I think Reza had probably been only trying to make you realize your hopes' futility and sacrificing your marriage just for a risky, emotional adventure."

"Saving your life wasn't just a hope. It was a mission, although I'm not a doctor—unless you also believe that your life hasn't been worth saving?" she asked so matter-of-factly I was simply stunned of her absolute trust, then, in her ability to save my life! Her belief and resolve even today sounded still more amazing or absurd for any sane person! *Yet I believed her!*

"No, in fact, I'd like to build a nice monument somewhere to appreciate your successful mission of saving my life," I said.

"Do you enjoy teasing me or just can't stop being funny for a minute?" she asked with a cute grimace.

"No, I'm serious. I'd mentioned it to Reza, too, when we met," I said giddily for my chance of using Reza's joke for fun.

"Did you really say that to Reza?" she asked with a giggle.

"Yes, I did just two days ago, right in front of our building."

"What did he say?" she asked.

"He said you deserved it for sure and actually accepted to pay for the cost of building the monument," I replied giddily.

"You'd never stop fooling around, would you?" she asked.

"No, I'm telling the truth… Ask him yourself anytime you want," I said and insisted more until Mahtab seemed to believe me at last. "He loves you a lot."

"I know," she said with a sigh.

"So give him another chance. He's come all this way just to protect us from some serious threats."

"But he's going to say the same things. He wants me to leave you and return to Iran, which I won't do under any circumstance, even if we're at risk and might even get murdered… Unless…!"

"Unless what?"

"Unless you've changed you mind and want me to go away."

"No, I haven't."

"Then I'm surprised you even consider listening to Reza and his intention to separate us for any reason, even the risk of death," Mahtab said so heroically I felt at sea again.

"I still think it's wiser to humour Reza," I said desperately.

"Are you afraid of him or Bijan? Are you afraid of dying?" she asked so matter-of-factly again I did not know whether to laugh about her naïve bravery, feel even prouder about her love for me, or get anxious about her dire fearlessness out of lunacy.

"Of course, I am. But I'd also like to keep Reza on our side."

"He'll never see our point."

"But we're not gonna lose anything just by listening to him."

"Maybe you're right," she muttered as if only humouring me.

"So will you see him if I ask you for turning him into an ally."

"I'll think about it. But I still don't know what you expect to achieve. We can't do what he wants. Right?"

"Well, it depends on what he wants, which we don't know."

"I do," Mahtab said sternly.

"You know I love you a lot already, right?" I asked seriously.

"Yes, I think I believe you," she replied with confusion.

"I promise to love you even more if you practise to become a bit more flexible and open-minded as well."

"You think I am stubborn and close-minded?"

"Sort of! But let's not argue about this issue, too. I know you're smart, but can be even wiser with a little more flexibility and listening to different viewpoints as well."

"I hope you're not insulting me subtly?"

"No, I just want to love you even more. Please let's hear what Reza has to say," I said with courage, while exhausted and fearful of her harsh reaction like the ones in Barcelona a couple of times.

"But how can we turn Reza into an ally only by listening to him if I ignore his advice to go back to Iran?"

"Again, we still don't know what he wants to tell you and you can always tell him no tactfully," I said with lots more patience and energy any human can muster in such a short span.

"I want you love me more every day, but my past dealings with Reza are still fresh in my head."

"That's why flexibility and open-mindedness are so important for an intelligent person like you."

"You sound wise and serious suddenly instead of clowning!"

"You see how flexible and open-minded I am?" I replied.

She burst into laughter. "And you're wearing me out, too."

"I think showing faith in Reza is a better strategy than making him angrier with us and friendlier with Bijan," I said with pride and conviction about my sincerity, which pleasantly superseded again even my earlier motive for pushing her to see Reza merely for getting my money from him. *I was surprised of myself, too!*

"Okay… If you think my conference with him will help us, I'll do it under one condition."

"What condition?"

"You must be present when he wants to make his big lecture and advise his baby sister."

"I'll make him agree with your *outrageous* demand!" I said jokingly. "That's how desperate he looks."

"Oh, how much I wish we could go hide somewhere nobody could ever find us. I should've brought more money with me, so that we could now elope."

"Do you think it's wise to go hide before you get your divorce from Bijan?" I asked. "We'd always have trouble adjusting to the environment even if we didn't have to watch over our shoulders all the time. You must focus on getting your divorce somehow."

"You're so naïve, Darren," Mahtab said with a sigh.

"I'm naïve?" I asked with surprise and humiliation after all that wisdom I had been supposedly dumping on her myself.

"Yes, you're naïve in this case," she replied with a charming grin, yet trying to hide her pleasure for finding her own chance of teaching me a lesson today herself.

"Why am I naïve?"

"Because you think my divorce would make any difference."

"It wouldn't?"

"Not much, I'm afraid."

"Why not?"

"Because you don't know Bijan. He's a very spiteful man and he'd never give up. Actually divorce would make him even more vengeful and dangerous."

"You probably know your husband better than most people."

"Yes, I do," she replied.

"Still talking with Reza wouldn't make the matter any worse. Let's see what he exactly wants," I said with love filling my eyes.

"I'm sure he wants me to talk to Bijan at least on the phone."

"Well, if that appears to be the only rational way to calm him and Bijan, it might be a wise thing to do, don't you think?"

"I don't know how to calm anybody."

"That's why you need Reza to help you," I said softly, trying to imagine her thoughts about my naiveté in that moment.

"Maybe you're right," she said with a sigh, but kept staring into my eyes with desperation, as if I were merely too naïve to understand anything or she abhorred even the idea of talking with Bijan. These Persian Moons, Mahroo and Mahtab, had ruined my pride and confidence, besides my delicate philosophies, with their incredible insights during the last two years!

It was too late to return Elizabeth's call when we arrived home exhausted from so much debate with Mahtab. Instead, I called Reza with the good news about Mahtab's consent to see him.

"That's great," Reza shrieked with excitement.

"Although she's imposed a very tough condition," I added.

"Oh, my god…! What does she want?"

"She wants me to be present as well."

"Well, you're right…! That's the toughest condition she could impose!" he said with a giggle. "But that's okay… Just try to be wise and support me as much as you can."

"I'll do my best. Sorry for missing your chance to talk behind my back and turning her against me," I said jokingly.

"I don't think even God could do that with my stupid sisters and your fatal effect on women."

"Should I tell her what you just said?"

"Oh, no please. Have mercy on me, my friend," he said.

He sounded thrilled like a child simply for a chance to see his rebellious sister next day in a café near his building. And I felt ecstatic for completing my plan that had many merits for all of us. So, I had to show my gratitude to Mahtab for coming down her high horses after such a long time only based on my simple reasoning. My physical and emotional strengths to make love to her that night was so commendable, so much as trembling in the end from terror and shame when Bijan's image of watching my great performance all along over his beloved wife manifested in the room for whatever bizarre reason. Our love travesty that night felt much more appalling than a mere sin.

Still sleepless and Bijan's phantom adamant to stick around with fury, Mahtab and I talked romantically for hours. It turned into another momentous experience with lots of tender thoughts and touching, as if we believed Reza would succeed in separating us tomorrow just for giving her to that nasty ghoul. She was an angel, I realized that night more than ever. Had not she proved so cooperative only based on her love for me?—all the more reason to keep her for myself, instead of letting Reza lure her. That was my final decision, which meant fighting for her with all my might and mind from that moment on.

Even after she fell asleep at last, I could not stop admiring her way of thinking and acting so differently from all other women I had known. I pondered how easily women could make us cherish them forever just by talking softer to us and hearing our sensible proposals more regularly, instead of always being controversial and bossy. I considered expanding this ingenious idea in a book called *The Secrets of a Smooth Marriage*, though it sounded quite impractical for women's taste if my knowledge of this gender's nature held water!—unless women now found my idea useful as a new potent gimmick for manipulating us even more!

Well, if I could not muster enough strength to paint again or find a gallery to sell my creations, maybe I could try to become a rich writer immediately and build a better and kinder humanity, too! *I needed lots of money to keep that sleeping beauty happy, after all!* I could not help T.J. become a good painter despite his efforts, so he became a cynical writer. But can he show me how to become a rich writer, rather than a listless, poor painter?

Nah... I must do some paintings soon to show to galleries or at least for calming my nerves from the hoopla around us.

Detective Stewart's mid-morning call was incredibly untimely after I had fallen asleep near dawn, finally. My hoarse, sluggish voice had possibly sounded sickly, but luckily, he did not fuss over my health again like last time! Anyway, all he wanted to say was that he had interviewed Jeff and few other people and was ready to discuss his findings and next steps.

"Nothing urgent," he said at the end, as if to validate my own cynicism about his call's value.

My silence, to ponder my timetable goaded him to continue, "Can you stop by today?" Now, he sounded like he had nothing better to do today and just wanted to fill his calendar.

After agreeing to visit him later in the day, I rushed back into Mahtab's bosom and slept another hour. When we finally left our cosy bed, we had merely enough time to see Detective Stewart before our rendezvous with Reza.

He took us to his office and closed the door. I introduced Mahtab to him merely for testing him playfully. With a cynical look, he reminded me swiftly that I had already done that in our previous meeting. He seemed eager to either prove his agility and massive memory or remind me of my slow brain after the coma. Mahtab's subtle grin reflected her appreciation of my mood to fool around again. *Or maybe the other way around*, I wondered! Maybe Mahtab worried about my slow brain, while the detective knew I was teasing him!

"I've talked with your friend, Jeff Nelson, and—"

"He's not my friend anymore," I interrupted Stewart curtly like a child perhaps, although I had still hoped to be funny. My mood today for horseplaying was starting to hurt and confuse even me rather than being amusing, I reckoned shamefully. Maybe it was the effect of my amazing time with Mahtab last night.

After a peek at Mahtab who giggled subtly again, the detective stared at me with disgust and continued, "He had nothing useful to say and we haven't found the thugs who shot you."

"But this morning you sounded like you had some clues and important stuff to tell me."

"Actually, I told you, 'Nothing urgent,' although a few points are useful to share with you about these guys..." he said calmly.

"Okay?"

"Well, they seem to be hiding and nobody knows much about them, either, although we're following a few leads."

"Doesn't Jeff know who they are?" I asked.

"Not directly. A few people, including the bartender who had introduced them to Jeff, seem clueless about their whereabouts. We're working on all these people and angles, anyway."

"They probably won't reveal the extent of their connection with the thugs, would they?" I asked with surprise.

"I have no reason to doubt Jeff's or bartender's claims about their limited connection to the thugs."

"Still they're both connected to the thugs even if it is not a lot. Aren't they guilty of something already?" I asked with frustration about this detective's cool and level of diligence.

"Not necessarily…"

"So what's new today?" I asked, trying to hide my irritation about his conclusions and dragging me here for nothing.

"Well, my reason for seeing you was mostly to give you this update, but also mention two important points," Stewart said.

"Okay?" I asked with curiosity.

"First, we talked with Mrs. Stanley who confirmed having seen, and spoken with, those thugs...," Stewart paused as though sorting out his thoughts. "She looked still anxious about having spoken with two killers. Then, she said she'd seen them around again in recent weeks a couple of times, but they hadn't talked with her or come close to your building."

Mahtab and I stared at him, rattled by his information and seeming cool stance. He peered at us calmly before continuing.

"So, if she's not hallucinating, these thugs might be stalking you and I wanted to give you a heads-up officially today."

"How have they learned about my recovery then, you think, if the bartender or Jeff hasn't informed them?" I asked.

"That's a good point, but we can't accuse anybody. Besides, I can't count on Mrs. Stanley's words alone. How sure are you about her words in general yourself?"

"I can't be sure, either," I said. "But, overall, the neighbours and I think she's a clever and observant person."

"So you realize my difficulty here," Detective Stewart said.

"I'm sure you're doing your best to connect all the dots."

"Are you staying in your apartment these days?"

"Yes, I am," I replied with stress. "I didn't until a few nights ago, but I must eventually feel safe to stay in my own place. How much longer do you want me to run away in fear of these guys?"

"We're doing our best Mr. Durant, but can't give you a reason to relax. Can you stay at a friend's place awhile until we get more information or at least these guys give up on finding you there?"

"No, I can't bother my friends forever. But it sounds funny to rely on the strategy of waiting for those guys giving up on finding me in that building. Don't you think a more proactive, permanent solution is necessary?" I asked with agitation.

"Of course, we're seeking the same result. Meanwhile, I wanted to ask you officially today to be as careful as possible, just in case I hadn't been quite clear the last time we met."

He sounded genuine for a second, so I stopped badgering him. "So, what is the next issue you wanted to talk to me about?"

"The matter of your charges against Jeff Nelson."

"Put him in prison for good, I'll say. He's responsible for this chaos and my likely death. Isn't that an attempted murder charge at least?"

"Well, it's not that simple. He claims he hired them to only talk with you and maybe intimidate you a little as a final resort if you didn't cooperate."

"But he'd agreed with the idea of bullying or hurting me."

"Yes, but only for punching you perhaps at most, but no shooting or killing. At least that's what he keeps saying."

"But Erica told me they may shoot a blank bullet to intimidate me. Both Jeff and Erica knew that they had guns."

"Empty guns…! He admitted he'd learned about this remote possibility from the bartender only after he'd hired the thugs and that was why, he insists, he asked Erica to forewarn you, while he kept looking for the thugs to cancel the contract long before the incident. The bartender confirms his claim," Stewart said firmly.

"I still think he's guilty and deserves some punishment."

"Do you confirm that Jeff had sent Erica to forewarn you, and hadn't he and Erica asked you to oblige the thugs and agree with their demands to let Elizabeth go?"

"Yes... She also said Jeff couldn't find the thugs."

"Here we go… You agree that Jeff wanted to stop them as soon as he'd found out they carried guns," Steward stressed with great enthusiasm and self-satisfaction for defying me.

"But he should've not started this dangerous game," I said.

"Well, who had started *this dangerous game* is still debatable, too, but all evidences at this time confirm his innocence about the shooting and his goodwill, in fact, to stop it."

"So you believe them?"

"Yes. Especially since Jeff seems remorseful and sincere. He swears he'd lost his mind initially when you'd stolen his fiancée and she'd simply abandoned him to come live with you. He kept saying, 'Darren started the whole damn thing himself.'"

"He's been saying that to everybody to exonerate himself."

"I don't wanna pass judgment, but if you stole his girlfriend of ten years, his frustration is understandable. We men go nuts when something like this happens," he said with a smirk and sarcasm that upset me. Then he peeped at Mahtab with a foolish grin, as if saying, 'Don't trust this guy'.

Mahtab looked disturbed about the nature of my past affairs and stealing my friend's fiancée. She was probably wondering how many lovers I had had when I had gone to Iran for Mahroo before flirting with Mahtab later in Barcelona, too. Maybe she saw me in a different light now after learning so much about my colourful past. In fact, all these information had been timely and handy for her, I imagined, to reassess her position after talking with Reza later today. In a way, I felt good about my scheme to bring her along to these meetings with Detective Stewart to help her decide about her plans better.

"I still think Jeff is responsible for my coma and pains."

"In fact, that isn't technically correct, either," Stewart said with a smirk.

"Why not…? Who is responsible for all this mayhem, then?"

"Technically, only you are responsible for getting shot, etc."

"Me…? That is my fault too?" I shrieked.

"Yes, it looks like it…," Stewart replied with a weird sense of satisfaction and sarcasm. Actually, he appeared relieved for the opportunity of raising this topic that had probably been his main intention of seeing me today.

"How can you say that?"

"Well, according to your own story and all the evidences, we can conclude that the thugs shot you only because you refused to give them your paintings peacefully."

"Did you expect me to simply let them take whatever they wanted?"

"No, all I'm saying is that it is always much wiser under some circumstances to humour hooligans instead of provoking them."

"Provoking them?" I asked in anger and disbelief. I could not have imagined that my earlier horseplaying with him might come back to haunt me so soon.

"Yes, in fact you seem to have been taunting them as well, again according to your own account of events and discussions."

"Taunting them? How did I do that?"

"Well, first you tell them you have the authority from Jeff to cancel their contract and then mock them by saying that you knew their bullets were blank. Did you say these things to them?"

"Yes, I did…"

"These words sound very humiliating if not intimidating even to ordinary people, let alone some loonies whose only job is to intimidate others themselves. It seems you have done your best to play with their nerves."

"But Jeff is the person who'd sent them… Don't you agree?"

"Yes, but they didn't shoot you because of their mission, but only because they got into a squabble with you directly over your paintings. They wanted something from you, wrongly of course, and you didn't want them to have it," Stewart said with a smirk.

"I just couldn't let them take my paintings!" I said with fury.

"Instead, you kept mocking them and raising their tension."

"This is really ridiculous now," I cried, totally flabbergasted.

"No, it's not, Mr. Durant. Jeff hadn't asked them to shot you if you refused giving them your paintings or any other property, had he?" Detective Stewart said so idiotically I considered filing a complaint against him instead of continuing this conversation.

"I'm completely astonished by your deductions today," I said.

"Well, I just don't want to repeat myself, but you knew those thugs had been trying to find you and waiting impatiently for a few weeks to do their job of bullying you and still you chose to intimidate them, instead of letting them do their job and go away as Jeff had sent Erica to tell you, too," Stewart said coolly.

"So, you're not going to prosecute Jeff for his involvement?"

"We can't. Maybe we could charge him with misdemeanour, but there's no way we can win with a criminal case against him, especially considering what you'd done to him and his possible state of mind during his bad decision to hire those guys. I know this punishment isn't enough for your hassles and pains, but only you are responsible for the shooting part itself, though the thugs might get serious punishment if we find them."

"The way you've found me guilty for so many things today, I'm afraid you might put me in prison instead of Jeff."

Stewart chuckled idiotically. "Maybe I should…"

"In fact, maybe you can even let those thugs also bring a case against me for taunting and provoking them, too," I said rudely and sarcastically.

"You see, you're now even trying to mock me for my opinion, instead of accepting the facts. Actually, you seem to enjoy teasing people a lot, Mr. Durant, don't you?"

"I'm sorry if I sounded sarcastic," I said timidly, hoping not to make an enemy of him as well. I had enough of them out there looking for me already.

"No problem. I just wanted to make a point and clarify things for you," Stewart said with a calm, reconciliatory tone himself.

"Thanks… You did a perfect job…," my loose mouth uttered and Stewart smirked, so I added fast. "So, at best Jeff gets only a slap on the wrist for everything he's done?" I asked.

"Yes, that's how it looks like…" Steward paused and chewed on some thoughts before continuing. "Unless!"

"Unless what?"

"From our investigations, it appears that Erica doesn't have any close relatives in Canada, right?"

"Yes, her parents came from Scotland. She was born here and had no siblings, either," I replied. "Why?"

"And you were still married when she passed away, right?"

"Yes, that's correct. Is this matter relevant?"

"Your only small chance is to pursue the matter as Erica's husband to punish Jeff at least with a civil case. And possibly a criminal charge, too, if you can convince us and the court that his actions have resulted in her death, especially if the thugs have pushed her over the balcony or she'd tried to run away from them or something like that."

"Are you saying you cannot do much about Jeff's role for my ordeal because I have survived on top of provoking the thugs, but I might be able to punish him regarding Erica's death?"

"It looks like it—only as a remote chance if you are adamant to go after Jeff somehow. Even that would be a hard task, but you have a better chance, then, if you're keen to punish him. I hope you understand my limitations here," he said.

"I do. Thanks for suggesting a way to punish Jeff, after all."

"You're welcome…"

"I'm sure you're doing your best, although you detest my role for stealing Jeff's girlfriend and then provoking the thugs, too."

"And all the other points I explained to you…"

"Yes. That I was asking for trouble myself," I stressed testily.

"Yes. I hope you realize I've tried to be as helpful and honest about everything as possible, despite your knack for argument."

"Yes, I'll think about everything you suggested today."

"Especially, be extra careful for a few more weeks or months. Go hide some place until we hopefully find the thugs."

I thanked Detective Stewart for his rather sincere suggestions and information as Mahtab and I left in a hurry to meet Reza.

"I feel bad about putting your life in danger," I told Mahtab in the street. "I don't mind dying, but hate any harm coming to you because of me. Reza surely wants you as far away from me and my enemies as well."

"Let's go to a hotel or something for a while, then," she said.

"It'll be expensive and inconvenient for us," I replied.

"We have no other option, do we?" she said.

"I can't think of anything right now."

"Don't tell these details to Reza, though," she said worriedly.

"Okay."

"By the way, I liked the way you challenged poor Detective Stewart and also the way you'd handled the thugs—driving them crazy and forcing them to shoot you," she said with laughter.

"I did a good job, ha?"

"You sure did! Were you suicidal..., maybe because of losing Mahroo and me?" she asked half-teasingly.

"Yeah... Maybe I was... But it all felt right at the time. And now that you mention, maybe you and Mahroo are responsible for my behaviour and its aftermath during those crazy days."

"It seems you had other girlfriends waiting for you, anyway?"

"No, don't change the subject. Only you two sisters had been the main cause of my suicidal behaviour around those thugs."

"But at least I've now made up for it by coming here and nursing you," she said half-seriously.

"Yes, you did. You've now redeemed yourself perfectly."

"Mahroo did it, too, by making our love happen," she said.

"True," I replied. I wished I could tell her that I owed Mahroo also for making me choose life over love at the end of my coma.

We discussed our new dilemma about a place to live the rest of the way to the café, to no avail.

The brother and sister were tense when they met in the café, which justified my presence even more than what Mahtab had felt. I tried to fool around about our funny situation, but those two were too anxious to appreciate my sarcastic humour. We relaxed a little after ordering food and drinking our coffees, yet nobody seemed ready to start the expected touchy conversation. Those two just nibbled on their foods passively, while looking amused with the way I ate fast to appear cool. Of course, I was famished, too, after all the energy Mahtab and I had consumed on talking and other stuff the night before, and then listening to Detective Stewart's frustrating comments this afternoon.

Reza's timid peeps and Mahtab's subtle tears were making me feel sad and guilty for my possible role, even so indirectly and innocently, in causing the mayhem around us. In return, I seemed to be seeking refuge only in food and the possibility of choking and dying to end this charade. That would be the fastest way of solving many problems and letting many people around the globe exhale a big sigh of relief. How could my existence be both so useless and tragic? I had already caused Mahroo's, Erica's, and Zia's deaths and I had spread lots of commotion during my short life already, including in my son's family. I had hurt Jeff, Bijan, Nazi, Reza, and Elizabeth, too, in recent months, inadvertently. All these events and pains happening because of me were too darn depressing.

Actually, a fatal choking could be deemed a divine relief, since no easier solution seemed at hand for so many emotional issues burdening many people, including myself. My conscience and psyche would also be relieved at last from carrying so much guilt everyday. And, best of all, my sinking spirit would not have to worry about a safe place to hide from our enemies on top of our looming poverty. No wonder I could not stop eating so fast and hoping for a timely miracle. *The miracle of death!*

Chapter Eighteen
Feeling Mahtab's Dilemma

Peering at my beautiful sister after so long, while she seemed amused with Darren gorging himself like a clumsy baby, I felt guilty for acting like a ruthless executioner for King Bijan. I was agitated and speechless about the touchy matter at hand, got more confused about the right thing to do, and questioned my right to influence her even a bit, if I could. My cyclical hesitation was annoying the most after mulling over this issue and believing in what was best for Mahtab. Still, the task of pushing her to abandon love to save many people, including this devouring lover boy, felt like my life's most sinful project with long-term emotional risks beyond the expected dangers.

"I'm stuck in a very bad position, Mahtab," I said very calmly at last. "That's why I hope you let me explain the situation before weighing the options together somewhat realistically."

She nodded and I continued, "In fact, I just want you to tell me what to do after hearing me out. I'm here to pick your brain and I really hope you have some good suggestions, because I don't." *Wow, I'd never imagined I had so much diplomacy in me!*

"What about?" Mahtab asked with surprise.

"The most important thing is to decide about our mother and Nazi. They don't have any close family members to rely on now that you're here and I have to travel all the time for business, not to mention for running Bijan's errands regarding your marriage."

"How are they?" Mahtab asked with some concern and guilt.

"Not so good at all after your departure. They miss you a lot. Our mother is very ill and would like to spend the last part of her life around you. With both Mahroo and Father gone so suddenly, she is devastated and now your absence and situation with Bijan is killing her faster, too. She has probably a few more months or at best two more years."

"I'm sorry… How is Nazi doing?"

"Terrible… She's already showing signs of melancholy and restlessness. She's still missing her mom and dad, of course, but was at least somewhat calm while living with you. She probably has Mahroo's and your genes, too, which makes controlling her too difficult for our mother or me. We can't help her and she'll be ruined if she continues on the same path without you around her."

Mahtab was quiet while Darren kept eating more wolfishly as my touchy account of the situation resonated longer and sounded sadder. I reckoned he was only hoping to hide his tension and shame by stuffing himself and pretending to ignore us, too. His guilty conscience was probably behind his boorish attitude and gorging. Mahtab stared at him curiously with a mix of passion and pity for his apparent tension before she started to sob subtly. Then, she peered at him again differently this time, maybe as a result of all the guilt she was suddenly feeling after my soothing account of our family's devastation. *Was my plan working?*

"I'm stuck in a mess, too," she said while looking straight into my eyes for the first time this afternoon.

"I understand," I replied in a soothing tone that felt sincere to me and most likely to Mahtab, too, in the way she looked at me with mercy. Our reconciliation felt more plausible every minute, while I was pleasantly surprised with the way I had chosen my words and made my pleas so diligently. I was proud of myself so far. Darren also seemed calmer now with no more food left to eat. He looked rather content and proud of himself for not only satiating his seemingly endless appetite, but also doing something right for me after so long.

"I miss mom and Nazi a lot, too, and feel guilty for not being there for them," Mahtab said. "I feel terrible, but how can I go back and face that horrible man who'll refuse to divorce me?"

"Still, facing him would be the fastest way to get your divorce if you're sure that's what you want. He swore he won't get mad at you and will listen to your conditions for taking him back."

"It's too late for reconciliation...," she replied. "Besides, I can't live in Iran and he'll never agree to go live in Europe or the U.S. with me."

"You can always impose that condition and see his reaction."

Mahtab's pensive silence suggested that my *brilliant* idea had impressed her like a magical revelation.

"That's a good gimmick to get rid of him!" she said giddily.

"Here we go… We already have a solution," I said happily.

"He probably wouldn't leave his family and political life in Iran to follow me for some uncertain future. He can't even find a job outside of Iran fitting his ambitions," she said, as if she had suddenly discovered the secret for eternal life

"I agree... So he'll divorce you," I said with reserved hopes.

"In fact, I've whined a few times already about my difficulty of adapting to life and jobs in Iran," she said with more triumph.

"And he knows that you've lived most of your life abroad."

"But what if he agreed? What if he called my bluff?" she said with a sudden panic, as if plunged into an icy pond.

"What is the chance of that… One in a trillion?"

"Well, he might be desperate...," she said with tension wittily. "I was silly getting excited about this option too fast. I'm sorry."

I nodded since Mahtab's conclusions sounded plausible. We men lose all our senses, willpower, and pride for love or a pretty woman. Still, her willingness to consider the option of traveling to Iran, or at least giving Bijan a tough ultimatum, was a good progress after only an hour of chitchat. I was happy.

At the same time, my candid discussions with Mahtab right in front of Darren with a chance for dumping him sounded rather insensitive and insulting, as though he had no say or stake in the matter. He appeared to be struggling to bear the humiliation and be as much supportive about the sensible ideas discussed around the table as possible. He was probably thinking, *Who am I in the big scheme of things? Just a nobody…, although I'll at least get my money!*

"Have you discussed the other complications with Mahtab?" I asked Darren to include him in our conversation for a bit at least before he ordered more food to soothe his melancholy.

"No… She already has enough issues to fret over," he replied sluggishly as if he had felt my shallow gesture of consoling him. He probably also recalled with pain my efforts to console him after Erica had asked him for a divorce to continue her affair with me freely!

"I think she should know some of the facts without discussing your private secrets today," I said diplomatically, while hinting the necessity of Mahtab knowing about his lovechild as well.

"What other facts and secrets?" Mahtab asked irately, staring at Darren who looked at sea himself.

"Bijan is threatening to send some hooligans to harm Darren and you if you guys refuse to act properly," I said. "He forced me to come here just to make you two realize his rage."

"You see what I'm saying now?" Mahtab yelled. "Is he a kind of person I can trust or respect?"

"In fact, he told me to stress that this is his last warning and your last chance to save your asses."

"My god…! Can someone who sends my brother to threaten me be a reliable person to spend my life with?"

"Not even in Europe or the U.S.?" Darren asked childishly for fun or maybe for revenge.

"Not even in heaven!" Mahtab replied with a grimace.

"But remember, he's saying all these things and behaving like an outlaw only out of love," I said. "He's just dying without you. Your house has fallen apart and he's gone totally mad."

Mahtab was upset again and I was losing ground for keeping her interest in discussing our options further. I could not think of anything sensible to say without upsetting her even more.

Luckily, Darren's timely question distracted Mahtab. "Did you ask Bijan if he still wants me to keep the secrets he'd insisted I must take to my grave?"

"What're these secrets about, Darren?" she asked sternly.

"I'll tell you if I'm allowed, especially since Reza just hinted that I'd better tell you," he replied before turning to me. "Did you ask him?"

"I did… He was angry about you trying to hurt him in return. He said, it'd only make your punishment more severe, but at the end he wouldn't care about you revealing the secrets, since he's now only interested in getting Mahtab back from you. That's all he wants these days."

"So, he's not worried about his father and other hot shots in Iran getting hurt, either?"

"Apparently not…," I replied. "He told me to tell you, 'You started this whole mess'."

Mahtab giggled tensely. "Many people are saying the same thing about you these days, Darren, aren't they?"

"Poor me. I've started all the problems around the world. I bet if the world war III begins, they'd blame me for it, too."

"Well… Bijan has a point, if you ask me," I blurted.

"Now you sound like Detective Stewart!" Darren said.

"Is that what other people say about you, too?" I asked wittily.

He ignored my joke and said, "Bijan's attitude shows his rage and obsession with Mahtab for sure, because he'd stressed to me that revealing the secrets may even cause a national mayhem."

"I told you… He's lost his mind and doesn't give a damn about his father or other officials," I said. "He only wants Mahtab back, which now makes me think he might actually even agree to go live abroad with her, even if it means never working or seeing his family again."

"That's right...," Mahtab added. "He's rich enough not to work for the rest of our lives even if we have a dozen kids."

"That's how lost and disturbed he is, eh?" Darren asked with surprise and pity and I nodded.

"What is this damn secret? Why don't you guys trust me to keep it to myself?" Mahtab asked Darren with stress.

"I'll tell you later in private even though Reza knows about it already," he said to her and then turned to me. "Do you also think it's okay to let out these secrets, then, eh?"

"I really don't know," I said. "It is up to you to weigh all the angles despite Bijan's attitude. You must consider other people who'd get hurt and react if you reveal their secrets."

"Why should I care if he doesn't?" he asked.

"I just told you a minute ago...," I replied sternly. "Bijan is simply out of his mind these days."

Darren nodded.

"Besides the ethic of keeping other people's secrets, you must worry about their reaction mostly towards you," I said. "You'll still be the main person they'll punish for revealing their secrets, not Bijan."

"And you think those people can hurt us even in Vancouver?" he asked with stress.

"I've already told you that both Bijan and the other group have enough power to chase and harm you anywhere."

Darren nodded with resignation, while Mahtab gauged him and me with curiosity about the secret and all those other possible sources of danger.

"I really appreciate your effort to see me today, Mahtab," I blurted. "I hope I've explained my concerns and maybe you can now think seriously and let me know what you want me to do with Bijan. I must go back to Tehran soon. I'm worried about mom and Nazi as I said, but I must go to Dubai for a week, too."

"Thanks for taking care of them, Reza," she replied.

"You're welcome. But my life is getting just too complex and crowded and I can't bear so much pressure for too long alone."

"Okay, I'll think and tell you my decision in a few days."

"That would be great," I said. "I also suggest that you come back to my suite right away."

Mahtab and Darren stared at me with surprise and stress.

"I'm sure Bijan will get his people to spy on us and it'd be wiser if at least you aren't staying with Darren..." I paused as Mahtab frowned, but decided to continue, "It's better to keep at least a decent appearance, instead of enraging him even more at this point, until we have a strategy to face the situation."

"I'll think about that, too," she replied testily at last.

"Isn't T.J. staying with you these days?" Darren asked me.

"Yes, but maybe you and I could swap these two refugees for a while at least," I replied.

Darren burst into laughter and said, "Is he already getting on your nerves?"

"No, he's not. Actually, he's been a good distraction for me, while the poor guy is in deep shit himself. Just imagine, at his age, still trying to sort out his life's basic elements and find peace with a family he's devoted himself to all along. He's deeply in love with them, while they hate his guts for being alive."

"What an ugly world we've made for ourselves!" Darren said.

"Poor T.J., he's a prisoner of love in a way, too," I said.

"So, we'll each have a prisoner of love to care for if we swap these two," Darren replied with a chuckle, pointing to Mahtab.

"That's true… But maybe we'll exchange these love refugees once more later after the storm settles," I said.

"That'd be great," Darren replied. "Say hi to him for me and perhaps we get together one night before you go back."

"That's a good idea to cheer him up, although you and I probably need lots of cheering up ourselves," I said and left after asking them if they needed a ride. They said they would like to walk around the harbour and Gas Town to ponder their options. I hoped they were planning to spend their last quiet afternoon and evening together before Mahtab agreed with my suggestion to go back to Iran or at least return to my suite.

As I walked away with baffling thoughts, Darren ran back to me, while Mahtab watched us with curiosity from a distance.

"Are you going to release my money now that I've done my part of the deal?" he asked giddily. "Convincing Mahtab to see you was the toughest job I've ever done, believe me! To be fair, in fact, you must pay me much more than you owe me!"

"Okay, I'll give you a cheque next time we meet, but Bijan shouldn't know about it. It's just another secret between us."

"Okay, that's fine. I really need this money quickly," he said and turned to leave, but stopped in his track and continued, "Do you think it helps to tell Bijan again that I will reveal the secret to everybody soon unless he stops badgering Mahtab and me?"

"No, I really believe he doesn't care at this point, but I can raise the issue again tonight when I talk to him. I'm going to tell him that Mahtab is considering his ultimatum and the option of going back to Iran under the right circumstance."

"Why do you wanna say that? I don't think she'll do such a thing," he said with stress.

"I know, but he'd given me only a week to sort this out or else," I said. "Its better to keep Bijan calm even for a few days until we know what we, especially Mahtab, would like to do."

"Okay. That is smart."

"But I don't think repeating your ultimatum to Bijan about the secret would be smart. It'll only agitate him even more," I said.

"I don't know… You judge and act as you wish…"

"But, Darren, can you be a bit less selfish and talk to Mahtab about her options realistically? Could you please make her realize her decisions at this point are too crucial to be affected by love or pride or other silly stuff?"

"I'll do my best," he murmured and sauntered away.

I started walking on the opposite direction, but could not help turning to watch the lovebirds going away hand in hand again. The scene of their desperate romance broke my heart and I began following them hypnotically for ten minutes at a good distance. They were the only two people in the world around my age whom I cared about so much. Watching them rekindled the memories of my complex romance with Erica again and the sad ending our decisions had caused us. How could I force my sister go live with a narcissist in a stuffy environment instead of testing her chance of having a lasting romance in her life?

The more I chased them and envied their blithe spirits soaring so fearlessly in the streets with absolute disregard for marital and social morality, the more my heart ached from a joyous emotion. I looked around nervously for a likely spy that Bijan might have put in charge of following them, while they acted so nonchalant about this possibility. I stopped following them near Gas Town and turned towards my condo with a big resolve to protect them against Bijan's tyranny the best I could. I wished them a chance to elude the feelings of loneliness and hopelessness the way T.J. and I felt nowadays. Comparing our tortures with the perceivable thrill that Mahtab and Darren shared had surely baffled me, too. Especially, T.J.'s desperate face around me these days had been a timely fluke for raising my conscious about Mahtab's long-term emotional needs contrary to my initial impression and resentment of her actions during the last 2-3 months. Overall, my official conference with her today felt absolutely successful—mostly for her benefit—while the outcome tickled me in the elevator going up to my suite! Now, grasping her dilemmas and choices felt most urgent to me compared with the time I had left Tehran with only one official goal: To enforce Bijan's desires. Certainly, a clearer picture was emerging after grasping her dilemmas better. However, I still had deep doubts about my role and her options, probably as much as Mahtab had.

T.J. was not at home. He had probably gone for a walk to stretch his legs and mind a little as well. I wanted to tell him and gloat about my success with Mahtab this afternoon without hinting the possibility of swapping him with her. At last, I went out for a snack and returned two hour later, still no sign of T.J.

I gathered my nerves to call Bijan and put his mind at ease somewhat with more lies. Despite his infuriating expectation to give him a progress report regularly, humouring him felt vital.

"Things are improving, Bijan," I said in a triumphant tone.

"In what way?" he asked with some reserved giddiness.

"At least she listened to my concerns for two hours today."

"That's good… Is she living with you these days?" he asked.

"Of course, she is. Where else do you think she lives?" I said, but immediately hated my hasty question—as though my sneaky subconscious had been dying to raise suspicion or a commotion!

"Is she there right now?"

"Yes…"

"Can I speak with her myself?"

"Let me ask her," I told him and then shouted a few words near the receiver before continuing, "No, she doesn't wanna talk to you this minute."

"Why not?"

"Just leave her alone tonight, Bijan. She's tired and pondering lots of stuff I've been telling her all day. We better not crowd her mind even more. Let's not ruin everything I've done today. "

"But I really must ask her a few questions," he said.

"Not tonight. Let her digest my good advice today."

Bijan did not respond as if contemplating my suggestion and trying to bask in all the hopes I was building for him.

"What good advice have you given her?" he asked.

"I've told her to come back to Iran and reconcile with you," I said with shame, fearing all these big lies haunting me later.

"Is she going to listen to you? Is she getting her sanity back?"

"I hope so. Let's give her a few days."

"What is Darren doing or saying about all these?" he asked, as if my earlier stupid question, 'Where else could she be?' had in fact done the trick my sneaky subconscious had intended!

"He's not involved with any of these things. In fact, he was quite angry when I told him you've accused him of betraying you and also threatening him."

"I'll deal with him myself later."

"Bijan, leave him alone. But he was glad that you don't care about his son's existence becoming public. He wants to be sure you really don't mind if he also talks about it with people in here and Iran. What if Sima's uncle hears that you've let Darren talk everywhere and maybe even look into the possibility of at least seeing his son?" I asked.

"Let's hope he's not that stupid. He shouldn't make the matter worse for himself."

"But he asked me to tell you that, 'You're the one who started this whole thing—about revealing the secret'," I said with glee.

"Then, tell him that the more headaches he causes me, the more severely I'll punish him. He can be sure about that. Give him my message clearly again. I'm not joking."

"But he thinks you have threatened him enough already. He asked me to give you an ultimatum of his own only because he feels cornered."

"Oh, he does, ha?"

"Yes…"

"What's his ultimatum?" Bijan asked.

"He said he'd tell the whole story and why he was jailed to everybody more publicly for retaliation as well, more than what is necessary just for creating some kind of contact with his son," I said vengefully against my earlier intention. Making all these exaggerations had simply felt delightful and necessary, although Darren had not meant to be so harsh and I was causing him extra danger inadvertently.

"Then tell that son of the bitch that I piss at his ultimatum. I don't give a damn if the whole world learns about the secret or Rafatti's wrath when it comes to my own interests, especially regarding Mahtab."

"Who's Rafatti?" I asked.

"Sima's uncle... the minister. You all must know I'm serious."

"Don't you care about your father and his honour at least? Don't you care if he and Rafatti become ferocious enemies?"

"Not really when it comes to Mahtab," he said with despair.

"Well, if that's how you think, then I cannot control Darren, either," I told him with satisfaction, anyway, against all logic! His rising madness was clear even from his casual disclosure of the minister's name contrary to what he had done until today.

"What do you expect me to say when you and Darren dare to talk to me this way and give me ultimatums?" Bijan asked.

"You'd better make up your mind, Bijan. Either leave him alone to keep his mouth shut or keep saying that you don't care."

"That's still what I'm saying to that son of a bitch."

"How can you simply refuse to choose a fixed strategy, but expect us to care and do everything as you wish?"

"Yes, that's still my position. He started the whole thing!"

"It'll be your fault, then, if he talks about his son. He says he has nothing to lose when you're intimidating him."

"Do your best, Reza, to make him understand my position and I'll do what's necessary to make things right."

"Okay, I'll do my best," I replied with a sense of defeat.

Thinking that women have so much power over us men felt too pathetic and heartbreaking again. The way Bijan's love for Mahtab had driven him to such degree of insanity and apathy even about his own parents and career was simply astonishing! Any more reasoning with him tonight, while he sounded more desperate for Mahtab every minute, seemed futile. In the end, I promised to contact him soon again, hopefully with good news about Mahtab returning to Iran. I had never lied so much in one day. I felt exhausted and useless.

"Call me in 2-3 days about her final decision, Reza, for your own sakes," Bijan stressed.

"Okay, bye for now," I said and hung up with rage, and then murmured, "Asshole…"

Chapter Nineteen
Retaliation for Fun

Reza looked bewildered, too, when I reeled into his suite quite tired and anxious myself. Passersby's antsy glares, as though aghast by an extraterrestrial in their midst, had affirmed the depth of despair and anger contorting my face, while I had staggered in the streets in a haze for hours after Feri's ugliest tyranny yet.

"Where've you been, T.J.?" Reza asked with great effort to appear alive himself.

"Walking in the streets after a row with Feri on the phone."

"Again…?"

"Yes… Now my life feels surreal completely."

"Why?"

"Feri wants a divorce," I replied with gloom.

"Oh… I'm sorry, T.J. That's terrible," Reza said

"Life is lousy already, but humans' tenacity to cause their own doom and gloom out of sheer arrogance is horrible."

"Hadn't you considered this possibility when you left them?"

"Sort of... Still hearing her ask for it so casually felt insulting and sad, like our twenty-year marriage had been only a picnic."

"So, you weren't quite ready to give up on her," Reza asked.

"I guess not..."

"What were you thinking, then?"

"I hoped she'd think a little and maybe miss me a bit, too."

"Gosh, you're as romantic as Darren and me," Reza said.

"I was hoping she'd get serious about our marriage, instead of behaving like a teenager at her age."

"Even all your research in family issues and years of personal pains haven't still thought you enough about modern women's tenacity," he said with a giggle.

"I know… I've tried to remain a bit optimistic and practical despite my deep cynicism showing in my essays."

"Is she serious or only testing you?"

"She sounds serious."

"Maybe she's only intimidating you to gain more control."

"Whatever... I'm tired of her attitude and games, anyway."

"So, this means the end?" Reza asked.

"Looks like it... Her disregard for other options, like marriage counselling or reducing her expectations, feels so cold and silly."

"Sorry, T.J.… But at least you're now free like me."

"Now I am just a homeless bum after a lifetime of working, saving money, and loving a bunch of ungrateful idiots."

Reza chuckled while pouring whisky for us.

"What am I gonna do now, Reza?" I asked.

"I've been asking myself the same question for years."

"You feel lost too?" I asked.

"Sort of… I'm stuck with Mahtab, Bijan, my mom and Nazi, Darren, and my boring business, including hundred employees."

"Don't forget me—a brand new burden," I added.

"Especially you these days, of course!"

"You feel stuck even with Darren?"

"Sort of... He looks at sea, too, despite having Mahtab around him...," Reza paused pensively. "...or maybe because of her!"

"Poor Darren... lost among women and possibly getting killed one of these days by a jealous husband or lover, too!" I said.

"He's messed up, T.J. You should've seen him today gorging himself like a pig, from tension, I'd say."

"It may also be partly the offshoot of his coma," I replied.

"So, for now, all we can do is to pound the pavements, think, and hope for a few miracles falling off the sky to save our asses."

"Soon I can't even do that!"

"Why?"

"My knees hurt and my brain is useless. Maybe I start gorging myself instead, then, like Darren. Maybe he's up to something!"

"Are we three gonna stop our race for the messiest life?"

"Expect it to get way messier as you age," I said glumly.

"Still remember you're not alone feeling so helpless."

"I miss old times when we discussed life and spirituality and felt wise. Will we ever be carefree again even for a few days?"

"I doubt it," he replied. "Then again, how useless our alleged wisdom and life philosophies feel now!"

"True! Our beliefs didn't even help us build a simpler life."

"Finding our place in life is not easy, anyway."

"Especially, raising a family stops us from building a personal outlook and an independent character. So, we feel lost," I said rhetorically, as if struck by a revelation after my daylong pain and rage in the streets in search of answers.

"Still, your divorce sounds weird and fast?"

"Well, I'd just avoided whining too much, although I hadn't imagined it'd get this ugly, either."

"So, you've been suffering all the time you were telling us to settle down, you sneaky snake?" Reza asked with a chuckle.

"Yeah… My marriage had been going south for a decade at least... Two years ago, I started feeling a subtle, persistent tremor in my body, even in my sleep. As it kept worsening, I saw my family doctor and he sent me for a variety of tests, CT scan, etc. At the end, they couldn't find anything wrong and the symptoms went away also suddenly after a few months."

"That's good news," Reza said, looking quite confused about my seemingly irrelevant story in the middle of our serious talk.

I enjoyed his funny bafflement before continuing, "During this few months of my suffering and frustration, worrying about a permanent ailment, Feri was looking around for nursing homes."

"You gotta be kidding me?" Reza asked in shock.

"No, I'm not… 'I think it's Parkinson and I can't take care of you,' she stressed at least ten times, as if now she'd become a physician over night as well.

'Can't we wait to see what it really is before you look around for a place to take me?' I asked her with disgust.

'No, we'd better be prepared. You should think about these things yourself instead of expecting me to take care of a cripple.'"

"How about your daughters? Didn't they show compassion?"

"Not at all… They all agreed with their mom and insisted that I needed professional care in a facility," I replied.

"That's horrible," Reza said. "After all your sacrifices!"

"I said I'd never talk to them again if they did such a thing, but they only shrugged and walked away."

"You and Feri have created a real family, haven't you?"

"We sure have. My point is that if a marriage slips gradually, it soon reaches a point of no return unexpectedly," I said.

"Then again, it's tough to stay on track with women's high expectations from life and their husbands nowadays?"

"Exactly! People are less patient and caring these days, much less than is required to keep a family together."

"So, we're all doomed, men and women, ha?"

"Yep. I threatened Feri today, but she only laughed at me."

"What'd you say?"

"That I'll give all my assets to charities. But she just shrugged."

"Meaning what…? She doesn't care?" Reza asked.

"I believe she thinks I don't have the guts to hurt my family; that I'm just too soft-hearted, like another one of my *well-rooted,* shortcomings that she's figured out cleverly."

"Then, she knows you very well. Even I think you're soft."

"I must've been. So, I should change myself at all costs now."

"Just to prove her wrong?" Reza asked with a giggle.

"Yes, I guess I should! Her arrogance to think I'm gutless is too disgusting and a big insult all in itself."

"But you still don't sound certain, ha?"

"Well, changing myself will cause lots of work and stress by itself, but letting people make me vindictive is disgraceful, too."

"Yeah, you're unsure even tonight at the height of your spite."

"But I must do it," I replied. "Shouldn't I?"

"I feel for you," Reza said. "It seems we're all doomed to be lonely and helpless despite our wit and wealth and all the love we exchange here and there."

"I agree. The whole humanity is trapped now in this alleged modern world... I'm certain about this at least."

"Still, oddballs like us live in limbo more than others."

"Yeah... Sometimes, I envy most people who've simply lost themselves in this shallow modern life filled with hypocrisy and social vanity," I said.

"Still, most of them are depressed somehow, anyway."

"That's true too," I replied.

"Anyway, your testy mood these days is justified," Reza said.

"What my eldest daughter, Rose, told me today killed me."

"She called you, too?"

"No, I called her to calm myself after Feri's call. I also hoped she'd jump and volunteer to discourage Feri as soon as I told her the story. And if not, I planned to recruit her to do that."

"So what happened?"

"I left her an urgent message, but she called two hours later with some kind of attitude and apathy. Still, I tried to be mature and control my nerves. After pouring out my guts to her pitifully about her mother's request for divorce and why it would be a big mistake for all of us, Rose interrupted me rather rudely.

'Actually, I told her to do it,' she said with pride.

'Why did you do that?' I asked her.

'Because she said she was unhappy and could've married a more sensitive man instead of wasting her youth on you,' she said so casually my brain went numb."

"My god…!" Reza uttered with bewilderment.

"At that moment I didn't know if I should kill her or myself."

"That's horrible… I agree," Reza said.

"Then, I went completely berserk when she asked me rudely and so matter-of-factly, 'Don't you think she could've found a better husband?' Her sarcastic tone alone could've killed you!"

"Just stop fooling me, T.J.!" Reza shrieked.

"No, I'm just telling you the God's honest truth," I said with a sigh. "Then, she said she had to go so casually while I was still in shock. I just can't believe my family's mentality and the sad truth I must bear about their horrible nature for the rest of my life."

"Even I'm shocked by Rose's attitude."

"I married her evil mother only to spare her life when she was just a helpless fetus, and now she repays me this way as a strong woman capable of putting some sense into her crazy mom's head and stop our family's demise. I'm sure they'll suffer much more than I would, but they don't seem to get it."

"What is going on in their brains?" Reza asked.

"I wish I knew. She sounded so stupid, like she didn't even realize that she would've not existed without me... if Feri had a different husband. Gosh, what's wrong with them, Reza?"

"I agree, it's just way beyond what I've ever seen or heard."

"I like to see their shock for not getting my last few millions."

"I didn't know you were that rich," Reza said with surprise.

"Thank god, I stopped making more money ten years ago."

"It's still a lot of money already…"

"Even worse, it's still growing fast in the crazy real estate markets in Vancouver and Tehran."

"You can find a few cute mistresses to forget your family."

"Especially in Iran, I can live like a king with several wives and mistresses. Pity, I also hate that lifestyle."

"Is there anything you don't hate, T.J.?"

"I'll have to think! But not trusting even my daughters hurts."

"Yeah, you're stuck, too... How silly our plans and aspirations feel now that we've lost even our identities!" Reza said.

"Although you guys might still have a chance. Just look at my family and learn a lesson before falling in deeper shit."

"Learn what? Stay single?" he asked.

"That's a great option for some enlightened people, but just get ready for more social chaos. Marriages, especially, will get even uglier every year," I said with a sigh.

"It's hard to know how to get ready, though, especially for oddballs like us...," Reza said.

"Especially Darren... He's screwed up the most," I said sadly.

"So, don't you think I'm also right worrying about the way he and Mahtab are duped by love now like teenagers?"

"Gosh! Did you start this long debate again only for justifying your meddling in Mahtab's life?"

"Yes, you caught me, T.J. But how can I just let them be and go away back to my other worries?"

"Didn't we discuss and analyse all these points already?"

"Yes, but after meeting them today, especially, I wonder if Mahtab knows how mixed-up Darren has always been about love and life... I don't think she can tame Darren, either."

"So now you think that not even her immense charm can do the trick, ha?" I asked jokingly.

"No... He's often rigid and reckless like a mule."

"You said he looked lost even now with Mahtab around him?"

"Yes, he did. He'd probably get fed up with Mahtab's free spirit and tenacity eventually," Reza replied. "She's so much like Erica in that regard as well."

"But they're hopefully smart enough to go around each other's personality flaws. Aren't they?"

"I doubt it when I weigh their characters logically... I already know how Darren and Erica drove each other nuts and I paid a price for it, too. Besides, he's just come out of a long coma and only God knows how stable his emotions and mind are now or later, especially around my moody, emotional sister. She's also been suffering the effects of a bad husband and living in Iran, a country she isn't accustomed to," Reza said.

"Yeah, they're most likely missing these crucial points..."

"Still, I feel both obliged and guilty for pushing Mahtab. I also know I've been all over the map about this matter too long, trying to reconcile these emotional and factual factors."

"Well, if they stay in love, they may learn to compromise in order to relate or at least don't get on each other's nerves all the time the way Feri and I did from day one."

"Thanks for the advice, anyway, but you're optimistic about people's ability to stay in love and keep compromising."

"All serious life decisions are risky and the bottomline is that living without a mate is not easy for Darren and Mahtab, either."

"That's true... You and I must also get ready to pay a big price for either having a mate or not," Reza said with despair.

"At least we oddballs realize our difficulty of being married and coping in society. This may be useful for Darren these days."

"Except that this affair's dangers are immediate and certain, so it feels even more foolish."

"Just let them be... They probably realize all these facts, but mention your worries to them, too," I said.

"As I said, you've been too romantic, despite the cynicism you portray and preach in your essays," Reza said with a chuckle.

"Of course...," I said. "And I know I've probably sounded all over the map today myself about marital pains and chances!"

"At least I had a good chat with Mahtab and left them with many tough facts to chew on," Reza said with a giggle. "I think I ruined their evening, but those lovebirds needed a reality check."

"At least you made them think a little. I wish I could've done the same with Feri and Rose. They don't even wanna talk to me."

"Yep, I ruined their evening...," Reza said with laughter.

"I wish I could've done the same... All I could do was to walk like a zombie all afternoon to find a solution, but only got more suspicious about my daughters' intentions for separating us."

"What intentions?"

"For one thing, they like to party and waste money without my occasional nagging. They're probably also thinking they'd get our money faster when Feri or I die, instead of everything going to the surviving spouse. Lonely people also die sooner. Those kids are sneaky enough to divide us and rule."

"Oh, gosh, T.J., you're just getting more paranoid every day," Reza said with a giggle.

"Maybe a bit more these days, but my long analyses today showed they're thinking only about themselves."

"So, you think your daughters have conspired to oust you to, 1) have fun without your nagging, 2) get their inheritance faster when one parent dies, and 3) make their parents die sooner as divorced, lonely persons," Reza listed my points to be funny.

"Exactly… You summed up my conclusions best."

"Well, actually you may have a valid theory," Reza said.

"So now I'm forced to counterattack, instead of just becoming less softhearted," I replied with loud laughter.

"What're you up to, now?"

"I think it'd be fun to make a plan with many odd conditions to negate my family's ideas and irritate them a long time before they get any of my money."

"You're getting soft again, but what kind of conditions?"

"For example, they won't get a penny as long as Feri is alive and until they're in their 50s at least."

"Really, T.J…!" Reza said with a chuckle. "You haven't just been walking in the streets wasting time, after all."

"Of course, not. It was quite productive, in a way!" I replied.

"Do you recall asking me last week if you were crazy and I said no?" Reza asked with laughter.

"Yep," I replied with a giggle.

"Today I agree with your neighbours."

"That's great, then, if my ideas sound crazy to you, too."

"Why? You want your kids claim your insanity and contest your will?" I asked confusedly.

"I'm including proper proof to make them fail after wasting time and money. I may need you also as one of my witnesses."

"You sound so sneaky today. In fact, your kids have probably inherited your own calculating genes."

"It's surely a factor, but mixed with their mother's evil genes has created a huge mess. They've made them much ghastlier than I've ever been or imagined possible for average humans."

"Still, ultimately their parents' crooked genes are in fault."

"That's why I mustn't be surprised about their nastiness when I've known all along how deeply they've inherited Feri's devilish genes and the way I've treated my own parents."

"That's right... You don't even have the right to be surprised," Reza said with a chuckle.

"That's why it's not fair to disinherit them totally. Another factor is that my own sly conscience gene led to creation of Rose who's now causing herself, Feri, and me endless pains."

"Not to mention encouraging Feri to ask for a divorce!"

"But thinking in this awful manner about my darling Rose makes me sad, too, while feeling horrible for being responsible for creating another devil."

"So stop all this nonsense, for your own sake at least."

"Unfortunately, doing nothing doesn't feel right, either."

"Why? You already admitted it's only their genes fault!"

"That's true, but anybody can become a better person if he or she gets smart and tries to curb the effects of his or her parents' bad genes, even as nasty as the ones inside Feri and our kids."

"So, now, the bottom line is that your daughters must wait an extra 30-40 years to get something from you?" Reza asked.

"Oh, no... They'll get an account of my estate regularly to see what they're missing and must wait for still longer."

Reza burst into laughter. "I hope you realize this gimmick alone will raise their chance of heart attack, while they curse your soul constantly as well, ha?"

"I know... But it's necessary to make them ponder the price of their lifelong apathy at least once a year."

"Still, I think you're nuts wasting your time on this project."

"If that's the price I must pay for doing at least one thing right in this world, so be it."

"Actually, it's genius to bug people much more after dying."

"People are the ones making us crazy, anyway," I replied.

"Of course! My sisters have driven me mad all our lives, too, but your family has done the best job on you. They get the prize!"

"My plan would at least make people think of me and laugh more often after I'm gone than when I'd been alive."

"And it also gives you the most important project of your life to keep yourself busy until your last breath."

"Absolutely... That's been a major factor all along."

"Honestly, if I had an ungrateful family like yours, I'd kick their asses outright. I don't have your patience," Reza said.

"That's how we all feel before having kids, but soon turn into marshmallows," I said with a sigh. "Actually, tell me how you'd kick their asses, and if it worked, I'll give you their inheritance."

"So Feri has been right about your soft-heartedness, after all."

"I guess... She knows how most parents, like her and me, are so helpless around our kids," I replied.

"I'm glad I'm at least not stuck with nutty kids or a wife."

"I'd felt their genes' wickedness when they were growing up, but I'd never thought they'd become eviler than the Devil. I'd also felt my family was losing their minds and respect for me, but had never imagined things will get so shocking and irreparable."

"You really mean it or are only too spiteful these days?"

"I mean it hundred percent, unfortunately and painfully…"

"Wow…," Reza uttered with shock.

"Still, I feel guilty for the mess they'll probably make out of their lives and the big price they'll pay for it in the future, too—"

Reza interrupted me, "Plus your guilt for causing their added pains from your necessary reprisals..."

"Exactly…. Then I'm also horrified and feel guilty about the kind of kids they might raise with such level of inferior mentality I've seen in my daughters. My poor grandchildren—just in case they carry some of my gorgeous, genius genes!"

"Don't worry... No smart man will marry your daughters."

"This has been my other worry all along, all thanks to Feri."

"She surely doesn't seem to have been a good role model."

"Her tenacity to stop me from explaining a different outlook to our kids has been despicable," I replied.

"So, neither of you taught them anything useful about life?"

"No… And that's the worst crime to inflict on our kids."

"Most parents have lost their own sense of reality, anyway."

"That's why each generation is getting worse in character and for relating to each other.

"And our cultures have also dwindled fast," Reza said.

"At least I can judge my own kids... Seeing them so lost in phony lifestyles and social vanity makes me wonder if those basic social rules in Iran serve people and families better than the loose values in this so-called civilized world."

"The problem is that we humans abuse our freedom stupidly, instead of understanding the purpose of mental freedom."

"Maybe bringing my family to Canada was stupid when I had major doubts about modern cultures already," I said. "I wonder if I ruined their chances of finding suitable husbands, too?"

"It's possible… But you had good intentions…"

"We always learn our lessons too late..."

"But don't say these words around people or in your writings. People will think you're not only crazy, but also rude and a male chauvinist," Reza said.

"For sure. I shouldn't jeopardize my gorgeous will's validity."

"Is life funny or what?"

"Especially by making us love a bunch of devils forever while suffering their endless evils," I replied with angst.

"I'm surprised especially about Rose who's always looked so calm and classy to me," Reza said.

"And I'm glad you didn't consider marrying her and cursing me every day until eternity," I said. "You owe me a lot."

"Absolutely! Thanks, T.J., for preventing a catastrophe and my eternal pain."

"Although Reza and Rose sounds like a match made in heaven! How about that?" I asked wittily.

Reza burst into laughter. "No, thanks...!"

"Don't you wanna do me a favour after everything I've done for you and you agreed *absolutely*?"

Reza laughed again and shook his head.

"Why not?" I asked giddily. "You think you have a chance to find a better mate than Rose and make a life together?"

"I doubt that as well... God likes to keep us on our toes until the end," he said.

"Ironically, suddenly my toes are hurting a lot these last few days as well in addition to my knees. God has kept me on my toes so long they're now ruined," I said seriously with worries.

"Really?" Reza asked with laughter.

"Yes... And I really think god is playing a funny game with all His creatures, but especially humans!"

"You revealed so much of your hidden talents today, T.J."

"I guess I did... But I hope you still think I'm not crazy."

"You're not. I'm proud of having such a smart, sneaky friend like you, especially for making me laugh during these hectic times. Thanks for being here these days," Reza said sincerely.

"I'm glad to have any value for somebody these days," I said.

"Do you want me talk to Feri or mediate between you two?" Reza asked while refilling our glasses with whisky.

"No, it's useless. Nothing short of my begging will convince that devil to take me back—maybe not even begging! She's made up her mind to find a young lover or husband and she might actually be able to do it."

"She's not so young or good looking anymore, don't worry," Reza said with a chuckle, hoping to cheer me up.

"But she's rich enough to find a bum or bimbo," I replied.

"You must think only about yourself, then," Reza said.

"I know… But it's hard after worrying about, and taking care of a big family for so long. Suddenly, I don't have a valid mission to pursue and don't know what to do with the rest of my life…"

"Are you crazy? You still have your nasty will to finish."

"Except for that project and writing, I mean… I feel useless otherwise."

"I don't even have that or a good idea about my future, even at my age when I should be full of ambitions and desires," Reza said after bringing some leftover chicken for us to nibble on, and pouring more whisky in my glass, which I kept emptying fast.

"Then, I must insist that you marry Rose to fill your life with lots of projects and joy, while thanking Feri and me every day for what we've created especially for you," I said giddily.

"Thanks for your kindness, but I'm not good enough for her."

We talked and laughed for another hour, sounding grateful for the opportunity of knowing each other to discuss our dilemmas so freely at least and bring short relief into our lives. These days, especially, my luck for having two smart friends had proven quite blissful, maybe as a part of a mystical fate.

"We'd better go to bed while we're in a better mood. Things will probably get even more hectic tomorrow," Reza said after a big yawn.

"Now you just had to ruin my hopes about things improving a bit tomorrow, didn't you?" I asked.

"I love your immense sense of irony or forgetfulness," Reza said sarcastically. "It goes very well with your endless paranoia and whining the whole night, doesn't it!"

"Thanks anyway, Reza, for harbouring and humouring a homeless avenger," I said.

"Glad to be of assistance, you vindictive devil. Now go dream some more tricks for your kids' inheritance!"

"Do you remember that old Persian saying, 'People kick their own fortunes'?" I asked with tears in my eyes.

"Yeah…"

"It applies to my family perfectly."

Chapter Twenty
Prisoners Swap

"We have tough decisions to make, Darren," Mahtab had said sombrely after our meeting with Reza, now suddenly sounding doubtful about her past position versus some emerging, plausible options.

"I know," that was all I had said, although her gloomy remark and tone had worried me all along.

We had then strolled in downtown streets in a pensive mood. We had touched and kissed occasionally, stealthily with fear, and exchanged random remarks, but otherwise remained locked in our thoughts. Reza and Detective Stewart had surely posed more urgent dilemmas on us today, while our options felt hazier and riskier every hour. So, we merely struggled with our emotions privately in a torturous silence.

Elizabeth had left another message on my answering machine and pleading to call her back as soon as possible. I had ignored her enough, mostly unintentionally, imagining she just wanted to convince me to let Jeff off the hook. At last, I brought myself to call her and agreed to meet on Granville Island the next day.

"Same place?" she had stressed with some tone of nostalgia, referring to the pub we used to go together those good old days.

"Okay," I had replied cautiously with guilt and hung up, while meeting Mahtab's probing eyes.

"I believe Elizabeth is still hoping to convince me drop my charges against Jeff," I told her.

"And you agreed to meet her?!" Mahtab asked sceptically.

"Yes... She won't give up until we have a chat *at least* and I may need her, too. I must deal with these simpler chores at least."

"Do you want me to go with you *at least*?" she asked tensely, as if mocking my sloppy use of 'at least' or its *special* meaning in this case.

"Why?"

"Just in case…"

"In case of what?" I asked for teasing and making her laugh.

"For not being alone in the streets now that those thugs are lurking around this building. She might even bring Jeff with her," she said seriously for protecting me—mostly against Elizabeth's charm, though, judging by a ray of jealousy in her eyes now that she knew about Elizabeth's role in the foursome love skirmish.

"I'll be safe, but if I'm murdered your decisions get easier."

"She was Erica's best friend, too, you said?" Mahtab asked.

I nodded and walked over and kissed her before we sunk into our private worries and thoughts again. I wished I could read her mind at that moment to decide least selfishly for her long-term welfare. Her choices were way riskier than mine, of course, while I abhorred my needs and preferences influencing hers. Despite our pledges, flourishing love, and wishing the best outcome for both of us, I liked to know what her best option was, never mind my needs. *I'm just becoming more softhearted and selfless every day, aren't I?* I pondered wittily with a giggle, which might have made Mahtab curious about my line of thoughts that second. Maybe she felt I was giddy for the chance of seeing Elizabeth the next day or maybe reminiscing about my old memories of her when she had been my lover.

Elizabeth looked frail and tense when we met in the pub. She was not as pretty as she had been in our accidental meeting right there just a few months earlier, which had led to our bizarre affair and Jeff's madness after she moved in with me.

"You look great, Elizabeth," I said.

"I hope you mean it," she replied sadly. "But you look good yourself, considering your ordeal. Sorry..."

"That's fine. It wasn't your fault too much, as I'd said before."

"Still you think it was my fault a little?" she asked.

"But I forgive you," I replied.

"Thanks…! Of course, I feel slightly guilty myself for Jeff's actions all because of me."

I only smiled at her while we ordered snack and beers to Cindy, who delivered her usual smirk to me, too, exactly like good old times, perhaps teasing me for my long reckless absence. She and other servers who knew me seemed surprised to see me around again after so long, most likely clueless about the ordeal keeping me away from my favourite pub all along.

"Were you out of town or something," Cindy asked at last.

"You could say that," I replied with a grin. "In fact, I was out of this crazy world for a while."

"You sound mysterious like usual, too," Cindy said and left.

"What'd you want to see me about?" I asked Elizabeth.

"About Jeff, as you'd probably guessed."

"Detective Stewart confirmed yesterday that he's guilty for what he's done to me and Erica. I'm gonna find a good lawyer and sue him for his last penny."

"But he didn't mean to cause that mayhem. His only mistake had been hiring two thugs to ask you forget about me."

"Yet his thoughtless act led to Erica's death."

"But you know that he'd done it merely out of jealously and desperation due to our action. You and I drove him to that state of lunacy, let's admit it."

"Still, he's caused me so much agony."

"Can't you forgive him for my sake at least and the damage our sinful affair caused that poor man?"

"Has he sent you to soften me?"

"No, he doesn't even know I'm meeting you. In fact, he'd go nuts again if he finds out I've even tried to talk with you."

"Do you really have to marry a crazy guy like him?"

"You know the answer, so stop bugging and humiliating me," she replied with grief pouring out of her eyes.

"Has he given you any details about those thugs yet?"

"No..."

"Do you think he knows how to find them?"

"I don't think so."

"Maybe he's lying only for protecting himself," I said just to agitate her, since I knew, according to Erica, Jeff had been trying to find and stop the thugs in vain even before the accident.

"How can you say this?"

"Because they seem to know I've recovered and are looking for me again."

"So?"

"Who do you think might've told them about my recovery? Who told you about it by the way?"

"He did," she replied. "But I don't know how he'd found out."

"Well, I don't know how he might've found out, either, but I believe he's the only person who could've informed the thugs."

"I don't think so, but you're scaring me with your ideas."

"That's good then, because he seems to have gone nuts."

"You really think so?"

"Yes. How much of the story has he told you?" I asked.

"He mentioned hiring the thugs and meeting with the police."

"Don't you feel badly at least about what happened to Erica because of his actions? Wasn't she supposedly your best friend?"

"I feel awful for what happened to her and I wish we could correct things. In fact, I wish we hadn't met and started this wild madness and causing all these catastrophes. But she'd been nasty to all of us, too. She wasn't such an innocent person, after all."

"Still she died for nothing; just for coming to my suite at a bad time when those hooligans had shot me. They were probably the ones who pushed her off the balcony to prevent her testimony."

"I'm really sorry for both of you, but sending Jeff to prison won't revive Erica or solve our problems, would it?"

"But I feel obliged to bring justice at least to Erica. She didn't deserve this," I said with some guilt about my ulterior motives' vagueness for following this case so vengefully.

"I don't know what to do," she said. "But I just can't let things happen to him and my life. I must either put all my trust in him and try to help him like a good fiancée or assume the worst about his character and leave him again."

"Then I'm the worst person to vouch for his character."

"One important point you keep forgetting," she said tensely.

"And what point is that?"

"That you and I—mostly you—caused his madness. That's the main thing I wanted to stress on today," she replied curtly.

"You think I'm the guilty person instead of Jeff?" I asked.

"Yes, I do… In the final analysis I agree with his comment, which he'd asked me to tell you and I did a few times already."

"His silly comment!?" I asked in a wrong way or tone.

"That *you started the whole thing*… You seduced me and made him mad. I agree with him hundred percent. So, you killed poor Erica, too, because you started the whole damn thing."

"Trying to make me feel guilty and drop my charges against him is understandable. But are you helping yourself by ignoring his guilt or marrying such a person?"

"Don't you think I've been fighting with the same maddening thoughts? I'm afraid of him sometimes and I feel pity for him other times. This is a new stressful dilemma all by itself, besides all the old issues I'd mentioned to you."

"So why do you defend him so much?"

"Because we'd caused his madness! When are you going to understand this?" she shrieked with such rage I felt horrible, for a second, about my role at the time in driving Jeff nuts, but more importantly, doing the same thing again to Bijan now.

"If I was selfish I would've insisted on my negative impression of Jeff," I said casually. "But you should decide for yourself."

"Decide about what?"

"If something is wrong with him or your relationship. Can't you still decide after eleven years of living with him?"

"I'd told you before, too, when we started our affair last year, that it's been hard to figure him out truly," Elizabeth said.

"Yet you're still planning to marry him and trying to convince me to ignore his actions, the same way you've always done."

"What else can I do?"

"Actually, you should thank and push me to prove the depth of his guilt. That way you can dump him, too, and go find a more suitable husband, or love him more if his innocence is proven."

"Darren, you're only confusing me again, instead of helping."

"I can't stop saying these sensible points. That's why I didn't think that our meeting was wise," I said with pain for saddening her, not to mention my selfish tenacity to refuse my own role and guilt in this matter*; or worse, about causing Bijan's lunacy these days as a new perfect parallel to my past sins.*

"Didn't we do all these analyses when we started our thing? I'm tired of it all," she said with tears gathering in her eyes.

"I'm only stating the facts again."

"Maybe similar thoughts had pushed me to see you, too?!"

"As I'd told you before too, you're afraid of losing him, while also remaining even more uncertain about him now."

"Yes, I remember your old advice, professor. Then I imagined you were saying those things about him just for keeping me for yourself. But now, you probably don't have the same incentive. You don't want me back in your life, I'm sure," she said slyly, which sounded more like testing my feelings these days or any residue of our old romance in my psyche. I merely ignored her cunning intention, while sensing her deep desperation in general.

Instead, I chuckled. "The best thing to do now is to force him find the thugs somehow to stop more troubles."

"What troubles?" she asked with surprise.

"They're looking for me again apparently. So, helping us to arrest those assholes would be the best way for him to redeem himself and prove his integrity to you."

"What if he can't or won't do it?" she asked with stress.

"Then decide about staying with him or not. You'll be helping yourself the most by learning about Jeff's role and guilt. Your influence over him is a big asset now for getting to the bottom of this mayhem and end it."

"You expect me to become a spy for you and that detective?"

"For your own benefit… It'll help you decide once and for all whether he's the right man to marry."

"And if not? What can I do next? Come back to you?" she asked either for teasing me or demanding a prize for her treason. *Again, not knowing which one felt unpleasant and unfair to me!*

So, I asked boldly for fun at least, "Do you even consider the idea of coming to live with me again an option?"

"Why not?" she uttered bravely but still mysteriously.

"Don't you worry he might send the thugs to kill us both?"

"No... I'm getting fed up with life, too, like the way you used to talk sometimes when we were together."

"So, that's my fault too perhaps, ha?" I asked and she laughed.

"Yes... Sometimes I think we could've made a good couple if odd circumstances hadn't caused our separation. Don't you think sometimes about the possibility of us being together?"

I still could not say if she was teasing me, trying to manipulate me to forgive Jeff, or really really wanted me!

"You were the one abandoning me when I needed you the most after my return from Tehran with so much distress," I said without knowing my motive to utter this mournful fact. Was it because I was already worried—subconsciously perhaps—about being lonely again if Mahtab decided to return to Iran? She had seemed rather toying with that option, after all! *Pathetic me!*

"I'm sorry. Maybe I made a mistake, but can we turn back the clock?" she said with guilt, which I reckoned might come handy later.

Now I realized Mahtab's wisdom about tagging along with me and displaying her ownership to stop the chance of Elizabeth abusing my vulnerability somehow. Yet I decided not to let down Elizabeth today to boost the chance of her cooperation *at least*.

"Everything has been happening too fast around me and my mind has rusted a bit during the coma, too," I replied. "So I can't answer your delicate questions today. Ironically, a few people have already asked to stay with me for different reasons."

"Sorry for asking such a silly question. But thanks for seeing me today. It has helped me a lot."

"So, are you going to grill Jeff now?"

"Yes, I will."

"Would you then share your findings with me?"

"I don't think so… It'd be a betrayal of his confidence in me and ruin everything. Don't you see these facts yourself?"

"But in case you wished to regain my trust, especially if you decide to dump him, I may be a good ally to have. I may even think about us again," I said, a bit ashamed of my hypocrisy again simply for abusing her connection to Jeff.

"You're a piece of work yourself, Darren, aren't you?" she said with a smirk and rose. "I must go. We'll talk later."

Gosh, these women are so charming and manipulating while they need you, then get so hostile promptly if we read their minds or resist their whims. How naively had I imagined only a minute earlier that she really cared for me and I could manipulate her myself? What a pathetic gender we are, we pompous men!

"Wait, I'm going too," I said and rose.

We stepped out of the pub and walked toward the market and the Aquabus platform. At one odd moment, we both looked up toward my apartment on the opposite bank as if the old memories and conversations in the same spot six months earlier ringed in our minds simultaneously. I wondered if she expected me to invite her, like the last time, to my apartment and maybe even make love together as tenderly, too. She had stronger incentives this time for seducing me, too, *at least* for making me forgive Jeff.

We reached the Aquabus platform and waited silently for a minute like expecting the other make a wonderful suggestion. But I only leaned and kissed her cheek before saying goodbye to her and stepping on the platform to board the Aquabus, rather rudely, while she watched me with tension. As the boat sailed away, I looked at my apartment again and wondered if Mahtab had been watching the confusing scene of Elizabeth and me at the Aquabus platform from the balcony with my big binoculars and wondering about my past or present relationship with her. I waved idiotically to the imaginary Mahtab on the balcony, just in case, but also as a repeat of this silly gesture a few months earlier for teasing nosy passersby and indulging my playful spirit.

Nearing my building, I noticed Mahtab and Mrs. Stanley chatting on the bench around the Creek. The scene was again too familiar, except that now Mahtab replaced Mahroo's position on the past occasion. Mrs. Stanley was probably making more gossips about me, the same way she had done with Mahroo six months earlier. Most likely, she did not even feel much of a difference between those two sisters. I wondered if I had yet succeeded in separating their presence and personalities fully in my own head.

"Good afternoon, ladies," I said giddily.

"Hello, Darren," Mahtab said with a pleasant grin.

"I was telling your friend about my interview with Detective Stewart a few days ago," Mrs. Stanley said eagerly.

"Yes, he told us. I had meant to talk to you myself," I said.

"What about?"

"He told me you've seen those guys again recently."

"Yes, I did. Twice… Once they were sitting in their car and once walking around, both times watching the building."

"You didn't talk to them, ha?"

"Of course, not. I'm not crazy to talk with killers."

"Of course, not!"

"But I should've walked by their car to get the plate number. I didn't think about it fast enough and that bothered me later."

"If you see them again, please call the detective right away or get the plate number."

"Yes, I thought so too. Maybe we can catch them next time."

"That'd be nice and you'll get a reward for it," I said.

"I'll keep my eyes open, then," Mrs. Stanley promised.

I made sure to fulfil my old pledge to myself to chat with Mrs. Stanley for ten minutes, while she looked pleased with my vastly improved demeanour today, but also her mission of catching the tugs. Then, Mahtab and I said goodbye to her and strolled away.

"What should we do about Reza's advice?" Mahtab asked.

"I think you should decide alone," I replied. "I'd rather only help you implement your plans."

"Are you undecided or only trying to be liberal?"

"A little of both, I guess," I said with a grin. She stared at me with scepticism, most likely about the meaning of my reluctance to decide. So, I continued. "What do you think we should do?"

"Maybe I'd better go back to Reza's place while we sort out other issues, although I also hate to leave you here alone."

"Don't worry, I'll survive somehow, I hope!" I said, but could not tame my itch to tease her a little in spite, or because, of our sombre moods. So I continued, "Besides, who said I'll be alone?"

"Don't tell me Elizabeth is ready to return as soon as I leave?"

I burst into laughter and luckily stopped uttering all the crazy words dying to jump out for teasing her more.

"No, don't worry; I won't do such a stupid thing. But if the thugs find and murder me, your life will get much easier."

"You've said this twice already...! Have you been expecting me to say I'll kill myself right away, too, if that happens?"

"No, never! Promise me you'll never do that...," I said giddily, glad for not adding, 'like Erica,' and proving my total idiocy.

"Okay, although replacing you might take a few weeks...," she replied with a giggle. "So I'll return to Reza's place."

"Okay... Let's minimize the chance of provoking Bijan."

"I also need Reza to keep sending me money from Iran."

"Making him an ally for our future fights is also useful."

"You sound relieved," she murmured with a sigh.

"I just want you to be safe," I replied, rather relieved all right.

"Did Elizabeth say anything about coming back?" she asked rather teasingly. Still, I was thrown off guard imagining women's miraculous intuition and tenacity to make wild, yet often accurate, insinuations so bravely!

"Are you kidding me now, too, besides leaving me?" I asked desperately to hide the truth.

"Thanks, Darren. I'm glad you agree," she said and kissed me. "Although you don't really seem to love me these days."

"Why do you say that?" I asked tensely.

"Because you sleep deep like a baby, eat like a giant, and your brain works fine," she said teasingly and we burst into laughter.

"I guess love has opposite effect on my sleep and appetite...! But how about Reza's idea of going back to deal with Bijan?"

"I have no plan yet... But Reza is right...," she said sadly. "I've been a bit selfish in recent months, only thinking about you and me. My mom and Nazi also need me, besides Bijan's demand."

"Thinking and taking one step at a time is the right strategy."

"I wish you could come with me," Mahtab said with gloom.

I burst into laughter. "To Reza's place or Iran?"

"Both," Mahtab said seriously. "Come hide in Reza's suite."

"I wish we could be together anywhere. But it's better that we live separately for a while. I'll miss you, but we can talk on the phone regularly—ten times every day."

"Hundred times…," Mahtab murmured and I nodded giddily.

We spent another splendid sleepless night together, savouring our last opportunity to be so close for a long time, if not forever if things got out of hand for one or both of us.

Early in the morning, I called Reza to give him the good news. We agreed to swap the 'prisoners of love' later in the day and we laughed about a few ways of teasing T.J. about the exchange.

When they arrived, I told T.J. to get comfortable in the spare bedroom, while I helped Mahtab and Reza. The idea of not seeing and touching her for God knew how long was ripping my heart. In front of the building, Mrs. Stanley asked Mahtab if she was returning to Iran *again* and Mahtab shook her head sadly, as we walked towards Reza's car. After Mahtab settled in the passenger seat, Reza turned and gave me a cheque for $30,000 furtively, exactly like paying me the ransom for giving back her sister.

"This is more than what my paintings were sold for," I said.

"Consider this only a loan. We'll settle the difference later. But for now, I'm keeping my promise to Bijan if he asks me to swear that I haven't given you the paintings' proceeds."

I nodded gratefully, then shook my head for all the nonsense teeming around us and all the lies we have been saying daily.

As Reza's car pulled away, my heart throbbed from Mahtab's departure and then faster from the sight of a car parked far away from our building with two guys in it. I considered approaching them furtively to check if they were the thugs or somebody else spying on me, or get the plate number at least. Luckily, I realized the risk of getting even slightly close to any suspicious people these days. I looked around to find Mrs. Stanley and give her the mission of checking out those guys, but no sight of her this once I needed her. I ran to my suite to fetch my binoculars and try to at least see them better or maybe read the licence plate. Yet, by the time I stepped onto the balcony with the binoculars, the car was gone. I kept looking around, but found only Mrs. Stanley reeling towards the building. I went back inside the living room.

T.J. smiled, apparently watching my spying on somebody or something so seriously with my binoculars.

"I guess I saw the thugs who shot me. Or maybe some other guys were spying on me near the building, but they're gone now or hiding," I told T.J., who kept staring at me with a sad smirk, as if eagerly open to the idea of thugs breaking into my suite that very second and ending both our miserable lives.

"I'm sorry to barge in on you like this. I still can go live in a motel if my stay is a problem for you these days," T.J. said.

"Stay as long as you wish. Actually, I need you these days."

"Why is that?" T.J. asked.

"For giving me both your mental and physical support."

"Yeah, just depend on me to kill both those thugs in a jiffy."

For an hour, T.J. and I whined about our dilemmas, especially his confusion after Feri's request for a divorce. To distract him, I told him how Mahtab and I had walked pensively for hours in the streets yesterday, wrestling with our romantic dilemmas amidst a dramatic situation. In the end, the poor guy looked overwhelmed, especially after I teased him about needing lots of his emotional support in case Mahtab decided to return to Tehran.

"Reza and I also walked a lot yesterday separately," he said.

"Many people appear to be walking or jogging to figure out their lives and praying answers fall off the sky!"

"Yes, I get that impression, too, but to me they look more like walking or running away from someone or something," T.J. said sadly, but maybe also stressing on his gloomier view of people's cryptic urges for sluggish meandering or energetic jogging.

"Could our two crude impressions be complementary?" I asked to humour T.J. now that he had tried to challenge me.

"I'd say you're the best person these days to solve this riddle."

"Yes, yes! You're right...! I'm doing all those things nowadays to restart my life," I replied and we burst into laughter. "Do you like to come with me for some jogging later today?"

"No, not today… My knees and toes hurt," T.J. replied.

I called Detective Stewart to give him an account of my exciting findings today. Luckily, he was in his office and took my call.

"Two things…," I told him matter-of-factly.

"Okay, Mr, Durant… Let's hear them!" he replied, sounding rather tired of my case and my corny vengeance towards Jeff.

“I believe I saw the thugs today in a car near my building.”

“So, you’re staying in your place despite my suggestion.”

“I don’t have any other place to hide and I need my life back.”

“It’s up to you… Did you get the licence plate?”

“No, I didn’t want to go near them.”

“Good decision…”

“But can anything be done about this matter?” I asked testily.

“Like what?”

“Maybe patrolling the building now that they come around so casually. I am a good bait maybe, now that I live here.”

“I’ll consider your suggestion. But how could you recognize them from a long distance?”

“I didn’t see their faces, of course, but they kept peering in my direction and seemed keen about my movements.”

“It could all be a kind of psychological reaction making you suspicious of anybody sitting in a car near your building.”

“Maybe… But they looked familiar,” I said, wondering if he now believed to be a professor of psychology, too!

“What is the other thing you wanted to tell me?”

“I like to stress on a point I made before and you dismissed.”

“Which point is that?”

“How do you really think those thugs have found out about my recovery so quickly and who do you think would most likely benefit from informing them?”

“It’s hard to guess,” he replied, which felt like another clue about his incompetence or fading interest in my case.

“It’s not too hard for me…! I think, and say again, only Jeff knew about my recovery and he knows that Erica has told me everything. Like the thugs, he wants to stop me from testifying.”

“We all realize these points, Mr. Durant. But as I told you last time, too, it’s only a possibility, not a solid evidence to charge him or even bring in for interrogation again. Besides—”

“Well, I’m not a detective, but don’t you think my deduction is very strong and implicates Jeff seriously?” I asked.

"Don't you think you might be paranoid about Jeff being a cold, calculating murderer?" Detective Stewart asked curtly.

"No, I don't," I replied with some spite that felt atypical of me. Deep down, however, I felt I was really pushing it and Jeff could not be a murderer in the way I had been acting, thinking, and talking about him with everybody. Maybe I was only hoping to push Jeff and the detective to find the thugs, so that I had one less worry these days. So my persistence to badmouth Jeff was both justified and ridiculous when looked from different angles! In fact, the detective could be right about my paranoia!

"Anyway, we can't act only on some hunches or accusations. We need real proof," he said. "Besides, I explained to you last time how you've played the main part yourself in getting shot."

"But I didn't quite agree with your findings about my part."

"Now, with your persistence, you're making me ask you a rather private question that has a major bearing on this case..."

"A *private* question?"

"Yes, I've been hoping to avoid it, but now I feel obliged to ask, anyway," he said sternly.

"So, what is your *private* question?" I asked sarcastically.

"Are you still seeing Jeff's fiancé, Mr. Durant?"

I was startled by the question and his possible insinuation.

"Well, I've seen her just to discuss the situation," I replied, quite unhappy about Stewart's new tactic and the odd possibility of spying on me instead of looking for the thugs.

"Well, I don't like to pry into people's private lives, but it is getting harder for me to judge your motives for accusing Jeff of a bigger crime while you're still in contact with his fiancé and maybe even more."

"I have no serious relationship with Elizabeth... I promise you," I said calmly, trying to control my frustration about his new silly allegation.

"But your promise is as legally valid as Jeff's promise about his role. In fact, your persistence may be construed as a way of getting Jeff out of the way to court his fiancé again!"

"I'm telling you the truth, Detective," I said with anger.

"That's exactly what Jeff says, too," he replied. "Besides…"

"Besides what?" I asked.

"Does Jeff know that you and Elizabeth are still in touch?"

"I don't think so…"

"Well, I hope you see the dilemma you've created for me."

Great… Now I had turned even Detective Stewart against me, as though I did not have a million enemies already!

"All I can say is that Elizabeth and I have no romantic affair."

"I'd like to believe you… But you must see my problem!"

"Sort of…! But I wished you believed me," I said pitifully.

"Again, I hate to pry in your private life, but for this special case, it'll help if you were in another relationship to mitigate the purpose of your contacts with Elizabeth," he said curiously, which sounded like a sly gimmick to make me explain Mahtab!

"Sorry I can't produce a love alibi to prove my innocence," I said with anger, quite upset about my inability to tell him and the entire world that I was indeed in love with Mahtab*, also sinfully… way more sinfully, in fact!*

"Anyhow, ultimately you're the only person responsible for getting shot. I explained the reasons before as well. Jeff didn't ask or provoke the thugs to shoot you. You did it yourself… and now still seeing his fiancé as well!"

"But we should at least find the thugs, so that I can rebuild a normal life. And I'm sure Jeff knows how to find them," I said.

"Okay… Leave it with me," he said. "But I also suggest you stop provoking Jeff again, at least until we catch the thugs!"

"How am I doing that?" I asked with exasperation.

"By still seeing his fiancé behind his back, of course."

I was itching to ask him how he thought Jeff might find out, but decided not to provoke him any further. After all, he could inform Jeff himself out of spite for me or merely for proving his point about the chance of Jeff finding out. He might at least give him a hint passively to raise Jeff's curiosity, maybe as a way of discharging his demented professional conscience!

PART III

One Lucky Man

Chapter Twenty-one
Painful Separation

The sound and scent of Mahtab back in my apartment, while she unpacked her small luggage in her bedroom, made me proud of my achievement. My calm, calculated approach had worked fine to win the first round and get ready for the big battle with similar tactics. She seemed to respond to my pitiful pleas better than she had reacted towards my logic and brotherly advice in the past. I had figured out this secret about women's keener response to sulking or sucking up, but had been unable so far to fight my pride and integrity to lower myself to their tactics or demands! Today, I was glad I had, though, hoping to master this diplomatic scheme for my future crusades. Now, perfecting this peculiar, potent art of negotiation felt admirable, instead of pitiful. If necessary, I might even shed some tears next time in front of Mahtab to make my case absolutely credible!

After Mahtab rested a bit, I invited her to a restaurant to curb her nostalgia. She said she was not in the mood to dress up or go out. So, using my new charm, I succeeded in convincing her to go without changing her casual outfit—a big revelation in itself!

"I wish we could ask Darren to join us, too," I told Mahtab in a soft voice after we sipped our wines and ordered our meals—*mostly perfecting my fawning regimen.*

"It's still not too late," she said with a cute mix of sarcasm and appreciation for my considerate attempt to include Darren in our thoughts at least. "Call him…"

"It is better not to be seen with Darren too much for a while. I'm almost sure Bijan has someone spying on us," I said, feeling sorry for mentioning Darren and opening the can of worms. My cajoling skills was still off, as it seemed to have backfired and I had failed a rather simple exercise.

"This is ridiculous, Reza," she said with angst.

"I know... I hate to be in the middle of this and making you unhappy with me. But I really need your help to settle this and other issues in a peaceful manner."

She nodded passively, which was still a positive, civil reaction considering all the pressure I was putting on her these days.

"I hope we can be friends and talk honestly and calmly even when we disagree or are under pressure," I said, wondering if I was pushing my luck too much by asking her to be friends.

"You've changed in recent weeks. What's happened to you?" she asked with surprise and cynicism.

"You're the only one who can understand and help me with my problems. I can't handle the situation in Iran alone," I said.

Mahtab only nodded again, this time with a cordial grin.

"I'd like us support each other like two friends," I said.

"We can try if you really mean it," she murmured.

"Then, may I ask you if you're really sure about Darren?"

"Yes, I do. At least I think so," she replied with a subtle angst.

"So, even you have some tiny reservation about the meaning and stability of love, especially for *a man like him*, don't you?"

"Everybody does… unless a person is totally stupid."

"Oh, dear Mahtab, I'm so glad you talk so intelligently. I'll do my best to be your friend and face our problems together."

"But what do you mean, 'A man like him?'" she asked irately.

"Well, he's a good man, but has had many upheavals and life challenges that have made him at least unstable emotionally and professionally. Even he's trying to figure out what kind of a man he is or wishes to be," I said as cautiously as possible.

"I guess! What do you think is wise for me to do?" she asked calmly, maybe for testing my intentions and expressed allegiance. Yet, I was too smart to fall into her trap and utter a direct opinion.

"You must decide on your own about Darren after weighing your mutual needs and temperaments. But, maybe it's best if you return to Iran awhile to sort out the pending issues and remove the present obstacles to be with Darren."

"I need time to think about it, as I'd said."

"How did all this happen, anyway?"

Mahtab shrugged and shook her head with a sudden sign of confusion and distress about a seemingly delicate matter. I just kept staring at her with affection and empathy.

"It is hard for me to know what happened and why I feel this way about him," she said at last. "But your question triggers a sore thought about my old jealousy towards Mahroo when I first saw Darren. For a moment that night, I wished I were in Mahroo's place instead of being married to Bijan."

"You felt jealous and desired Darren that soon?" I asked with shock mostly about Mahtab's sudden courageous candour.

"I'm confessing since I like to get a big load off my shoulder."

"Wasn't it the same night Mahroo passed away?" I asked.

"Yes... You and Darren arrived early that night and Mahroo was still at work in that depressing rehabilitation center."

"Yes, I remember. We came early for him to talk to Bijan."

"I've felt terrible all along for what happened to her that night, while I'd felt jealous of my own sister because of Darren."

"You were drawn to Darren right after seeing him?"

"No. Maybe Mahroo's way of adoring and explaining him for months had affected my perception of him already. But when she gave me his painting, too, something strange happened and my feelings for him grew mysteriously the more I looked at it."

"That damn painting has been demonic all along! I don't even understand why Mahroo gave it to you when she loved it herself."

"I was surprised, too, but I feel horrible when I consider the chance of causing her death with my desire to be in her place."

"Don't be silly. These thoughts are merely a symptom of our love for Mahroo. But your confession also shows that the root of your feelings for Darren is vague and bothering you, too."

"Reza, do you think I have stolen Darren from Mahroo?"

"No, I don't think so…," I said with gloom and confusion, never expecting such deep emotions hurting my frail sister.

"I wonder if a mysterious hand grants our wishes to show its magic or mercy, or just punish us at the end for our evil desires?"

"Why do you even consider these superstitions?"

"I don't know! I'd never believed in this stuff."

"Just don't even think about these things," I said in distress.

"I can't, Reza… I feel so guilty for what I might've done or what I'm doing now," she said in tears.

"Oh, my god... I'm just stunned with your confession today."

"Don't you think I jinxed and killed Mahroo with my stupid desire for Darren?"

"Of course, not. I really appreciate your trust in me, Mahtab. But I'm now suddenly more concerned about you than ever."

"You are?" she asked with sarcasm and pity again.

"Yes… Discussing things with you feels even more urgent now," I said, trying to raise her trust in me without angering her.

"I'm glad for this chance to make these confessions," she said with pain. "I've suffered a lot for hiding this feeling with guilt."

"You haven't shared these thoughts with Darren, either, ha?"

"Oh, no, never… Please promise me you won't mention this matter to him or anybody else ever."

"Of course… Don't worry about it," I replied with distress.

"Sometimes, I think I must give up Darren simply out of guilt. But often I believe Mahroo also wants me to love Darren."

"I also think that is what Mahroo prefers, if you really care for Darren," I said with conviction, amazed of my change of attitude about her affair so suddenly and the possibility of Mahtab having in fact goaded me to tell her exactly what she had never imagined I would ever say. What was happening to me and what was Mahtab doing to my head, the way I was indeed now begging her to love Darren, just to stop her sense of guilt for killing Mahroo. Meanwhile, as a related clue, I pondered mentioning my dream about Mahroo ordering me to leave Mahtab and Darren alone. Thank god, I stopped making Mahtab more confused with some nonsensical notions or my dreams.

My job to console and advice Mahtab had become many folds more complex in just one hour, since I had tried to be her friend. I had put myself in a bizarre spot beyond my imagination. Now that she had spilled her guts to me and sought my advice, I felt helpless to think straight myself. Now, I could feel how both options of loving or leaving Darren seemed hurtful for Mahtab in different manners. I needed a holy guru myself to guide me in this highly emotional saga.

"My advice is to do not decide anything too quickly," I said helplessly only as a show of support. "Let's go home and relax. We have overworked our brains in recent days a lot."

"Okay… I believe I love him, anyway," she replied nicely.

"Good... Since we're clearing the air and starting a friendship, I also like to ask you something that has bothered me," I said.

"What is that? What other truth you wanna drag out of me?"

"Something about the night I arrived from Iran and saw you guys in my bed," I said cautiously.

"What about it?" Mahtab asked with surprise timidly.

"Were you two laughing at me after I yelled at you and went to the living room?" I asked.

Mahtab burst into laughter. "No, not at all… Silly…! It was for something that Darren said."

"What did he say?"

"He asked in a very serious tone, 'Do you think we can blame Detective Stewart for this, too?'"

"Who is Detective Stewart?"

"He's the detective trying to find the thugs who shot Darren. He'd told us it was safer for Darren not to stay in his own place. So we decided to blame only him if anybody ever found out and complained about Darren living in your suite or hiding with me."

I burst into laughter myself realizing the gist of the anecdote.

"Did you give him an answer?" I asked with a chuckle.

"After we could finally stop our hysterical laughter, I told him I really enjoyed his wit even in such an awful situation."

"I'm glad you two could keep your sense of humour when you knew I was dying of shame and rage in the next room and hearing your seemingly mocking laughter going on and on."

"Well, he was really funny and we couldn't waste the irony in that moment, despite the misery we all felt."

Back in my apartment, Mahtab returned Darren's call before I returned Bijan's, who asked for an update and a chance to talk with Mahtab. When she refused again to talk with him, I asked her to at least talk loudly near the phone to humour Bijan.

"I don't feel like talking to anybody tonight," Mahtab yelled near the phone for Bijan's benefit.

Bijan sounded thrilled at the end of our conversation about hearing Mahtab's mesmerizing voice despite its harsh tone and rejection. He even said so timidly, which sounded rather romantic to me instead of pitiful like usual. What was happening to me so fast, getting so soft and caring even towards people who were causing me so much pain and hassle, if not considered my enemy altogether? For a moment, I felt the torture, humiliation, self-pity, and loneliness that poor Bijan must have been enduring in recent months. The hope and energy that even Mahtab's rude remark near the phone, about her reluctance to talk to him, had given Bijan was simply an eye-opener. How sadly helpless we men are around women and about love, despite our vast arrogance. Wow! Our poor, pathetic souls! Bijan's… Mine… Darren's… T.J.'s…!

The next day, Mahtab and I had a long but calm argument when she insisted on visiting Darren alone or together somewhere. To repeat certain facts to her and maintain my diplomatic approach with both of them was taking a big toll on my nerves. However, I kept reminding myself to remain calm for my sacred goal.

"Why can't we see Darren together?" she asked again when I had assumed the matter was settled for a day at least. Gosh, these women are really stubborn and have a lot of stamina for arguing!

"The point is that you can most likely assess your long-term options better if you put Darren on the side awhile to handle your marital and family concerns first."

"But we can't simply take him out of the equation," she said with stress, reminding me to be careful.

"I'm sorry, I meant it's better to handle Bijan and your feeling for Darren separately...," I said quickly with terror. She sounded like a teenager falling in love with another juvenile like herself.

At last, I convinced her to stay away from Darren a few days and instead go to Whistler with me today. All the years I had been in Vancouver, I had hardly gotten a chance to explore the natural beauties of this province. Mahtab had not done much sightseeing here herself, either. Thus, I thought it was a good time to do so, especially for Mahtab.

We drove on the shoreline highway carved on the side of big rocky mountains next to the Pacific Ocean. The breathtaking view made us stop in many spots to absorb the majesty of nature and take a few picture. Besides a joint picture with Mahtab that I once asked a man to take, I photographed her pensive face mostly looking into the distant horizon and expansive waters—quite similar to the mood of the woman in Darren's epic painting. We walked around the lake at Whistler and in the cosy village, visited an art gallery, and then sat for lunch at a café.

"Why don't you go back to Tehran and bring mom and Nazi here with you?" Mahtab asked.

"I've been thinking about this option and talked to mom about it, too. But we both thought it was not a good idea at this point."

"Why not?"

"For one thing, she's not sure if she likes to live in Vancouver, especially if nobody knows about your final place of residence. She thinks you might return to Tehran even if you divorce Bijan. Or you might go live in Europe or somewhere else. She likes her house and friends. Nazi is not a Canadian resident and we don't know who'll take care of her if mom leaves us. Besides…" I paused in time, wondering about the wisdom of raising family issues on a day we had allegedly dedicated to relaxing our minds.

Mahtab stared at me tensely, so I continued, "The main hurdle is Bijan again, of course. As soon as he realizes that mom and Nazi are on the move to Canada, he suspects that it relates to your final decision to not return to Iran. So, he'll start intimidating you and Darren immediately as well as our mom. We're still trying to keep a civilized relationship with Bijan to keep him rather calm and friendly with us, while we all wait for your return."

"So, mom and Nazi are his hostages?" she asked tensely, which justified my earlier plan to avoid raising these topics today.

"The situation will get ugly if mom and I show any sign of detachment towards him, too. We've kept him close for now."

"I understand… That is wise. Thank you," she said.

"Mom is very diplomatic and clever. Bijan respects her more than his own mother. She's a potent weapon for you."

"I see your point…"

"So, Bijan would behave himself if you just make a short trip to Tehran and decide about your marriage and family."

"I'm thinking about it, as I said."

"When do you think you'll decide?"

"I don't want to rush. I need more time."

"Can you give me an estimate at least? A day or a week?"

"A few weeks at least."

"Wow… that's too long. Bijan won't wait that long and I can't leave mom and Nazi alone more than a few days."

"I'm facing a tough decision, Reza," she said with a grimace.

"So I'd better go back to keep things calm over there and wait for your decision. I'm worried about mom."

"That's probably the best," she said with a sign of relief.

"I don't know how to deal with Bijan much longer, but I don't wish to push you more, either," I said.

"Good... Can you pick up Mahroo's portrait that is in Bijan's house, the one that Darren painted in Barcelona?"

"Okay, we'll do that. But will you talk to Bijan for a minute on the phone when he calls tonight and tell him that you might be going to Tehran soon. That will help me keep him quiet awhile."

"Is that really necessary?"

"Yes, it'll help me a lot. Try to show flexibility on the phone."

"I'll think about it..."

"Besides, a short chat with him might give you an impression about him if you return to Iran and how to handle him."

"Maybe... I'm not sure..."

"When I return to Tehran, I'll also take mom and Nazi to visit him as a sign of things getting normal amongst us."

"That's a good plan."

"Anytime Nazi calls him Uncle Bijan his whole body shivers from excitement as if given a free pass to heaven. He loves her only a little less than he loves you."

"Is she calling him Uncle now?" Mahtab asked with surprise.

"Yes, we've taught her to say it to keep Bijan feel connected."

"You're cunning, too, Reza, even more than mom."

"What do you mean?"

"You've apparently been using an old woman and a cute child all along to control Bijan."

"He's not a bad man, after all, except that loving you so much has driven him crazy."

"Okay, I'll talk with him tonight just for you," she said with satisfaction, sounding more cooperative and wiser every minute.

"We'll use similar tactics on him to keep him on a leash when you come to Tehran, too, even if you still want a divorce."

"I'm glad we're allies, although you don't let me see Darren."

"It's only for a while. It's a good strategy in the long term."

"I bet you've been cunning me all along, too—becoming my friend, supposedly, to make me do many things," she said wittily.

Her intelligence to humour my manipulations all along was pleasant. She could not be fooled and I must have sounded rather reasonable to her, besides my growing knack for fawning. It all felt like a big achievement and boosted for my self-image.

"I'll never have that kind of power over you," I said.

"You have… Making me talk to Bijan, abandoning Darren and not seeing him, considering going back to Iran, and all the other stuff you've been making me do, you sneaky bastard," she said with a giggle and I joined her in laughing. "Worst of all, you convinced me to go out to a fancy restaurant in rags last night."

I leaned and kissed her cheek and we hugged for the first time after many years. She wept, as if family sentiments had raised her nostalgia for Mahroo, Darren, or both—now stuck with me!

"You should trust me and do some of the things we can agree is good for you as well as Darren," I said when she was calm.

"Do you still like Darren?" she asked. "Are you afraid Bijan might hurt him?"

"Yes and yes. He's a good man but rather reckless and also unlucky. So your association with him worries me for you a lot more than I worry about him, of course."

Mahtab nodded pensively, which made me think how much I could or should keep her away from Darren. Was she going to see him again right after I left Vancouver in a few days?

She could hardly wait to call Darren as soon as we arrived home and thanked each other for the pleasant day at Whistler. They talked behind the closed doors for two hours on the phone like teenagers. When I spoke with T.J. later, we laughed a little about those two juveniles, as he confirmed Darren had also gone to his room and talked quietly, behind the closed door. We had only a short chat before I rushed to prepare something for supper. When Mahtab emerged finally from her bedroom, looking quite happy and rejuvenated, I was famished and sorry for waiting so long just to have our dinner together. Then, as we sat down, the phone rang and I had to spend another twenty minutes to give Bijan a progress report before passing on the phone to Mahtab. She spoke rather civilly with the poor man about two minutes and promised him that she was considering a trip to Iran soon to settle the outstanding matters between them.

"How did Bijan take your promise?" I asked her.

"He sounded excited and polite," she replied.

"That's the whole point. Our plan is working, no matter what he's thinking and hoping."

Mahtab nodded and then we finally sat to have our supper.

Three days later, I was ready to return to Tehran without any clue about Mahtab's plans, though she appeared counting the days and hours for my departure to see Darren and make her final decision —in each other's naked arms, most likely. I did not push her for not seeing Darren, either. I had done my best to discourage her and now it was time to let her be.

When I called Darren to say goodbye, he insisted to give me a ride to the airport early in the morning. Humorously, I wondered if his generous offer was part of the lovers' plan to ensure I left Vancouver. What could I do with these two fearless lovebirds so restless for my departure to resume their travesty? Crazy fools! Apparently, I was the only person truly worried about Bijan's wrath and the big chance of all of us being under surveillance. I stressed this fact to Darren again, too, on the way to the airport and advised him to refrain from seeing Mahtab.

"Are you sure it is wise for Mahtab to return to Tehran and confront Bijan if she is not going to reconcile with him?" Darren asked with concern. "He might make things really hard for her."

"Do you remember your answer when I asked you a similar question and you promised not to influence her decision?"

"Yes."

"I'm doing the same thing. We must let her decide alone. This is probably the most difficult and crucial decision of her life," I said with angst. The painful separation between these two lovers had singed my spirit more than they realized, especially after she had confided in me about many issues recently!

"But you seem to have been influencing her all along, Reza," Darren objected. "She suddenly seems rather ready to go back."

"She knows all the facts better now, I believe. That's all!"

"You're sure?"

"Yes, I promise too. And stop thinking that you're her only concern and the only person she loves."

"I realize that, but she's now suddenly different."

"Her new conclusions are hopefully based on all the relevant information she'd been ignoring for a few months that she'd been in Vancouver and thinking only one dimensional—about you. She's facing the reality better now and I'd like to ask you again to leave her alone."

"I won't impose myself on her," Darren said. "That's the best I can promise you."

"Also remember that Bijan most likely has a spy following Mahtab at least and things could get nasty, especially for you. Focus on her welfare even if you like taking risks for yourself. Seeing her anywhere will be risky." Darren did not answer, so I continued, "You've caused my family lots of grief last four years. Give us all a break a few months at least. Be a man!"

Darren still kept silent and I realized my remarks might have been slightly too harsh, although I had thought during the last few days about the necessity of making him appreciate the gravity of the situation we were all facing, thus letting Mahtab make her decisions wisely. I had apparently achieved my sacred mission—going by his timid silence. I felt pleased with my ultimatum, but tried to think of a humorous topic just in case I had upset him.

"Has T.J. mentioned the details of his recent skirmishes with his family leading to his present homelessness?"

"Yes he has, poor guy. He's suddenly in a bad place, too, like you and me. He looks so lost and desperate."

"Try to focus on him more and help him think straight again."

"Instead of seeing Mahtab, you mean?" he blurted wittily.

"That too, yes. Maybe this project can reduce your obsession with Mahtab," I said.

"I will. He suddenly looks much older than his age and quite heartbroken. He reminds me of Dervish Ali sometimes."

"Poor Dervish Ali... I haven't seen him for a long time. I don't even know if he's still in prison or alive. My family problems have ruined my business and personal obligations as well."

"If you see him, give him my best regards," he said.

"There's something I should get off my chest," I said, hoping to raise his sense of responsibility and guilt, too.

"What's that?"

"Bijan and his father have stopped following Dervish's case after Mahtab came to Vancouver, you recovered, and their wild imaginations grew," I said with a heartbreaking sigh to crush his conscience.

"Oh, I'm sorry. Have you mentioned it to Mahtab?" he asked.

"No, I forgot. But it's a good piece of information you could tell her as well."

"Does Dervish know?"

"No, I haven't told him that you and Mahtab are the cause of his longer detention and possible death these days… Otherwise, he would've been released by now."

"Are you hoping to make me feel even guiltier?"

"I guess so. You and Mahtab must know that Dervish Ali is now a dying hostage for your actions as well."

"I'm sure you'll never tell him about us!" he said tensely.

"I hope I never have to tell him you two are killing him, too."

"Thanks…! I'd felt badly about my role in many people's fates already without you adding this new guilt to my conscience. I hate all these mixed complications."

"Let's hope we get a chance to rescue him in time," I said with pleasure about my sly gimmick agitating Darren.

"You really made my day today, didn't you?" he whined.

"I must at least try to see Dervish now that I can't help him."

"Tell him I'm sorry without mentioning my reasons," he said.

"Okay… Meanwhile, you take care of T.J."

"I'll try, although I don't know how or if he lets me. Actually, he wanted to come along, but now I'm glad I didn't bring him to witness my humiliation."

"Sorry, Darren, for being frank this early in the morning, but I'd meant to say these words to you without Mahtab around us."

"I appreciate your efforts to save us, especially Mahtab," he said sincerely, though his sentimentality also sounded sarcastic.

"I hope you mean it!" I said, trying to show his subtle sarcasm was not missed. Then I giggled. *He is a clever man after all, like me,* I mused, peering at him with further appreciation for his pure nature. I was leaving my dear sister's fate in his hands, after all.

"Absolutely," Darren replied with a silly giggle of his own, apparently trying to outdo me in our dire knack for sarcasm and humour mixed slyly.

"Can you take care of things here, especially Mahtab, for all our sakes, while I face big battles in Tehran?"

"I'll do my best," he said.

"If I happened to die, protect her with all your might."

"Don't worry about Mahtab. But don't die yet."

"I can't promise. Some spirits have been pushing me recently to do something about my measly existence," I replied, pleased with my tongue for not revealing whose spirit has been travelling all the way to Tehran and goading me to jump off my balcony. *I wondered if Erica had been looking for me and calling me all along in Tehran or knew I'd come to Vancouver?*

"At least don't die before taking care of Bijan somehow!"

"I'll do my best…"

"And I'll take good care of Mahtab, anyway, even if you're not around!" Darren said giddily after stopping the car in front of the international terminal at the airport.

We got out of the car, shook hands, and I walked towards the terminal with great confidence in him. Still, my witty paranoia liked to think that he would go park his car somewhere nearby, maybe even in a 'no parking' zone, just to rush back to make sure

I really got on that plane and out of their hairs. I wondered giddily if Mahtab had told him to do just that. I hoped those two fanatic lovebirds were smart enough to elude making a big mess of their lives, but what more could I do? What a silly game love is!

During my long flight, my attempt to stay optimistic and hopeful about things working out fine for Mahtab and Darren triggered a deeper concern in my head about the meaning and purpose of *hope* for managing our existence, as a forceful drive for modern humans' psyches. We three petite philosophers had studied this topic a few times as well. On the one hand, I have pondered and abhorred my dire inability to enjoy a simple mentality driven by hope like most people in the world, mainly under the influence of religions. Or was I merely naïve about other people's innate knack for simpler perceptions of life based on hope and religions, and thus an easier routine existence in line with crooked social norms? It seems our ultimate helplessness also triggers the notion of hope to soothe our sinking psyches in line with our dreams for a magical turn-around.

On the other hand, I have gradually begun to believe that we may live more naturally and truthfully if we could abandon hope in all our thoughts. It is a tough conviction to embrace and it takes plenty of time and courage to learn how to live without the hope for a stable or happy existence. It is tough to train our minds to adopt this life's reality—such a radical conclusion—about hope as a practical life philosophy. Achieving this goal has remained a challenge personally, in particular, when I still *hope* for all love affairs to succeed. Or even more foolishly, *hope* to help Mahtab on that matter myself! Certainly, these conflicting notions were so unhelpful these days, while I strived to invent a wise strategy for helping Mahtab fulfil her hopes for both of us. Nevertheless, the idea of abandoning hope has prospered in my psyche as a plausible option or divine ambition, if not a genius life path.

Here we go again…! My inability to relax and take at least a nap during long flights is so bothersome, almost as irritable as my indecision about the role of hope has been in recent years. I have never been much of a conversationalist around strangers to open up to passengers in order to curb my erratic thoughts. Anyway, I squeezed my eyelids and *hoped* so uselessly to fall sleep! *What did I just tell you about hope?* This topic of hope alone would not let me rest! *And these long flights might ruin my brain totally!*

What is hope, where did it come from, and in what period of human history? It is simply our naïve trust in a supernatural force rewarding us for some reasons (our goodness, for example) or just randomly. Hope is a derivative of 'faith' then. We put our faith in that supernatural force to help us. This is what religion is made for: to raise people's dependence on 'faith' in order to live merely based on hope and fantasy—often the hope of going to heaven or being able to put some sense into people's numb heads, especially Mahtab's and Bijan's at this grave time.

Before religions—when people had lived mostly according to their instincts and adaptation forces—no definition or application had probably existed for 'faith' and hope! Just a few millenniums back, before philosophy and religions, maybe humans were not stalled or fooled by so many devious devices, especially love and hope, which are now ingrained in our essence apparently. Now, we strive to seek refuge in so many illusive concepts out of sheer despair and fear. Did our ancestors ever rely only on themselves and no supernatural force, like all other creatures? Now, we weak, wicked humans use many traditional and modern jargons, such as fate, luck, hell, heaven, positive thinking, and love, casually to soothe our pains. We keep building fancy churches and mosques and spend many hours praying hopefully for miracles.

Now, it seems almost impossible for anyone to live even a day without a mix of hope and socializing. Yet, if one could master this tough challenge without losing his or her identity and spirit, he or she would most likely acquire the ultimate maturity and wisdom, along with serenity as most tangible rewards for being.

What am I turning into?

Chapter Twenty-two
Cost of Free Accommodation

The prisoners swap, which had been furtive, fast, and funny, had also availed the opportunity of seeing Mahtab briefly for the first time. Her resemblance to late Mahroo stunned me, although I had heard about it and been anxious to judge it myself. Reza took her suitcase from Darren and walked towards the elevator, while I stood politely with my huge luggage and a big load of agony, pondering the humour of human behaviour. Darren told me to go settle in the guestroom, and then ran after Reza and Mahtab.

The humiliation of being transported nonchalantly from one sad location to another like a broken piece of furniture, while Reza and Darren joked about the 'prisoner exchange,' was only a small cost of my sudden homelessness. The bigger hassle was a sense of civil obligation to prove my innocence and the crimes posed upon me rather than being a convict—as a main provision for this prisoner exchange. I had to recount the long, pitiful sagas of my family's new atrocities to the new warden all over again. However, repeating them felt sadder and cruller every time, as though sensing a higher pinnacle of human folly and my share of stupidities with more humiliation and astonishment, especially the roots of my misery—meeting and marrying Feri.

Luckily, in the end, my long account of my homelessness root proved plenty to qualify me for Darren's charity, too! The ironies of my old age traumas offering hilarious tales also felt useful at least for making us relax a bit and subdue our worries briefly. Darren's sly requests to elaborate on my family's shoes, Rose's role in Feri's request for a divorce, and my reprisal plans showed the depth and oddities of my fate perfectly. His loud laughter made me wonder jokingly if I should start charging him extra for my tales besides the free accommodation; *unless his jubilation pertained to his relief about Mahtab's departure!*

I was wrong... Soon, the mood got frightfully bleak when Darren felt obliged to whine a lot himself about missing Mahtab and his continuing love misfortunes. He did it also out of duty to soothe my pain or to shut my mouth awhile. Worse, we soon felt the need to outdo the other to get more sympathy, entertain and calm each other, or justify our inadequate energy and sympathy the other person sought desperately—all as part of our friendship duties! Our efforts to empathize, rationalize, or substantiate our situations and the misery of our wrecked lives only burdened both of us even more, especially since we strived to analyse the incidents and our fates both practically and philosophically, too—maybe as an educational endeavour in itself.

So, Darren's refusal to take me along when driving Reza to the airport had initially felt like a clue about him getting sick and tired of my presence and grievances already. Then, I realized their intention to exchange some last minute wisdom and whining, while I needed a break from Darren even more. Reza had already made a few tough requests from me the day before his departure.

"Make Darren think straight, T.J.," Reza had stressed.

"I can't think straight even myself!" I had replied.

"At least push him to leave Mahtab alone next two or three weeks, so that she can decide with a clear head."

"I don't know how but will do my best," I had replied.

"Pretend being sick and needing his help if necessary," he had said. *Now, I had to become a great actor and liar, too!*

"What else?" I had asked with sarcasm but he was pushy.

"Keep warning him about the risks of going anywhere alone or with Mahtab and facing those guys who shot him."

"Apparently, the police have also told him that. The other day, he said he'd himself seen those guys around the building."

"Here we go. This is a big excuse to stop him from seeing her. Become his bodyguard to keep Mahtab safe, too," he had giddily.

"You mean, guard him away from Mahtab's body?" I had asked childishly for teasing him.

"That'll also keep her safe from bigger threats around him."

"Bigger threats than Darren himself? Is it possible?"

Anyhow, my homelessness had brought me lots of extra work and lying to stop Darren from going anywhere without me, on top of the hassles of going with him everywhere, for fulfilling Reza's request. Then, Darren started to believe Mahtab had *changed*, probably due to Reza's ardent advice to her, like the one he had apparently given him on their way to the airport. His mood had become so pitiful and demoralizing that the free accommodation I enjoyed in his apartment felt less worthy every day. In two days, my pains and stress had grown in many bizarre ways unrelated to my main miseries, while I still tried to fathom the reasons for my beloveds' rebellion and vile attitude. I had been crying privately a lot since moving in with Darren. On the other hand, my wifeless life felt so wobbly and weird I stirred his whining intentionally sometimes, rather ironically, to either forget my own agony for a while or die faster from so much nagging around the house. For instance, my abrupt loaded comment to him the other day felt like a masterpiece:

"Reza has surely made Mahtab think!" I said slyly out of the blue after a long silence in the room.

"Yes, she's in a different world suddenly," he replied glumly.

"But ultimately, she is the one who must make so many tough decisions along with some serious thinking after so long. She's in fact behaving rationally these days at last, instead of letting her feelings for you alone dictate her decisions," I said, wondering if I was pushing his nerves a bit too much

"You're right… That's why I love her. But I'm also afraid of losing her, T.J.," he said solemnly with pitiful eyes. "I've lost many lovers in one year and I'm desperate to have a stable life."

"I get it… I had the same ambitions. Now look at me! This is the result of my lifetime goodwill and efforts for a stable life."

"That's true. Just witnessing your situation makes me sadder when I imagine it happens to most of us," Darren said.

"Sorry for reminding you of life's tyrannies. But also imagine Mahtab wrestling with many emotional issues these days besides you," I said, as if paid by the Devil to tease him to the verge of lunacy. He looked so sad I felt *a bit* sorry for starting this chitchat only for fun or a break from our silent, sad reflections.

"Yeah. She's stuck in a tough position. I must be less selfish."

"Remember this pledge and let her be awhile," I said, thinking that I was doing a great job of obliging Reza while showing the Devil's sense of humour.

"I have no other choice, anyway, while she's avoiding me," he replied with gloom. "But this anticipation is so darn painful."

"Just be patient... Ask your doctor for some tranquilizers."

"It's useless... Not knowing her thoughts or plan, plus the fear of living without her has crippled me. I've got too attached to her and don't know how to live alone, especially after the coma."

"Why don't we start going to the gym every day?"

Darren only stared at me pensively.

So, it was official now! Darren was truly in love! Or else, he had gone cuckoo without Mahtab. I was so certain I considered calling Reza and telling him so, too. Maybe Reza would relieve me from my mission of containing Darren with all types of tricks or reasoning, although my 'bodyguard' duty was reducing my own negative thoughts and bitching.

"Do you know a good lawyer, Darren?" I asked, hoping to amuse him for a few minutes and make up for my horseplaying.

"A divorce lawyer?"

"I may need a divorce lawyer eventually, too, but first I like to speak with an expert in estate planning and inheritance."

"An expert in disinheritance, you mean?" he asked with loud laughter, suddenly hyped up for some clowning of his own, as I had hoped for to change the mood in a gloomy room.

"Just a lawyer with a good sense of humour," I replied.

"I only know the ones Erica had chosen for our divorce. They seemed like decent people compared with all the stuff we usually hear about lawyers."

"Let's see if they can help me have some fun when I'm in heaven, then," I said.

"Okay... In fact, I'm glad you reminded me. They'd asked me to contact them a long time ago. Are you all set for irritating your family?"

"Yes, with our growing depression on top of other dangers, I hate to die without a proper estate plan. Your sad eyes and sighs alone might give me a heart attack soon."

"When I was Iran in 1985 and depressed, Reza gave me a few books and one of your manuscripts to read and restore my spirit."

"Which one?" I asked.

"It was called *Doubts and Decisions for Living*, I guess."

"Oh, yes. That was the first essay I wrote," I said.

"The beginning of that manuscript was most intriguing."

"Yeah, the story of my reasons for immigrating to Canada."

"The first line says, '*The night my first child was born my life changed forever—for better or worse, I would never know.*'"

"Yes, that's still true today after all these years."

"And you still can't decide if it'd been *for better or worse*?"

"No. I was right when I said, 'I would never know.' I still love them despite their wickedness. Yet, I must show my anger out of principle, while also feel sad about the necessity of reprisal."

"You're a complex man, T.J.," Darren said.

"Or some kind of a lunatic," I replied dolefully.

"Sometimes genius and lunacy mix..."

"Whatever it is, it has only caused me extra pain, especially when I see most people can ignore facts of life and live casually."

"Kids are particularly mixed-up nowadays, so you must be patient with them," he said.

"Reza told me that you have a son in Iran," I said hesitantly.

"That's true—fortunately or sadly, I would never know!"

"So now you know and bear the pains of parenthood, too."

"Not as much as you do, but my pain is for not knowing if I'd ever get a chance to see or have any relationship with him. That's a different kind of pain, I guess."

"Yes... I know that feeling nowadays when I wonder if I'll see my daughters enough in the future or have a relationship with them ever. Most parents feel this pain these days, especially when one spouse destroys the roots of family relationship deliberately, the way Feri has done it in our case."

"So our desire to see and build a relationship with our kids is permanent, isn't it?" Darren asked with gloom.

"Yes..., for most parents. Do you miss your son a lot?"

"Yes, although it may sound strange to miss someone you've never seen and didn't even know existed until Bijan told me."

"Why can't you see him?"

"The family wants to keep the origin of the baby confidential mainly for protecting the mother's and family's honour."

"Maybe it'd be easier in the long run to forget all about him."

"I've tried all along. But since Bijan pretends not to care about keeping the secret, the idea of finding out more about my son and maybe even seeing him has grown. What do you think?"

"I don't know, Darren. Both options will cause you lots of pain one way or another…; that's all I can easily foresee."

"My feeling about my son is stressful, but also heightens my fear of losing and never seeing Mahtab as well."

"Yeah, many emotional issues have suddenly gotten mixed up in your head, too, aren't they?" I asked.

"Exactly… So forgive my possible moodiness in the next few days or weeks," Darren said with gloom.

"Don't worry… I'm used to your and Reza's moods," I said, while hiding the whole truth. It did not feel right to tell him that having those two grouchy, needy friends with their emotional problems had indeed helped me mitigate my self-pity as well as my reservation about old age being the main factor for my rising negative feelings about modern women.

Witnessing men's grim lives regardless of marital status and age showed how and why we men lose our identities readily and have now become the weak gender. Thank god, many other testy, intelligent men were around to share our grief and unorthodox views on the matter, too, while I jotted down my radical theories with diligence, vengeance, and persistence as fast as I could find any spare time to return to my computer. Besides keeping me amused, these two young friends helped me build a more realistic outlook through our philosophical reflections, while I made notes about the variety and enormity of human emotions complicating relationships. All along, I admired Socrates' profound advice, which I have kept forgetting to recite to Darren and Reza as well: *If you get a good wife, you'll become happy; if you get a bad one, you'll become a philosopher.*

Poor Socrates! What a messy fate he must have endured!

Yet, all these blissful friendships, distractions, and self-pitying positive thoughts, as well as my reflective writings, had not still mitigated the deep pains of missing my family, even Feri, while suffering the fact that they did not miss me even a bit. How could they, like most modern women maybe, be so selfish and uncaring towards their husbands and fathers? Quite the opposite, they still accused me, and men in general, of conceit and insensitivity. They claimed I was self-absorbed and aloof because I did not enjoy their shallow mentalities, materialism, and pretensions. I had not complained much about their hollow lifestyles, yet they had taken offence even of my subtle distaste for materialism as a rooted, ruinous social foundation. In fact, the way they took my lifestyle opinions so personal and offensive had felt truly bizarre to me, I tell you!

Still more bizarre was my radical dilemma about the logic of blaming my family's mentality and attitude too much. They were naïve victims themselves, after all, born into phony societies with customary vanities, and just imitating others. They simply could not think and act differently. Maybe I must even forgive their low image of me and finding me so oblivious of their impressions of life. In fact, maybe I must only blame myself for my inability to join the mainstream. Perhaps I was an alien, after all, as my neighbours' rising rumours attested! Another fact surely not missed by my family was the way most men have been pliable to their families' superficial impressions of life so conveniently. In particular, my bizarre reluctance to behave like other *seemingly successful* men—in full subservience to their family's demands and wasting their times and energies to get richer and socialize shallower—was probably quite obvious and too irritating.

About a year earlier, a bunch of families and mine went to a picnic and did all the normal things to amuse ourselves the entire day. When everybody seemed bored again, anyway, a sneaky woman, who recognized and enjoyed my knack for controversy tried to stir some fun and commotion by provoking me. She asked for my opinion about ***gender differences causing so much marital conflicts***. I frowned and asked her why she expected me to have valid ideas worth mentioning in the crowd. However, she remained vague, while insisting on knowing my opinion. Beyond her routine sly scheme to provoke me, she had probably intended to trigger some sore memories in Feri's head as well, or simply reassess Feri's harsh views about me. Her motives for any of these scenarios could be fun to study as well, but let us skip all that extra torture here.

Anyhow, so stupidly, excited about my rare chance to whine about women openly within such a conceited group, I said, 'Two main categories of men exist nowadays: First, modern men who have become too passive and needy and lost their interest to build a certain identity and role in the family. Second, old-fashioned, ignorant men who still try to dominate their families themselves.

Thus, it seems men are now stuck within these two extremes, instead of building a healthy identity for themselves at a time women have been too eager to enforce a superficial identity for their gender.' In my naïve mind, I tried to sound constructive in fact. Yet, as expected, most men took my comment to heart and one called my opinion an insult and a sign of my ignorance and chauvinism. Then the men's uproar stopped right away when a well-respected, pretty woman in the group shouted, 'He's right... Modern men have become passive and lost their identities.' *She was surely very smart and brave, too, I must add!*

Nobody peeped, as though her verdict had ended the need for any more debate. Especially, the loud man who had attacked my observation so harshly shut up and looked intimidated the most. This was a momentous event for me for so many reasons worth listing here: **First,** I was amazed and flattered that a wise, pretty woman had agreed with my touchy findings and took my side when everybody else was attacking me. **Second,** to me, her agreement showed not only her fairness and open-mindedness, but also her realization that men's lack of proper identity is not helping women in general. To my astonishment, in fact, she had explained this point very intelligently about any woman who does not realize this deep cause of marital conflicts. **Third,** it showed feminine courage and power, which I truly believed had always been the case, but now rising too fast out of control in the new era. **Fourth,** the abrupt silence by the crowd after her strict observation proved my point mostly about men's timidity. None of those sly, haughty men dared to even peep at her. **Fifth,** Feri was angry with me a couple of weeks and refused to have sex with me, which again proved men's helplessness in relationships these days even for expressing a general opinion, let alone acting upon their sensible beliefs. **Sixth,** I basked in the small chance that the woman had defended me only out of spite for Feri, while Feri becoming jealous of another woman taking my side. If I had a few women defending me regularly, Feri would either go nuts or begin to worship me herself. *I'd worship that woman myself* *like a slave if she gave me a chance. After all, I've become a needy, passive man myself!*

Most of all, **Seventh,** that event also confirmed the old saying, 'Behind every successful man is always a powerful woman.' I won that day in front of that big crowd only because an influential female had come to my rescue—but not my own lousy wife. As expected, of course, even my seeming success to make a point about men's frailty was tentative. After that picnic, my already depleting status in that group, amongst both men and women, sunk even deeper and people avoided me more openly. Worst of all, my daughters and Feri became more hostile towards me. The fact that men have become so weak with lost identities is not hard to prove. Merely their reluctance to see and accept this fact makes the situation sad and funny. They show no courage and interest to ponder and do something about this flaw constructively, which ironically hurts women the most, since ultimately no relationship can shape properly unless both genders have definite, strong identities that coincide in a teamwork setting and create synergy for the welfare of family. The prevalent mishmash of women's superficial and men's shallow identities would never help them personally or in their marriages.

Lost in my daydream and the ideas I was pondering to include in my books, Feri called to inform me of the outstanding credit card statements and bills. The nerve of this woman!

"Pay them yourself," I said with vengeance like a child.

"Okay," she said calmly, which made me feel amazed, for a second, of her unprecedented sense of cooperation and even the possibility of missing me, too. But she ruined my fantasy quickly, "Transfer six thousand dollars to my account immediately."

"Pay it out of your own money. You're the one *supposedly* making all kinds of money these days."

"Why should I pay for your daughters' expenses?"

"They're 'my daughters' only to pay for their extravagance? You turn them against me and let them spend so much, so now at least pay their fees for torturing me the same way you do."

"You're the one who's tortured us for years."

"Just go away and leave me alone."

"How about the money?"

"Forget it," I said with tension.

"Then I'll hire a lawyer to deal with you," she yelled.

"Do as you wish. You can't intimidate me anymore, darling."

She hung up, thank God. Yet I knew I should prepare myself for some form of retaliation and a long war. I had been imagining this day long ago, though. Actually, I had anticipated all these scenarios and agonies—like a divine warning—the day I had agreed to marry Feri *solely for integrity. A divine warning against integrity is a huge puzzle and revelation in itself, though!*

Feri had insisted on getting married in many subtle manners until I had agreed out of desperation about ever finding anybody slightly in line with my views of a sensible relationship, while *my sneaky conscience gene* had been pushing Rose's case, too. So, anytime I have tried to be fair and honest, I have wondered if my chronic pessimism about modern relationships had played a big role from the start in my passive approach towards Feri and her hostile views of me all along in return.

On the other hand, Feri had been confirming my suspicions about modern women and relationships quite perfectly also from day one. Therefore, I had never been able to trust her and her judgments enough or change my negative perception of modern relationships. I had failed to envision and support an active, friendly environment for us to flourish within. Instead, as the only reasonable remedy to tolerate our marriage, I had strived to create a liberal setting for sharing our resources and lives, which she had refuted and resented as well. As a first step, I refused to give her the control she craved to have over my assets like most other women. Naturally, my resistance to put all my income into our joint accounts had upset Feri. Instead, the more she had persisted on this matter, the more I had felt and feared her fierce obsession to run my life altogether. So we had begun alienating each other from the start and become estranged more every day just because

I had refused to submit to her instinctive controlling mentality. In fact, I have often been amazed of my foresight all along even as a young husband when we are vulnerable against feminine charm and demands. Then, her sense of failure to tame her husband like other women—as a modern marital milestone nowadays—had surely enraged her deeply. In fact, my refusal to be a submissive husband with endless greed for wealth to satiate her materialistic mentality had made her restless to see me as poor and powerless as possible at least, while she played her role keenly to attain this goal, too!

Thus, at the end, today, my marital demise was merely the outcome of my general caution and sensible pride to elude Feri's desired level of control over me. Now, I was thrilled she could not access my bank accounts these days to waste everything out of spite. Then again, I had never expected loneliness and gloom after raising a family being so torturous—a new wisdom to remember about family life, too, especially before building one. Alas, this new lesson could not help me now, although it might be useful for young people planning to marry, especially oddballs like Reza and Darren. So, I jotted down these depressing points diligently to include in my essays.

Swiftly, however, my general melancholy today raised a huge wave of self-doubt about both the validity and purpose of my writings as a personal ambition. Then, my old sense of self-pity got thicker, the more I reread my words of wisdom, wrestled with various questions and doubts about my future, and abhorred Feri and people for no reason other than my disbelief or disapproval of their values. I wondered whether my views and knowledge of psychology were enough, in fact, to do proper analyses and draw valid conclusions? What would my writings' value be without ample contacts, scientific observations, and immense objectivity? Were my contacts with Darren and Reza enough to write simpler books or only cheap novels? My goals now appeared conflicting and making a decision felt tough. What were my options, then? Should I take the torture of meeting and bearing people as a basic necessity for becoming as great a writer as I aspired, or give up writing, too? That was a new obstacle to sort out fast, too, among million other pending doubts and decisions at the time. Should I take the risk of missing the reality in hopes of finding my soul in seclusion and perhaps even the salvation I craved and deserved after living with Feri so long?

I reckoned life nowadays has become too dynamic and I could not rely merely on my experiences or observations to write about people and gender conflicts. Nor could I keep observing only my aristocratic friends and write about them as the main causes and symptoms of social disorder. Their lifestyle was most educational and useful, I reckoned, yet it showed only a fraction of atrocities inflicting humanity. Our politicians, leaders, clergy, and scholars were also playing their big roles in ruining the world.

I also shared these harsh facts with Darren later that evening to distract his mind and mitigate his pains about Mahtab's sudden aloofness, including less phone calls. He looked desperate and asked me silly questions about love, while listening to my ideas blankly and thinking only about Mahtab. My efforts to console him felt absurd, while he seemed eager to raise and curse Reza's elaborate scheme to convince Mahtab. Luckily, I could control my big mouth from getting into this touchy topic again as much as he tried. Still, we were merely driving each other nuts! What a lot of losers we three friends had turned into!

"Do you have a clear view about modern relationships, T.J.?" Darren asked at one point.

"I have some ideas… Do you like to read one of my essays?"

"Can you give me just a recap for now," Darren replied. "I'm not in the mood for reading anything these days, either."

"Well, let me find a short paragraph in my notebook," I said.

Relationships can potentially satisfy many of our basic needs for sex, belonging, compassion, security, and maybe even selfless love, as a likely reward for finding our soul mate. Therefore, companionship has turned into an urgent need. Yet, we sabotage our chances of reaping even its basic benefits, since we idiotically think it can **(must)** *also bring us plenty of happiness and love. Yet, in fact, we should be prepared to pay a big price—mostly emotional burdens—for carrying our relationships, while we also lose our chance to explore the mystical notions of happiness and love on our own, perhaps in a simple lifestyle, if not solitude.*

"So, you're saying that, in the end, relationships nowadays are often useless and painful for finding our personal salvation and peace, ha?" Darren asked

"I guess so…! But a more important fact is that most of us can't either avoid or remedy this reality. Most of us are incapable of replacing relationships and family life with an independent way of filling our lousy lives," I said trying to sound a bit positive this late in the evening with his messy mood and all!

Darren got up, said goodnight rather testily, as though I was responsible for all these sad realities about love and existence—and maybe even for Mahtab's sudden aloofness! He turned and waved at me with a dry smirk and left me alone to wrestle some more with my depressing thoughts.

Staring at the walls, alone, now the fear of old age struck me with another wave of self-pity along with a dire sense of reality. With age, we all feel our direr need for compassion and peace naively, which we also assume family can provide, while we lose the opportunity of finding peace on our own at least—alone. What a conspicuous, yet outlandish, dilemma! We like to rely on others, mainly our spouses, to not only fill the gaps in our hearts, but also manifest themselves as valid purposes for our pathetic existence. We just prefer to fool ourselves and ignore that we are all too sick and needy ourselves these days to save even our own souls, let alone grasp or care about anybody else's agonies and needs. We cannot fathom the purposes of our own beings, never mind fostering others', maybe as a role model or idol. Nobody can help anybody due to our vast preoccupations and insecurities.

Finally, I felt tired and depressed enough to march towards the bedroom and close the door quietly.

Chapter Twenty-three
Be a Man

Reza's rather rough order, 'Be a man, Darren,' on the way to the airport, had banged my brain often. T.J.'s reminders to let Mahtab decide on her own also sounded bizarre, as though Reza had left his deputy to enforce his decree sternly in his absence! My own nosy conscience agreed with T.J. and Reza. But, most of all, I was merely at the mercy of another lover again! So, I just tried to fool my spirit by praising my own goodwill in making Mahtab think deeper, even at my expense! I was also happy for not confronting Reza or telling on him to Mahtab and T.J. about his rude tone near the airport. Be a man!!! *It still singed me!*

Reza had surely not dared to talk to Mahtab so direct. Still, his coaxing tactics with her had apparently worked perfectly, since she had sounded more mysterious every day, while stressing on Reza's advice to stay vigilant. Now, sometimes I regretted and cursed myself, mostly humorously, for pushing her so diligently to be open-minded and humour Reza in the first place, especially since she had been adamant not to do so. Instead, maybe I should have stopped Reza from butting in our affair?

Anyway, I was simply forced to *be a man,* after all, in hopes of keeping Reza an ally for a presumed higher cause and praying that he had not succeeded in brainwashing Mahtab completely to abandon me. Now, our telephone conversations were also getting shorter and gloomier, as though she were drowning under a lot of pressure or had travelled to a different planet. *Oh, dear God, why do You keep sending me all these moody, mysterious mates or are all women this way? Giving us dejected men even this bit of information can save us a lot of extra hassle and pain..., even if you don't like to tell us why you've made them this way, anyway! Please only tell me at least...! Am I not your special being?*

My familiarity with these two sisters' chronic moodiness was partly helpful in bearing Mahtab's confusing attitude, although it rendered a concern all by itself. Maybe time had come for me to smarten up myself and get out of this big mess now that she was giving me a perfect chance. Yet, I felt homesick without her, like a helpless patient at the mercy of two numb nurses, Mahtab and T.J., hoping that her spooky silence and his endless advice end soon. I had never expected so much disgrace and confusion, even beyond what Erica had caused me for years, as added side-effects and necessities of love! *Just imagine what Bijan is going through, then, asshole,* I told myself at some moments of truth.

T.J.'s full-time attention and accompanying me everywhere as my bodyguard was both cute and annoying. Even funnier was forcing me to tag along anywhere he went, just to prevent my solitude even a minute. Now, he was taking my earlier precaution about facing the thugs and other enemies very seriously. Yet, his pesky, bizarre attachment felt more like a serious scheme to deter my attempt to see Mahtab, too, despite my repeated promises to him about letting Mahtab do her thinking alone. Being supervised by a desolate old man with some mysterious motives of his own felt funny at least, anyway.

Strangely enough, often I did not feel still ready to take care of myself. I felt confused, lonely, and helpless, as if in a semi coma, only subconsciously alive. I wondered with anguish if it was just another side-effect of the coma or related to my moot affair with Mahtab and the unbearable thought of losing her again. What if she decided to go back to Iran and never returned. How could I adjust to the idea of living without her? I loved her so much, I realized with both thrill and terror. So, should I force her to see me and listen to my pleas to stay at whatever costs to both of us? Thank god, Reza's and T.J.'s standing orders imposed some level of self-control and selflessness on me. I had to curb my blazing temptation to see, talk, and make love to the woman who had now captured my being completely. Even weirder, my immense attachment to her in such a short time made me feel more often for Bijan, who had loved, and lived with, her for so many years. Poor guy! *He didn't even have the luxury of other women waiting around to court him the way I did!!* I tried to tease and laugh at my sinking self in any silly manner I could. *I had enough worries of my own already, so fussing about Bijan as well made me more anxious regarding my erratic personality!*

When we planned to go out, T.J. watched our surroundings and drove my car if necessary, while I humoured his rising knack for teasing or appeasing me alternately during our bizarre forced commutes. Only once, he agreed to let me go out with Elizabeth alone. She had called and asked to see me again, as she allegedly had very important information to share with me. I asked her to say it on the phone, but she insisted to congregate at our Granville Island rendezvous again—maybe hoping to try harder this time to rekindle our old, mushy memories! *Hadn't I already bragged about many women eager to seduce me? Forget Mahtab!?*

Detective Stewart's warning to me to stop provoking Jeff by meeting his fiancé behind his back hit me, but I did not care, like a mad martyr or spitefully, nor did I share it with Elizabeth on the phone. I was also looking for an excuse to ditch T.J. for a few hours, although I still welcomed his daily attention to my affairs. So, I asked Elizabeth to pick me up in front of my building if we really had to go to the pub and yet her consent to make this extra effort felt curious. T.J. escorted me downstairs and gauged her curiously, as though checking the reliability of the babysitter he was trusting me to, or maybe he was mesmerised by her beauty the way he often lost himself around pretty women, at least prior to his supreme cynicism about women in recent months.

"This meeting may raise some eyebrows," I told Elizabeth as I sat in her car.

"Like whose?" she asked while peering at T.J. curiously.

"You know! Detective Stewart also advised me against seeing you. Even T.J. is anxious about our meetings," I said.

"Why is he following you around and staring at me like that?"

"He's my bodyguard, in case Jeff's thugs return to finish me."

"It's not gonna work," she said mysteriously and sped away.

"Why? Are you planning to kill me today yourself?" I asked with a chuckle, recalling our old-time trickeries.

"No, not today…," she replied. "I'm only kidnapping you."

"And then?"

"It's up to Jeff and the thugs to decide your fate."

"I should've guessed from the way you insisted to see me."

"Well, just relax now and be quiet until I'm done with you."

"Why are doing this, Elizabeth?"

"Because I can't sit back and let you destroy Jeff and me."

"I hope you're going to abuse me sexually first at least?"

"I haven't quite decided yet. It all depends on your level of cooperation and my mood at the end."

"Stop the car this minute or I'll jump out."

"Doors are locked and you can't escape," she said.

"Please have mercy on me, Elizabeth. I beg you…"

"I begged you to forgive Jeff but you just kept harassing us."

"I'll do whatever you want, please Elizabeth. I forgive Jeff."

"It's too late now… Stop begging… I've made up my mind."

At last, Elizabeth parked her car and we got out giddily. It felt refreshing to repeat our old routines of playing games and fooling around with each other the way nobody else could, or cared to, do with me. I walked to her and kissed her on the cheek, as we strolled towards the pub. I was suddenly so horny I might have cheated on Mahtab if Elizabeth was willing to help me get my revenge on Mahtab with her mysterious attitude driving me crazy these days—not to mention out of spite for Jeff and Detective Stewart. *What a corrupt, impressionable lover I have always been!* I mused with guilt and shame while praising Elizabeth's sexy body, especially her long, shapely legs, and recalling our special sexual routines just a few months earlier. *Maybe old, naughty Darren was finally emerging out of the coma, too!*

"It's good to see you still have the mood to horse around in spite of living with Jeff," I said. "I've always enjoyed your goofy personality as I'd told you in the past many times."

"We could've become the goofiest couple, Darren, if you'd only been a bit more serious about us at the time I stayed in your place and you promised to love me," she muttered woefully.

"But how did you expect a goofy person get serious?"

"If you loved me enough, you could," she replied giddily.

"Things got out of control. It was my fault, I admit."

"What a pity. Sometimes I miss you," she said solemnly.

"I've missed you a few times as well, especially for horsing around together and laughing like kids."

"That's why I insisted on seeing you. I'm using every excuse to see you," she said with some traces of passion and desolation.

"Are you all right, Elizabeth?"

"I don't know… I don't know what I'm doing."

"What's happened?"

"Oh, nothing new. I'm just confused about so many things, including my relationship with Jeff."

"Welcome to the club. My friends and I are badly stuck in our relationship conundrums these days, too."

The way Elizabeth sounded for half an hour, I was starting to think she did not really have any information to share with me today, but only used the gimmick to meet me. It felt like she was fed up with Jeff and considering dumping him, so retesting her chance of luring me back as her lover. Her intention felt bizarre, but plausible considering everything we knew about each other.

She could be thinking around those lines, but how about me. For a moment, I also entertained the option of reconnecting with her if Mahtab was proving to be so moody or going to leave me with no foreseeable prospect. This bizarre idea made me wonder more about both my mental stability and commitment towards Mahtab. Did I really love her or was only fooling myself again with this love affair, too? What a moron I have turned into! *You are really getting out of control, you sullied seducer!*

I pitied my bewildered mind and conscience as Elizabeth and I chatted freely like good old times rather numbly.

"Anyway, enough about my hectic life. Let me give you the information I dragged you here for," she said swiftly in a serious tone that ruined all my fantasy about her possible thoughts and all the other nonsense I had entertained in my silly mind like a child.

"Okay," I replied solemnly.

"I confronted Jeff and got more details about his involvement with the thugs."

"That's great. I hope he's been honest about everything."

"Yes, he is and has enough proof if necessary."

"What did he say that is new?"

"He says that in fact Erica had been behind the whole thing from the beginning."

"You see…? I told you he'd find some new nonsense to fool us. Now he's blaming poor Erica for everything since she isn't here to defend herself."

"He's telling the truth. Erica had forced him to find somebody to kick your ass, so that you'd let me go back to Jeff and she'd lure you back for herself. He has Erica's cancelled check for her share of payment to the thugs. The bartender knows everything about Erica pushing Jeff to do it, too. If you want, I can give you a copy of Erica's cancelled check. Maybe you could also ask the police to talk to the bartender and confirm Jeff's claim."

"Are you fooling with me again?" I asked edgily.

"No, I'm not… Actually, Jeff said that Erica's secretary gave him the cheque and a copy of the newspaper clipping with your picture on it to pass on to the thugs. If you like, you can also talk to her to confirm this fact and the exact date it happened."

I was suddenly at sea, more than I had been in recent days. I could not believe my ears and Elizabeth's harsh accusations about Erica's direct involvement in my and her own misfortunes.

"Have the thugs killed Erica, too?" I asked dumbfounded.

"Jeff doesn't think so... But what if she'd arrived just in time to witness the shooting or something like that?"

"That's right... What does Jeff think about this possibility?"

"He thinks they would've shot her, too, instead of dragging her all the way to the balcony or pushing her in front of people and alerting the whole neighbourhood," Elizabeth replied.

"It makes sense... So he thinks she just jumped herself?"

"It looks like it. I can't think of any other possibility."

"Why would she do such a silly thing?" I asked.

"Well, even more reasons come to mind now."

"Like what?"

"First of all, she might've felt guilty for causing your death if she thought you were dying. She might've also felt fed up with her life, or she might've done it out of sheer love for you."

"I doubt the last possibility, although she insisted she'd loved me all along when we met the night before the accident."

"So, it's possible," Elizabeth said.

"Nah! But a big shock could've made her or anybody insane for a second to act silly," I said, as all three reasons that Elizabeth had suggested sounded plausible to me, too. *Although I liked the last one the most and found it more appealing and plausible now as well!!*

"I had felt, and you also said it yourself, she was feeling too depressed and lonely those last months of her life," she said.

"Yes, that's true. I felt it and she also mentioned it to me with lots of anguish," I replied.

"Jeff said the detective has some information that also makes it unlikely about anybody else being involved with Erica's fall."

"I guess Stewart mentioned something similar to me, too."

"What'd he say?" she asked.

"Apparently some bystanders had testified that they'd seen nobody else on the balcony, while she'd been screaming or trying to talk to them before she jumped or fell," I replied.

"So you already knew she might've in fact jumped herself."

"Still, it is hard to believe a selfish person like Erica comes to that low level of self-esteem and do a crazy thing like that."

"What had she been trying to tell the bystanders?" she asked.

"Maybe she was telling on the thugs, so they pushed her?"

"Maybe... Have you gone to visit her grave?" Elizabeth asked.

"No, have you?"

"No, sadly, I haven't yet. Do you know where she is?"

"Yes, I have the address!" I replied.

"Give it to me, or even better, let's go visit her together one day next week."

"I'll let you know. In fact, let's go there and do some kissing or other stuff to irritate her."

"You still like to do those stuff with me?" she asked giddily.

"Maybe. At least for teasing Erica," I replied, wondering if kissing or other stuff on someone's grave was only disrespectful or strictly forbidden by civil or religious laws!

"Okay, let's go one day." She looked as horny as I was.

"We'll see… But going back to Jeff's involvement, does he know where the thugs are, so that we can wrap up this matter? If we catch them, I can decide about Jeff's guilt faster, too."

"I was hoping you'd forgive him now that we know Erica had been behind the whole thing."

"I still need time to think about letting Jeff off the hook. But first I should consult with Detective Stewart."

"I believe Jeff…, about Erica pushing him until he'd finally asked the bartender to help him."

"Well, Erica could be really pushy sometimes, I know," I said.

"When she wanted something, she went all the way... Do you recall the day she came to your apartment when I was living with you, just to force you dump me?"

"Yes, I remember it. She almost succeeded, too," I said with a chuckle, recalling how she had seduced me, how tenderly we had made love, and how naively I had promised to reconcile with her, too, all in a matter of thirty minutes or so. "But, you proved even more tenacious than she was. Or you really loved me, ha?"

"Maybe I did, Darren… So forgive Jeff… He'd been merely another victim of Erica."

"No, I can't, yet," I said, amazed of my grudge, considering my consent about Jeff himself being badly manipulated by Erica.

"Won't you do it for me?" she pleaded.

"Yes, if I do it, it'll be only for you, but no promises today. Bring all your proofs and I'll talk to the detective, too," I said.

"Okay... Actually, Jeff said he'll give all the evidences about Erica to the detective now that disclosing Erica's involvement seems essential," Elizabeth stressed with triumph.

"Why hadn't he done it from the beginning?" I asked.

"He said he wasn't expecting to be accused, but also thought this information had no use, especially since Erica was dead and never been in contact with the thugs personally."

"Well, Maybe he's right," I said.

"Why did you tell the detective that we meet?" she asked.

"I didn't. He somehow knew it or tricked me to confess. I also wondered if he was only testing my honesty."

"And you confessed without thinking?"

"Yes. Besides I thought you might've told Jeff yourself."

"Are you crazy?" Elizabeth shrieked.

"Now I worry about this detective's loose mouth or deliberate hints about us to Jeff out of spite or whatever," I said giddily.

"Maybe he's crazy like you and likes to provoke Jeff himself for fun or something."

"Yeah, he sounds crazy sometime… We'd better go back if you're done with me today," I said.

"Sure, but let's plan to go visit Erica's grave together."

Elizabeth drove back and walked with me all the way to the front of my building leisurely. I wondered if she was trying to ensure my safety or hoping I would invite her in for whatever reasons, maybe even another quick reminder of our sexual thrills—maybe as a practice for what we had talked about doing when we go visit Erica's grave! But I only thanked her for escorting me and said goodbye, again wondering whether I had left her with a sense of rejection. Then I thought I was really so full of myself these days for whatever silly reason… perhaps! *Was this another lingering symptom of the coma, hopefully?*

In return, a divine punishment put me in my proper place and I felt the agony of rejection ten folds myself as soon as I arrived home and returned Mahtab's call. We chatted ten minutes, while I tried to sound calm and prove that her seeming aloofness had not shattered me; and she probably fought her nerves to stay patient and humour me for a bigger cause. Still, her soft, gloomy voice agitated me all along, while I fought my negative gut feeling. At last, she gathered her nerve to reveal the main purpose of her call.

"Darren, I'd better go to Iran awhile, after all," she said sadly.

Although I had imagined these words and this moment in my head for the last ten days, I could not think of a suitable response or reaction to her heart-shattering announcement. She had played this hurtful stunt on me so callously once in Barcelona, too.

"Darren…? Are you there?"

"Yes, Mahtab, I'm here. Just trying to think."

"Sorry, my love. I've been thinking a lot, as you can imagine. I'm devastated by my own decision. But it seems wiser for both of us to face the facts and challenges head on. We can't run away from this matter forever," she said.

"Are you going to reconcile with Bijan?"

"Oh, no… At least I don't think so at this time! I'd like to get my divorce, hopefully, and come back to Vancouver, perhaps, if you still want me to return."

"Of course, I do. But do you think it is possible?"

"Most likely, but it may take some time."

"How long do you think?"

"Probably a year or so depending on Bijan's mercy."

"If that's your decision, I live with it. I wish you all the best."

"Will you wait for me?"

"I will if you ask me to wait."

"I'd like to ask, but don't know how things will go and how long it'll take. I don't wanna put your life on hold," Mahtab said.

"You didn't like when I called you Mahy once, but you have been rather slippery since I've known you, after all, like a mahy."

Mahtab burst into tense laughter. "But I've been forced into these decisions… I'm not slippery like a fish, believe me!"

"Will you at least call and keep me posted?"

"Of course. I'll stay with my mom and talk to you regularly, probably more than we've been even here in Vancouver the last ten days. Why haven't you called me more often?"

"Because everybody told me to leave you alone to think and I thought you also preferred that."

"I guess… Staying alone has helped me think realistically. I get carried away emotionally fast when I'm around you."

"Now we can admit, I guess, that everybody, especially Reza, had been right advising me to leave you alone to think."

"Yes, they were all right about our inability to understand the facts and make a proper decision if we stayed together or met too often these days," Mahtab said.

"Now look at the outcome!" I said with despair.

"But I still love you a lot and would like to spend the rest of my life with you after taking care of problems."

"Although we don't know if and when we can reunite and if I'm still alive!" I said.

"But then, if we're both still alive, our relationship will be wonderful without always worrying about people chasing us."

"Do you think Bijan will let us be even after divorce?"

"I really don't know. But at least our relationship won't look sinful or too provocative. The rest remains a matter of fate and how vengeful those people will be," Mahtab replied.

"Yeah... Animosities will continue even after your divorce."

"I wished you could also come to Tehran, maybe secretly."

"Alas, it's impossible. I'm sure they'll find me again and cause problems for both of us," I said with angst.

"So it's not the matter of money now?" she asked playfully.

"No…Now that I'm not poor you still leave me"

"I'll give you more if you come quietly," she said wittily.

"Thanks... When're you leaving, then?"

"In four days," she replied.

"Is it okay for us to meet at least once before you go?"

"No, I don't think so. We'd better not screw up everything now that I've decided to make some peace with Bijan."

"I understand," I said.

"Besides, if we meet, we may feel worse than we do already. It'll make things more difficult for both of us."

"Okay, but I've missed you a lot and now it feels like I'll never see you again despite our promises," I blurted with gloom.

Mahtab was silent and I felt she was weeping quietly. I just waited for both of us to gather our emotions. My feelings and the situation again resembled a similar scenario six months earlier with Mahroo before her departure to Tehran, even in terms of our last minute chitchat and promises about seeing each other soon. But then, I never saw her again, although I went to Iran to gauge my sudden infatuation for her right in the middle of my affair with Elizabeth. Instead, she had simply died at work accidentally in Tehran in the same evening we were going to meet.

"Should we take the risk of meeting on the way to the airport? Is it too much risk?" she asked.

"No. That's an excellent idea…"

"Okay then. Let's do it. Pick me up in front of the building. I'll wait outside with my luggage."

"Maybe I should bring T.J., too, to make it look more normal and innocent. He's been going everywhere with me and driving me around, anyway."

"Yes, that's a good idea," she said as if relieved. "Bring T.J."

After hanging up the phone, I felt sadder and lonelier than I had been for days about another seemingly promising love affair going down the drain. Mahtab's last words rekindled yet another incident when Mahroo had asked me to bring T.J. with me when going to visit her again late one evening after we had returned from a night out together dancing and fighting at the same time. That visit had turned into a shocking, funny experience. And now reminiscing about it brought me some relief to soothe the painful idea of not seeing Mahtab for a long time, if ever.

T.J. tried to convince me that her decision to go back to Iran sounded very logical and I must respect it.

"I have no other choice. But I have a hunch she'll never return to Vancouver. I've lost her too," I replied, now cursing myself so much more, half-wittily again, about pushing Mahtab to talk to Reza and be open-minded in the first place. I had not imagined the cost of opening someone's mind would be so costly and come back to bite me personally.

"You're probably right and that maybe a better solution even for you in the long-run as well," T.J. said.

"Why are some of us so unlucky with women, or is there something wrong with me?"

"Both…," T.J. replied with a chuckle.

"You don't like the idea of me marrying again at all, do you?" I asked with a giggle. "You're afraid of me disproving your glum theories about marital relationships these days."

"I'm only hoping you won't make another mistake or raise a bunch of ungrateful children like me. Just remember all these free advice I'm giving you. Maybe I won't be around long enough to witness your fate, but I hope you can disprove my glum theories by living happily ever after with a great mate."

"I hope so!" I said with gratitude for his odd way of consoling me at this time of my greatest misfortune with love.

"Besides, if I'm gonna be alone for the rest of my life, you'll be more useful to me unmarried," T.J. added giddily, most likely for teasing me, or maybe not!

I knew that even T.J. believed some lucky people, and maybe even he, had a small chance to find a right companion and build a good family. We just could not guarantee we were one of those lucky people. Still, the chance of at least seeing Mahtab once more kept my nerves a bit calmer for the next three days.

On the fateful day I was supposed to take Mahtab to the airport, she called me early in the morning just as I got out of the shower.

"Don't come to pick me up, Darren," she said with a strange tone without sounding sad or anxious but mostly serious.

"Why? I really want to see you at least one more time."

"Not today," she said in a soft, mysterious voice.

"T.J. and I are ready to go pick you up right now," I pleaded.

"It's not necessary."

"But why?"

"Because I'm not going to Tehran today."

"Why? What has happened, Mahtab?"

"I'll tell you later. I've been a little sick these days and I might have to see a doctor today, too."

"But you're still going back, ha?" I asked with confusion.

"Yes, I think so."

"Can't you even tell me the cause of this delay? Is it your sickness?"

"Yes… I'll explain everything later."

"Do you want us to go over and help?"

"No, I'm tired right now. I didn't sleep well last night, either. I also need some time to think alone and sort out everything," she said, starting to sound too mysterious all over again!

"Okay… Let me know if you need my help," I said.

Naturally, I got worried about Mahtab, but deep down, I was both thrilled and curious about her change of plan. Meanwhile, I began thinking cunningly about any possible scheme I could or should put into motion *immediately* to keep her here for myself. I hoped her sickness was not serious, but even the remote chance of that being the case added to my anxiety.

Chapter Twenty-four
A Changed Man!

Mahtab's call four days earlier with the news about her return to Tehran had thrilled us all. I celebrated the possibility of regaining some control over my life after ending such exhausting, horrific dealings with Bijan and Mahtab. Immediately, I called Bijan and gave him the fantastic news. He got ecstatic and timing felt perfect to make a gesture about boosting our relationships all around. I told him my mom and I liked to talk with him about Mahtab in advance. As I had expected slyly, he felt obliged to invite us to his house with a hint about asking his mom and aunt, too, so that the family got a chance to meet after so long. So now, everybody was counting the days, coordinating everything with great enthusiasm for her majesty's arrival.

With so much excitement and goodwill in the air, my mom, Nazi, and I visited Bijan the next evening with both optimism and wily intentions. Especially, my mom wanted to *prepare* him.

"We should give her plenty of time and space to adjust while she stays in my house," my mom blurted almost as we arrived.

"Isn't she coming here, then?" Bijan's mom asked tensely.

"No, she likes to stay with Nazi and me awhile until she knows the right thing to do," my mom replied with a show of despair and hope.

"Do you think that's the right way to do it?" Bijan's mom asked while peering at her son with pity.

"Yes, I think it's better this way, too," my mom replied.

"Oh…? Why is that better?" Bijan's mom asked with stress.

"Because we shouldn't push her. We must be diplomatic and let her decide what she likes to do on her own," my mom replied and then turned to Bijan. "If you want to increase your chance of having her back in this house, you must give her room and act tactfully around her. In fact, staying alone in this big house with you may depress her fast while your relationship is not normal."

"I guess you're right. This house feels depressing nowadays," Bijan replied solemnly.

"Yeah, she should relax first without feeling guilty or getting stressed right away," I added immediately.

Anybody could feel what my mom and Bijan had confessed. Even though we talked loudly and Nazi ran everywhere with ceaseless energy, the house felt like a ghost-ridden manner with a deadly aura seeping through its foundation. Compared to the times Mahtab had lived there and ruled the affairs, a spooky chill and vacuum besieged that haunted mansion, while a bunch of desolate servants moved around in a haze. I felt jittery even more than the last time I had come here to visit Bijan. He himself now looked thinner, paler, and more miserable, while also bearing his mom's stealthy, pitiful peeps at him. Such a powerful man being driven to this horrible state and looking so frail and glum, all for a woman, felt pathetic and disheartening. I wanted to run away, but we had to be patient and pretend to enjoy the dinner and Bijan's awkward efforts to look calm and courteous.

"My mom and I will go to the airport to welcome Mahtab, anyway," Bijan said while her mom and aunt nodded.

"Do you think that's a good idea?" I asked.

"Of course it is," Bijan replied.

Bijan's mom added, "Yes… Mahtab joon must know we all welcome her back and she can feel free to return to her own house if she likes to do that."

"That's fine if we don't ask her directly," my mom said with a mixed tone of diplomacy and warning.

"But she must know I'll do everything to make her return to this house easy. This is her home even if she decides to stay with her mom at the beginning," Bijan said.

"We also like to have a welcome party for her here or at my house," Bijan's mom said. "It'll be a big party like the ones we used to have with plenty of relatives and friends."

"Hopefully things will soon feel normal like before and you'll have many big parties here again," my mom said tactfully.

"Is the day after her arrival all right?" Bijan asked giddily.

I looked at Bijan and his mom with stress. It was difficult and cruel to ignore so much goodwill, but I doubted Mahtab was up to it. "I think it's better to wait and choose a date after she's here," I said.

"No, let's plan this party now, anyway, at my house," Bijan's mom suggested. "I hope Mahtab joon won't refuse to come to this gathering that is mainly in her honour."

My mom and I looked at each other and felt obliged to be nice and polite about this matter. So we nodded helplessly. As ladies got engaged in their chitchat and planning for the party, Bijan asked me to go to his study.

"So, my mom and I will pick you guys up to go to the airport together in four days, okay?" Bijan asked ecstatically.

"Yes, okay," I replied, while pitying his desperate plot to raise the chance of Mahtab going to his house instead of ours, just in case she felt merciful or cornered—as a one in a million chance!

"Do you think *she* will be nice to me again?" he asked.

"Let's hope so. Try to gain her trust gradually even if it takes a few months before she is ready to discuss your situation more favourably. Don't rush her."

"She'll see that I am a changed man and I'll do everything she likes," he said desolately.

"Just be patient," I replied, trying to imagine his pain the way he looked and sounded so awfully helpless but hopeful. His total submission reminded me of Mahtab's concern about the chance of Bijan even agreeing to go live abroad as a main condition for taking him back. He already seemed broken enough to do that and everything else for her as he had readily confessed plainly so pathetically.

"Will you talk to her, too, if she wants to stay at your mom's house at first?" he asked, looking more pathetic by the minute.

"Talk to her about what?" I asked.

"Just keep telling her that I have changed and will do anything to make her happy. Encourage her to return to this house and talk to me more productively. Will you...? Please..."

"I'll do my best," I said as we started toward the family room. For a split second, I felt for him despite his regular arrogance and spite. Then, I thought Bijan's mental state was definitely worse than mine and Darren's put together, just because he had been attached to Mahtab for many years helplessly, maybe worse than a heroin addict is doomed. An addict could at least always hope to buy heroin from one source or another!

"It was all Darren's fault that she changed so fast," Bijan said.

"No, I think she's still grieving Mahroo's death. That was a big shock for her and things started going sour after that tragedy."

"But why did she get mad at me or go to Vancouver?"

"She was, and probably still is, confused. She still can't accept Mahroo's death… She's still sad," I said aloud as we arrived in the family room and I repeated the same fact to the audience, too.

"Yes, that's an important point... I'm glad you mentioned it, Reza, about Mahtab still mourning Mahroo," my mom said.

"It was horrible. We're all still in shock," Bijan's mom added.

"We must help her accept Mahroo's death like the rest of us," my mom said casually. "By the way, Bijan, can you get someone to bring Mahroo's portrait down and put it in our car?"

"You want to take it to your home?" Bijan asked.

"Yes, I think it will help Mahtab to relax and gradually accept Mahroo's death better with that painting around her."

Bijan nodded hesitantly, then went upstairs at last, brought Mahroo's portrait down and took it to our car when we were leaving. Fulfilling one of my promises to Mahtab felt gratifying.

The prospect of things starting to feel a bit normal again around my family had boosted our spirits, while we counted the minutes for Mahtab's arrival anxiously. So, her unexpected, weird call the day before her arrival was infuriating.

"Aren't you on the plane?"

"No, I missed it. I'm here in Vancouver," she replied.

"So when is your flight?"

"I don't know yet… I'll let you know."

"But do you have a plan?"

"It'll be at least two weeks later," she said.

"How do you think Bijan will react when I tell him you've changed your mind again?" I asked with frustration. "The poor guy has been ecstatic about seeing you."

"Just tell him that I'm sick or something and postponing my travel for two weeks," she replied diplomatically, which sounded rather weird considering her normal tenacity. *Have I or Darren succeeded in opening her mind a bit at least?* I wondered wittily!

"Are you coming back in two weeks for sure?"

"I hope so… But to be honest with you, I'm not sure."

"This is bad news, Mahtab."

"I know, but, for now, you just tell everybody I'll come in two weeks. I'll tell you the exact date soon," she said calmly.

"Mahtab, what's going on? You sound mysterious again."

"I told you, I'm not feeling good," she replied testily now.

"Did Darren make you change your mind?"

"No, just leave him alone. I'll talk to you later," she said.

"No, I can't leave him alone and Bijan will kill him."

"He didn't even know until I called him this morning. In fact, he and T.J. were supposed to give me a ride to the airport."

I tried to control my nerves and sound normal when I called Bijan to give him the news as soon as Mahtab hung up.

"Hi Reza, I was about to call and thank you for sorting out everything so nicely," he said giddily like a child. He sounded so ecstatic and civil after months of outrage I loathed ruining not just his tranquility, but mostly my recuperating pride and respect after bearing his insults for so long.

"You're welcome, but—"

"It's also okay if she decides to stay at your mom's place first, but how soon do you think you can convince her to come back to her own house or at least talk to me in private?"

"Bijan, Mahtab just called from Vancouver."

"Why? What has happened?"

"I don't have much detail, but she's missed her plane."

"So, when will she arrive?"

"She didn't know yet," I said timidly.

"Did she at least tell you her reason, or only bullshitting us again?" Bijan asked tensely.

"She's apparently fallen sick and doesn't want to travel in that condition," I kept lying desperately to keep him calm. "She wants to do a check up next week before travelling."

Bijan was quiet a long time and maybe even trying not to cry on the phone, then finally said goodbye to me abruptly. I called Darren and left a message, wondering if he was with Mahtab at that very moment, possibly clutched together in my bed again.

Staring at the park through the window, I despaired, ready to cry from frustration and confusion. I paced the room impatiently for Darren's call. One hour later, the phone rang and I jumped to answer it. But it was only Bijan quite furious now.

"I'm really angry, Reza. My mom was angry, too, when I told her that Mahtab is not coming. She's invited a lot of guests and is embarrassed to cancel the party. I feel ashamed in front of her and my family again."

"What do you expect me to do, Bijan? I told you all I know."

"I hope you're not bullshitting me, too. I've had it with all of you. I'm running out of patience and if she doesn't arrive in two weeks, I won't be responsible for anything," he yelled.

"Calm down, Bijan. Just give her room a bit longer and let's wait and see what's happened. Do you prefer her take the risk of dying on the plane?"

"I'm not gonna let her make a complete fool of me and laugh behind my back with Darren. Make sure they understand what I'm telling you today," he stressed with anger.

"I'll tell her again. But you take it easy, too," I said with angst and frustration. I had had it with his threats and yelling at me like ordering one of his servants around.

"No, I can't take it easy when people humiliate me and my family all the time. Just give them my last warning."

"You know something, Bijan?"

"What?"

"Suddenly, I'm starting to feel happy about Mahtab's view of you," I said with an astonishing, rather divine, satisfaction. In fact, all my despair and confusion a few minutes earlier, before his call, seemed to have evaporated in a jiffy. The whole situation seemed much clearer to me now so swiftly, all thanks to Bijan himself!

"Why is that?" he yelled in bewilderment.

"Because you just proved you can never control your temper and you are not a changed man contrary to what you've been asking me to tell Mahtab."

"If you guys expect me to accept all your bullshit, you're wrong," he shouted again.

"Then I don't know how you can expect me to believe you have changed and convince Mahtab, too."

"You'd better stop arguing with me and instead listen to what I'm telling you."

"And what is that?"

"I won't let this masquerade continue forever," he yelled.

Suddenly, I felt I could not let him treat me like a piece of dirt any longer. I had run out of patience to accept all his abuse just for the sake of helping Mahtab and my mom. As he began to talk, I just hung up the phone and felt so great for doing it, too. Getting Mahroo's portrait out of his house before things possibly getting totally out of hand now felt so timely and satisfying.

I called Darren again right away with great hopes to drag some information out of him about the situation in Vancouver. Luckily, he answered the phone this time.

"Did you make her change her mind, Darren?" I asked.

"No, I had nothing to do with her decision and I haven't even seen her for almost two weeks."

"So what happened? She told me she was coming home only a few days ago."

"She'd told me the same thing and then called this morning to say she didn't need a ride," he said.

"Didn't you ask her why?"

"I did, but she didn't tell me."

"Can you find out and tell me what she's really up to?"

"I'll try," he replied.

"Bijan has given me his final ultimatum. He told me to tell you both that if she doesn't return in two weeks, he'll send you to hell. He sounds totally crazy and I'm tired of the game we're playing, while he's also driving me nuts here."

"I don't know what you expect me to do, Reza."

"Whatever is necessary…"

"I have no control over Mahtab, but I'll pass on your message to her. To be honest, I'm also getting tired myself of her mood changing every minute these days."

"So, you don't want her anymore?" I asked, unable to resist the chance for some humour in the middle of the mess that kept getting deeper every day.

Darren burst into laughter. "Well, I still love her too."

"So, she must come and get her divorce from this asshole as soon as possible. He's just lost it now and he can't be fixed."

"Should I tell Mahtab this as well?" Darren asked.

"Yes… Absolutely!"

"Do you realize that conveying your message about Bijan to her might put the last nail into his coffin and most likely abolish the chance of her keeping her promise and returning in two weeks?" Darren asked with great surprise.

"Yes, I know my words might affect her decision, but I must be honest with her. I can't hide my impression of Bijan from her anymore," I replied with surprise myself, but with conviction.

"Wow…! This is amazing! I'll tell her! Thanks, Reza. You're a wonderful man," Darren said with such compassion I not only believed him, but also felt deeper about my mission to help them.

"Will you call and fill me in as soon as you talk with her. Can you do me this favour?" I asked.

"Okay, I promise. I'm sure she'll be thrilled to hear your new, strict suggestion to divorce Bijan."

As though I had not hung up on him a few times already after our rows, Bijan kept calling me every day for any news regarding Mahtab and her reason for changing her deadline to return. Love and rage had destroyed even the last grains of his pride! I just kept saying I still did not know and he simply got angrier every time before I hung up on him again. The turmoil worried my mom and me, but I tried to keep things calm and prayed that Mahtab's and Darren's next calls would be good news. At last, she called ten days later with a final blow to all our hopes and nerves.

"Reza, I'm not going back to Tehran, after all," she said in an unprecedented, pitiful voice.

"Why?"

"Your message thru Darren helped me finalize my decision. I'm glad you agree I must get my divorce, so please help me."

"How can I help you if you don't come to get your divorce?"

"Believe me, this is the best way I can help myself under the circumstance. I can't face Bijan anymore. Just trust me."

"Fighting with Bijan long distance is your best option?"

"Yes… But do you think you still have it in your heart to help all of us. I know I'm asking you a lot after causing you so much grief already. But I'm in a curious position that makes my return to Tehran impossible and maybe even dangerous."

"You sound so mysterious. What's going on, Mahtab?"

"I can't explain my reasons now, but I promise you'll support my decision to stay in Vancouver for now when we talk later."

"But your decision will start a chaos here," I shrieked.

"Didn't you already say that facing Bijan in person is hard?"

"Yes… But we'll fight him together if you come home."

"No, I can't... I can't even look at him," Mahtab said.

"Does at least Darren know your reasons and agree with you?"

"Yes, but I've asked him not to discuss them with anybody."

"So, what do you expect me to do?" I asked.

"Everything... I'm asking you too much, I know. But you're the only person who can help me."

"How?"

"I want you to send me money, arrange for mom and Nazi to come here, stop Bijan and other people who're planning to hurt Darren and me, and then find a way to get my divorce."

"That's all?" I yelled with frustration.

"No, but let's concentrate on these simpler chores first," she said with a giggle.

"Are you crazy?"

"I guess I am… But I need your help. Please help us…"

"Us? You mean you and Darren?"

"Yes, plus Nazi and mom."

"I don't know how to respond to your crazy request. In fact, not helping you seems like the best option for me. Maybe you'll get smart and return to Tehran if I don't even send you money!"

"No, I won't go back, but I don't want to become a burden on Darren, if I can help it. I need money until I get my residency and a job myself."

"I'll send you money, but must think about those other things you're asking me to do. Do you think I am a superman?"

"Yes, you're my superman and you'll find ways to do all those difficult things."

"You have so much trust in me, but also a lot of nerve to ask me to handle all these issues here single-handedly."

"Because you're the only one who can help me. Darren can't go to Iran or do anything there. Just think about my request and tell me soon if you'll help. I hope you won't leave me alone here to suffer and do everything that must be done on my own."

"Mom is going to be devastated when I tell her the news. She may not survive all these turmoil."

"Then, don't tell her and others the truth. Humour everybody and lie on my behalf until we, mainly you, find real solutions."

"Of course... Mentioning your plans will start a chaos for sure. Just let me think for a few days," I said. The horrendous amount of lies we humans tell one another daily just for basic survival, even as a sincere, conscientious person, was driving me crazy!

As much as I liked to help Mahtab, I could not imagine how I could tackle the huge obstacles she was expecting me to conquer. I ambled in the streets, the nearby park, and my suite for hours, pondering the risks of getting drawn into Mahtab's affairs still deeper or finally coming to my senses and excusing myself from jumping into some dicey territories. I just could not fathom any means of achieving the goals she had listed. Stopping Bijan's wrath and getting her divorce felt particularly beyond my power. In fact, my involvement could only worsen the matters on many fronts. Then again, Mahtab's pathetic appeal on the phone still resonated in my head and I felt she was sincere and in a jam. She had sounded desperate, like begging me, which had felt weird for the person she had always been—so independent and proud.

After four days, I realized I could not abandon Mahtab at such a critical time, despite the foreseeable hassles for months or years to come. I just had to jump in wholeheartedly, trust her reasons for starting a nasty war, and fight for her with all my might. In fact, I had to think like a crafty general with strict plans and move diligently in several fronts with conviction. Ensuring Mahtab's safety in Vancouver was certainly my first priority, since Bijan's reprisal was inevitable in line with his two-week notice. Yet, the toughest task was to find the right timing and way of giving him Mahtab's message as tactfully as possible, too. God knew, how fast and furiously he might react to her dire rebellion.

Waiting any longer for Darren to return my call and tell me about the situation on the other side also felt impossible.

"I was gathering my courage to call you myself," Darren said.

"Courage? Is the situation so bad also over there?"

"We're ashamed of causing you so much headache, but things aren't easy for us here, either," he replied.

"Thanks, but I couldn't wait anymore. Things will get nasty soon here and most likely in Vancouver, too, as soon as I inform Bijan of Mahtab's latest decision."

"You haven't told him yet?"

"No, I've tried to stall him, while weighing my ability to help you two."

"She is your sister!" he pleaded.

"Still, I had to decide about getting even more into this mess."

"But you are not, right?"

"No, I can't leave her alone, although I may regret it later."

"Great… That's wonderful."

"I don't know how great it'll be soon…," I said with despair. "But she's my only sister and I feel guilty enough already about Mahroo's fate, too."

"It's wonderful how you talk about Mahtab. She'll be happy to hear your decision," he said.

"But do you think we should let her run this show, Darren?"

"What do you mean?"

"I mean, is it wise for you and me to submit to her whims and take big risks? Maybe the best way of helping her is to send her to a psychiatric facility to cure her perhaps," I said with gloom.

"I know what you mean. Sometimes, I've wondered myself," he replied with stress. "But in this case, I think she's right. So I have no hesitation helping her in any way I can."

"Do you realize that your life will now get many folds more dangerous?"

"Of course, I do… I'm not daft," he replied with a sigh.

"And I guess you have a role in her plans, ha?"

"Of course... I'm equally committed," he replied with a giggle and an air of mystery. "I love her even more now…"

"Even at the risk of getting killed for her stubbornness?" I asked cynically.

"Absolutely…," he replied with conviction and thrill. "We'll marry eventually, I hope."

"That's great. But at least give me a hint about her reasons for not returning to Iran and finalizing her divorce first?"

"The bottom line is that she can't face Bijan or get stuck in Iran for months."

"Why…? Why can't she talk to him in my presence at least?"

"You said yourself that he's now lost it totally and his words and actions are unreliable. She can't take the risk of going all the way to Iran just to test what you've already told us. Besides, Bijan won't give his consent again if she asks for an exit visa."

"Yes, that's true. He's a madman now…"

"Actually, I can say, you started the whole thing," Darren said giddily. "She decided quickly after I gave her your message."

"But did she have a good reason before my comment about Bijan's madness?"

"Yes. After listening to her, I agreed that going to Tehran or explaining her reasons will make the matter worse for all of us."

"I hope you two see my situation here. Should I start a war?"

"Just be brave… Be a man," he replied with a giggle for using my own phrase a few weeks earlier on our way to the airport.

"Okay, I'll try to be a strong man…, but now I'm starting to worry about your sanity as well after this long argument...," I said. "Are you sure you're okay?"

"Don't worry… She thinks I'm absolutely wise like her!"

"They asked the sneaky fox, 'Who's your witness?' It replied, 'My tail.'"

"Another Persian proverb, ha?" Darren asked with a chuckle.

"Yes... Aren't they cute?"

"Yes, you just focus on all the things she's asked you to do."

"Still, you two sound crazy from where I stand."

"Do you remember your similar cynicism about Mahroo's sanity and wishing you could send her to a therapist, too?"

"Yes. Do you also remember having the same doubts yourself about both my sisters off and on?"

"Yes, but it's different now…" he replied. "How many times are you gonna ask these questions?"

"Until it makes sense to me, too, before dying in the war she's begun. Can't you give me at least a clue?"

"No… Just trust us…"

"Okay, then… I'll trust you loonies and hope for the best."

"Just do that…! Help us," he replied in a sincere tone. "And I'll do whatever I can for her here."

"In that case, the first thing you must do is to arrange for her safety right away," I said. "That's your job now…"

"What do you mean?"

"She shouldn't stay in my apartment."

"Should I bring her to my place?"

"No, everybody probably knows where you live, too. "

"So what?"

"Talk to her about my concerns. Ask her if she can think of a place to hide, perhaps with my mom's friends there. Otherwise, take her out and hide her somewhere safe, maybe in a hotel or something until we find a more permanent solution. And be extra vigilant."

"Are you sure we need all these difficult precautions?"

"Yes, we can't take any risk and you're stalked by some thugs at least yourself. Talk to her and make a plan quickly."

"So, you'll tell Bijan about her final decision?"

"Not the whole truth, but still hell will break loose when I start talking, even if I say she's only delaying her travel plan."

"Okay, Reza. Thanks for helping us," Darren said.

"Still, not knowing her reasons makes me guess silly things and worry about her even more… I hope you guys realize that?"

"But it's for the better," Darren said.

"There's something else I'd like to ask you," Reza said.

"What?"

"I've been working on a plan of attack here in Tehran and get ready for the war."

"Okay…?"

"I may need to contact Sima."

"Really?"

"Yes, she might be the right strategic point to penetrate the enemy's barricade and activate my main battle with Bijan."

"You have a war plan already?"

"I've been studying my options and Sima seems the right place to start. So I just wanted to give you a heads-up and make sure that contacting her is okay with you."

"Yes, that's fine with me. Do you know how to find her?"

"I'm hoping she still lives in the same building you used to live when you knocked her up."

"Yes, that's a good place to start. Good luck and thanks a lot."

Consoling my mom while telling her about Mahtab's new plans was another tough task. We, mainly Mahtab, were ruining her last years, but other concerns, including Nazi's fate, were evident in her contorted, pensive face. So, I spent a whole day with her and Nazi, while all these family consoling and supports had put my business and personal life in jeopardy.

Sending my mom and Nazi away was the first, and supposedly the easiest, step before I could start my fight with Bijan. Even so, raising the matter with her again and again as subtly as possible was becoming too tough in itself.

"So, have you thought enough now about going to Vancouver and living with Mahtab and Nazi?" I asked my mom for the fifth time in the last four days, while I could not explain the urgency to her or push her too much.

"I told you, I'll feel lonely living there. Here at least I have some family and friends. What am I gonna do in Vancouver?"

"Mahtab is there and you also have some friends, right?"

"She's busy with her life and my friends aren't close enough for this stage of my life. I have only a few more years, Reza."

"I know it's hard to leave your home and friends just because Mahtab wants to live in Vancouver."

"But I must also think about Nazi. She needs a young mom. Don't you want to get married and take charge of Nazi, too?"

"I don't know when that will happen," I said.

"But if you marry soon, Nazi will be safe and I don't have to go anywhere," my mom said.

"Let's not count on me getting married anytime soon, if ever," I replied with guilt, yet the idea of finding and marrying someone as an urgent project in my busy schedule, just to accommodate my mom, made me giggle.

"Why? Why don't you choose someone? So many girls like to marry you."

"I don't think I can be a good husband or father," I said, now worrying also about the roots of my inability to build a family. *All these new topics unrelated to main issue causing all sorts of fresh arguments and thoughts were wasting a lot of our energies and time at such a critical point!*

"In that case, we must get Mahtab to adopt Nazi. Nazi won't be happy living with anybody else other than you or Mahtab."

"Do you still need time to think about going to Vancouver?" I asked. "Or if you prefer, maybe I'll take only Nazi with me and let Mahtab take care of her."

"But I hate to be away from both Nazi and Mahtab. Do you wanna kill me with your crazy ideas?" she shrieked.

"Sorry mom…," I replied timidly with angst.

"You think Mahtab will never come back to Tehran?"

"No, she sounds serious about living in Vancouver, although I haven't still told Bijan. I should find a way to stall him as long as possible with hope or perhaps do something a bit drastic."

"Like what?"

I only shrugged. "Don't mention our conversations or the chance of going to Vancouver to anybody, not even Nazi."

"I won't…"

I left my mom late in the evening, wondering if there was a way to make Bijan commit suicide as a rather typical act for a desperate husband in deep love with a tenacious, unfaithful wife. Assuming that I had the guts to be so sinister, did I have the right or duty to persuade him to be a real man and do the right thing for his own honour mostly, but also other people's happiness? That simple option could solve all the problems. I would not have to do all those extra work and everybody else could do as they liked or live wherever they wished. Instead, he had become only more vengeful every day. Actually, by refusing to accept his defeat gracefully, he only kept proving our consensus about this man's inherent weakness and inaptness as a husband. He surely did not grasp the meaning of love, at least not according to T.J.'s and Darren's elaborate definitions—now forcing my mom to leave her home and family, too. He simply did not seem even capable of realizing the best option for a man in his position: Suicide.

Of course, another option would be to kill him myself, since he was not a good man, anyway, on top of being so gutless to do the honourable act of suicide when such a great opportunity was gifted to him so generously! *I wished I had such a great excuse to end my own life!* Besides, he was a ruined soul with no value to himself or anybody else, and without any chance of redemption, the way Mahtab had treated him. He was better off dead now for his own sake at least! *I would've not persisted on this matter and offered all this wisdom if I weren't quite sure about his welfare!* Well, if I did not have the guts to end his vain, painful existence myself, it was not hard to find someone to do it for me, *and for him especially,* at a good price. *Thank god, so many useful thugs lived amongst us to handle these necessary, humanistic chores. Now I appreciated the value of their services much better.*

I hated being so vengeful and thinking like a murderer, but I was getting too desperate, merely due to Bijan's desolation and lack of pride. Still, I decided to keep this proactive option in mind, at least as a last resort! How could so many men be so empty of manhood? *It seemed that T.J., Darren, and I were the last three real men alive—even though so terribly lonely and damaged!*

Luckily, I decided to deal with Bijan as civilly as possible at the outset. In particular, it seemed appropriate to repeat the potent phrase I was an expert on now after using it on Darren at the right time with good results... "Be a man, Bijan!"

The fact that Mahtab and her plans were changing even my character and triggering such evil thoughts in my exhausted brain this late in the evening was quite disturbing and possibly a clue about my looming madness as a result of being around too many loonies for years. Yet, all these radical thoughts made me chuckle as I drove in the empty streets of Tehran towards my apartment late in the evening.

Gosh, Tehran could be a nice city to live in if it didn't have so much traffic and smog during the day!

Chapter Twenty-five
A Devious Devil

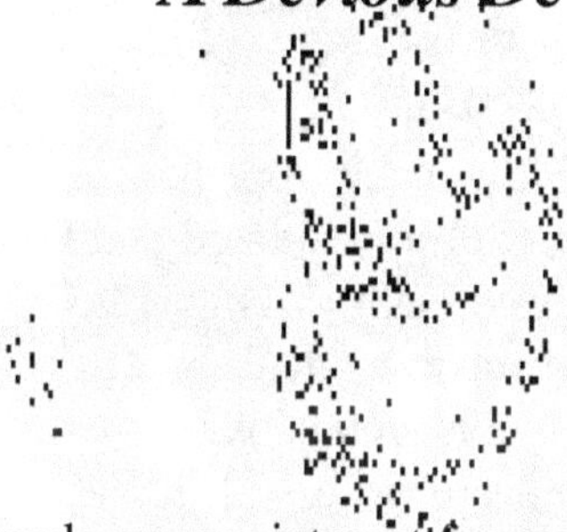

Darren made an appointment for me to discuss my elaborate inheritance plans with the lawyers he knew on the same day he was meeting the senior partner about some outstanding issues. Meanwhile, he got busy to find a safe place to hide with Mahtab according to Reza's latest instructions. He asked me if I preferred to go with them or take the risk of staying in his place alone. I said I definitely preferred to stay put in hopes of dying if the thugs came to kill him and instead had to do with me for now.

I met Larry, a junior staff at the law firm and explained my needs to him patiently and diligently.

"Mr. Olaee, we have never done such a vindictive estate plan as far as I know," Larry told me with a teasing tone and smirk.

"So, my case will help you expand your expertise and offer it to many clients who'd have similar needs," I said with a mocking tone of my own. "I bet the number of testy people needing this type of planning for their nasty families is on the rise and will surely turn into a lucrative business for you".

"You think so?" Larry asked pensively with a chuckle.

"I promise… You'll make tons of money," I replied.

"Yeah, maybe. But it'd be a big challenge for us and we must study many legal angles to satisfy your rather odd requests."

"So what're saying? Are you able to help me or not?"

"I can't answer today. I'll have to run your ideas with a senior lawyer before giving you an answer."

"Okay, I don't think I'm in a rush to die."

"Are your assets in Iran under your name only and does your wife know about them?"

"Yes and yes," I replied.

"And all these arrangements must coincide with your divorce settlement, I presume?" he asked with apprehension.

"Yes, I need your help with my divorce and handling some asset distribution quarrels. Especially, I'd rather keep the assets in Iran out of our discussions with my wife."

"How would that be possible, you think?"

"Well, I don't have to share them with her according to the Iranian laws, so just make sure she won't be able to file a claim if I ever brought any money to Canada later."

"This is getting really tough," Larry said rather edgily.

"Maybe I should talk with a lawyer more familiar with special estate planning circumstances. Do you have such a person?"

"Yes, but if you don't mind, let me get the preliminary data and discuss them with her. She must prepare herself before going over the details with you. Is that okay, Mr. Olaee?"

"Sure, okay. What other information do you need?"

"First, let's see if I've got your main intention right at least..."

"Okay...," I murmured.

"You want to make it hard and lengthy for your family to get some inheritance, but don't want them to be destitute or wasteful with money you think they don't deserve in the first place," Larry mimicked my words along with my sardonic hints. He was trying to be cute, while hiding his frustration with me.

"Yes, it seems you've got the gist of it, especially about them not deserving my generosity!"

"So you need an administrator for a long time. What's a good estimate of your net wroth including your Iranian assets?"

"Over seven million. Even if half of it is kept in real estate, the growth in a few decades will be substantial by the time my kids finally become eligible to get any money."

"Yes, I bet it will be, especially in Vancouver's market."

"Well, it seems wise to have an administrator, then," I said.

"Yes. With that kind of money you can have an administrator or anything else you want," Larry said with a much kinder tone suddenly.

"Okay then, add an administrator," I said with a chuckle as if ordering a sandwich.

"One administrator...!" he uttered wittily while jotting it down.

"Yes, a very clever, rigid one...," I added with my own wit. "It'll help if he or she has a good sense of humour, too."

Larry frowned and asked, "So your daughters will get the first twenty percent of the estate upon their mother's death, another twenty when they're at least fifty years old, and the rest will be distributed based on the details and conditions you'll specify later in line with their needs, age, and marital status, right?"

"Yes. But still send periodic statements to them," I said gaily. "I want them to see how much money belongs to them, but can't touch until specific conditions are met."

"Oh, boy… You're really planning to stick it to them, aren't you?" Larry asked with a chuckle.

"Oh, yes… Make sure you mention it to the senior lawyer, too." I said, he burst into laughter, and I continued, "Just wait until I give you all the other details."

"You have still more conditions?"

"Of course… What I've told you is only the tip of the iceberg. I bet you and the senior lawyer will enjoy the details even more!"

"Please tell me all your conditions, so that we can work with the total picture."

"I can't give you everything today. But as an example, their potential entitlement for some eventual inheritance should not be used as collateral for borrowing from banks or similar stuff. Also, the unused portion of my estate goes to some specific charities as soon as I can find some eligible ones, or else find other options."

"It's getting more complicated by the minute," Larry said with a sigh, as though already giving up on me as a potential client.

"Maybe I should talk to another law firm, too?"

"I don't know how that would help your situation or how to advise you today. Just let me think and talk to others in the firm about your needs and contact you in a week or so."

Darren was waiting for me in the lobby.

"How did your meeting go, T.J.," he asked giddily.

"Not good… The guy sounded rather pessimistic about doing what I need," I replied.

"So, basically, your ideas drove the guy nuts, too, eh?"

"Yes, they did… How was your meeting?"

"It was very productive indeed; way beyond my imagination. The angels are blessing me left and right these days, it seems," he replied with a secretive grin.

"I'm glad at least you feel jubilant after so long."

"Thanks. So what're the snags with your estate plan?"

I explained my conversations with the junior lawyer while driving toward home, but stopped at a coffee shop for lunch first. I was dying to know the purpose and result of his conversations with the senior partner and the cause of his eerie jubilation. Yet, he stayed reserved even after my subtle probing for information. He had been mysterious enough already recently, hiding the cause of Mahtab's sudden change of heart about returning to Iran and all, like I was not his old confidant anymore. So, I stopped prying and tried to be happy about his rising spirit.

Feri's unexpected call and edgy tone made me curious and jittery. She sounded breathless and talked in a muffled voice, like trying to conceal her conversation from someone around her.

"Can we speak privately for a minute?" she asked.

"Yeah... Is everything okay?"

"No, nothing is okay anymore. Your daughters are following in your footsteps and driving me nuts."

"Oh…? That is new…!"

"They have your stubborn genes," she said.

"What have they done now?"

"They want to leave me, too."

"Where're they going?"

"Rose wants to go live with her boyfriend and Noshin wants to go live alone or get a roommate. They're suddenly too restless and don't listen to anything I say."

"Welcome to the club. That's what I've been feeling last ten years while you and your daughters have only contradicted me."

"Can you talk to them or do something?"

"Didn't you hear what I just said?" I asked. "When was the last time they or you listened to me?"

"They're going to ruin their lives if you don't stop them."

"Hadn't I told you the same thing and you always took their side. You never backed me up whenever I tried to put some sense in their silly heads?"

"But now you must do something about your daughters…"

"Now suddenly they're my daughters again?"

"What am I gonna do, then, if you aren't doing anything?"

"I don't know. At least you'll still have Leila, I guess, right?"

"Thank God, she's still too young. But she's also given me her notice already about leaving after high school," Feri said.

"At least you have her for now. I don't even know how often any of my daughters want to see me, if at all."

"What's happening with these kids, all running away from their families so hastily?" she said with angst.

"You've spoiled them too much like most other parents we're associating with, besides all the garbage society is teaching them."

Feri sighed and started weeping, while I stayed quiet patiently with a torn heart myself. Our rotten kids had two heartbroken parents now. This was the reward of sacrificing our lives for them. That was how our daughters were paying us back. The new development saddened me, but Feri getting her punishment for all the wrong things we had done, consciously or not, was rather satisfying. Personally, I had often been forced to behave against my will and wisdom, while dreading the harsh consequences of our lifestyle and disunity haunting us for the rest of our lives. Now, my fortune for not witnessing my daughters' decisions and departure felt like a small blessing. All afternoon, I had felt a bit guilty after my lengthy interview with the lawyer. Now, however, I was keener about my spiteful plan against my daughters' lack of compassion and traditional ethics. Oddly enough, I also felt a tiny bit of pity for Feri, the way she sounded so miserable today.

"Do you wanna try your luck to stop their silliness?" I asked.

"Of course. I prefer they stay here until they find a husband."

"So are you ready to help me for once?"

"How?"

"By giving them an ultimatum."

"What kind of ultimatum?" she asked with cynicism.

"Tell'em we'll both disinherit them if they keep doing crazy things or don't treat us nicely."

"How many times you wanna use this stupid threat. Don't you recall how casually they ignored you when you said it before?"

"Yes, I realize their idiocy and lack of sense for money, but then they thought they'd get your money at least."

"I doubt any kind of threat will work on these kids."

"They have no brain, I know. But it doesn't hurt to tell'em once more for both of us."

Feri was quiet for a while, surely disgusted for being put in such a tight spot, but also considering it as her last resort.

"I may tell'em, but don't think it'll work. They're simply too eager to go away and have sex every night."

"Then they'd better be ready for the consequences."

"I'll tell'em what you wanna do, but they'd probably only hate you more for it. Do you still want me to say it?"

"Only if you'd say we'll both do it, not only me."

"No, I changed my mind," she said tensely.

"You chickened out already… in two minutes?"

"I won't say anything about doing it myself, but I'll say you have five times more money than me, which is true."

"You see, you're still afraid of them, instead of helping them learn something by showing our unity even this once," I said.

"Whatever… Do you still want me to tell'em you have lots of money and are very serious about disinheriting them?"

"Yes. In fact, tell'em I have ten times more money than you."

"You do?" Feri asked in shock with anger.

"Yes, just tell'em…"

"I will, asshole, but I don't think it'll work," she said tensely.

"But it might if you say you do it, too. This is your last chance to help yourself and them."

"I'll think about it, but I don't think I'll join in your threats. And you'd better get ready for their harsh reaction."

"How worse can they treat me? You think they'll kill me?"

"They might. They're just getting so out of control," Feri said with a tense humour, sounding rather horrified for once by the kind of relationship that our family has built for itself out of mere stupidity in the midst of this pervasive social mayhem. She most likely also knew how devilish their daughters were, like herself, even capable of killing me!

"To be honest, I'm trying to learn not to care about them or anything else anymore," I said with gloom and shattered nerves, tears gathering in my eyes.

I knew Feri had always been too timid around her daughters to oppose, let alone threaten, them. But she would surely repeat my trite ultimatum to them and the extent of my hidden assets for a slight chance of dissuading them from leaving her, but mostly to ruin my relationship with them for good. What a silly women she has always been!

Feri was quiet with an apparent air of helplessness.

"Any other bad news you wanna dump on me?" I asked.

"I'm gonna put the house in the market if you don't wanna give me some money."

"If you're still serious about our divorce, selling the house is the right thing to do. I don't think either of us would like to live in such a big house alone without our kids."

"I will, then…"

"Do you ever sense the chaos and pain you've caused?" I said.

"You still believe everything is my fault, even our daughters' plan to leave home?" she asked with despair.

"Of course, I do… You couldn't teach them anything useful. Instead, you taught them lots of garbage and crooked notions that this damn society is dumping on us."

"That's bullshit. You started this whole thing by leaving home and giving your daughters more nerve to do the same thing."

"No, that's not the reason... Just the opposite. They were just waiting for an excuse to dump us and go away. After playing you all along and causing our division, they're taking advantage of the situation now as two weaker, desolate parents. They even dared you to ask for divorce and you let them. If we'd instead shown them the power of our unity, they would've not dared to divide and destroy all of us. That's a pity."

"Yeah, that's a pity you've destroyed my life and now our daughters. I hope you burn in hell forever," Feri said and hung up abruptly, leaving me in deep agony at a new height of despair. *How can any human be so silly like her?*

I truly believed—and suffered for it all along—that Feri had ruined her daughters' lives by being such a horrible role model with her demented lifestyle and mentality, contradicting me all the time, and hindering my chance of getting close to my kids at their young ages. She sabotaged my attempts to give them some notions of reality for choosing a humbler attitude and worldview. So, ultimately, we can even say Feri had not loved her own kids properly by the way she had misled them, instead of grasping the reality of life herself and teaching her daughters, too. She did not even mind her daughters lose their chances for a less hectic, if not a very comfortable, life by all the money they could get from me —all merely for abolishing my relationship with them. Besides her crooked teachings, surely our daughters' looming fate related to the effects of Feri's evil genes transferred to them, while my fabulous genes, especially that infamous *conscience* gene of mine, had seemingly suffocated under the pressure of Feri's evil ones. It had failed to give our kids even a basic compassion towards their parents. *Am I such an objective, modest person myself or what?*

Darren noticed my gloom when I emerged from the bedroom. He had certainly heard at least my loud voice and screams at the end, fighting with Feri on the phone behind the closed door. So, he had insightfully prepared two large glasses of whisky already and we plummeted onto the couch. "Are you ready to move again to a new location?" he asked with a chuckle.

"Are you kicking me out, too?" I asked with surprise.

"I am kicking both of us out of here."

"Why?"

"It is not safe for us to live here."

"Should I look for an apartment or something for myself?"

"No, we'll both go to a new place tomorrow. Then we'll also bring Mahtab to stay with us. We'll hide there for a while."

"Where's this place?" I asked Darren.

"I'll explain everything to you and Mahtab later. But things are starting to work in our favour swiftly at all levels, although we're still facing a few serious threats."

"That's great… You deserve a break."

"The way destiny works and things suddenly start to improve feels bizarre or magical," Darren said with an air of mystery.

"It's encouraging that at least you sound happy and positive."

"Thanks, but don't tell anybody about us moving out of here."

"Okay…But as I said before, I don't mind staying here alone or even getting killed by the thugs," I said in hopes of getting my privacy here until hopefully getting murdered.

"I know and I don't mind, either, except they might force you reveal our hiding place first," he replied with a chuckle.

Darren's fast-growing optimism felt surreal, while he enjoyed being secretive about its source. His jubilant mood after so many years was both soothing and shocking enough to boost even my dying spirit a little. He was spreading a timely source of energy we needed to face many dilemmas and threats and I was grateful to benefit from his fortune, despite my tiny envy when watching him sing and laugh so lightheartedly out of the blue.

"So we're moving tomorrow night, you said?" I asked.

"Yes, we'll sneak out late in the evening from the garage."

I had not really meant to drag my family into my wistful world of literature and story telling, but it was getting harder every day to write about anything else when ninety percent of my thoughts revolved around them. This psychological necessity felt like a new nuisance jeopardizing my ambitions for scholarly reflections and contributions. Then again, my family had been the cause of my agony, dismal destiny, meditations, and writing in the first place. So, sparing them felt hard, especially because I wished to fathom the sources of my suffering, and also because my broken family's stories were apparently humorous and educational, too, according to friends and Larry—the petty lawyer. I recalled Feri's objection a few months earlier about my likely intention to write about her tyranny and I had assured her that I had more important things to dwell on. At the time, I had cringed upon the idea of informing the entire world about the potential depth of human evil just by portraying Feri. But, in recent weeks, this juicy idea had felt more relevant and inevitable every day in line with Feri's rising cruelty and my deeper gloom. Recalling her objection to write about her was now *especially* encouraging me to do just that out of spite as well. In fact, I wondered whether this idea would have ever found such a focal attention in my literary world if she had not brought it up herself! *What a sly, spiteful devil I have become!*

Accordingly, I began to believe that I should at least admire Feri's foresight about her looming role as a main character and topic in my writings. Maybe I must even thank her for putting this splendid idea into my head. *But should I do it in person, maybe along with a beautiful gift, to show the depth of my gratitude?*

These thoughts also demonstrated how a devious devil like me is created every minute in this weird universe nowadays, mainly through a torturous mechanism we call marriage. I had never imagined that such a devil resided so deep inside me, too! Still, even a sadder realization was that only other people, mainly my dear family, had awakened this devil deliberately to cause so much pain for myself and others, along with a sense of obligation to propagate my feelings!

In the end, reflection and writing, mostly about Feri, felt like a viable venue to soothe my compiled sufferings before and after our separation, while filling my days with this soulful hobby as well. She would be the main heroine in some of my novels with lots of room and liberty to show her talents! I could write erotic novels about her flirting and dirty affairs with other men. I could write educational essays about her arrogance, and ignorance. I had millions of stories that revealed the ultimate depth of human stupidity. Sadly, my twenty or so remaining years would not be long enough for finishing my books only about her, even if I worked ten hours a day, though I had many other topics I wished to tackle, too. I must surely write about the way she had ignored my forlorn parents to the point I had lost my connection with them myself. I never had enough compassion and patience for them, anyway, but she ruined my basic relationship with them. I took her side mostly to secure my marriage, while alienating my parents. Then, we left them to come to Canada. They did not like to come with us or even for a visit simply because of Feri's nasty character. My mother's health was poor already, but Feri made her feel much more miserable as not only a person, but also a helpless witness to her son's imminent demise.

My way of treating my parents had always saddened me, but the clarity of my failure to keep a civil contact with them and my sense of guilt grew ten folds after Feri's request for divorce. I felt horrible for breaking their hearts repeatedly in the past out of my sheer gutlessness and sense of practicality. They had not even seen and enjoyed their grandchildren enough. Then again, I was glad that our distance had at least limited my parents' knowledge of their granddaughters' depth of vanity and malice. I was also glad I had kept my mouth shut about this matter in fear of making them even sadder for their old son as well as the entire humanity with all the extra-special devilry that Feri and her daughters were inflicting upon it. Being ashamed of your kids instead of proud, especially before your parents, seemed to defy all natural laws!

Ironically, though, my helplessness to even express the risks of my family's imprudence to them still worried me the most. I just could not stop being a conscientious and concerned father, apparently. Instead, learning more every day about their rising recklessness with no discipline and foresight never stopped being shocking, hurtful, and humiliating, while also raising my own devilry urges. Giving up on Feri after years of patience, waiting for her reform, was excruciating enough already, but witnessing my daughters' horrible minds was immensely tough and painful when they were just unable to grasp any practical sense about life, while getting more self-absorbed and extravagant.

My father's single visit after my few half-hearted invitations turned out quite embarrassing in itself, although he spent only two days with us. The poor old man came all the way to visit his grandkids like other normal families, but was sorry the first day. Then, he went to a hotel after Feri's bad treatment and temper. He had possibly assumed Feri had matured after raising her own kids and sensing parenthood. However, he realized his mistake the first night of arriving in Vancouver.

My father is a smart man and a good judge of characters. He had told me not to marry Feri and my mom did not like her at all, either. So maybe some of Feri's behaviour towards them and me had been only retaliatory and the outcome of my parents' initial coldness towards her. To her credit, Feri has always been keenly receptive and cunningly spiteful. The irony was that I could not tell my parents that marrying Feri had been such an excruciating decision for me, since saving my daughter's life had felt like an honourable gesture for any conscientious person. Still, I had hoped deeply that my parents had guessed my reasons for marrying her already. I had desperately prayed they knew I was not an idiot to make such a plain mistake, especially after all their hints about Feri's unsuitability. Still, even if they had doubted my sanity at the time, they, like many other people, had guessed the cause of my madness when Rose was born only seven months after the wedding. So kindly, everybody had pretended it had been merely a premature birth in spite of Rose's healthy condition and speedy release from the hospital. What a lot of tactful relatives, hoping, praying, and trying to keep my shaky family together!

All along, living with Feri in confusion, while mourning my stupidity and humouring my dumbfounded, anxious parents and relatives had been a torturous journey. Still, I had hoped that some miracles would not only change Feri one day, but also give my parents enough reasons to reconcile with her and respect their son like old time, before I had appeared like a complete fool.

So naively, I had always dreamed of the day I would have the courage and conviction to swear to my parents that Feri's brain had started to work a little at last and it was prudent to give her another chance to prove herself. I had wished a day would come to feel proud of being Feri's loyal husband. Alas, my dream never came true, and instead she got wilder and viler. Now, I had to inform my heartbroken frail, parents that they had been right all along and I had been foolish. I wanted to tell them that I had known my stupidity even then, before the wedding. More ideally, I hoped they would also gather the courage and confess they had known all along that I had not been so daft to marry her only out of love or for any likely quality. I had hoped to regain my pride someday one way or another. Instead, we had to wait twenty years for me to announce my divorce, confess to my lifelong, painful knowledge of my horrific mistake of marrying Feri even for Rose's sake, and suffer the consequence of my well-publicized stupidity! *At least this important fact—my innate stupidity—is established now forever! This wisdom has been the most tangible outcome of this doomed marriage!*

As a rejected, humiliated father, now I felt even more for my parents, all thanks to Feri's efforts and success again to turn our daughters against me. Now, I finally felt too ashamed for having done similar atrocities to my own parents in the last two decades, although never intentionally at least!

Nevertheless, it was time to beg for my parents' forgiveness both in person and in my books. A short trip to Tehran might also boost my spirit, after all, despite the humility of returning to Iran with my tail between my legs, looking straight into my parents' sad eyes, and hinting about my dreadful failures. Yet, I was now determined to do just that like a real man at the age of 55, finally.

In the end, the only silver lining for my shattering family life has been my chance to keep myself busy a few decades during a long retirement by analysing my lousy life. Initially, writing had manifested only as a refuge for solace and survival in solitude. But, soon, I began to believe that all the torture in my married life had in itself been only God's wisdom and blessing to reform my life path and enjoy a productive, long life when we have nothing useful to do with our remaining years even if we happen to have a caring family. How else all these end-of-the-life privileges would have materialized if I had not married Feri? Meanwhile, my relationship with God has also appeared to be soaring faster, the more my family has ignored me. So, now with these radical beliefs making me put my blessings in proper perspective and think fairly, I feel even more obliged now to acknowledge Feri for being such a piece of work. At least the last years of my life could indeed be fulfilling with a chance for self-searching and self-cleansing, while thanking god and Feri for their ironic roles in my fate. Having so many stories to ponder and propagate felt blissful for various ends amidst my dire gloom.

On the other hand, so much noise with Darren around all day, and soon maybe Mahtab and others, too, was making it too tough to concentrate on my work as much as I desired. I just prayed I would at least get a quiet room for myself in the new place we were planning to sneak into tonight.

Chapter Twenty-six
Spooky Fortune

Mahtab's decision not to return to Tehran was exciting news already, but I got ecstatic when she explained her reasons finally two days later. I felt heaven had opened its door to me and my life was about to change forever now that she had chosen to stay with me.

Of course, Mahtab had asked my opinion and stressed, with her witty charm, that if I had any reservations about her decision and reasons or worried about Bijan's wrath, she would pursue her other option and return to Iran in a couples of weeks.

"No, my darling, your decision and reasons are perfect and I don't care about Bijan's rage. I love you, Mahtab," I had said giddily, despite the anxiety behind my foolish show of bravery.

"But, Darren, we shouldn't tell anybody about our secret for now," Mahtab had insisted on the phone.

"Not even Reza?" I had asked.

"No. We shouldn't bother and confuse him with side issues."

"You call this a side issue?"

"For the time being, yes."

"Okay… I love you and your side issues," I had replied.

"In fact, we must get ready for war even with my family."

"I agree... Let Bijan and others think you'll go back soon."

This phone chitchat had taken place three days earlier after Reza's call from Iran. Things had been changing fast around us, but I had not yet gotten a chance to tell her about the outcome of my conversations with my lawyers yesterday. Thus, I called to inform her about T.J. and I moving to a new location later that evening and that she would join us the following evening.

"This would be against Reza's order," Mahtab said.

"No, it's not… He's now issued a new decree. He thinks you won't be safe alone, especially in that apartment."

"Why?"

"He said the risks increase drastically when Bijan's two-week notice is up and he tells him about your delay to return, again."

"Where's this place we're going to hide," she asked.

"I'll explain when I see you. Can you pack and be ready to move out tomorrow night?"

"Okay."

"T.J. will come to pick you up. Open the garage door for him when he arrives and buzzes you. Then, go hide in the backseat before he gets out and brings you to our new home."

"Our new home? Is it big enough for three of us?"

"Yes, we'll have lots of space. And don't tell anybody about your move or related issues."

T.J. and I spent several hours cleaning the house and did a major grocery shopping in anticipation of Mahtab's arrival. Our home looked impeccable with plenty of food and fruits, just in case a war began and we could not go out much. In the evening, T.J. left to collect Mahtab and followed a scrupulous scheme to ensure the secrecy of our new place and her relocation.

Mahtab was impressed with the elegance throughout the house, too, the same way T.J. had been the night before upon our arrival. I took Mahtab and her luggage to the big master bedroom with an eloquent ensuite and hot tub.

"This is your private suite," I whispered to her. "I'm using the next room and T.J. is in the basement for his privacy and quiet."

"It's good keeping a decent appearance while T.J. is around."

"I thought so, too," I said and kissed her lips after so long. "I missed you so much."

"But come and hold me all night, anyway."

"Absolutely… I'd been dreaming about tonight a long time."

"Me too," she said with a sweet smile.

"Come down for a snack and drinks if you aren't tired," I said and left her to unpack or whatever.

T.J. had already poured us cognac and started Mozart's songs and sonatas when I arrived in the family room. He looked relaxed on the comfortable sofa with a triumphant grin. The new setting was certainly a major improvement over the accommodation he had been sharing with me in my tiny apartment. Mahtab arrived soon as well, freshened up, and looking also happy. Recalling the mansion she lived in with Bijan in Tehran, I could imagine how claustrophobic living in either Reza's or my place during the last three months had possibly felt to her. Now we all felt relieved, although I still could not believe my luck with so many blessings in just one week!

"This is my house now. So feel free to do as you wish."

"This is your house?" T.J. asked with shock.

"Yes, it's mine."

"Did you win a lottery?" Mahtab asked.

"No. Apparently, I own this house, because Erica and I were still legally married when she passed away. I lived here a few years, too, before our separation," I said.

Now Mahtab and T.J. also looked pleased with our fortunes being linked together so miraculously at such a timely manner.

"So you're sort of back at your old place," T.J. said.

"Yes, sort of… It always belonged to her, though, while I'd felt like an unwelcome guest."

"This is a really beautiful house, Darren," Mahtab said.

"Yes. Erica has tried hard to decorate it so elegantly. Still, she complained about feeling too lonely living here alone."

"How can such a beautiful woman feel lonely?" T.J. asked.

"It's possible… I feel for her," Mahtab said. "But I couldn't imagine she had such an amazing taste even after witnessing her talent in doing Reza's suite."

"Alas, not even all that talent helped her relax and be happy."

"You've been a lucky man, Darren. Now I know why you've been missing her so much all along," Mahtab said.

"Yes, I've been lucky... First Erica and now you."

"Did you paint that portrait of Erica?" she asked pointing to the large tableau on the wall.

"No, I hadn't even seen it until last night," I replied. "Now the question is what to do with it?"

"I thought it was her... She was beautiful," she said pensively.

"Should I take it off the wall now?" I asked. Nobody peeped, while we all kept staring at Erica's portrait hypnotically.

"Do you think it's a good portrait of her?" T.J. asked.

"Yes, it is... You can even see her sly charm," I said giddily.

"You might miss her even more now in this house!" Mahtab said at last in a teasing tone along with a hint of jealousy.

"Maybe a little more. But I also feel closer to her spirit now—for living in the space she's created for us."

"Especially, inheriting this cosy place just in time to hide from your enemies feels weird," Mahtab said.

"Good for you," T.J. added. "At least we'll be safe here."

"This is the second miracle that has happened to me in the last few days, which makes me feel so blessed suddenly."

"Second miracle?" T.J. asked. "What was the first one?"

I winked at Mahtab who looked amused by T.J.'s curiosity and my sly grin.

"Well… Isn't it obvious? Can't you see Mahtab sitting here with us instead of being in Iran now," I said with a chuckle, while Mahtab looked at us with delight.

"Oh..., of course. You're one lucky man," T.J. said.

"I know Bijan is very spiteful, but still wonder how far he'd really go with his threats?" Mahtab said with a sigh.

"Are you saying we might be just too paranoid about so many sources of danger?" T.J. asked mostly Mahtab.

"No, I think we should trust Reza's judgment on this matter," I replied. "It's better to be cautious and proactive, as Detective Stewart also keeps telling us."

"In fact, the number of your enemies is probably growing faster than you think," T.J. added.

"Maybe... Thanks for staying here and being our bodyguard."

"We've put you at risk, too, T.J.," Mahtab added.

"Just the opposite... I was actually hinting about the risk of harbouring a man with a long list of his own enemies," T.J. said.

"You have a long list of enemies, too?" Mahtab asked.

"Yes. Besides Feri, now my daughters also have good reasons to kill me before I get a chance to sign my nasty will," T.J. said with laughter. He then recounted his recent conversations with Feri and warning their daughters about his plan to disinherit them if they do not act wiser and be kinder to their parents.

"So they must now either change themselves overnight or kill you quickly before it's too late, ha?" Mahtab asked with a giggle. "You've really put them in a tight spot!"

"Killing you is much easier, of course," I said with laughter.

"Of course...! They can never change, let alone overnight... Besides, I promise you my family is wilder than all your enemies in Iran and Canada put together," T.J. said, while offering proof with humour about being in danger more than Mahtab and me.

"It's sad when families fight amongst themselves fiercely for basic stuff," Mahtab said with gloom. "Look at all of us."

"It's not too odd if Feri wants me dead. But the idea of my daughters killing or even hating me so much feels so unnatural, I'd say, besides being painful," T.J. said.

"What kind of genes and education have you given them?" I asked slyly for fun, knowing T.J.'s sensitivity about this matter. I did it in the same spirit I knew he always teased me on sensitive issues, in particular during those two painful weeks of my forced separation from Mahtab. He did it in good taste and knew I was noticing his intention to make us laugh and relax.

"You know my opinion, you sly agitator," T.J. said. "You ask these silly questions to laugh at me some more, aren't you?"

"But Mahtab doesn't know… You'd better tell her, too."

"It's all related to Feri's rotten genes, spite, and training, plus all the garbage society teaches people," T.J. said and we laughed. "They've now proven perfectly that narcissism is hereditary!"

"Okay, T.J., I agree you're in more danger than we are—"

T.J. interrupted me, "Once we were having our super together like a magical fluke and arguing when Rose said, 'You think all four of us are always wrong and only you're always right about everything.' I laughed and replied wittily, 'Yes, it's just the matter of your genes, not consensus! My claim isn't far-fetched at all and you've finally caught my drift…'"

"Why did you give them an ultimatum, then?" Darren asked.

"I guess I wasn't thinking clearly when Feri was pushing me to act. Stupid me! I hope they don't learn where I'm living now."

"Should I buy you a gun to protect all of us, then?" I asked.

"It's not a bad idea," T.J. replied and we laughed again.

"Let's make sure we activate the alarm every night until I get you a gun," I said while giving them the code.

"You're surely caught in an emotional web as well, like us," Mahtab said. "It's tough, T.J., I know…"

"Especially since he's such a gentle person," I added.

"My only consolation is that, now with me out of the picture, those four will only drive one another nuts," T.J. said with a sigh.

"Yeah, you're right...," I said. "They'd been using you as a punching bag so far to release their frustrations, ha?"

I called Reza and told him about Mahtab living with me and T.J. in a safe location. Despite his curiosity, I told him it was safer for him not to know our hiding place for now. He was getting ready to go see Bijan and give him new excuses for Mahtab's alleged decision to delay her return again. However, he stressed he was certain Bijan would not believe him anymore and the prospect of war escalating in all fronts was looming.

"Have you contacted Sima yet?" I asked excitedly about any kind of information regarding my fatherless son.

"No, but soon," Reza replied. "Should I tell her you said hi?"

"I see no harm in that, do you?"

"Not at this point…," Reza replied.

Mahtab also spoke with Reza and looked happy about his plan to help her and Mahroo's portrait moved to their mom's house.

"Reza is really becoming a good ally for us," she said giddily.

"I'm glad you made peace with him."

"Me too," she replied with a sense of triumph of her own.

"Didn't I tell you it'll pay off to be flexible and open-minded?"

"Yes, you did…!"

"So, will you listen to whatever I say from now on without any delay or driving me nuts?" I asked in front of T.J. and we laughed.

"Yes, my lord… Who's Sima?" she asked, while T.J. tittered.

"Oh…," I whispered. "She's my son's mother. Reza thinks he can use her to face up to Bijan and my other enemies in Iran."

"So Mahtab knows about your son, too," T.J. asked.

"Yes, we shared our secrets last week. Now, you both know about the son I have not yet seen, but was sent to jail for in Iran. He's already caused me lots of physical and mental pain within a few months of his birth and before we even meet."

"What did I say about kids?" T.J. said. "It'll only get worse in the coming years, I promise. Still, my kids are the nuttiest ever!"

"So you definitely want a gun and your nagging will continue, eh?"

"Yes, I've just only begun!" T.J. replied with a tense giggle.

Besides the advantages of having a safe place to hide, being back in the house I had shared with my once beloved Erica was fun. I felt guilty for enjoying it so much more now without her in it!

Still, her spirit and my mixed memories of her in this space haunted me. I reminisced our romantic evenings, but also the nights I had fled to the guestroom away from her vile vibes or the idea of my beloved wife loving someone else. Still, her house felt like a perfect place to raise a family with Mahtab, so I decided to keep it, while hoping Erica's spirit would not bother us out of love or spite. I hoped we could now make peace even if it was proven that she had been the main culprit in hiring the thugs who had shot me. *So generously*, I reckoned, the wealth she had left for me inadvertently somewhat made up for all the pain she had given me all along, especially at the end. Causing her own demise, just to make me wealthy and safe, was enough punishment for her and I had already forgiven her.

I had not mentioned the extent of my sudden fortune not even to Mahtab. Besides the house, plenty of cash in Erica's accounts and her partnership share in SDI now belonged to me. According to the lawyers, SDI had now become a major software company and my share was worth millions of dollars. Last week I was a desperate destitute, fussing about finding a job or a gallery to sell the paintings I was hoping to do if I ever gathered enough energy, and I was almost sure Mahtab would go back to Iran and leave me with the pain of losing her, too. Now, I seemed to have it all. Oh, God, how can I thank you for all this wealth, that Mahtab, and... all the rest of it?

Still, the idea that *only* Erica's death had brought me a timely relief in many ways tickled my conscience. The high chance of her soul being furious about my inadvertent possession of her assets, merely because she had died prematurely without a will, was my new source of anguish adamant to restore my mood to its messy level only two weeks earlier before my sudden fortunes. I could not elude these taunting ideas, while I promised my restless spirit to find a way to settle the matter with Erica's angry soul somehow. Judging by my conscience's whining and verdict, my mere forgiveness of her crimes against me was apparently still not enough for her spirit to forgive me in return and let us be. I abhorred these silly thoughts and a few small nightmares since we had moved into her house. I yelled at, and tried to strangle, my nosy conscience, while I planned to do everything possible to ensure Erica's testy ghost would not turn this place into a haunted manor. As an ironical scenario for my psyche's fun, I even played with the idea of the entire saga, including her suicide, being her own gimmick, as her last resort, to bring me to this house just for torturing me for years! Meanwhile, her stern portrait on the wall appeared to be watching us closely, while I feared removing it!

Another bizarre side-effect of living in Erica's house was my rising compassion to the point of even believing Jeff about being just a puppet for Erica to separate Elizabeth and me. Elizabeth's pleading to forgive him was also a factor to do so! Let Elizabeth have a chance for happiness as well, I had decided, *so generously again*! I was just waiting for the evidence she was going to bring to prove Erica's role to do my final review of Jeff's case.

Above all, forgiving Erica and Jeff, and feeling mercy towards Elizabeth, triggered a profound thought: Maybe I was not such a terribly conceited devil I had assumed to have become, after all! Maybe some hope for my redemption existed, despite my endless sins of seducing other men's beloveds with so little compassion for those broken souls, especially this very last one—Bijan!

Then, it occurred to me swiftly that even my forgiving attitude and mercy had been, at the end, only for indulging myself—to justify my entitlement to all these seeming fortune and salvation! *What a conceited, lousy human being I have become, after all!*

I met Cameron, my new partner at SDI, to discuss my options.

"You can stay a silent partner, be a supervisor as an active partner, or sell me your share," he said after offering his sorrow for losing Erica as a very professional partner.

"I'll keep my share and maybe return as an active partner."

"Fine, I'll be glad to see you work here. Also… I believe you and Reza are good friends, too, right?" he asked with hesitation.

"Yes, we are very good friends, in fact."

"That's great. I've tried to raise his interest to work with SDI like before, but he's been rather aloof after Erica's departure."

"Oh, don't take it to heart. He's been very busy during the last year with so many catastrophes and family issues," I said.

"Would you tell him that I like to use his expertise and I can prove to be as good an associate as Erica had been for him?"

"Okay, I'll tell him. Is Erica's secretary still working for you?"

"Yes, why?"

"I'd like to ask her a few private questions, if possible."

"Yes, of course. You can use Erica's office to do it. I'll ask my secretary to get her come and see you."

"You've kept Erica's office still empty?"

"Yes. Except for odd occasions when a colleague uses it, I haven't assigned it to anybody. If you decide to become an active partner, you might like to use her office."

"Okay, I'll go there and wait for her secretary," I said and left.

I sat behind Erica's big desk with an eerie feeling. I had taken over her house and business, and now I could have her impressive office and maybe even her secretary as well. Surely, driving her spectacular BMW had also been fun these days! How could her ghost not go nuts watching me enjoy everything she had worked for so hard for ages to indulge herself? What a crazy universe!

Erica's pretty secretary arrived with a cup of coffee for me and expressed her condolences.

"Thanks... I just like to ask you a few questions about Erica's last days before the accident," I said.

"Sure," she replied with an alluring grin, *maybe even dreaming to be my secretary soon!*

"In particular, I'd like to know about the day a man called Jeff came to get a newspaper clipping and other documents from you, the ones that Erica had asked to pass on to him. Do you recall?"

"Yes... It was the article about your paintings," she replied.

"So what happened?"

"Just as you said. He came by and I gave him the clipping I had photocopied and a small envelope, as Erica had asked me."

"Do you remember when it was?"

"About five weeks before her accident."

"Are you sure?" I asked.

"Yes, absolutely. I can find the exact day if it's important."

"I'll let you know if I need that. Thanks for the information."

After she left, I lingered another fifteen minutes and basked in the possibility of coming to Erica's old office and bossing a few people around the way she did. Especially, harassing my arrogant supervisor when I had worked at SDI as a technician felt like fun.

Mahtab, T.J., and I tried to build a relaxing environment and daily routines for us, while we dined out almost every night. We still commuted cautiously, though. The likelihood that anybody could guess our present residence was small, but we tried to stay vigilant about the chance of someone seeing us by accident, in a café or restaurant maybe, and following us. I did not mention the spooky pleasure of living in Erica's old house to Elizabeth, either, when we met briefly a few days after our move. We met again in the same Granville Island pub for colleting the evidences about Erica's role in hiring the thugs.

The date on the copy of the check Erica had given to Jeff matched the date Erica's secretary had mentioned to me about Jeff's visit to collect it. Erica had been the mastermind behind the plot and manipulated Jeff as another weak man like me and Reza. Elizabeth was happy after hearing me forgive Jeff, so much so she kissed me firmly on the lips like old times as we left the café. *Being merciful tasted so good!* I wished Detective Stewart and Jeff could have seen that big kiss filled with a nostalgic reminder of another confusing, interrupted romance!

"Have a great life with Jeff. I hope you two can make each other happy," I said with passion after we stopped sinning.

"I hope you also find the right person to love," Elizabeth said.

"You mean it? Do you think anybody would ever love me?" I asked teasingly.

"Perhaps not as much as Erica and I did."

"And now see what happened to all those wasted loves."

"But don't give up," Elizabeth said with a mix of pity and wit.

"I won't," I replied, quite certain that I had already found the love of my life—the one waiting for me this minute at home and possibly fretting over my tenacity to humour Elizabeth's repeated requests to meet me. *Was I driving poor Mahtab nuts already? What if she'd seen me kissing Elizabeth with my binocular?*

The next day, I called Detective Stewart to say I agreed with him about the low chance of proving Jeff's guilt beyond his naïve intention to intimidate me a little. I also confessed to him that my investigation showed that Erica had been in cahoots with Jeff and fallen off the balcony most likely by accident or when eluding the thugs, if not jumping out of desperation. I did not speculate on a few possible causes of her desperation and jumping—perhaps for her plot backfiring or out of guilt for causing my seeming death. On the other hand, I was dying to fool around with him a little by insisting on the *high possibility* of Erica committing suicide *only* out of love for me. I wanted to sound so full of myself just to drive him nuts. The gag felt too hilarious to bypass! Yet, in the end, I managed my juvenile urge, while *still* promising myself to use this trick on him another time perhaps. Deep down, still I gave only five percent chance that Erica had killed herself for me, although my fat ego and romantic heart abhorred my cynicism—*I mean, the low chance of her suicide merely out of love for me! Was Erica my Floria?* On a positive note, though, these idiotic thoughts kept rekindling Erica's memories with both joy and pity.

Accordingly, the urgency to speak with Erica's soul and settle a bunch of outstanding issues between us, especially the matter of enjoying her assets and status against her wish, had grown daily since we had moved into her house. At last, it seemed imperative to talk to her in private—*only after a long debate with my devil self about honouring Elizabeth's outstanding request to go there together and the opportunity of teasing Erica's spirit with our goofing around her grave.* I told Mahtab I was going out alone for a few hours. She gazed at me with surprise.

"I've been planning to go talk to Erica for sometime," I said to put her mind at ease. She nodded with confusion, but held her pride to ask me any question in spite of her curiosity boiling over. *Yeah, I was really driving her crazy already.*

At the nearby florist, I bought a bouquet of red roses I knew Erica loved. So often, when we had lived together, I had brought her red roses for special occasions or expressing my eternal love to her. The florist seemed to have a vague memory of me going there regularly a few years earlier. Like in the past, I asked the woman for one of their cute little cards that read, 'I will always love you, my darling.' She peeped at me with a subtle admiration for my mushy sentimentality and maybe just remembered me for using the same phrase so many times before.

I laid the roses next to Erica's gravestone and read the gloomy inscription on it. Her lawyer had told me about her resting place and the fact that they had managed her funeral with the help of her secretary at SDI. They had done a great job to find that cosy corner in the cemetery for her and choosing a fancy tombstone deserving such a brash, creative person. Standing in reverence, plenty of her positive attributes amused my mind for ten minutes. Then, I sat on the cute platform next to her grim grave, imagined her tiny, sexy body down there, and started talking to her.

"I've come late to see you, but you've been in my thoughts and prayers everyday. No, I'm not joking, not even about praying sometimes. Nothing to worry about, but just an air of divinity has bemused me after my coma. I haven't yet grasped it, though, the same way I never figure you out. They say this spiritual notion happens to many people who've had a near death experience. Anyway, I've come to tell you that I will always love you and remember you in a divine manner. But I also like to get some old grievances off my chest about how you treated me, while insisting that you loved me as much as I loved you.

"All along, you kept me in limbo as your lover or husband. Even today, I don't know what to think of you, although I've whined a lot about your knack for insulting and hurting people, especially me. Then again, I've always felt that, deep down, you are not a bad person, and in fact, you have often shocked me with your soulful sentiments and qualities. Often, I even believed you loved me, but then left me callously to love someone else. You asked for a divorce, but stopped your lawyers to finalize it. You tried to reclaim me with alluring words of passion and eternal devotion, but then hired some hooligans to harm me. You fought with me for a painting, and then when I finally gave it to you, you died and left it for me again along with all your other assets. You snubbed me when I worked for your firm, but then made me a director and owner of that company inadvertently. So often, you prayed to God to kill me when we argued, but then jumped from the balcony when you thought I was dead or dying. You died for whatever mysterious reason, but then only your fall saved my life, although you would keep me in suspense forever about the chance of jumping off the balcony only out of love for me, guilt, or loneliness! I've mourned you everywhere since coming out of the coma: in my building, looking at your dying spot; in your house, looking at your portrait on the wall; and here now, looking at your beautiful tombstone, but then I must stop soon, because now I really love someone else!"

A bee came fast and furious and kept circling near my ears or sniffing the roses tentatively, like the way Erica played with my sentiments so often. It rushed at me a few rounds before returning to the roses, paused at several blossoms one at a time, as though undecided which one to suck. I waved it away, but it kept rotating its routine to sniff the roses before hurrying back to bug me. Erica had always loved flowers and enjoyed going to parks, especially Queen Elizabeth Park, but she feared and hated bees.

"Oh, my darling, have you sent this bee to bug me now that I've come here to cherish your soul? Aren't you happy that I've come to visit you? Even now, you confuse me, the same way you did so cleverly all those years you lived mysteriously. I never knew what to do with you. Can you send me a signal about your wishes? Are you sad about my chance to enjoy the wealth you worked so hard to accumulate? Are you angry about my delight with a woman who loves me as much as you said you did?"

Staring at the bee's sudden boisterous love affair with roses one by one and sucking their nectars so selfishly sank me into a deep trance—still musing over Erica, emptying my heart to her, and hoping to get a sign about her peace with me in spite of the inadvertent reverse of luck in our lives. The bee settled awhile on a particular blossom with an unprecedented curiosity and care, as if keeping me amused or bemused—indeed quite successfully—before vanishing swiftly. Then I felt its fast impact and sting pain, slapped the spot, and stared at my palm with the shattered flesh of the devil bee right in its middle.

I laughed lightheartedly when I wondered if Erica had been reincarnated as the bee I had just killed. If so, killing her twice already was very cruel of me! Maybe God had turned her into a bee, since she hated bees so much. *I hoped it had liked the roses and their nectars at least before dying again!* She was stung by them a few times when she had gotten close to flowers in our or other gardens we had visited together those good old times. Our conversation once after a bee had stung her rolled in my head.

"These bees are really selfish," she said, while scratching her beautiful hand that was swollen, red, and itching like hell.

"See who's talking?" I said with a chuckle.

"Are you insinuating that I am selfish?" she asked irately.

"No… I'm just saying it…"

"You see how you never let us have a civil conversation?"

"I'm sorry… I was only fooling around…"

"You never seem serious about my points," she said. "You always kid around like a child."

"I'm sorry... Why do you think these bees are selfish?"

"Well, they come to my house, suck my flowers' nectar, then sting me for even walking near the flowers they apparently feel they own," she said with her own peculiar sense of humour to make me happy, but maybe also to nag about my inadequate care all along about her sting itch and pain.

"They're stupid too," I added. "Let me see your hand again."

"Why are they stupid?" she asked as I kissed the bee sting.

"Because they usually die if they sting humans or big animals."

"Assholes… I hate them invading our garden all summer and ruining my fun around my flowers."

"In fact, Erica, they seem to have a special interest in you and your flowers. They seem to love our garden more than I see them buzzing in the whole neighbourhood or around me."

"It looks that way, doesn't it?" she admitted with angst. "The more I hate them, the more they come around to bug me."

"So maybe they're smart and spiteful like you, not even caring about dying as long as they hurt you first," I said giddily.

"You enjoy watching them bug me, ha? Don't you think you do it enough yourself already?" she asked.

"Is the bee sting gone now that I kissed it?" I asked wittily.

Erica burst into laughter. "No, not even your kisses are useful these days. In fact, it's made it worse. What'd you do?"

After an hour of reminiscing and chatting, I kissed her tomb, promised to return soon for more chat—maybe with Elizabeth next time—, and turned to leave. But a crucial question hit me swiftly and I looked back at her grave again, "By the way, honey, what do you want me to do with your portrait on the wall?"

The bee sting jolted me, as if hinting her spirit's rage today—hearing my patronizing words for an hour and then being insulted about her portrait's future, too! For a person hating bees so much just for sucking her flowers, watching me enjoy daily everything she once had owned and enjoyed must be feeling like hell!

I stopped at the florist and bought another bouquet of red roses for Mahtab with the 'I will always love you…' card attached.

She stared at me with surprise this time and asked, "Did you lose the other one you bought two hours ago?"

"No, this one is for someone else," I replied with a giggle.

"It's good to have so many people to express eternal love to in just an hour," she said with sarcasm or confusion, I could not say.

"It is, isn't it…?" I said and turned. "I am one lucky man!"

Chapter Twenty-seven
A Formidable Alliance

"I'll do whatever you think is right for us to do, Reza," my mom said with anxiety and resignation after two days of thinking. This was the first time she had spoken to me so submissively, so I was shocked and perturbed witnessing such a domineering and outspoken woman pushed into this position in her final years. The idea of moving to Vancouver and living with Mahtab was putting a lot more pressure on my mom's poor health after all the horrific episodes during the last year. She had looked pensive and gloomy in recent days, apparently wrestling with many dilemmas clouding her brain at her age. I bet going so far away from her daughter's and husband's tombs was a big pain in itself for her.

"Thanks, maman… It is better for you to go away, instead of being in the middle of all the chaos that will start in a few days."

"Have you told Bijan about Mahtab's decision yet?"

"No, and I don't think I can ever tell him that Mahtab is not coming back at all. Please make sure nobody suspects anything about your travel to Vancouver, not even Nazi. I'll get the papers for you and Nazi and reserve your flight for ten days from now."

"Ten days? That fast?"

"Yes, the sooner you leave the better. You need more time?"

"At least two weeks," she said.

"Okay," I replied with nostalgia about their looming absence.

"It'll be hard for me to live in a different city at my age, Reza. But I'll do whatever you say. I'm doing this only for Nazi and Mahtab; otherwise I don't care about Bijan's revenge and the war you're talking about."

"Thanks maman. That's the right decision. Nazi needs a mom and Mahtab is the best person for this job."

"What's gonna happen to the house?" my mom asked.

"Don't worry about these stuff. You just get ready to go."

"You'd better send Mahroo's portrait to Vancouver, then. I guess Mahtab wants it there," she said with gloom.

"Of course... I'll get it wrapped and shipped. If you want a few other small items, like picture albums, put them all aside and we send them all together."

The following two weeks, I spent most of my time with my mom and Nazi and helped them with packing and all the other details, but mostly suffered the idea of not seeing them for a long time or ever. I also kept studying and refining my plan to contact Sima's family and begin my crusade against Bijan, whom I humoured every day with bigger lies and promises about Mahtab's return. Raising even a slight suspicion was imprudent until my mom and Nazi left Tehran. Finally, I took them to the airport and watched them go away with tears gathering in our eyes. Then, I breathed a sigh of relief and got ready for my attack the next day.

With a pocket full of large bills, I went to find Sima in the same building Darren had lived when working in Tehran. I checked the residents' directory at the front of the building and luckily found my target. Apartment 808 was listed under the name Arshadi—most likely the parents of Sima and Colonel Arshadi that Bijan had mentioned to me. I paraded the large brown envelop in my hand keenly like an important document, while the guard at the entrance watched my snooping around the directory suspiciously before coming towards me at last.

"Can I help you with something?" he asked curtly.

"I must deliver this document to the right person."

"Who're you looking for?" he asked.

"Is this Mr. Arshadi the father of Colonel Arshadi and Sima?"

"It is Mrs. Arshadi, yes."

"Is she Colonel Arshadi's and Sima's mother?"

"Yes, I believe so, but Colonel Arshadi doesn't live here."

"Okay, that's good, thanks. They're the right people, then."

"Buzz the intercom and talk to them."

I gestured with hesitation to buzz the intercom before turning to the guard.

"Can I instead trouble you to pass this document to Sima Khanoom privately?" I said with a grin, while taking out a few large bills out of my pocket. I put them on the top of the big brown envelop I had been showing off all along and extended my arm towards him. As he still seemed hesitant, I took a few more large bills from my pocket and offered the upgraded pile to him again. At last, he took the whole pile, but kept staring at me, as if memorizing my face, then nodded.

"Please give it to Sima Khanoom only, just in case she must prepare her mother for the news first," I said very carefully.

The guard nodded while gauging the brown envelope. I took out my pen and wrote 'Ms. Sima Arshadi' on the envelope while he held it. I thanked him again and left.

My letter introduced me as Darren's friend eager to discuss some important matters with her. Along with my phone number, I had emphasized to keep my request private.

Sima called me the same evening with a timid excitement about my possible good news. She had probably imagined I had a message from Darren for a reunion and perhaps even marriage. Poor girl! I did not wish to disappoint her on the phone, either, while eager to draw her sympathy to help me. Anyhow, it felt we both were keen to explore the potentials of exploiting each other for our personal needs or dreams.

So, we met the next day at the entrance of the park near her building. As I had hoped, she arrived with a child in the stroller. Accordingly, I had brought my camera just in case my hunch materialized. I said hello to her before leaning to look at the baby.

"It's a beautiful baby," I said.

"Thanks," she replied.

"I'm Reza Azimi, Darren's friend," I said and she nodded. She looked quite smart by the way she was gauging me warily with no interest to assume I knew about the baby and other stuff. My job to divulge my knowledge of their secret tactfully without triggering any negative reaction by the family felt direr than I had imagined. Timing was crucial and I had to be careful with regard to my ultimate goal. I hoped she would say something revealing about the baby, perhaps as an attempt to test me.

"Darren worked for my company for three years and we've been good friends for even longer," I continued.

"That's good...," she replied softly.

"He asked me to say hi to you."

"Hi...! How is he?"

"He's fine now after a health issue," I said without getting into details, and luckily, she did not dwell on the matter, either.

"Is he coming back to Tehran again?"

"I don't know exactly, but I don't think so," I said.

She only nodded and peered at me with disappointment, but also more curiosity and suspicion about my reason for seeing her.

"Still, I'm sure he'll be thrilled to know how you're doing these days, especially with your baby and all," I said slyly.

"So, what has he told you about us?" Sima asked.

"He said you were close friends when he lived in Tehran."

"What else has he told you?"

"That you're a nice person and hopes you're always happy."

"Tell him nobody's *always* happy. But I'm happy enough."

"I'm sure he'll also be happy when I tell him that," I said.

"Has he told you anything else about *us*?" she asked slyly in my opinion, while I was eager to know whom she was referring to by *us*, Darren or the baby? I let the matter go for now!

"Actually, he told me about a particular secret only recently, although he often shares his thoughts with me."

"What secret?" she asked with a subtle sarcasm and giggle, yet looking keen to give me some hints.

"He was forbidden to discuss this big secret that had also been the reason for being jailed when he came to Tehran six or seven months ago."

"He was...? I didn't even know he'd come back or jailed."

"Yes, he came and went to jail directly for doing so," I said.

"Just for coming to Tehran?"

"Yes."

"Why?"

"Because your family didn't want your secret to come out."

"But now Darren knows the secret?"

"Yes, he does... He found out after he was released from jail."

"And you know everything, too?"

"Yes, he recently told me," I replied.

"Did my family really put him in prison to keep the secret?"

"Yes, and then forced him to promise to never come back to Tehran, contact you, or reveal the secret to anybody," I replied.

"But he still told you?" Sima asked.

"He told me just recently after he felt forced to talk about it."

"He was forced to tell people?"

"Yes... That's my main concern, too."

"Who's forcing Darren to do that?" she asked with a phony grimace, yet looked amused about the secret coming out.

"That's a long story I will share with you when we trust each other and agree to help him and stop the rumours, too," I said.

"Had he come back to Tehran to see me?"

"I honestly don't know. I found out about the reason for his imprisonment only recently and I didn't know he'd been forced to leave Tehran and never return."

"I didn't know any of these, either," Sima said with distress.

"It's good that you know the truth at least now, and about his long torture in the prison," I said solemnly.

"I miss him often and I wish to see him again someday."

"Maybe you guys meet someday, anyway, who knows!"

"So you really know his secret?" she asked with a chuckle.

"I do, and I hope we're talking about the same secret," I said with a peek at the baby in the carriage.

"It seems that we are," she said giddily as if relieved, but still showing a mix of reserved suspicion and curiosity.

"I have not and will not reveal it to anybody else," I said. "In fact, my intention for meeting you has been to stop the possibility of this secret spreading any more. I hope you can help me stop some people from talking too much."

"So you definitely know everything?" she asked again.

"I guess I do."

"Tell me what you know."

"That beautiful baby is yours…"

"And…"

"And Darren's," I said cautiously.

She stared at me hesitantly. Her facial impression was hard to read, despite the seeming joy from the idea of my and Darren's knowledge of the baby.

"Is he happy that he has a fatherless son?" she asked at last.

"All I know is that he misses him like any father. His inability to talk about him or see him, not to mention his imprisonment for this matter, has tortured him a lot."

"So he likes to see his son? Is that why you've come to see me?" she asked.

"Not exactly… My main intention is to stop the possibility of a bad situation for your family if the secret comes out."

"So now you guys are worried about the secret coming out more than my family has been all along?" she asked with angst and surprise.

"Yes, sort of."

"Is he ashamed of having a Persian son?"

"No, just the opposite. He doesn't want anybody jeopardize his son's welfare even if it has to be at his expense."

"Wow..., I didn't realize he was such a devoted dad!" she said with amusement and sarcasm.

"Yes, he misses him… What's his name?"

"Darius."

"He believes that if your family thinks keeping the secret is best for Darius, he'd respect and support your plan. He doesn't want some people take advantage of the situation and sabotage everything your family has been doing all along."

"Who wants to do that?" Sima asked with agitation.

"As I said, it is a long story I'd like to explain to your family, especially your uncle," I said. "Is it possible to meet with him?"

"I must ask my mother but I'm getting confused," she replied.

"I understand, but it is best for me to talk to your uncle who is a minister in the government, I gather. What's his name?" I asked.

"Rafatti," she said, confirming the name Bijan had mentioned.

"Could you tell Mr. Rafatti that I'd like to see him in a rather private manner? It is very important."

"I'll ask my mother."

"But please don't let anybody else, especially your brother, Colonel Arshadi, know about me at this point."

"I should ask my mother if that's okay as well," Sima said, while I felt pleasantly surprised about a young woman asking for her mom's permission so much—so unlike my dogged sisters and Erica, especially. Then again, perhaps Sima's polite attitude these days was merely an offshoot of her new wisdom after not asking for her mom's permission years ago about sleeping with Darren and making Darius!

"Of course... Also ask both your mom and uncle to keep even our meeting secret for a short while, until I explain everything."

"All right…," she said.

"Please do everything you can to arrange this meeting for me with your uncle. This is important mostly for Darius."

Sima nodded and I continued, "May I take a few pictures of Darius and send them to Darren? It'll make him very happy."

Sima hesitated ten seconds before finally nodding. "But don't mention it to my family in case you see them."

"Okay... They'll object, you think?" I asked.

"I'm sure they will. Tell Darren to keep them secret, too."

"Okay, I will, and thanks for letting me make him happy," I said and then took half dozen pictures of Darius. He was a very cute and alert boy. He stared at me and into the lens with great enthusiasm. I asked Sima, and she agreed eagerly, to hold him in her arms for a few pictures of them together.

"I'm taking a big risk letting you take these pictures," Sima stressed. "Tell Darren to be very careful with them."

After Sima left, I felt a bit jittery about the risks of revealing Bijan's recent recklessness regarding Sima's family secrets. He was doing it to punish Darren and restore his own family honour. And now I was ratting on Bijan for saving my family. I walked a long time around the park pensively, amused about the way we were all ruining other families' lives and honours for the sake of our families and personal pride. At last, it felt honourable to give Bijan one last chance to stop his threats before I continued my plan with full force. I called and learned he was on his way home. So I drove to his house and waited half an hour before he arrived in a sadder state than the last time I had seen him. He was startled seeing me and got anxious, possibly taking my unexpected visit a clue about more bad news again.

"Can we go to your study?" I asked carefully.

He nodded and started walking ahead of me.

"What's up now?" he asked after we plummeted onto the sofa and stared at each other tensely. "I hope you have good news."

"Mahtab has decided to stay a bit longer in Vancouver. I'm sorry, Bijan," I said edgily. "She isn't in a condition to travel yet."

"Is she really sick?" he asked.

"I think so, but don't know exactly what's wrong with her."

"She's sick mentally… That's all, I'm sure."

"Leaving with you in Iran certainly hasn't been easy for her, anyway," I replied with satisfaction.

Bijan did not peep, but rage contorted his facial muscles and he blushed while playing with his unduly long beard, like trying to calm his nerves. He had occasionally grown some tidy beard in the past, as if wondering how it might help his looks and career in a beard-loving Islamic regime, while realizing Mahtab's aversion for a bearded husband. Now, especially since my last visit, three weeks earlier, it seemed to have grown too disorderly so fast. His messy appearance alone was obviously a sign of his rising stress and apathy towards life, work, and people.

"So that is her decision, ha?" he asked at last. "And she has not given you any real reason for it or a clue about when she'll return, ha?"

"No… But maybe it's better to forget about her altogether if you are not willing to let her be and decide freely about the time she feels ready to return," I repeated the phrase I had prepared and rehearsed giddily for days for an opportunity to warn him about the low likelihood of ever getting Mahtab back in his life. I wished I had the guts to add, *Time has come at last, Bijan, to commit suicide like any honourable heartbroken lover and get this masquerade over with.*

He trembled and stared at me with disgust, anger, and despair, as if I had confirmed his own sense of finality and any hope for Mahtab's return to Iran, let alone into his life. Maybe he even read my mind about the *honourable thing* for him to do now!

"I can't ignore the disgrace she's caused me and my family on top of my pains after all my love and devotion. My parents had warned me about her and her kind of unreligious mentality, but I defended her. Now see what she's done and how she's disgraced all of us. First, she kills my son by purpose or her depression and now this mess. I'm avoiding even my parents to minimize the embarrassment I've brought to them and the whole family."

"You're still too young to let these simple setbacks ruin your future. Find a more suitable wife for yourself, maybe a religious one this time to make your family proud, too."

"Unfortunately, I can't put her out of my mind and I can't let Darren get away with his betrayal of my services and honour."

"Be a man, Bijan...! It is time to do the right thing, mostly for your own sake," I said firmly, as I could no longer hold back the sentiment I had been nurturing and rehearsing to dump on him on an appropriate occasion as his best option.

"I'll give'em a lesson they'll never forget even if they survived the punishment and pain I'll cause for them. Mark my words."

"Just let it go, Bijan… Please be more forgiving, at least for saving your own soul. Revenge is not going to change anything for you, but could make the situation get really out of hand."

"I don't care about anything anymore as I'd told you before."

"Just divorce her and get on with your life… Forget her… She'll never be capable of making you happy, so get rid of her," I said as calmly and compassionately as I could manage.

"No, I won't do it. They can't get away that easy."

"I think I've done everything in my power, Bijan, to keep things under control, but if you want to be vengeful and irrational, then I must wash my hand and only think about myself and my family from now on," I said.

"Do as you wish," Bijan shouted.

"Okay," I yelled back and left.

How vastly humans' brains and characters differed in terms of seeing the facts of life and reacting to them amused me as I drove towards my office. We do not even learn good lessons from the exact situations and cases around us. I was particularly pondering how Bijan had not learned a lesson from Zia's wise decision only a few months earlier to end his misery when his heart was broken by Mahroo's apathy. How Zia had seen this simple fact and made the right decision quickly was admirable when this idiot Bijan still could not see and admit the reality of his defeat and make the same smart decision Zia had! Instead of doing the right thing for all, especially himself, he was getting more adamant to hurt all of us, especially himself again. Two brother-in-laws thinking and reacting so differently was just amazing, especially since their wives looked so alike and had very similar personalities! Most amazing about human brain was the way mine worked!

Days went by torturously slowly as I waited anxiously for Sima's call, while imagining Bijan activating his plot for revenge already. I regretted visiting and agitating him further before discussing my plan with Rafatti and securing his allegiance for a counterattack against Bijan. I cursed my conscience for making me give Bijan a last chance to smarten up. All I could do now was to feel lonely and homesick without my mom and Nazi, yet I felt proud when they called from Vancouver. I also gave Darren a heads-up about my recent fight with Bijan and the chance of his quick retaliation. I told him about my meeting with Sima and his son as well.

"His name is Darius and he's a handsome and friendly guy," I said without saying anything about taking Darius's picture.

"Thanks a million, Reza, for everything you're doing."

"You're welcome. Just make sure you protect my family there instead and keep my meeting with Sima confidential."

"Just rest assured! T.J. is doing a great job protecting all of us and he's now even asking for a gun, too, to do his bodyguarding as professionally as possible," he said for teasing me, we laughed, and signed off giddily about the prospect of learning more about Darius in coming days and months through Sima as well.

After a week, Sima called at last and said that her mom and uncle Rafatti have agreed to see me the following evening. With a box of fine pastry, I arrived at Sima's residence and met her family. Exchanging pleasantries with strangers who gauged me with suspicion and curiosity felt awkward. So I started rather abruptly.

"Thank you for agreeing to listen to my concerns," I said.

As they nodded, I addressed Mr. Rafatti. "I believe you know Bijan Taymori."

"Yes, I know him very well," Rafatti replied.

"He is my brother-in-law."

"Oh… That's good. I'd been wondering who you were."

"I've also learned about Darius's background recently since Bijan seems not quite concerned anymore about the matter your family had insisted on keeping confidential."

"Why? What is going on Mr. Azimi?"

"My sister has decided to ask for a divorce, so Bijan is angry with me and my family and friends, including Darren."

"Why Darren...? Has he seduced your sister as well," Rafatti blurted with such bluntness I almost fainted and fell off the chair. His vulgar tone and attitude also shocked Sima and her mother.

I had imagined the high likelihood of Sima and her family connecting Mahtab's request for a divorce with Darren as soon as I mentioned the facts. Yet, doing so had appeared necessary for pursuing my plan and possibly putting a leash on Bijan. I knew I was walking on thin ice, but was not expecting such a coarse comment by Mr. Rafatti so fast.

"I don't think so, but Bijan has gotten the same impression, because she has gone to live in my suite in Vancouver, which also happens to be the city Darren is living now."

"So you also live in Vancouver," Sima asked, while her mom and uncle stared at me curiously.

"Yes, I live in both Tehran and Vancouver."

"I'm still sort of lost, although your story is getting weirder and more upsetting every minute," Mr. Rafatti said with a smirk, while Sima seemed immersed in her deep thoughts after a shock. The idea of Mahtab in Vancouver had most likely ruined Sima's rising hopes in the last few days about seeing Darren soon and possibly marrying him.

"The point is that the war between Bijan and Darren could also affect others for no good outcome," I said dramatically.

"I know what you mean but explain anyway," Rafatti replied.

"Well… While Bijan is threatening Darren with some form of retribution, Darren is making his own counter-threats in hopes of stopping him. He's telling Bijan that he might break his promise to him about keeping the secret about Darius and maybe even make plans to establish his rights to see his son at least."

"In that case, a war might also start between certain families in this country, plus new troubles for Darren," Rafatti said.

"I've heard about that possibility from both Bijan and Darren as well. But Darren and I are doing our best to prevent this."

"But it's still Darren's fault if our secret comes out," Rafatti said with anger.

"Not really," I replied. "Bijan had started divulging the secret much sooner to me at least in order to explain the source and level of danger Darren was in. He was hoping we could pressure Darren and force Mahtab to return to Tehran."

"What danger? I still don't understand!" Rafatti said.

"Oh… Apparently, Bijan had heard about Colonel Arshadi's intention from the beginning to punish Darren regardless of your family's calm approach. So, Bijan has found and given Darren's address in Vancouver to the colonel. He's also told me to warn Darren about Bijan and Colonel Arshadi joining forces to punish him. He's kept telling me that he's been the only one all along stopping the colonel who is very serious and powerful," I added.

"Are you telling me that my son is collaborating with Bijan?" Mrs. Arshadi exclaimed.

"Yes… That is one problem, of course. But the main issue is that Bijan now says he no longer cares if Darren or others reveal the secret to the whole world if that is the only way to achieve his goal of bringing Mahtab back to Tehran," I stressed slyly without shame, hoping to stir everybody's emotions.

"So both Bijan and Darren are gone crazy. I'll deal with both of them," Rafatti said.

"But there's a big difference in terms of their motives," I said.

"What's the difference?"

"Well, Bijan has revealed the secret to many of us already and doesn't seem to care if it spreads fast everywhere. But Darren hasn't done anything yet. He's only saying that if the information is out there, he might as well use it only out of desperation and fear of Bijan. He's saying all these things in hopes of stopping Bijan's intimidations."

"It's a silly situation, Mr. Azimi," Rafatti said, while Sima and her mother stared at me in bewilderment.

"So you realize that I'm caught in the middle of this skirmish and hoping to bring some kind of sense to these people," I said.

"Yes, the outcome will be much graver than Bijan and Darren could imagine," Rafatti said in fury, then stood up and began walking around the room with distress. Sima and her mom also looked angry and helpless, while tears filled Sima's eyes. She left and returned fast with Darius, as if worrying about him or merely letting even the baby hear firsthand the irritating complications his short existence has created already!

"I'll kill Bijan if he wants to be a son-of-a-bitch," Rafatti yelled with conviction, while peering at Darius in Sima's lap. I felt he was trying to assure his sister and niece about his resolve to disallow any complication and dishonour inflict the family.

"I just wanted to let you know what's going on and possibly stop this war that might get out of hand," I said with pride for my role as a Samaritan, but also the seeming success of my plan. Rafatti was nicely agitated well beyond my initial hopes.

"Thanks for letting me know. I'll certainly do something about this matter," Rafatti said, while nodding repeatedly with distress as a gesture of his seriousness.

"Of course, another reason I wanted to see you was to let you know about your nephew's role behind Bijan's threats."

"I must talk with him, too. He's sometimes quite stubborn and he's apparently still angry."

"That's why Darren feels cornered and has asked me to help him. But he's also worried about Darius's welfare and only trying to prevent troubles in any manner he can."

"So, now Bijan simply doesn't care about his actions harming us more than it hurts Darren, ha?"

"Apparently not…," I said proudly.

"I'll have a chat with his father."

"Bijan in fact told me plainly that he cares about nothing at this stage, not even his father's rage about his actions."

"We'll see about that. It seems he's simply gone cuckoo for a woman. He hadn't appeared such a wuss to me, ruining his and other people's lives just for a woman," Rafatti said with a smirk.

"I've told Bijan the same things. I've tried hard to calm and convince him to divorce Mahtab now that he doesn't trust her, but I can't do it alone apparently. He's simply lost it these days. His messy beard alone shows his degree of distress and insanity," I said like an angry devil on his darnedest mission with no limit for humiliating Bijan.

"All these information about Bijan sound really odd to me. He'd appeared quite strong and committed to his father and his own official responsibilities."

"I'm surprised too, but I guess love can always break down even the strongest men."

"What a pity! What a bunch of weak men we've turned into."

"I agree hundred percent," I said diplomatically. I had never badmouthed anyone so tenaciously and giddily in my life, while witnessing and enjoying its success firsthand as well!

"Anyway, I'll look into this."

"I'll stop Darren from talking about Darius to anybody else as long as I can. I'll keep the secret myself, too. But please stop both your nephew and Bijan from harassing my family and Darren,"

"Okay, Mr. Azimi. Thanks for coming to us..."

"I'm glad I did and thank you."

"You seem to have a big battle of your own with Bijan if your sister wants to leave him, especially if she has a relationship with that jerk, Darren," Rafatti said.

"Yes, I do. I feel trapped, but must protect my sister and other family members."

"That's an honourable fight you've taken on and must win. You look like a good man. I'm just surprised you're still friends with that infidel. This Darren acts like the biggest fiend on earth I've ever seen," he said, while peering at Sima with disgrace.

"I know he has some weaknesses, too, like most men," I said in a sombre tone to calm him.

"If he was here in Iran, I would've certainly had him hanged this time as a fiend on earth."

"He has some good qualities, too," I said with a teasing tone.

"I hope so, just in case Darius has some of his genes."

"Are you married yourself?" Mrs. Arshadi asked with a grin, as if looking for a husband for her disgraced daughter.

"No, I haven't found the right person, either," I replied, trying to read her thoughts at that moment as well as Sima's. I peeked at Sima stealthily, who looked quite attractive and smart based on my limited conversations with her.

"Some nice girls are always around from good families that you can choose," she said pleasantly.

"That's exactly what my mother keeps saying, too," I replied with a chuckle.

"Because she loves you, I'm sure... You might not need to go too far to find the right wife for yourself," she said while peeping at Sima with a grin and praising her furtively.

"Thanks for your advice. I'll keep my eyes open," I said with a grin, imagining Sima as my wife. I'd already seduced Darren's wife, so I might as well marry his mistress and raise his child as my own, I mused giddily as I stood up to leave.

"Is there anything you want me to do?" I asked Mr. Rafatti.

"No, just leave everything to me. I'll contact you when and if necessary. Are you going to be in Tehran for now or going back to Vancouver?"

"I'll be around for now," I replied. "Thanks again for all your help. I knew you were the only person who could do something before it was too late."

"If you have to see me, let Sima know and we'll meet again."

Chapter Twenty-eight
Confessions of a Testy Writer

Three joyous months now since Mahtab, Darren, and I had fled to his luxurious house. Mahtab's mom and Nazi had also joined us two weeks later upon arrival from Iran. We all had our private rooms and still one bedroom was empty. I offered to go live somewhere else, but Darren insisted quite graciously that my presence was still useful while the potential threats to all of us were not over. He suggested that I move to his old suite when my safety there was no longer a concern—"Except that Mrs. Stanley will try to seduce you, T.J.," Darren stressed a few times giddily.

"And that's the mother of all dangers, ha!" I replied.

"The kind you can't avoid or remove, either," he said. "She'll be always around anytime you get out of your suite. And you don't have my willpower to resist her charm, I'm sure!"

Darren had been in a great mood all along, which still felt odd after years of witnessing his uptightness bizarrely mixed with an uncanny knack for horseplaying. Now, he did mostly the latter, like a man appreciating his magical rebirth and growing fortune amidst the joyous noise and hoopla, mostly due to Nazi's running around. Like Darren, her spirit had risen drastically as well for having Mahtab back in her life. For me, living with these kind people was a blessing and I thanked God for granting me such a timely, huge refuge now that He had taken away my own family from me unfairly so hastily. That was my sole consolation these days, because loneliness might have killed me already if Darren had not pushed me to stay there. I strived to repay his generosity in any way I could, mainly as the family chauffeur, while Darren still minimized driving alone. He was rather upset-minded, which also affected his driving reflexes—unless he pretended all that, so generously, merely for justifying my presence.

"Now what?!" resonated in my head more often, though, the more Darren insisted my role as a bodyguard and chauffeur was essential! This primitive existential question kept haunting me in spite of the fun hoopla around Darren's fast-growing, boisterous family, which ironically raised my sense of loneliness and need for a long-term solution. *Just see what has become of me! After a lifetime of drudgery and triumph, only for serving my family, I'm now reduced to such meagre being. And must be thankful for it, too. What an unfair world we're living in!* And, still, I considered myself one of the lucky ones on our doomed planet!

My writing projects were put on hold as well, as the hoopla hindered my focus to build great ideas and phrases. Instead, my theory about prolonged solitude being the main factor for serious contemplation and writing was now proven to me unequivocally.

We visited Darren's suite regularly to check on things and bring some more of his stuff stealthily. We often went to a coffee shop and waited awhile as an added step to ensure nobody was tailing us to our new residence. Darren looked in the rear mirror and behind us to warn me of any chaser, as I drove strategically through narrow, quiet city roads to avoid any likely danger. He had come up with this brilliant security routine, so I argued with him about its flaws and hassles only once to no avail. Of course, he at least admitted to his rising paranoia and uptightness along with a bigger urge for teasing people rather childishly!

For one thing, he goaded me to enrol on various dating sites. I was curious myself to explore the idea, at least as my hands-on research about relationships. It could be an amusing, educational hobby, if not a sensible idea for all healthy persons to rectify our loneliness and restore our dignities, I reckoned. What a ridiculous idea and approach, however!—trying to build our lives around other people's whims and emotions! We are too naïve about this matter and I had to affirm this sad truth the hard way after dating a few dozen women who had expressed interest in knowing and taming me. Within months, I lost my interest and hopes gradually about this pitiful adventure having any meaning or meaningful outcome, at least at my age. I had never met or spoken with so many nuts before my short period of catastrophic on-line dating experience. *What is really happening to us lonely humans?* was now a huge new dilemma I could not dismiss!

On the other hand, my deplorable attempts to connect with a woman my age or younger had turned into a laughing matter for Darren. I went on for hours whining about the way women tried to cajole and manipulate me with their naïve tactics for their evil ultimate agendas. Then, as they realized, like Feri, that their petty schemes would not tame me, they got angry and dumped me for no reason other than my honesty about my needs and views.

So many strangers showing immense enthusiasm to meet me felt odd and made us laugh. Yet, my dating masquerade had also turned into a serious project for Darren and me. When we had nothing useful to babble about, we analyzed each case or women overall—beyond our customary clowning. We reviewed their profiles together and wondered about people's nerve in the way they sounded so full of themselves with so many absurd demands from a person they were hoping to date and marry. How could all these haughty, needy people mix or even imagine the chance of building any kind of relationship remotely possible. Many of the pictures already showed what a mean person he or she was and some looked utterly ugly, yet demanded handsome and romantic partners with high qualities, most likely for financial support, too!

Many people from distant cities and countries wanted to chat with a plan to meet up soon. This showed so many things, but mainly their desperation for a suitable mate after failing to find one in their own big cities. Some long-distance interests—as far as Europe and Asia—sounded like mere adventure and a chance for touring a nice city if I offered the free accommodation. At least they were willing to pay for their own airfare! Some were trying to use me for emigration and some requests for meeting seemed like gimmicks by some crooks for swindling desperate old men, such as asking for airfare to come visit me. *What a big lot of petty people and morbid minds,* I wondered.

Despite its depressing and degrading nature, my pathetic dates had proven quite educational and amusing for Darren and me, as two online-dating critics hiding in the big house with plenty of time to waste and clown like two useless teenagers. He laughed like crazy and found more opportunities to fool around about my best and last option: to date Mrs. Stanley, after all!

"Well… That'd be the best way to get this whole shenanigan on dating sites over with at least…," Darren said giddily. "I'm exhausted myself watching you suffer on those sites, too."

We also discussed many topics about human behaviour and how we turn into juveniles quickly when our immediate worries about subsistence subside. We had become great examples and proved this theory so energetically during our house confinement along with lots of clowning. Thank God, humans must make a living a lifetime! *He knew what He was doing in this instance!*

Sometimes, Mahtab, and later her mom, felt obliged to jump in as well and offer their advice during my dating stories and my elaborate accounts of my hopeful admirers. Mahtab's mom kept telling me to go live in Tehran and take as many good wives as I desired. Alternatively, I could go find a young, pretty mate and bring her here to drive my family and friends nuts. Luckily, my pride rejected these pitiful options. My slim hope to establish a simple relationship with my spoiled daughters, eventually, was another hindrance, although I kept working diligently with my lawyers on my will, anyway—merely perfecting the details of my cunningly laborious inheritance plan. It was starting to look like a huge masterpiece! I reckoned if I could not finish any book soon, I could always publish my three-volume Will and Testament!

Luckily, this chapter about an old man's dating adventures also ended soon when I realized my incapacity and impatience to face what women expected these days. I admitted I would most likely remain a single author forever, while the idea of dating in itself was a wasteful ambition for cynical, old folks like me. The time and effort we invest merely for spending a few hours with a woman is not worth the hassle involved, in particular considering the amount of pretences and nonsense we should exchange to impress one another non-stop for no good purpose whatsoever. Women appeared absurdly stubborn, unnatural, demanding, and selfish. I imagined men were equally rotten and idealistic. Yet, I could not be a good judge of that myself due to my lack of enough data. Women can best judge men's mental decay in modern society. Surely, men's innate vanity has been historical and also proven perfectly by my old friends' behaviour. But it was hard for me to guess how spoiled and useless men have also become for dating purposes nowadays, in spite of their overall submissiveness appeasing most modern women. Anyway, Darren and I had proved, rather scientifically, that the prevalent dating format and practices were hopeless—until humans grow up a lot!

By the way, Feri had gotten suspicious about my whereabouts and disregarding her phone messages—usually more bad news —for a few days. She listed our house after forging my signature and I did not even object. As both the owner and the listing agent, she possibly swindled me, too. When it was sold, I just signed the papers and took less than half of the proceeds. She bought a suite to live with Leila and our older kids simply honoured their whims and left with no regard for Feri's pleas or my threats. They had shrugged off my supposedly scary ultimatum, which in return, boosted my resolve to become more creative with my estate plan. At the same time, my kids causing me so much extra work and thinking at the age I should sit back and relax was infuriating. Ironically, the only way to stay sane was to keep inventing new sinister ideas, calling Larry to concoct ways of putting them in my damn will, and waiting for Darren to buy me a gun!

Our hideout secrecy had also caused the hassle of indulging Mrs. Stanley longer every time we visited Darren's old place to check on things. She seemed to be wandering near the building more often every day in hopes of finding an unlucky soul to drag into some kind of chitchat. In particular, now we had to coax her longer and keener to prevent her suspicion regarding our absence. Sometimes, I wondered how Fluffy felt about always wandering outdoors, much more than the poor dog got a chance to sit in a warm corner and ponder its own gloomy existence in the hands of a forlorn old master getting more desperate daily. Bringing Fluffy along every time looked odd, especially if she assumed that tiny thing could protect her, too. That exhausted dog looked so fed-up, I imagined it would most likely just sit and watch if any intruder came to rob or kill its master. Then again, Fluffy was probably Mrs. Stanley's only excuse for being out there, rather than walking alone aimlessly, so many hours every day.

"Are you still worried about those hooligans?" Mrs. Stanley asked Darren once a few weeks after we had moved out.

"A little...," Darren replied. "Why do you ask?"

"'cause I don't see you around. Are you hiding in your suite?"

"Yeah, that's why… But I've also hired myself a bodyguard," Darren said, pointing to me. "You'd seen T.J. before, right?"

"Is he your bodyguard…?" she said, staring at me with great pity and scepticism.

"Yes... T.J. is staying with me until they catch those thugs."

"He doesn't look tough enough to me," she said, still gauging me curiously. She probably hated my guts to advertise and take on this bodyguarding job.

"Oh, yes, he's tough. He's a martial art expert. Tell her T.J."

I smiled. "Yes, I'm dangerous. Anybody coming close to him better be ready to meet his creator. I'm gonna get a gun, too."

"Is everything quiet around the building these days," Darren asked her. "I haven't seen them around here recently, have you?"

"Yes, I think I've seen them again once or twice," she replied pensively. "But this guy (pointing to me pitiably again) doesn't really seem to cut it… to handle those hooligans, I mean. Well, that's my honest opinion. This time I insist, since you'd ask me." She just did not want to let the matter go; now looking obsessed with Darren's choice of bodyguard and my ability to protect him. I was truly insulted, but kept my composure with lots of effort!

"No, you just show them to T.J. and he'll take care of them," Darren said giddily, equally persistent to continue this chatter at my expense. He was enjoying the new topic for teasing me now that my dating adventures had become less serious and amusing.

"You see...! You don't believe me again as usual... He looks too old for this job," she said so rudely I wanted to jump and kill her just to prove her wrong about my old age and frailty!

Instead, I blurted, "Just don't worry, Mrs. Stanley… You only show them to me or call the police next time you see them."

She peeped at me briefly, as if struggling to find any reason to change her verdict. Rather, she soon looked fully pissed off about my nerve trying to convince her, too, after fooling Darren already.

"Okay, we'd better move along," Darren said at last.

"So now you live in our building, too," she asked me softly, like showing some pity, after all, or just adding me to the list of building occupants she must monitor.

"Of course, I do."

Her swift curiosity amused Darren again, while she grilled me with silly questions and I strived to humour her for Darren's sake.

"He is single too," Darren said as we started going away.

"Then we must talk more soon," she yelled from a distance.

"Sure," I yelled back before whispering to Darren. "Why did you say I'm single? She'll now keep looking for us more often."

"You're right. It slipped my tongue," Darren said with worry.

"You'd better keep your mouth shut when we see her next time," I said like a real bodyguard, even after all that humiliation.

"You're lucky I didn't tell her which dating sites to look for your profile," Darren replied with a giggle.

After that day, Darren got sillier every day about the merits of marrying Mrs. Stanley. "Just to show Feri," he insisted.

"Your clowning gift just keeps flourishing with less worries."

"We're not safe yet… But do you think I've turned into a jerk these days just because I feel a bit safer and happier?"

"Not a jerk, just a bit juvenile," I replied.

"I'm only kidding about your dating misfortunes. But do you now understand my old complaints about the difficulty of dating any woman regularly and you teased my inability to commit?"

"Yes, I do. Forgive my past ignorance and claiming you were just a whining womanizer," I said.

"Okay, I forgive you… Your present dating torture has been good enough punishment for you," Darren replied.

"Thanks... Still, the situation is five times more pathetic and painful for my age group," I said.

"Why is that?"

"For one thing, watching women in their fifties and sixties talk and behave like teenagers drives you nuts. I thought only Feri was like that, but most women I've dated so far have been the same way. They're phony and act like we owe them the world. They wanna be spoiled and they wanna tame you somehow."

"My age group is the same way, don't worry!" Darren said.

"Maybe, but at least you may call it immaturity and tolerate it because of their youthful beauty. But how can you justify all that nonsense coming out of an old ugly broad?"

We laughed before I continued, "Besides, at my age, we've usually had lots of bad experiences that we're hoping to make up for and do not repeat in a simple, sincere new relationship."

"No, we don't learn anything even from our failed marriages," he said with a sigh. "Anyway, welcome to the real world, T.J."

"At least Mahtab and you make a good couple and give us some hope. She sounds mature and smart," I blurted with envy.

"Yes. I wish you and Reza also find smart mates like her."

"Too late for me but Reza needs a mature wife. Then, you two will probably forget your single old friend, too, like the rest of my married friends," I said pitifully, showing my psyche's unrest.

"Don't worry; we'll try to remember not to forget you… But maybe you should marry Mrs. Stanley, anyway, for caution."

"Here we go... Back to your juvenility...," I said testily.

"But she just seems like a perfect match for you... You like dogs too, don't you?" Darren asked. "What if someone jumps in and asks for her hand before you make your move?"

"I hope this house confinement ends soon before you turn into a fulltime clown," I replied.

"You're right T.J., about us becoming juveniles without any job or immediate worries boiling our brains. Still, some research is needed to prove this theory of yours," he said.

"You'd be a perfect subject for this study, but I'm probably acting equally silly around you, too. I'm feeling weird myself."

"Yes, you're catching up fast and I admire you for that!"

"Oh, gosh, what's becoming of me without a family?" I said.

"By the way, what happened with that sexy Sue?"

"It didn't work out, either."

"It's strange!" Darren said. "You seemed more vigorous and horny around women when you were married."

"I was naive before dating and realizing I hadn't been missing much and luckily lost my pitiful lust in the process as well."

"You should've appreciated what you had. You should've obeyed and spoiled Feri, instead of envying my freedom and fun idiotically all those years!" he said with loud laughter.

"I think Saadi Shirazi said this Persian proverb, 'The sound of kettledrums is pleasant only from a distance'," I said.

"So, now, you deserve some punishment," Darren replied.

Darren's rising spirit boosting his ironic fun over my dating drama had been both pertinent and perturbing. That particular day, however, his spirited demeanour made me dream, with envy, about my own chance for better days ahead as well, despite my failure in finding a proper mate so far. Darren's sudden change of fortune was a perfect proof, after all. How could I dismiss hope and the possibility of finding happiness and peace contrary to my experiences and philosophy, especially now that luck seemed to be the main or only factor to find one's soul mate and a tranquil life? How could I dismiss the scene of some people's thriving relationships around me? Still, believing in the value of hope and luck felt absurd as much as I gauged and reproved my pathetic conviction about life being inherently torturous, the way I had felt, experienced, and stressed as my final philosophical verdict about existence. Instead, a new theory jumped at me as a more fundamental, fatalistic verdict: That humans' crooked genes and innate urges are too weird and destructive to allow harmony and teamwork in relationships, thus their looming demise. Then, were Darren and Mahtab immune from this likely scenario?

So mysteriously, Darren's notice about relieving me of my chauffeuring chore for the family had sounded like telling me I was now good for nothing anymore, so I might as well merely keep myself busy with writing or something until I would finally succumb to death. Thus, at this point, I moved to his old suite to perfect my art of solitude and resume my writing seriously just for survival—*now that I was forced into seclusion, had no family or job, and my chance of finding a suitable mate had vanished.*

Still, I prayed to God to let me live healthy another 30-40 years for finishing my projects and annoying my family and friends in the process, although all those extra years would only feel like a longer torturous imprisonment. Besides my rising zeal to test the value and validity of my philosophical beliefs, Darren had encouraged me to keep on writing for helping others with my theories, too. He had stressed giddily that my grand findings might at least make some singles lighten up, reflect, and laugh a little like us about modern relationships' ironic tortures. Thus, we argued and laughed over all kinds of radical theories before we approved them for inclusion in my books.

For example, we agreed that about 70% of people are crooked due to their genes with 20% pushing themselves to pure evilness.

So, I admitted fully that my family's crookedness and animosities towards me should have not surprised me also due to humans' innate evilness. I must have not simply expected my daughters to be compassionate, honest beings, against all odds, just because they were mine, I loved them a lot, or I had assumed my kids would be exceptional—*maybe a bit like their kind, wise dad!* This last minute liberalism and enlightenment helped me relax a little, stop blaming my kids' natural urges so much, and maybe even forgive them partially—around 70%, without changing the gist of their pending legacy, though. I just wished they would live long to feel old age and parental pains the way I did before they would get a chance to destroy my wealth and laugh behind my back. Maybe they would read some of my books, too, and finally grasp my sense of humour or source of cynicism as well, maybe as *confessions of a testy father turned philosopher!*

According to this significant *newly approved scientific theory*, at first it seemed Feri deserved a reprieve as well, as she was just another crooked human, after all. Thus, I had to forgive her, if we assumed she was a human. *I've always been so fair and factual, after all, as I'm pretty sure you've also fathomed all that by now.* Luckily, however, I realized fast that Feri belonged to the 20% category in this revelatory theory—the pure evil ones—who did not deserve amnesty due to their intentional meanness and malice their entire lives way beyond their innate urges and genes. *Was Feri's case now settled for good at last, then?! Not quite…*

Because anytime a family story made me laugh, my playful conscience gene bugged me to forgive her, anyway. My psyche sometimes sided with my cunning conscience gene, too, when writing witty fictions boosted my spirit enough to merit the idea of absolving Feri, after all, at least for her ironical role in stirring essential thoughts in my head. Even my dull research and serious essays regarding marital and family conflicts in modern societies had raised my spirit when those findings had kept supporting my sad personal experiences. Regardless of its scientific value, all these self-exploratory research had cleansed my spirit at least.

In fact, my spirit, psyche, and conscience conspired together to pardon Feri. They insisted I would have remained a useless, greedy, and shallow person with no clue about other options for living outside the dark box if Feri had not pushed me out of our gloomy marriage into a fertile self-imposed exile. So forgiving Feri for being such a nutty wife felt spiritual, too, without hindering my whining and writing about her, of course. *I wished Socrates were around nowadays to help me with these dilemmas, although he'd most likely give up on me and my overdiligence soon, too!*

At last, my rejuvenated, juvenile spirit, with its growing knack for clowning in recent months, gauged the opportunity of fooling around with Feri at least, just for humour. I laughed for a minute imagining the scenario of calling and asking Feri to meet me just for giving her the good news in person.

"Hi..., it's me...," I would say in a gloomy tone.

"Yeah...! What do you want?" she would reply with attitude.

"Can we meet for a very important talk?" I would ask.

I believed she would accept to meet finally, while imagining and enjoying just a series of fantasies about me begging her for reconciliation, her opportunity to brag about it to her idiot friends and daughters, and her subsequent power to control me and my assets forever, if she took me back. Then, she would spend hours concocting amazing ideas about playing hardball and humiliating me an hour before showing pity and giving me another chance to cherish her. She even prepares her opening words to set the stage.

"So, what's this important matter you've dragged me here for?" she would ask triumphantly.

"I thought it was important to tell you in your face that I've decided to forgive you!" I would say sincerely with delight and a sense of divine enlightenment for finally maturing into an angel. Her shock and disgust, while glaring at me in absolute disbelief, exactly like I had imagined, would make me burst into laughter. Then, she would explode with laughter herself and mock me for turning into a complete loony now! We would be laughing our hearts out together for the first and last time in our lives!

This hilarious scene was not just a theatrical imagination or dream, but a valid projection based on my spectacular knowledge of Feri's personality. In fact, I was so certain I planned to share it with Darren as another plausible theory and *possibly* prove it by calling Feri and enacting that scene *if I really felt up to it*! I just feared Darren might push me to do it right away even if I was not ready to look into Feri's eyes or talk nonsense to her. He might even try to tape the whole scene furtively for posterity.

Naturally, my spiteful views and dreams also reflected my hidden hurts and sore memories piled up last twenty years. They showed my regret for not divorcing Feri two years earlier when she had cheated on me with a petty, married man among our new friends in Canada. Hearing noises and giggling in the bathroom, when I had returned tired and edgy from a camping trip two days ahead of the schedule, I found them naked in the hot tub. I left and stayed in a motel two nights before going home nonchalantly according to the scheduled time, though the three of us had stared at one another for ten seconds, speechless. Feri showed no shame or remorse, not even a word or apology for her adultery, as if she had only exercised her primary constitutional right. The whole episode had felt offensive since the guy was a big loser by all accounts. He had not even a single quality over me, except for a head full of hair. I must have killed them both or at least Feri right away; or divorced that bitch at least. Instead, I had waited two years for her to build her guts to ask for divorce, maybe from so much pent-up confusion and guilt. Ironically, signing the divorce papers with spite had brought me a huge relief, so much so I had wondered about my stupidity for not pursuing this basic means of salvation sooner myself. How silly the extra pain I had borne felt just in hopes of saving my marriage and daughters' future by a miracle. What a dreamful man I have always been, especially in terms of hoping to guide my kids build stable lives, while they had persisted on messing up their beings any way they could as soon as possible! *Discovering the immensity of our naiveté more every day is an excruciating experience in itself for some of us!*

My parents sounded old when I called them to announce my marriage's collapse, *as well as their parental hopes for my life's stability the way I hoped for my kids!* They sounded surprised and tried to console their elderly lonely son the best they could. Still, their voices, words of wisdom, and empathy did not reveal if they were sad or relieved about my marriage's final blow. Were they maybe even thrilled furtively about my misfortune due to my own stupidities and disregard for their wisdom and advice? The idea of consoling a son approaching sixty fast had probably felt funny to them as much as it had felt humiliating to me, yet I appreciated their kind, parental attempts to cheer me up. In return, my decision to go visit them soon elated their spirits.

"How soon do you mean?" my mother asked giddily.

"In a few months, as soon as my divorce is complete," I said.

"Do you want me to look around for a more suitable wife for you this time?" she asked.

"I don't think I should marry again."

"I think you should. So many good women in Iran can take good care of you. You've suffered enough and I'd like to see you get a break in your life before I die," she replied, while her voice declined and I could hear her weeping.

"Maman, don't stress yourself. I'm fine here."

"You're not going to work anymore and you don't wanna get married, either. So, what're you gonna do the rest of your life?"

"I'll find something to do, maman, don't worry," I replied.

I could not tell her anything about my writing obsession out of desperation, as I feared ruining their impression of my sanity for good. They would have surely cried or laughed hysterically, like myself, as they had persisted on raising me as a practical person with great appetite for wealth and status. They would disbelieve me if I told them that I had realized finally, only near the end of my being, the vanity of my struggles as a successful banker based on some crude ideologies and ambitions. After listening patiently, with immense concern, to my stories and excuses for becoming a great writer, my mother would surely insist even more to find me a faithful wife to forget all the nonsense I was telling her about my new mission in life! The thought of disturbing my parents with my pathetic life story at my age and their funny attempts to rectify my mistakes, mostly by finding me a new bride, made me both amused and sad after our telephone conversation.

In fact, I still concealed the depth of my writing obsession from everybody. I only claimed it kept me amused now that I had no incentive to work or make money. Besides irritating them, my response most likely sounded as bizarre as the one that mountain climbers often give for their seemingly pointless and dangerous adventures to reach a remote summit: *Because it's there!* Besides Feri's main role in my special case, the novel word-processing facilities were surely goading millions of desperate, bored people like me to merely seek refuge in writing now that they had failed in life, especially with their families. Writing has been giving us a chance to elude the mad society and people, hide in a quiet corner behind our computers, punch the keys, and ponder the vanity of existence. It was a good relief from so much grief. *Thanks Evelyn Berezin, for making this new toy and preventing many suicides.*

Actually, the therapeutic value of my writings became clearer to me as the amount of ideas pouring out of my active, ambitious mind kept growing. I also sensed and cherished deeper my earlier spiritual intuitions about my fate's active role to push this life path on me for personal salvation, if not another mystical purpose to wait for patiently as well.

Most of all, of course, my calling felt imperative for distracting my mind away from the awful reality of existence per se, which I could neither elude nor honour like another enigma keeping me in limbo. Not knowing if my erratic fate reflected a divine luck or a punishment was an added pain. *Had Feri been a blessing in disguise or a curse in the skies?*

My deeper confessions in the next few pages probably attest to many awful human urges that erupt erratically, especially if we feel empty without a serious family life and bear the side-effects of living with a carefree guy like Darren. My subtle envy towards his brisk luck was the simplest and least destructive example of humans' appalling and funny urges that not even an allegedly enlightened man like me could elude. Surely, the last five months of close association with Darren, while teasing each other all day, had felt blissful. However, my mood and personality changes felt alarming, too. I had not imagined being such an impressionable person at my age, letting Darren turn me into a clown the same way Reza had made me a pot smoker.

Anyway, skip the rest of this chapter if you are bored of my whining and reflective confessions as a testy writer.

As a major factor agitating my psyche, the huge discrepancy between my dreams and destiny appeared astonishing, frightening, and embarrassing to me. I had always imagined I would be lucky *at least* enough to marry a gracious, graceful, and gorgeous lady who would love me as much as I would cherish her, if not more, all our lives. Instead, I had ended up with a wicked, gawky, and ugly slut for many torturous years, before being left alone to rot in despair. This cruel discrepancy had felt like some divine lesson or retribution, way beyond a mere bad luck, which I could neither accept nor ignore in order to learn full resignation due at my age. Maybe it related to my error of pushing Homa out of my life or a fair punishment for a major sin that God had taken to heart—something too vile to let go, despite all my repentances! I knew I had committed many of those, but always wondered which one God had loathed the most!

Still, it felt imperative, as part of my punishment perhaps, to gauge the reasons for my marital failure scientifically as well and establish how much of it had been my fault or avoidable. *Of course, even if I admitted guilt, I feared it would only raise my sense of self-pity instead of helping me bear a woman better!* Thus, I read many books about modern relationships and drew on my suitably fitted academic background, marital experiences, and online dating after separation to perform methodical research.

Accordingly, this research focused the theme of my writings, while affirming the difficulty of finding and keeping a suitable mate in our presumed modern society. Actually, relationships felt like a fundamental social pandemic and I was now on a sacred mission to gauge the depth of our social numbness and madness. Ironically, my failure to amuse my mind with a decent mate—if not that gracious, graceful, and gorgeous mate I had believed to deserve—had led to my tenacity to become such a critical, testy researcher and writer about relationships—although this mission had soon felt holy as well! Feri ruining my chance for even the basic merits of marriage had in fact made this sacred research quite urgent and vital for saving humanity besides my soul!

Still, my efforts felt pathetic, like a revenge on my karma, yet the alternative—to keep looking for a soul mate to soothe my loneliness and replace my writing addiction—would have killed my spirit slowly along with deeper humiliation and torture. More amazingly, I persevered with my research even after admitting the high likelihood of wasting my life on a subject that nobody seemed to care about despite relationships' growing pains.

Then, as writing felt precious for my meditation and reaching a sense of spirituality, my old inner conflicts about my initial goal still lingered: How could I become a fine author if my goal for writing was mostly to forget about life and people who caused this global chaos? These conflicting objectives often stirred a fog of self-pity that obscured my observations and judgements about the world. How could my writings be truthful if I chose seclusion as a refuge? How could my views of people's psyches stay sharp without enduring contacts and study of their routines, thoughts, desires, and miseries? These were big hurdles and roots of dire prejudices that could spoil any writer's outlook and objectivity, in particular one seeking the truth and aiming for the stars!

Even worse, the necessity of indulging people for validating my writings, made me wonder if it meant I needed their approval of my efforts, too—for both humouring and studying them so artfully! That was the way Darren had felt earlier in his career, thus letting self-pity ruin his life, while doubting the value of his efforts and profession. How awful his low self-image must have felt when Erica had looked down at him and his passion. That was now exactly how my family and friends viewed me as a lost cause. I felt a bit insecure already when I sensed people's furtive pity and teasing of my pathetic attempts as a writer… *And surely not just a mediocre one, either,* which I seemed eager to prove to them and set their minds straight! *Life's odd conflicts are endless!*

In the end, the best I could do was to try to spend at least 20% of my time with people and outside the house in order to justify my writing efforts alone at home, although even this minimal sacrifice could jeopardize my main reason for becoming a writer in the first place!—to find 'who I was' along with some peace, both attainable only in solitude.

Wasn't this the biggest dilemma anybody has ever faced?—to indulge one's snobbish friends and sullied humans merely for literary purposes and professional obligation. It was surely a dire challenge and irony!

I also realized at last that my problem, as had been the case for Darren, was related to my own doubts about the validity of my observations and reflections away from the daily social hoopla—without fussing a lot over people's motives behind their deeds and desires. Then, I took the risk and challenge of self-reliance, too, like a sacrifice to possibly rebuild my identity without letting people's view of me sour my spirit. I had to ensure my self-pity and critical worldview would not contaminate the clarity of my perceptions and the value of my conclusions.

Luckily, I learned and admitted that my essential urge to write was merely for self-exploration without fretting over its rewards or becoming a social scientist. My objectives were valid enough to persevere and never doubt myself again, the same conclusion Darren had reached after years of agonizing about his painting passion and getting spiritual advice from our guru, Dervish Ali. Afterwards, only the incentive to fathom the purpose of my life —after two decades of marital pains—would goad me to plough on. I just wanted to grasp my being through contemplation and writing, after all!

Surely, the confessions of this testy writer have been ambiguous. On the one hand, counting my blessings about miracles and joys of living, even during such trying old age, has amply made up for my cynicism about existence. Even the dire pain of being out of place in Darren's house among a jovial crowd had felt worth the privileges of friendly voices and smiles around me on top of the luxurious service. The peculiarity of that lively setting had well mitigated the ongoing sad news about my dwindling family.

On the other hand, no amounts reprisal against my family—mainly for amusement—have still alleviated my loneliness pains. Instead, haggling with finicky lawyers over my will's new details that my sneaky mind invents *regularly* has been an added agony in itself. Surely, my beloveds are guilty also for my brain's weird tenacity to fathom nasty plans against my conscience, psyche, and spirit's likings. Still, I must stress that letting my kids make me this way has been irritating the most. Realizing and loathing my spite in the last stage of my life has been a hurdle for a man trying to explore spiritualism as a path to salvation and peace. I had never meant to sound so mean and grumpy in a novel. I also wondered if many authors have suffered from similar dilemmas or committed suicide, after all. Had Hemingway, for example, struggled with, or acted based on, similar thoughts?

Sadly, these confessions also lead to a big atrocity on my part as a duty to amend Socrates' advice (page 333) respectfully by adding: *If you get Feri, you'll become the nastiest and testiest philosopher ever born.* I wished he had met Feri, *and perhaps even married her, instead of letting her make me a better philosopher than he'd been until a few years ago!*

These perturbing thoughts, so late in the evening, goaded me to turn on my computer and retrieve the poetic recap regarding my existence that I had started the night before. I decided to work some more on this compilation of my latest literary efforts, which reflected the gist of my growing apprehension about my present state of mind, but could also serve as a tribunal for the futile life I had imposed on this pretty planet that is perishing fast under the weight of human folly. Maybe I could get Reza to recite it as part of his eulogy if I ever chose to allow a memorial service for me. *Nobody would come, anyway!*

At two a.m., I finally accepted the following summary about my pathetic life before going to bed.

I came to this world without my decision,
I strived to grasp my being, but reached no conclusion,
I hoped to live it, anyway, but never gained a real motivation,
I searched all corners of the world for the truth, but saw only vast devastation.

I planned my steps diligently, yet it caused only more frustration,
I trusted fate often as well, still it caused only more anticipation,
I argued a lot *all for what*, besides causing only more separation,
I loved a few with all my heart, but it caused only more desperation.

I believed in finding happiness, yet it only proved to be an illusion,
I suffered instead all the way, yet nobody believed my suffocation,
I reached a point of resignation, yet still kept my sacred reservation,
I felt people's daunting misery, yet most had no comprehension or compassion.

I got cynical and sinister, but it merely ruined my spirits' attention,
I forgave my enemies sometimes, but it only raised their retribution,
I cried my heart out, but it only heightened my chronic trepidation,
I laughed like a loony many nights in seclusion, but wept again in the morning out of sheer confusion.

So why had I lived for so long, as if bound by a divine resolution,
So how had I felt all along, besides deploring human condition,
So what was it all about, still wondering with a mystical suspicion,
So where would I go at last, wishing to know with no superstition.

I dreaded death, about going this time, again without my permission,
I imagined a god in charge of existence, to obey without hesitation,
I doubted His wisdom for making me, with such dire determination,
I hated the most, about my creation, the notion of coming and going without even a simple consultation.

Chapter Twenty-nine
Good News All Around

Mahtab and I were thrilled about her mom and Nazi now living with us. *Persian Moons*, Mahroo's portrait, had also arrived among other stuff shortly after they had two months ago. Mahtab had hung it in the family room to ensure Mahroo was among us most often. I had already removed Erica's portrait from that wall with pain and guilt and hid it in a closet for now! I was undecided about its fate, but intended to get Reza's input on this matter, too! Maybe he wanted it. *Erica hadn't yet offered a clue herself, either!* Reza had kept us abreast of the pending issues he was sorting out before joining us in Vancouver, perhaps for good. The main issue bothering Mahtab, and somewhat me, however, was the matter of the big secret we had kept from her family.

"Darren, we should tell my mom one of these days," she said with mixed feelings of guilt and gaiety.

"You think it's time to do it?" I asked tensely.

"Yes. I'm probably looking weirder every day. We'd better tell my mom at least before she asks an embarrassing question."

"Does she know about my secret in Iran?" I asked.

"No. I don't think so."

"Then we should tell her that as well."

"Not now… Let's shock her with a tough surprise at a time."

"Do you wanna do it right now?" I asked bravely.

"Right now…? You think so?" Mahtab asked with panic.

"We might as well get it over with."

"Okay…"

"Do you wanna do it together or alone?" I asked.

"Together, if you don't mind. I'm afraid she might kill me if you're not around to protect me."

"Okay, let's go do it, then," I told her with a grin, although my nerves were shattering.

Mahtab and I went downstairs to the kitchen where her mom was preparing the supper. Nazi was playing upstairs in her room.

"Maman, Darren and I would like to tell you something," she said rather calmly with a timid grin.

"What is it, dear?" her mom asked kindly, although Mahtab's prelude had already alarmed her.

"You know that Darren and I love each other and would like to marry as soon as my divorce is final."

"Yes, it seems we are stuck with this Mr. Darren one way or another," she said with a presumed humour in broken English. "But God knows how long it'll take Reza to get your divorce. Maybe years, because you are not there yourself and Bijan is still trying to hurt us."

"Yes, we know all this. But we're going to marry eventually," Mahtab stressed.

"Okay, when the time comes we'll discuss it… to put this shame behind us if you two still like to marry," Mahtab's mom said with some tension and confusion before recoiling to resume her work.

"But I wanna tell you something important today," Mahtab said courageously, while I braced myself for a catastrophe.

"What is that?" her mom asked with angst about discussing a touchy topic that had apparently upset her enough already.

"I'm pregnant...," Mahtab whispered.

"What?"

"I said I'm pregnant."

"Oh, that's terrible!"

"No, it's not. We're happy about it," Mahtab said right into her face bravely, while I avoided eye contact with her mom.

"And you wanna keep it while still married to someone else?"

"Yes. Darren and I discussed it sometime ago and decided to keep the baby."

"Sometime ago? How long?"

"Over three months."

"My God!" Mahtab's mom exclaimed, dropped the wooden spoon in her hand on the counter, lurched to the family room, and plummeted onto the sofa.

Mahtab poured a glass of water and gave it to her. She and I sat on the other sofa side by side, far away from her mom's reach in case she decided to kill or slap Mahtab at least.

"So, that's why you didn't return to Iran?"

"Yes, I couldn't let people watch me get bigger every day and maybe even have the baby before my divorce. I couldn't go to court with someone else's baby in my belly or lap."

"I don't know what kind of daughters I've raised. Both you and Mahroo have caused our family a lot of disgrace already and now this. What am I supposed to do with you?"

"We won't tell anybody, not even Reza. That's all! Hopefully everything will work out before anybody sees me or finds out about this secret."

"Why didn't you get rid of it?"

"Because abortion is wrong. But Darren also preferred to keep it after we discussed the added risks in our situation."

"Because he doesn't understand our culture or family honour, does he?" Mahtab's mom barked while glaring at me.

"He left the decision to me. Do you get it?" Mahtab snapped.

"But he agreed with you," she yelled at Mahtab before turning towards me and shouting at me with a glare, "It's all your fault."

"As usual, everything is my fault these days," I said.

Mahtab burst into laughter, peered at me, and said, "Yes, you started this whole thing for sure."

I burst into laughter myself, "Yes, I did. So, I might as well accept all the blame," I said with a grin. "But I'm not sorry…"

"I am a bit guilty, too. But you're guiltier, at least for painting that *woman in the white dress* that began all this chaos," Mahtab said wittily before kissing my cheek.

"So what're you gonna do?" Mahtab's mom asked.

"Nothing… We'll just have to wait another six months."

"Your father is lucky not to witness all this disgrace."

"I'm sorry he's not around to see his new grandchild."

"You two don't even look ashamed of yourselves for all your silly decisions and actions!"

"Not too much," Mahtab replied teasingly.

"Because you're crazy…"

"But you should at least be proud of me for not going back to Iran with a baby. That was a good decision, right?" Mahtab asked with a chuckle as though demanding a reward as well. Then, she walked towards her mom and kissed her left and right to make up. At last, her mom smiled, shook her head with despair, and started towards the kitchen.

"I think it's a boy. Don't you wanna have a grandson finally?" Mahtab said giddily, following her mom towards the kitchen.

I was glad this embarrassing secret was shared with Mahtab's mom, while we awaited the right time to dump the other secret on her later. Nazi rushed down the stairs and ran towards Mahtab, who smiled at her with deep affection and open arms.

"Are you gonna have a baby soon?" Nazi asked Mahtab.

Mahtab and I burst into laughter, while Mahtab's mom shook her head in the kitchen. I wondered if Nazi had overheard a part of our conversations even though we had mostly whispered.

"I hope so, dear. Why do you ask this question so suddenly?"

"Because I like to have a sister to play with me," she said quickly and rushed back up the stairs.

"Let's go outside and do some gardening, Darren," Mahtab said. "I'm thrilled Nazi thinks of me as her mother." I nodded.

As we started trimming some bushes, Mahtab exhaled a sigh of relief and said, "I'm glad I got this secret out of my chest, but telling it to Reza would be even more embarrassing."

"Didn't you tell your mom we won't tell Reza?"

"Yes, but maybe telling him is better, to keep his trust in me."

"Let's hope at least Bijan doesn't find out for a long time, if ever," I said with a thunder of shame and fear rattling my spine—from the guilt of not merely having a child with his wife, but also the chance of indirectly contributing to the death of his unborn son. Mahtab's words about her love and worries for me affecting her health before miscarriage still irked my conscience. *Gosh, how much damage I have caused this family!*

"Where did this stupid bee come from?" Mahtab asked irately.

"I don't know…," I replied firmly, although I had a hunch! *Stop it Erica,* I whispered.

Slowly and furtively, T.J. and I eventually moved my painting supplies, canvases, and the *Tosca* painting from my suite to the new studio in my house. Pondering and saying 'my house' still felt odd even after five months, while I felt guilty for enjoying it more every day. In particular, the gardening chores that Mahtab and I liked doing together regularly had boosted our spirits a lot, although we joked about a particular bee chasing us anytime we went out there. I wondered if Erica's spirit watched us every step of the way and got angrier, especially about Mahtab helping me build a big family—the topic that Erica had shied away from all along. I wondered what supernatural power had made her buy this big house with the ultimate aim of accommodating a large group of people these days. All those years that Erica and I, or Erica alone, had lived here, at least I had doubted the wisdom of having such a huge house. Thanks to her amazing foresight, it had now solved many tough issues for a bunch of love refugees, new immigrants, and homeless people.

While counting my blessings and believing I had had enough luck for one year, Detective Stewart called and asked me whether I could identify the thugs if I saw them. I told him I might be able to do so. So, he asked me to go visit him the next day.

T.J. and I met Detective Stewart in his headquarter, but then a police car took the three of us to the morgue. He took only me to the cold basement of the building and an attendant showed us two bodies one after another.

"Are these two the ones who shot you?" Stewart asked.

"I guess. Especially the one with the goatee looks familiar," I said. "I didn't know you wanted me to identify their corpses!"

"That's the best we could do for you, Mr. Durant."

"That's good enough for me," I replied giddily.

"We haven't found anybody to identify them officially. We might show their pictures to the bartender and Jeff as well, but how sure are you about these corpses yourself?"

"I'm pretty sure, although they looked livelier, then. And they were so full of themselves, in fact. Now just look at them."

He burst into laughter. "You think that's what killed them?"

"It looks like it! But didn't you guys kill them?"

"No, we found them like this near a crushed vehicle, but the one with the goatee had a gun wound as well."

"I didn't do it, either, just to clarify before you blame me for this, too," I said giddily for teasing him and he grinned as well.

"I hope so, but your own input can best help you decide how much to relax now. We've also found their residence and some paintings. So that is another good clue if you can describe them."

"This is great news. When can I have them back?"

"I'll call you to come and pick them up in a week or so," he replied, then asked me to describe the stolen paintings.

My newest luck to have my paintings back amused me, as T.J. drove us from the police station to our home. I recalled the chaos that one of those paintings—the *Woman in the White Dress*—had caused for many people in the last four years, including Mahtab's pregnancy according to her recent witty comment.

"The thugs got what they deserved," I told T.J. after telling him the story that Stewart had told me about them in the morgue.

"The good thing is that we don't have to worry about them anymore and you don't need a bodyguard, either," T.J. said. "But I still need the gun you'd promised to buy for me."

"Of course! But don't stay in your apartment too much. Come and visit us as often as you can take a break from writing."

"Sure, but I've been a burden long enough," T.J. said.

"No, you have not. But I think my apartment has been a good option for you if you prefer more privacy."

"Yes, it has, at least for getting back to serious writing again."

"And being near Mrs. Stanley, too, you devil?" I asked with a chuckle as we arrived home and got out of the car.

Mahtab was gardening, so I went out and kissed her.

"Have they arrested the right guys?" she asked.

"It's more than that," I said and explained the story to her.

"So, we now have one less worry," Mahtab said.

"They'll release my paintings in a few days," I said giddily.

"That's great... Do you recall our long fights in Tehran over *Persian Moons* and the *Woman in the White Dress*?"

"Yes, I do. But—"

"Now we'll hang them side by side and enjoy them together forever," she interrupted me with thrill.

"But do you also recall my arguments in Tehran about the possibility of this painting being cursed. I wonder if it'd also had something to do with the thugs' horrific demise."

"Were you serious or only trying to fool me to give it to you?"

"I was serious and you mentioned your own bizarre senses around it leading to *this*, right?" I said while touching her belly.

"Yes, but I still love that painting, too. *Persian Moons* is our sanctuary for cherishing Mahroo, but the *Woman in the White Dress* put me in love with you before bringing us together at the end, despite the misfortunes along the way..., not to mention this miracle," she replied while rubbing her hand all over her belly.

"I love that painting, too, but I'm also worried."

"Are you sure you're not superstitious."

"I don't know, but it's better to be safe than sorry," I said.

"It's such a momentous painting to give up," she said.

"But now we, especially you, must decide whether to bring it into this house with the chance it might be cursed," I said.

"I don't know...!"

"Didn't it cause my near death, Erica's death, and now the thugs' demise, plus Mahroo's confusion and stress before ruining her marriage as well as yours when she gave it to you? A demon seems to be living in that painting, all thanks to Vincent."

"Well, you've sacred me enough, too," she said.

"I may be superstitious, but I'm worried, mainly for our kids."

"Is it in the police station now?"

"Yes, but it'll be released in a week or so."

"Can they keep it a few months until we decide?"

"Or until the station blows up or the Police Chief is killed?" I said with loud laughter.

Mahtab also burst into laughter. "That'd be a good test," she said jokingly as we went inside. "Let's think about it, then."

"I wonder if Vincent would ever stop his game!" I muttered.

Nazi rushed over to kiss both Mahtab and me. What a pretty and compassionate young girl she was turning into. I have always loved her dearly like my own daughter. For her sake, especially, bringing the *Woman in the White Dress* into this house did not feel wise. Like Mahtab, I loved this painting, but taking risks with it was a deliberate challenge of our luck. Was Vincent's spirit still keen to play tricks on people and have fun through that painting?

Mahtab and I discussed the *Woman in the White Dress* during the following ten days a few times in vain. Our options felt silly or unethical one way or another. At the same time, neither of us had the guts to take the responsibility of bringing it into our house. When Detective Stewart informed me that my paintings were released, I promised to go pick them up in a few days. Thus, the pressure for a decision was mounting when I received a surprise call from Jerry, the owner of the Elixir Art Gallery. We had not spoken for over a year now after he had cancelled our contract for representing my paintings.

"I just read the new article about your painting," he said.

"Which article?"

"Do you recall the reporter who did the publicity article about your paintings over a year ago?"

"Yes."

"She's been following the story after you were shot and your paintings were stolen, when you came to, and now that the police have found the thieves and your paintings. She's written another short article about the paintings in the paper yesterday."

"I haven't seen the article," I said.

"I can give you a copy if you can't find the paper yourself."

"Thanks. Did you say she'd also written another article earlier about my recovery?"

"Yes. Do you have any plans for these paintings now?"

"No, I haven't yet decided about one of them," I replied.

"Which one?"

"The *Woman in the White Dress*."

"That is actually the one I'm interested in. If you like, I'd be happy to show it in our gallery and put a big price tag on it, too."

"How big?"

"At least one-hundred grand or maybe even two-hundred."

"You think so?" I asked with surprise about my luck again.

"Yes… This reporter has apparently been obsessed with this particular painting and its story even before your accident and more so now. In fact, I'd be happy to renew our contract and start showing and selling your other paintings in our gallery, too."

"It's a good suggestion, but I don't have any other paintings at this point. I haven't been in the mood to paint yet."

"That's even better. Maybe it's also better to only display the *Woman in the White Dress* in the gallery with lots of publicity, while telling people that it'll be auctioned later, most likely after you start painting again, if you ever feel like doing so."

"So, you'll keep it on display and its price keeps rising as long as I don't do any new paintings?" I asked giddily.

"Yes, it sounds like a fine strategy for publicity," Jerry replied with a chuckle himself as if he had read my mind. *Wow, that was a huge incentive in fact to stay lazy and never paint again, too!*

"All right, then… Actually, can you send your people to pick them up from the police headquarter after we sign a contract?"

"Yes, that'd be my pleasure if you can come by and sign the paperwork, tomorrow perhaps?"

"I need the other painting myself," I told Jerry.

"I'll get my people to deliver that one to you, then," he said. "Are you still living in the same address?"

"Yes, deliver it to the same address to T.J. Olaee," I replied.

After explaining Jerry's offer, Mahtab uttered a sigh of relief too, for leaving everything to fate instead of making a decision about the painting. Now, we could also visit it in the gallery as we wished, while it hopefully stayed on display for a very long time. Mostly, I loved my big excuse for not painting or procrastinating a long time to delay Jerry's plan of auctioning the *Woman in the White Dress*! *Am I a sneaky person or what? Or at least too lazy still to paint again!* We also hoped the new owner, when and if it happened, had the power to negate the likely curse chasing this particular painting of mine—unless he or she was by accident such a greedy, wicked person that we would not care one way or another! Jerry himself had been a tricky individual, although I hoped no harm came to him!

"Do you recall my idea about us opening an art gallery?" I asked Mahtab after she agreed to go with me to the gallery.

"Yes, I do."

"So look around the gallery tomorrow," I said. "Maybe we can make Jerry an offer in a year or so to buy his gallery."

"Okay... Unless the gallery blows up because of the *Woman in the White Dress*!" she said wittily.

"So let's wait three years to make sure the painting's curse is removed or impotent in a gallery."

Yet my main goal of taking Mahtab along was to show her off to Jerry in retaliation for what he and his mistress, Nora, had done to my painting career all due to Jerry's infatuation for Nora. Then again, if he had not cancelled the contract, because of my side affair with Nora, I would not have been forced to go all the way to Tehran for selling my paintings, meeting Mahtab and starting such a splendid love affair. Maybe in my deepest subconscious, I was also grateful to Jerry for his indirect role for my luck to find my dream mate that now I wanted to show off to him and make him jealous. I wondered if Nora was still the gallery manager and would get the pleasure of meeting Mahtab with me the next day!

"I have a surprise for you, too," Mahtab said.

"Another surprise? Don't tell me you're carrying twins?"

"No, but it's almost like that," she said giddily, while giving me an envelope.

I opened the envelope and found half dozen photos of a baby.

"Whose baby is this?" I whispered.

"Yours," Mahtab said.

"Mine…?" I uttered as my heart sank.

"Yes, and Sima's."

"Where'd they come from?"

"Reza had sent me the images and I had them printed for you. He looks like you."

"Yes, he does," I replied.

"We must keep these pictures secret, too, according to Reza's request," Mahtab stressed.

"Yeah, okay, sure."

Mahtab and I were so mesmerised looking at the photos we did not notice her mom entering the family room and staring at our amused faces.

"What has Reza sent? Pictures?" she said with excitement and walked towards us eagerly.

Mahtab and I were caught off guard and did not have time or the guts to react and hide the pictures. We just stared at her until she was near us and looking at the pictures.

"Who's this baby? Don't tell me it's Reza's baby, is it?"

Mahtab and I stared at each other and her mom awhile with embarrassment before I said at last, "He's my son."

"You have another child?" Mahtab's mom shrieked with a grimace. "How many kids and wives do you have?"

"Only one son and no wife. My ex-wife died as you know."

"Is he your son with her?"

"No, he's not. He and his mother live in Iran and don't wanna have anything to do with me, either."

"I'm not surprised! They're smart…"

"I'm not such a bad person, I promise you...," I said hesitantly with some doubts about the matter myself!

"How many other secrets you two are hiding from me?"

"No more secrets, I promise," I said giddily, hoping not to give a frail old woman a heart attack. I rose and kissed her cheek.

"Maman, this is another secret. Don't mention it to anybody, not even Nazi," Mahtab said, rose, and kissed her mom, too, as we grabbed her arms and went to the nook for a cup of tea.

"Gosh, how many secrets we should keep," Mahtab's mom said in a rather hypnotic manner while shaking her head all along.

She did not seem to have a heart attack today, thank God.

At the end, everything had worked out nicely in terms of bringing Mahtab's mom into our conspiracy about many hidden secrets, too. Now we could just sit around and watch Mahtab's belly get bigger every day, while her mom and Nazi kept staring at her with some kind of admiration and anticipation. T.J. seemed happy in my suite, but kept joining us regularly for dinner and chatting before returning to his place late in the evenings.

"How is Mrs. Stanley these days?" I asked T.J. once, mostly out of curiosity and courtesy, so unlike my usual joking habit.

"She's fine, but keeps asking for you. She really misses you."

"Say hi for me, but still don't tell her I don't live there," I said.

"But she seems too eager to find you. Are you eluding her?"

"No, why should I do that?" I asked nonchalantly.

"Because she seems to be pregnant, too."

"Are you kidding me?" I asked in shock.

"No… Are you sure you haven't made a son with her, too?"

"I'm glad your sense of humour is growing so fast, T.J."

"Actually, my sense of humour is getting too wild and a bit annoying now even for my own conscience," T.J. said with pain.

"Why do you think this way? Humour is always good."

"But it seems I'm catching your demented sense of doing silly jokes with people; and it didn't feel right afterwards when I did it a few times with Mrs. Stanley."

"So you're now joking with her, too, you sneaky lover boy?"

"Yes, I'm afraid that living with you for so long has turned me into a jerk like you in terms of playing tricks on people…," T.J. replied with a chuckle.

"So what tricks have you played on Mrs. Stanley?" I asked.

"I keep asking her if she's seen the thugs almost every time I see her and she says 'yes' while asking me to be careful."

"You still haven't told her they're dead?" I asked with thrill about turning T.J. into a rather playful man at his age as well.

"No, I haven't and I won't tell her anytime soon, either."

"You, bastard… If you wanna tease her even more, tell her that they've kidnapped me," I said with loud laughter.

"That'll be really fun, but she'll scream at me for not being a good bodyguard, after all, according to her sound prediction," T.J. replied. "In fact, I've kept telling her that you're afraid to get out of your suite every time she asks me why you're not around. She thinks you've been hiding in your suite all along."

"You're really getting out of control," I said with a chuckle.

"All thanks to you," T.J. replied with some hesitance. "She's also asked me a few times if you've bought me a gun yet."

"I'm really glad that our cohabitation has been so effective in making you such a tease and a fun person," I said with a giggle.

"Well… I'm also rather glad for becoming a clown, all thanks to your generosity and taking care of me when I needed a real friend. Thanks Darren…"

"You welcome... How're your writings going?"

"Great, in fact. My technique is improving fast as well. Your apartment is really making it easy for me to concentrate and keep on ploughing... This house was getting too crowded and noisy for a serious author like me."

By the way, after Jerry, the gallery owner, told me about the few articles in papers about my recovery and the thugs' demise later, I realized Jeff and the thugs had probably learned all these facts through those articles. I had driven Detective Stewart, Elizabeth, and myself nuts about this matter for so long, all for nothing. Feeling stupid, I hoped the detective would not find out and call me to rub my presumably genius proof of Jeff's guilt all over my face. Instead, I was now too curious about this reporter. I recalled how she had been intrigued about the *Woman in the White Dress*'s background and story when I had recounted it to her in our interview and she had written it in her first article about a year earlier. But why did she still seem obsessed with it and me?

Sometimes, I also reflected upon my conflicting conclusions about life being more important than love when, in reality, I had chosen Mahtab in spite of the risk of dying, and more in line with classic love stories and lovers' unconditional devotions. With the dilemma of life versus love now in limbo again, I have also been wondering if anything in human existence superseded their being per se. Accordingly, now I recognize and cherish that traditional belief: that more crucial than life, for me at least, was our legacy and maybe pride and principles, or all together—a legacy of pride and principles. If so, I had to work a lot more on my character in coming years. My pride was fine, but building more humility would help my enlightenment a lot. *Then it occurred to me that when we have no real job or worries, we spend lots of time and energy on philosophy, too!*

Accordingly, I wondered how lazy Socrates had been!

Chapter Thirty
The Big Reunion

My regular telephone conversations with the jubilant gang in Vancouver energized me enough to pursue my mission with an immense sense of purpose. My mom, Mahtab, Nazi, Darren, and T.J. sounded ecstatic about their new lives forming in the right directions, while insisting that I join them and live in Vancouver as soon as possible.

"Cameron wants me to convince you to come work for SDI full time in Vancouver," Darren said with an odd sense of duty one time. "Erica was the main brain at SDI and now Cameron is under lots of pressure, while the business is still expanding."

"He's a tough person to deal with, though," I replied.

"I guess I should also mention that now I own 50% of SDI—Erica's share. So, don't worry about his personality, Reza; you'll be working mainly for me," Darren replied.

"Oh…! I'm glad to hear that," I said with surprise.

"Besides, I'm sure you'll learn how to handle Cameron, too. And if you like, I'll also sell a part of my share to you. I can't contribute much, but will stay in the company for now."

"I'll think about it. It might not be a bad idea to live near you guys, too. But selling my businesses here and in Dubai will delay my travel to Vancouver even more."

"We'll wait for you...! You can even have Erica's office and secretary," Darren said with a chuckle for sweetening the deal.

"That'd be the biggest incentive—to sit on her chair!" I said.

"And when I go there, I'll sit on her chair, too," he replied.

"Aren't we two driving poor Erica's ghost nuts?"

"Especially after everything she did to kick us out of her life."

"I miss her a lot… Don't you?" I asked tenderly.

"I do. Let's share her company, too, Reza!" he replied slyly. "Let's also hang her stern portrait that I've hidden in the closet these days. She can watch us do a good job! What do you think?"

"I agree, although we may get tense or emotional often when she keeps staring at us," I said half-teasingly.

"Don't worry; we'll manage her as long as she doesn't talk."

"Ironically also, I'll be working for you after bossing you all those years here in Tehran."

"But, I'll be a tough boss, unlike you...!" Darren replied.

"You see how the universe fools around with us?" I asked.

"Yes, I could never imagine things reverse so much so fast."

"T.J. keeps reminding us, too. Doesn't he?" he asked.

"Yeah..., he's the best example himself," I replied.

"By the way, have you seen or heard from Dervish Ali?"

"No, I've been so busy, but I'll try to contact him very soon."

"Give him my best regards, Reza," Darren said.

Darren's persistence that I work for SDI had felt reasonable, yet bizarre, since he knew my apprehension regarding Cameron's antsy personality as well as the extent of my business obligations in Iran and Dubai. Then again, I could imagine Darren's sneaky, real interest in the matter. He wanted me there, so that he could just sit back and do nothing himself for the rest of his life, while I handled Cameron for him, exactly contrary to what he had slyly told me about not having to worry about Cameron myself! Of course, that clever Darren seemed to have a valid point, as I may indeed be the best person to keep Cameron in order, after all, *not that I wished to brag about my managerial and coaxing skills, especially after my handy practice on Mahtab!*

Four days after my conspiracy chitchat with Mr. Rafatti in Sima's place, Bijan appeared at my front door late in the evening in total distress with an even longer and messier beard.

"Now you're acting against me, too?" he asked with agitation.

"You've put me in this position yourself. I told you things will get out of control and you said you didn't care."

"So you confess to be the one talking to Rafatti."

"I had to before it was too late. What'd he tell you?"

"He said he's heard rumours about Darren intending to reveal their secrets... He wanted to know what I knew."

"What'd you tell him?" I asked giddily.

"I said I knew nothing about his intentions," Bijan replied.

"Did he believe you?"

"I don't know, but he wants me to get to the bottom of this rumour in a week," he said, quite rattled, which was a good start.

"So what're you gonna do?" I asked with great satisfaction.

"Coming to see you was the start... to satisfy my hunch about you being the spy. What do you think you can gain by messing with me, Reza? You think you can fight with me now? I'll just crush you and your family."

"You think so?"

"You'd better believe it," he yelled.

"I suggest you calm down and realize you're making things more difficult mostly for yourself," I yelled back.

"You're lucky I haven't broken your neck only out of respect for your mom. I'm going to see her tomorrow and tell her that if you don't stop your rumours and Darren's stupidity, then do not expect me to stay cool or let you turn Rafatti against me."

"They're gone," I said proudly, but felt sorry right away.

"Gone where?"

"They went to Vancouver to see Mahtab."

"They did? Without telling me, not even a simple goodbye?"

"She didn't think she needed your permission," I replied.

"So, that's it? She is against me now, too?" he asked tensely.

"She's simply fed up with your attitude and hurting Mahtab and the rest of us."

"Will they return soon?"

"I don't know. Mahtab is alone and sick in Vancouver."

"This makes the matter so serious, then," he said with a glare.

"Whatever... But you better smarten up and stop your threats."

"Listen, Reza. If you wanna team up with Rafatti to fight with me, I'll ask Colonel Arshadi to take care of you, too. He's already found your suite as well as Darren's and he'll go there himself soon or get his people to take care of him and Mahtab."

"Now you listen, Bijan. This is my last warning to you, too. Now go away," I yelled at him while opening the apartment door for him to get out.

Bijan kicked and knocked down the side table with the lamp on it before leaving. Promptly, I called and asked Sima to tell her uncle that the situation was worsening. She called me back two days later with a message and an address to visit her uncle three nights later. Then she asked me whether I had time to see her the next day in the same park we had met the first time. I agreed.

I arrived a bit early and waited for Sima, who came with Darius in the stroller again. After some preliminary chitchat, at last she asked solemnly, "Do you think Darren will marry me now that he knows we have a son?"

"I think you'd better not count on Darren as a reliable man."

"Is it because he's gonna marry your sister?"

"Nobody knows anything about this matter and it's important not to spread rumours and make Bijan madder, either."

"So the rumours may not be true, ha?"

"I don't know. I hope they aren't."

"You should worry for your sister, then," she said slyly.

"Of course… I worry about the rumours and my sister being attracted to him somehow, if not having another Darius as well," I said wittily but pretended to be really worried.

"He'll ruin her life, too, the same way he's destroyed mine."

"So why do you still hope to marry him?"

"Mostly for Darius having a real dad," she said with a sigh.

I nodded and she continued, "Although my feelings for him aren't all vanished, despite his attitude and hurting me so much."

"I know… He has that odd effect on women and spoiled other people's lives, too, but doesn't mean to hurt others. He's just lost and I guess you also know this," I said, hoping to calm her.

"Yes, I know," Sima replied in a genuine tone.

"You are a smart woman," I said.

Sima peered at me pensively with a grin. She seemed to have grasped my hint about her slim chance of reunion with Darren. Probing me had probably been the whole purpose of her request to meet and I was glad for the opportunity to set her mind straight with no hope for taming this wild Darren.

"Thanks… Can you tell him, anyway, that I miss him?"

"Yes, I will."

I took another bunch of pictures from Darius playing on the grass. Then, Sima picked him up and put her face next to his, stared into the camera seductively, and asked me to take a picture of them together as well. I did.

"Give him this picture for sure," she said.

"Okay… I'll send him all of them…"

"Tell him that Darius needs a dad…"

"I will," I promised her before we departed.

It felt weird to have similar unflattering discussions about Darren with various people regularly, including the one right after leaving Sima. I called Dervish Ali's house and his wife said he had at last been released from the Evin prison three weeks earlier. She checked with him before conveying his consent to see me that afternoon. Dervish Ali looked quite frail and impatient after nine months of imprisonment in such horrible conditions that Darren had already explained to me based on his own experience and contacts with Dervish Ali in the same prison cell.

I had felt terrible during the last eight months about my family affairs hindering Dervish's chance for release, which only Bijan and his father could facilitate. Guilt had singed my spirit often and I had wondered how I could dare look into his eyes. Then, I tried to console my conscience and justify my focus on Mahtab, since she was the only person left to help me with family duties. Of course, Mahroo's and Erica's deaths had also drained my mind and energy all along. Still, I felt the need to come partially clean to Dervish.

"I'm sorry we could not help you," I told Dervish with shame. "Bijan has turned against my family now."

"Why? What happened?"

"Mahtab has decided to divorce Bijan," I said.

"Your family has been going through turmoil, too, like mine. I heard about Mahroo's accident, too," Dervish Ali said.

"So many deaths for nothing, especially Zia's and Mahroo's."

"You know that Mahroo and Darren drove Zia, my darling nephew, to that sad state of mind and ending."

"Not intentionally," I said with shame, recalling my reasons again for eluding Dervish. He had most likely felt my seeming apathy in the last four months and built deeper grudges against all of us, including Darren.

"How is he these days?" he asked with sarcasm.

"He's been having his own problems."

"He's a big sinner going by what I've learned about him."

"He's not a bad guy, though… He was actually worried about you and asked me to make Bijan help you, too."

"Why is Mahtab divorcing Bijan?"

"She can't cope with Bijan's Islamic ideologies, but her travel to Vancouver to nurse Darren made the situation worse."

"So, this is also Darren's fault, right?" Dervish asked as if he already had some magical insight.

"I don't know, but you never know with Darren," I replied, wondering if there was a special place in hell for the biggest liar of history! Even worse, I was tired of this troubling thought messing my brain thousand times every day after every lie!

"I bet she's now attached to Darren, too, like her sinful sister."

"I'm telling you this stuff in private, since I trust and respect you. I have a tough task ahead to get Mahtab's divorce."

"Why you?" Dervish asked.

"Because she doesn't want to fight with Bijan face to face."

"But she went to Vancouver to be with Darren, right?"

"No, not really… She'd apparently only felt an urge to help a dying man."

"What was wrong with Darren?"

"He was shot and remained in a coma for three months."

"Was he shot because of a woman, too?" he asked as if he knew this fact already as well.

"I don't know… But it's possible…," I replied timidly again.

"It's just amazing how he causes all these mayhems. So many people die because of him, but he survives even such seemingly fatal accidents. He survives even when he deserves to die for his treasons at least."

"He's lucky in many ways, but he's had his share of bad luck, too, as you saw it yourself when he was in prison with you."

"He didn't even know why he was in prison," he said with a smirk. "But now I'm sure he deserved it, whatever the charge had been. In fact, I bet, it also related to another woman, am I right?"

"I don't know… He never told me," I lied for the hundredth time in this meeting alone because of Darren.

"Well, he's been a nasty man at least in some ways, although he's tried to redeem himself sometimes," he said kindly.

"Yeah, he's lost his soul through a daunting fate," I said.

"Is he okay now?"

"Yes, he is... He asked me to give you his best regards and tell you that he was sorry, but didn't say why."

"He's got nerve, sending me his regards!" he said tensely.

I grinned and stared at him with surprise. "Do you still have grudges against him?" I asked.

"Actually, I forgave him when he asked me in the prison," he replied with a sigh. "But now I wonder… I guess he fooled me, too, to forgive him…"

"Are you sorry now?" I asked with a giggle to tease him.

"I should've killed him in Evin when I had a chance," he said half-seriously. "Maybe Mahroo and Zia would be alive if I had."

"He still has many fierce enemies to finish him, anyway."

"Don't count on that! He'll probably outlive all of them, too."

I burst into laughter. "He always talks about you as his guru and friend. He'll be surprised if I tell him your new sentiments."

"He'd felt my anger towards him," he said. "Did he tell you I almost crushed his empty skull in the Evin cell we were sharing?"

"No, he didn't. Why did you do that?" I asked.

"I lost my sanity when he confessed to being in love with Mahroo and coming to Tehran just to gauge his feelings for her."

"Why would he say that? He knew Zia was your nephew."

"He said he wanted to come clean and clear his conscience for both loving Mahroo and possibly causing Zia's suicide. Then, I appreciated his odd honesty, but now I'm not sure if I can ever forget his role in Zia's suicide. And now he's apparently doing a similar stunt with your other sister and brother-in-law…"

"Maybe you should've killed him, after all," I said jokingly.

"Yes, I should...! I'm sorry I stopped strangling him in the last second."

"You are?" I asked with surprise witnessing even a divine man so spiteful and frustrated because of Darren.

"Yes, my life would've not changed much if I'd done this service to humanity. It might've also saved Mahtab's and Bijan's marriage from the sound of the story you're telling me. And now he says he's sorry for something that I don't even know about!"

"Maybe other people's lives, including mine, would've been easier these days, too, if you'd finished the job," I said wittily. "I agree with you that all these mayhems are your fault."

"Sorry, I made a huge mistake. It's a pity those other people in Vancouver also failed to end his miserable life."

"Well, don't worry too much… As I said, still a good chance exists that another group or maybe even Bijan takes care of him soon," I said jokingly.

"I doubt it… More likely Bijan would commit suicide, too," Dervish Ali said with a tense chuckle. I giggled about the chance of his witty premonition *hopefully* coming true to set us all free.

"I really don't know how much to blame Darren or my two wild sisters," I blurted a fact that I could confide only to my guru.

"My sentiments exactly… I'm glad you mentioned the main problem yourself," he said with anger and angst.

"I'm sorry…"

"Both your sisters seem to have been touched by the devil. But Darren is also guilty of something," Dervish said.

"He sure is! I'm also going nuts dealing with all these messes they cause for so many people merely for love apparently."

"Yeah, Darren was confused about love as well. He asked me a lot about it and then hurt himself and others with it, anyway."

"Now that we're talking so candid, I'd like to confess my own sense of guilt to you again as well in confidence," I said.

"Okay, go ahead and confess if you think it'll help you."

"Often I think that if only I hadn't fallen in love with Erica, maybe she was still alive and married to Darren, I had not hired him to come to Iran and seduce both my sisters one after the other, many deaths had been avoided, two marriages had not broken, you had been released from the prison long time ago, and I had not felt responsible and suffered for all these chaos."

"I couldn't imagine you've been feeling guilty about all these catastrophes as well," Dervish Ali said with surprise.

"I feel also embarrassed when I still have to defend my sisters and sometime even Darren, especially to you. But what can I do? It's also funny that we all feel guilty for these mayhems."

"I understand. You've been caught in these messes mostly out of pure obligation, and yes, we've all been guilty somehow..."

"Especially you, for not killing him when you had such a big chance!" I said teasingly.

"I agree… I'm the guiltiest of all for not finishing him."

"Even now, everybody still expects me to clean up after their messes, including Darren," I said.

Dervish Ali peered at me with angst. "Don't worry too much... But I don't know if I should accept his regards or put a curse on him, as I'd intended initially in Evin. I must think about it."

"That's fine. Let me know when we meet again, if it's okay?"

"That's okay, Reza. You're not a bad person yourself, despite your sisters' actions and your choice of Darren as a close friend."

"How's your health now," I asked.

"Not very good. It is deteriorating fast and people in the Evin killed a good part of my spirit, anyway. I'm not allowed to talk to people or have religious meetings, but at least they released me to die near my family and not in the Evin."

"Yeah… At least you survived the ordeal," I said.

As scheduled, I met Mr. Rafatti in his huge house. Bijan's and his father's mansions had always both impressed and depressed me already. However, entering the foyer of Mr. Rafatti's palace, I was flabbergasted. Still, I tried hard to keep my composure for the main purpose of my visit. In a country where so many people are stricken by severe poverty, occupying or even visiting these kinds of extravagant dwellings felt like a major sin.

I was directed to Rafatti's study where he sat on the couch with a younger man who glared at me with a chilling effect.

"This is my famous nephew, Colonel Arshadi," Rafatti said wittily with a cute chuckle without bothering to introduce me to him, too. Apparently, the good Colonel knew me and they had been chatting behind my back while waiting for me. I was certain Bijan had already created a terrible impression of me for the tough looking Colonel.

Colonel Arshadi shook my extended hand with reluctance as if unsure about making peace with me or trusting my intentions.

"My nephew and I have discussed your concerns, Mr. Azimi. I asked him to come here tonight as well, so that we can agree on everything together," Rafatti said, peering at Colonel Arshadi who nodded a few times with subtle hesitation, as if cornered.

"Thank you," I said cordially.

"We do not want Bijan tell us stupid things or cause friction among us, right?" Rafatti stressed, staring mainly at his nephew.

Colonel Arshadi was peering at the floor, but the silence made him look up at Rafatti and nod again.

"What has Bijan told you, Reza?" Rafatti asked.

"He told me he's teaming up with Colonel Arshadi to find and punish Darren and me," I replied.

"Is that true, Hussein?" Mr. Rafatti asked his nephew.

"Yes… But I have been looking for Darren myself, anyway," Arshadi replied irately, but also as a show of pride and defiance.

"That's all in the past now, right?" Rafatti asked his nephew.

Colonel Arshadi nodded without looking at us.

"So, Reza and Darren shouldn't worry about you bothering them or helping Bijan, right?"

"Right," Colonel Arshadi murmured. "Just for you, Uncle…"

"Thank you Hussein. If you're in a rush to leave, go ahead. Reza and I would like to talk some more," Rafatti said.

"Thanks, Uncle," Colonel Arshadi said before staring at me. "You guys don't worry about me, although I'm still angry with Darren. He'd better do something really good for my family to make up for his big travesty." He then rose and shook hand with me rather cordially this time before leaving.

"Are you satisfied, Reza?" Rafatti asked after his nephew left.

"Yes, thank you. I hope Colonel Arshadi keeps his promise."

"He will. I've talked to him before, too. I didn't know he's still so mad, but I convinced him to forget about Darren and do not let Bijan influence him. So you guys don't worry about him."

"But Bijan is still threatening both Darren and me," I said.

"I think I can also fix that problem. I've already expressed my concerns to his father and he promised to get his son to back off."

"I really appreciate your help, Mr. Rafatti."

"That's all right. I'll wait a few days before talking to Bijan as well. I think he's still manageable despite his sudden madness."

"I hope so… Thanks again…" I said.

"I can sort of understand his situation, losing both his wife and honour because of Darren."

"I hope he'll back off... I've started my sister's divorce, too."

"You have to do that for her as well?" Rafatti asked.

"Yes... I've also hired an attorney to help me," I said, hoping that all these extra information would be useful. And it was!

"I'll help you with that as well," he replied. "Let me know which court your case is filed in and I'll get the job done much faster and smoother than your lawyer can do alone."

"Oh, that would be wonderful, Mr. Rafatti. Thanks a million. If I can do anything for you in return, please let me know," I said sincerely, amazed about my success to gain Rafatti's support so much more than I could have imagined even in my dreams.

"You just make sure Darren does not do anything stupid to ruin our understanding," he said. "He mustn't reveal our secret or try to get involved with Darius at any time."

"Absolutely… I promise… He would've not even raised the issue if he'd not been threatened by Bijan or pushed to confront him for helping himself and my sister."

"I understand and that's why I've helped you."

"Thanks again," I said.

"If you have any more problems with Bijan, just let me know. I'll force him to agree with everything quickly."

"I'll be forever in your debt and hope to repay it very soon."

"In fact, there's something else that maybe you or Darren can do for us," Rafatti said.

"What's that?"

"Can you guys help in hiring a good immigration lawyer in Canada for Sima and her mother? They think they can make a better life for Darius and themselves in Canada and I'm starting to believe that it might not be a bad idea."

"Of course, we'll be happy to hire the best lawyer and ensure he does it in the right way. Do you want us to start right away?"

"Yes, look into it and keep me informed. Maybe it's best to give Darius and Sima a chance for a better future in Canada."

"Both Darren and I think the same way and would help you and Sima as discretely as your wish."

When I left late in the evening, we felt like friends, way more than two strong allies, capable of trusting each other totally. Now, I did not even mind his choice of living in that castle, after all!

Meanwhile, the more my spirit had kept crashing during my squabbles with Bijan and other rascals trying to hurt Mahtab and Darren, the more the idea of living in Vancouver had sounded appealing to me every day, too, even before Darren giving me all those extra news and incentives. Eventually, the idea of working for Darren also felt not merely tempting, but rather inevitable. So, I set out to sell my businesses in Tehran and Dubai rather cheap to leave fast. It had been a rough four months for me, after all.

Exactly as Mr. Rafatti had promised, things proceeded smoothly. Bijan's attitude changed drastically in a matter of days. His father and Mr. Rafatti had apparently gotten through his rotten head to dump his resolve to hurt Darren, Mahtab, and me. It seemed he might commit suicide any minute, after all, the way he looked so miserable and timid the few times we met to discuss things and in the court during Mahtab's divorce process, as if hypnotized or lost his will to live. *He was a changed man at last, after all, in a depressing way, though! All because he had failed to change in a positive manner! Or at least do the right thing like Zia!*

Yet, ironically, I suffered my mixed feelings about him, too!

On the one hand, I enjoyed my success to push him indirectly into this precious position for his divine salvation at last, looking more ready to do the honourable thing for a man in his situation every time I had met him! On the other hand, I felt sad for him as yet another forsaken human and believed he did not deserve so much humiliation and betrayal in his life at such young age.

Still, it took me four months to finalize Mahtab's divorce, which was the last pending task for me in Tehran. All along, I'd kept Mahtab, and sometimes Darren too, appraised of the court's proceedings and my plan to join them soon. I sold my business and properties and transferred all our monies to Vancouver.

I met Sima regularly and took more pictures of her and Darius. She looked so innocent and beautiful suddenly. She also sounded quite smart to me, contrary to what Darren had told me about her. I wondered how much of his views had been accurate or driven by Sima's possible erratic behaviour around Darren due to her love for him. Accordingly, the chance of my affection for Sima growing too far made me giggle tensely, as this ironic possibility felt less outrageous every time I met her. The way my life and Darren's have been mixing over the years and the way I had been drawn to women that he had damaged felt bizarre. It seemed like I had been born to clean up after him when he kept going from one love affair to the next and messing up things. So, the chance of his demonic fate also inflicting Mahtab worried me as well sometime, but nothing I could do about this matter now. I had simply resigned!

In my last meeting with Sima before my departure, I promised her to find a good lawyer to do everything Mr. Rafatti had asked me to do for their immigration to Canada. We chatted for three hours, while we watched Darius running around sloppily—falling and jumping on his feet again and again. Sima looked so much prettier every time we met and happier about the mere hope of seeing Darren again and starting a joyous life in Canada. Or else, I was falling in love with her myself maybe. I wondered if my mom would be glad or go nuts if I told her that I was falling in love with, and maybe marrying, Darren's past mistress and adopting his lovechild! Didn't she always insist that I needed a wife? So, if I married Sima, it would be her fault, after all!

I also met Dervish Ali a few times during my last days in Iran. Every time he looked more frazzled and thinner. I took pictures of him when he looked somewhat healthier. In our last meeting, he was lying listless and sounded hardly coherent. His wife said doctors had lost hope and he could not walk or talk more than two minutes at a time if at all the entire day sometimes.

"I won't be able to see you for a while, Dervish Ali," I told him with tears in my eyes as I was getting ready to leave.

He stared at me and nodded but did not ask why.

"I'm going to Vancouver to see my family and maybe also work there," I said with sadness for the high likelihood of never seeing my guru again.

"Ali's hand upon you. Send my regards to that greatest fiend on earth, too," he murmured with difficulty.

"So you've decided to forgive Darren again instead of putting a curse on him?" I said jokingly.

"Yes, I've forgiven that devil again. Besides, it seems that my curses always work," he muttered with a mysterious tone, which made me wonder if Mahroo's death had been one of his curses that he was pondering and hinting, and maybe even regretting.

When I mentioned my plan of surprising the family to T.J., he insisted to pick me up at the Vancouver airport himself two days later. However, I was the one getting a bigger shock when T.J. and I arrived at Darren's house. They were surprised, of course, but seeing Mahtab in that condition threw me off balance, while I kept staring at her and Darren with my jaw dropped to my chest.

"What is this?" I asked dumbfounded, pointing to Mahtab's huge belly, while almost jumping to punch Darren in the face.

"This is my new son," the devil replied before bending and kissing Mahtab's belly and then her cheek. "Now I have two sons whom I haven't yet met."

"This one you'll see in a matter of days," she said with joy.

I was angry with them for keeping this exciting news all to themselves during the last nine months or so. Yet, I felt jubilant to be part of this crazy family. I bent and kissed Mahtab's belly, too.

"Why didn't you tell me?" I asked Mahtab.

"Isn't it obvious...? I didn't want you lose your focus or feel too guilty for helping me."

"Was this actually the reason you didn't return to Iran?"

"Yes, this timely miracle probably stopped the possibility of choosing a different path for myself and maybe all of you, too," she said triumphantly, pointing to her belly.

"I forgive you," I said while giving Darren a big pile of new pictures I had taken from Darius during the last five months.

Everybody glanced at the pictures, but Darren stared at them a long time with nostalgia, perhaps wondering about the prospect of meeting his first son someday soon, too, while his second son would surely amaze him much sooner.

"So, I see you've met Dervish Ali, too?" Darren asked.

"Yes, we met a few time and he let me take his picture."

"Did you give him my regards?" Darren asked.

"Yes. He sent his regards to you, too," I replied. "He took his time to make that decision, though…"

"Oh…?"

"In fact, he almost put a curse on you, but changed his mind at the last minute," I enjoyed teasing him along with a hint about his effect on so many people already in his short miserable life.

"I know I have not been a great guy. But I'm trying to make a better use of myself and my life, I hope sincerely," Darren said.

"I hope so too," I replied with a chuckle. "I've tried really hard, especially the last six months, so that you get this big chance to redeem yourself."

"Thanks... I'll try really hard!" he said giddily.

"This is really your last chance, Darren," I replied.

"Okay, I think so, too... So, how is Dervish Ali?"

"Not so good, Darren. He is dying."

"Oh, I'm sorry," he replied.

"It's probably unfair to say this, but after my last meeting with him, a few time I've gotten a sense that perhaps he'd put a curse on Mahroo," I whispered to Darren.

My comment jolted Darren, as if he already knew about the curse that had killed Mahroo. He did not even look into my eyes.

"He also told me about attacking you in Evin after you had confessed about your affection for Mahroo. Is that true?" I asked.

Darren's face showed his turmoil. "Yes. He almost killed me with his bare hands. He was really strong for such an old man…"

"Did he put a curse on Mahroo?" I asked abruptly after my sly prelude to get a straight answer out of him.

"I don't recall," he replied, yet his eyes betrayed him—that big liar! So, what had killed Mahroo, after all: Dervish's curse, Mahtab's jealousy, or Vincent's games? Had that cripple war veteran in the rehabilitation center been responsible alone or just a means?

"We've hurt one another, even that poor Bijan," I said. "He'd even bought two of your paintings from the gallery in Tehran."

"How do you know?" Darren asked.

"Gallery owner told me. He'd been following your situation and informing his clients, including Bijan, after I'd told him you were shot," I said.

"Were they all hoping that I die soon so that my paintings' values might shoot up?"

"Maybe... He said he'd informed Bijan of your recovery, too. That was something I'd been curious about for sometime myself. He also said that a reporter in Vancouver has been writing about all these events regularly. Was he right?"

"Yes... Thanks, Reza, for everything you've done for us."

"Still, we all must watch for Bijan's possible revenge," I said.

"Really...? Mahtab has also kept saying that he's so spiteful."

I nodded and then asked, "Are you excited about your kids?"

"Oh, yes, of course… I'm dying to see my sons."

Epilogue
Gibberish Chitchat

Life is painful and pointless in general, gets baffling and challenging on occasions, but can also become idyllic during some fleeting periods of our lives. This revered resignation after decades of struggles, triumphs, and reflections helps me ward off many moments of relapse and suicidal ideas. The irony of recent, weird love affairs around me also pervades a crude sense of hope about luck and joy erupting erratically like another mystery of the universe to muse and amuse ourselves. The oddly mixed large family around Darren and Reza remains a perfect, *enviable* clue. Still, my morbid destiny and mood obstruct my shoddy efforts to embrace this corny mumbo-jumbo regarding God's wisdom as a divine faith, not to mention my old grudge against hope! Instead, Reza's remark last year about life being a humiliating, exhausting journey still competes with some positive viewpoints in my brain. *Ironically, my confidants have heightened my cynicism, too!*

Sima, her mom, and Darius have also arrived from Iran, now giving Darren the joy of hugging both his sons together, while Mahtab and Sima appear quite friendly to everyone's amazement.

Besides Mahtab's fine nature, I guess women detect each other's moods and obsessions fast intuitively; and that is why Mahtab does not feel threatened by Sima. Actually, Sima's infatuation for Darren appears to have faded away. Instead, she now seems quite taken with Reza whose fascination with her is supported by his hints about getting cosy with her—maybe after getting Darren's blessing first, *this time*. Mahtab has noticed this cute revelation, too, and welcomes Reza's chance to settle down soon as well. Reza's mom, on the other hand, monitors the situation tensely and rolls her eyes sporadically.

Surely, the ambience feels odd with all these swift connections and plans among a bunch of goofy characters mixing naturally like they had grown up together. The jubilant crowd in the house exchanging love, making noise, and laughing on top of babies' howling is simply amazing. Darren who has never had a proper family is possibly most enchanted. His fortune and euphoria after years of struggle with existentialism seems surreal now. In return, his infinite kindness to me still energizes me during my gloomy downfall. The miraculous hoopla around Darren has helped me handle my dilemmas rather easier, bear my family's tyranny, and remain active, although I am mostly alone now in his quiet, old suite that I might buy for myself soon. I am also thrilled to be the lucky person closing this book of love stories erupting amidst endless family turmoil. Maybe I get a chance to write the sequel to this love story, too, if a million people ask me in the coming years and I am still alive. *Hopefully, the new tales would also prove the absurdity of my sardonic cynicism in these final pages, after all!*

So romantically, I like good endings for all love adventures, too, but cannot forget the realistic reflections and findings about life and relationships that we three eccentric buddies had pained one another with for years. My fresh experiences and research supports my scepticism about the stability of our fortunes and the chance of these mesmerized characters living happily ever after. Cagily, I wonder how long this romantic serenity would last.

Then, I feel sad about my negativism, hide my silly thoughts, and pray that only my old-age traumas are stirring my paranoia about new revelations ruining the peace we are enjoying nowadays. I feel also uneasy about writing this rather unsettling Epilogue for such a wonderfully ended love story. Maybe Reza and Darren made a mistake choosing me for this final reality check due to their rising family obligations, besides their fear of jinxing their fates by any rumination. In fact, they seem adamant these days to avoid the kind of thoughtful chitchats about life that they loved to raise in the past frequently! Nevertheless, they must have known that asking a realist like me to do a final recap was risky. Leaving this delicate task to me also indicates how we humans usually make further and bigger mistakes when family responsibilities leave little time and appetite for reflection.

Accordingly, you may wish to skip the rest of this evocative Epilogue that mostly show my crabby conclusions about life and people with no effect on the ending of this book. Only if you are keen to listen still some more to a grumpy old man's whining and learn what happens to us when we age, be my guest, keep on reading the remaining few pages…

Of course, it is crucial to acknowledge first the way Darren's good fate has saved my life as well as Reza's in a timely, magical way. We both were vulnerable and suicidal when Darren *wisely* used the chance of bringing us together to share his friendship, family, and fortune. Especially, after causing so much hassle for Reza over the years, it seems he has made it up to him perfectly in many ways and Reza is happy and grateful, too, especially for bringing Sima into his life.

What really goes on in their heads nowadays is hard to guess, yet we tell one another often, like a ritual perhaps, that we must count our blessings, while they *still* treat me quite cordially.

"You're now part of this crazy family, too, T.J.," Darren often tells me with humour to make me relax when he calls and insists to join them or when I say I do not wish to bother them too much.

"You're not as much of a bother as you think," he adds.

The irony of this full turnaround haunts me, though, when I recall the times I had been a rather happily married, mature man indulging two carefree bachelors wandering around the world helplessly *or hopefully,* in rotation or simultaneously, trying to find a mate. Now they are settled with large, cohesive families, while I am staggering alone and fearing my fate if Darren and Reza also lose interest in me or get overwhelmed with their growing families' infinite demands. Life's games and ironies are frightening and funny in rotation or simultaneously as well!

Sometimes, we also try to replicate our old habit of reflecting on our evolving fates and philosophies as three pensive friends. Some of you might have appreciated the gist of our dialogues and associated with our sentiments about the vanity of human efforts and existence as well. At least our gibberish chitchats have been reflective, focused, sincere, and infrequent, although at the end they have still often felt as futile as life itself. I go nuts witnessing most people these days wasting their precious times and energies to talk nonsense and lie constantly in person or on the phone just to go through another day, to impress or fool one another, soothe their pains, or make more money. Why are we so persistent to abuse our neglected brains so much with trivia and controversy? *What a pathetic species we have become!*

I do not know what Darren and Reza have learned through their reflections and how they can apply their divine beliefs within their busy family settings. Personally, my ongoing reflections and discoveries about myself and life are still the only way to satiate my spirit. I might share more of those findings with you later. However, a basic wisdom I hope to apply forever is that although my *life without a wife* feels wobbly and weird, I am quite certain that *wife without a life* is ten times more humiliating and painful for any wise man. Anyway, I just try to stay healthy and content through reflection and putting the strings of words together while basking in my rising writing aptitude and projects.

Mrs. Stanley also visits me sometimes when I take a break from my frantic writing, which she insists to read and I refuse for many reasons. She is a broken soul, too, but I am getting used to her, which shows the depth of my loneliness and despair, despite the few good things happening around me. Now, I count her as a blessing, too, without mentioning our meetings to Darren to avoid giving him more ammunition for teasing me.

Reza and Darren's visit two nights ago got heated especially. They came by mostly to smoke pot after a year, take a break from their family commotion, and fool around with me in the privacy of my apartment. The only drawback of Darren's sudden duty to run a large family is that we hardly kid around when I visit them. We cannot relax in our manly mood, smoke pot, and talk silly like before. Ironically, with fewer issues to nag about these days, we get bored and crave our old gibberish chitchats, *while we can!* Yet, my heart breaks a little when Darren speaks about death, particularly mine, so freely as the final phase of our friendship and smoking ritual.

"We'll smoke joint secretly while you're still around," Darren insists, as if doing me a favour before quitting as soon as I die or their kids grow up. All good things end, we agree, including my mostly aimless existence nowadays. He is probably only joking, yet I am not thrilled about this particular topic!

Not his jokes about death per se, but the notion of my looming end is oddly unsettling! Now, I guess I hate to die before grasping a plausible view of life and God somewhat. I prefer doing it on my own, instead of hoping to ask Him some silly questions in person! And most likely He refusing to answer even then, in heaven!

Anyhow, a few puffs of a potent pot ignited our light chitchat towards higher domains inevitable during such occasions.

"So, how do you like this building?" Darren asked.

"I like it. But it feels spooky and quiet without you around."

"Yeah…? Really…?" Darren asked with surprise, probably wondering if I had meant to imply something funny or sinister.

"Yeah… Your absence feels weird!" I replied truthfully.

"Does she say that, too?" he asked.

"Who?" I asked jokingly as I knew whom he was implying.

"You know who…!" he mumbled, stoned so fast already.

"She misses you, always asking me about you and sending her regards. Should I call and ask her to come over to see you?"

"Who're you guys talking about?" Reza asked.

"Mrs. Stanley, of course," Darren replied before turning to me. "So, you have her number and everything, ha, you devil?"

"Yes, I do. Should I call her?"

"Is she still asking to see your gun?" Darren said giddily.

"Not only that, she wants to read my writings, too...," I replied. "But there's no point teasing her. She's very lonely too."

"I know, T.J. Why are you so grouchy tonight?" Darren said.

"It's a pity young people nowadays are so impatient and rude sometimes with the elderly." I said, wondering if my testiness was another clue about my rapid, untimely aging and looming death.

"Sorry, T.J.," Darren said. "But you seem to be hiding some secrets from us! What's going on?"

"Nobody realizes our despair, especially without a family or a mate," I said testily, wondering if in fact imagining and fearing death were the main causes of old people's grumpiness?—rather than merely a natural symptom of aging!

"Now, you're starting to sound in love, defending her with such energy at the cost of irritating us?" Darren replied giddily in a soft tone. "But you know that I like and respect both of you."

"Thanks, I'll tell her. And sorry for being testy tonight," I said, hoping to end this silly conversation.

"I didn't mean to upset you, either, old man!" Darren said.

"Don't worry... I think I'm a bit sensitive these days," I said.

"No, you're right, T.J. We usually see the elderly as grouchy, senile people," Darren replied. "My dad has proven it, too."

"Exactly the way I'm sounding and proving it right now."

"It's all because life is so hectic and people are too stressed to bear others enough. That's all...," Reza said, trying to calm things —the role I used to play before when Darren and Reza argued.

"True... Emotional and financial issues drain our energy and compassion to remain tactful," Darren said.

"Still, ignoring or mocking elderly is awful," I said, amazed of my stamina tonight to exhibit the world's consensus about old folks' grouchiness. Despite Darren's provocation, my tenacity to prove this point tonight felt most admirable! Maybe pot had made me sound so heartbroken tonight. It usually makes me candid and sentimental for no goddamn good purpose.

"We all sound silly tonight, but finding you a wife may slow down your senility," Reza said with a giggle.

"That's what my mother keeps suggesting, too," I replied.

"I bet she likes to find a good one for you herself," Reza said.

"Of course... It's typical of Persian mothers," I replied.

"That's right. My mother has been torturing me to find a wife, but now she frowns when I mention Sima."

"That's exactly what my mom did to stop me from marrying Feri, but now is dying to find me a wife just for highlighting my idiocy forever about ignoring her initial advice."

"Anyway, find yourself a mate soon before turning against us young people completely," Darren said with a giggle.

"What're you busy with these days, T.J.?" Reza asked to change the subject again, I guess.

"Well, I'm writing about the last chapter of my meagre life."

"That's probably why you're so sensitive, then," Darren said. "Don't think too much about dying, old man…"

"My nasty will is also causing me a lot of grief and tension," I said with a sigh.

"I told you to forget it before going totally mad," Reza said.

"So, what new trick you're cooking now?" Darren asked.

"It's secret for now... But it seems I should prepare my final resting place myself as well," I replied, hating my loose tongue.

"Resting place? What the hell is that all about?" Darren asked.

"You can read all about it in *My Lousy Life Stories* novel—in the last chapter—when it's published."

Reza and Darren burst into laughter and I joined them.

"So, you're gonna build your coffin or dig your grave yourself to save money?" Reza asked.

"No, it's actually for wasting lots of money... to build a fancy mausoleum for myself if I find a good location for it."

"This is a strong pot, for sure," Darren said. "Do you smoke every night, T.J., maybe with Mrs. Stanley?"

"Senility goads crazy acts, but I should build this mausoleum also because I can't rely on my family even for burying me. I fear they may even vandalize, or piss on, my grave if it's in the open."

"Let's stop smoking for good after this last joint," Darren said.

"I knew you won't take me seriously," I shrieked.

"I do... So when will it be ready?" Reza asked.

"In two years or so. But don't tell anybody. It's secret until I die," I said with a giggle, while they kept laughing.

"You're really serious, ha?" Darren asked.

"Yes. If I put walls around it, I'll call it T.J. Mahal with a huge plaque at the entrance," I said and we laughed again.

"Mahal in Persian means 'place'," Reza said to Darren before turning to me, "Have your statue built for the entrance, too."

"So, we can go to *your place*, this T.J. Mahal, and smoke pot before and after you die, eh?" Darren asked.

"Yes, I'll give you guys keys to come around after I'm gone."

"Who else is gonna have a key? Your kids?" Reza asked.

"Nobody else, I guess," I replied. "But statue is a good idea!"

"If you build it, we will come...," Reza said giddily. "Darren and I will visit you often when you're gone and laugh about these crazy times and all these gibberish we exchange after a joint."

"You have any other friends these days, T.J.?" Darren asked.

"No. I had many even here in Vancouver, but not now. They all started hating my guts and I couldn't bear their hypocrisy and pretensions any longer," I replied.

"I know what you mean!" Reza said, peering at Darren. "I'm already tired of the way people and friends act, even at my age."

"You see, Feri was a whore flirting with everybody, but my old friends competing to take advantage of our obvious alienation and seduce her looked just too pathetic."

"Were they that obvious?" Darren asked.

"Oh, yes… Even worse, the way they peeped at me timidly or stealthily with a mix of guilt, spite, arrogance, and pity for me was just too humiliating but hilarious," I said.

"This time, I know what you mean!" Darren said sarcastically —a repeat of Reza's comment a second earlier—gazing at him. "Do his words ring any bells in your head?"

Reza peered down in silence, looking reluctant to open the old can of worms about Erica incident for the hundredth time, usually when smoking pot. Then, he swiftly looked up with glee to make a retaliatory comment that sounded so timely and wily, "I wonder how poor Bijan is feeling these days! Do you still remember him, Darren, and *why you've been two bitter enemies*?"

"Yes… Honestly, I'm ashamed of our gender becoming so helpless in the hands of women," Darren replied.

"At least you've finally found the right mate," I told Darren with envy. "You're *one lucky man*."

"Anyway, building T.J. Mahal is a superb idea," Reza said.

"Read how the idea dawned on me in *The Final Plan* in my novel. It'll sound hilarious, except to my ungrateful family."

"It'll still sound crazy to people, too," Reza said. "But overall, I like your stamina to stick it to your family, especially Feri."

"Still I suffer the most," I said. "I hate both my spite and envy sometimes towards some lucky families."

"You do?" Darren asks fretfully, mainly about my envy, I bet.

"You have only three daughters, T.J., right?" Reza asked.

"I thought you knew!?" I replied.

"I just recalled how odd and mysterious you'd sounded when I asked you this question a few years ago. Then, we weren't close enough to ask what you meant."

"Did I say, 'As far as I know'?"

"Yes, I remember now… So what'd you mean?"

"I've often doubted my kids' legitimacy, especially these days, but I may also have a few sons who don't even know I exist."

"Are you now inventing these stories just to compete with me even on this matter?" Darren asked.

"No. My youth had been a bit crazy, too," I said nostalgically. "But you've been luckier on this matter as well, Darren—to find and boldly disclose your lovechild's existence." He ignored me.

"That's another side of you we discover tonight," Reza said.

"Actually, I have strong hunches and info about a son at least and feel bad for not seeing or getting to know him," I said.

"You're really getting out of control," Darren blurted giddily.

"At least I've had some fun pretending to have a wise son in my novel. Mixing facts and fiction is what I like about novels."

"Any chance I am one of your sons?" Reza asked wittily.

"I doubt it, although I've always liked you like a son... I even gave you a chance to be my son-in-law at least and you refused like an idiot, but it's still not too late," I replied and we laughed.

"Still, no thanks... But why do you doubt your kids' origin?" Reza asked slyly in hopes of juicier secrets or laughing matters.

"Mostly because I think if they had just even 2% of my genes, they would've been much better humans," I replied seriously.

"You've sure sounded oddly dramatic tonight," Darren said.

"Sadly, I might've raised a few bastards with horrible genes belonging to Feri and some perverts, while missing the joy and outcome of my splendid genes nurturing some fantastic boys out there with weird last names, whom I'll never see. What a life!"

"Anyway, go build your mausoleum quickly before you have a heart attack and die from all these silly thoughts," Reza said.

"Although I might outlive you guys," I said teasingly.

"You think so?" Reza asked with a grimace.

"No, Feri thinks so," I replied.

"She said that?" Reza asked.

"Yes. Once I overheard her whining to her mother about my family's high life expectancy. She said, 'He's not even gonna die soon. He's gonna live a thousand years like his damn parents.'"

"I bet you'll never run out of stories about Feri," Reza said.

"I have 20 years of funny and humiliating memories about her idiocy. But an angel told me an amazing secret recently, too."

"Now angels talk to you, too? What'd she say?" Reza asked.

"She said, as soon as Satan realized God had a son who was preaching and saving people, he decided to react before Jesus could purify humans for good and run him out of business. He began building a daughter to charm and dissuade Jesus. But this project got too complicated and took him a millennium to perfect, and by then Jesus was crucified. Satan was sad for having such a fully wicked daughter wandering around uselessly, except that her showiness and shallowness, revealing her lack of pride, had driven Satan crazy! So confused and furious, he couldn't even choose a name for her.

"Anyhow, another millennium of serious thinking and teaching her his biggest tricks, while getting tired of her constant nagging, Satan decided to call her Feri and make her my wife to torture me. He'd either gotten angry about my war against him to reform myself at last or hoped Feri can revive my old talent for devilry."

"It sounds like a plausible theory to me," Reza said giddily.

"No, it's not a theory… It's a true story," I replied seriously. "I've received firsthand info and evidence about it."

"You have thousands of real stories about Feri to entertain the world and still make up more tales, too," Darren said giddily.

"As I said, it's a real tale that the whole world must know. In fact, Satan had been so pissed off about wasting two millenniums on building Feri after realizing that humans' inherently flawed nature can't be reformed even if God had hundred sons and sent them all to the earth. God couldn't rely on humans to correct His design error even if He went to New York Himself. The angel revealed that Jesus' efforts have helped purify at best a few dozen humans in the last two millenniums," I said and we laughed.

"She's right," Reza said. "It's strange how human brain can invent such incredible ideas and achieve huge scientific goals, but it's incapable of learning the right stuff to help humanity."

"Yes. After all these great prophets, gurus, and philosophers, we're still so stupid," Darren added.

"In fact, it feels so weird how we humans insist on sabotaging our existential needs, often intentionally," Reza said.

"Especially by marrying the Devil's daughter," I said.

"Still, wasting so much time and energy to punish your family feels absurd, T.J. Is it really worth it, you think?" Darren asked.

"Yes, it is... I'd never imagined reprisal could be so much fun, despite its horrendous pain for people like me, too," I replied.

"But also making us laugh now and later in your mausoleum. We'll try to keep your memory alive after you die," Darren said.

"And I'll try to send clues from the heaven in return," I said.

"Just let's hope your theatrical final plan won't drive you nuts before completing it," Reza said.

"Too late, I'd say!" Darren added. "He's starting to sound weird and scaring me like my dad."

"Well, I'm getting old and grouchy, too, I know," I replied.

"You also look older with that white beard," Darren said.

"Nobody realizes what I'm feeling and saying these days," I said testily while loathing my inability to control my oblivious whining. *What's really wrong with me tonight!*

"Why did you grow a beard, anyway?" Reza asked.

"I did it two years ago to irritate Feri for a short while only," I said. "But now, I don't have an incentive or energy to shave."

"You see, you're confessing how you've been driving that poor woman nuts yourself," Darren said.

"Maybe... But I was about to shave it when she started going around and telling everyone that my beard showed my lunacy on top of my declining hygiene. So, I couldn't shave it anymore, could I?"

"Yeah, you're nuts… It's now official," Darren said.

"Dye it a little at least," Reza said.

"That'll look even sillier and a total waste of time," I replied.

"You sure sound grouchier when we smoke pot, T.J.," Reza said as if confirming Darren's point a few minutes earlier.

"No more pot for you…!" Darren said and we giggled.

"So how is your dad these days? Are you in contact with that poor man?" I asked Darren, hoping to cool down myself at least, while irritating him a bit as well.

"The same way, like you, still insisting that I go live close to him in Toronto, but he can't decide about coming to Vancouver himself. I don't know what I can really do for him, but the way you talked tonight has been really helpful for my decision."

"I'd hoped my grumpiness would be good for something, but not for ruining your dad's tiny chance for your mercy."

"Yes, T.J., your record whining has made me feel a bit guilty, but also rethink the idea of pushing him to come to Vancouver."

"Don't you think you should still help him?" I asked curtly. "You just confirmed my point about the youths' cruelty."

"And tonight you proved the reason! How much energy and patience you think even the youths have?" Darren asked.

"Gosh, now I must feel guilty for your poor dad, too," I said with a sigh. "He's probably gonna die alone like me."

"You guys think I'm cruel with my dad?" Darren asked.

"I do. I know how lousy he feels," I said and Reza nodded.

"Okay, then. I'll bring him to Vancouver to enjoy his lunacy together, especially his bizarre, new sense of divinity."

"Fine, maybe he can enlighten us, too," I said giddily.

"At least he can join you and Mrs. Stanley to start the loonies club and conspire against me," Darren replied.

"Well, we might actually get along nicely," I replied solemnly before an idea for retaliation attacked my brain, "Are Sima and Mahtab getting along still?" I asked him with a moronic giggle, as if itching to agitate him the way he had teased me all night, but regretted my silliness right away. This damn pot kills my senses nowadays. I had never felt so cynical and critical one moment and so light-hearted and silly the next.

"Yes, my dear Mahtab is very kind to Sima," Darren replied.

"I'm so proud of my beautiful, open-minded sister, taking care of everybody, especially those three kids," Reza said.

"It's a pity, but maybe a good thing, that Sima and Darius are going to live with Reza," Darren said.

"Oh, are they?" I asked.

"Yes," Reza said with glee.

"You see how Reza always steals my women, T.J.?"

"You two are the weirdest friends I've ever had," I replied.

"At least I'm safe with Mahtab, *I hope!*" Darren said giddily after he took a long drag on the pot and passed it on to Reza. "That was a big factor when I decided to marry Mahtab."

"Do you wanna irritate Feri even more, T.J.?" Reza asked.

"Sure... Do you have any good ideas?" I asked.

"Donate a bunch of benches in your memory to all the parks in Vancouver, too," Reza replied.

"Wow… That's a great idea! How much are they?"

"Less than a thousand dollar, I imagine," Reza replied.

"Like I weren't crazy enough, you guys invent more amazing tactics. I love it!" I said and we laughed more about all those odd ideas apparently floating in midair inside that marijuana smoke. It was surely quite an inspirational joint! *I wondered how we could think of any good ideas and do any philosophizing in the future if we were planning to quit pot?*

"Glad to be of assistance," Reza replied with a chuckle.

"Okay then, let's put hundred memorial benches in Vancouver parks, but five or six in each North Vancouver park."

"Don't you wanna go national or international?" Reza asked.

"I'll think about it… Is it possible?" I asked mockingly.

"I guess so…," Reza blurted with laughter. "Then your family can't stop basking in your memory any park they go to."

"Not even in Europe…!" I replied gaily.

"Make sure to write a bunch of truly memorable tributes for the plaques on the benches," Darren added.

"Yes, a big variety of funny one, to be different in each park."

"Just fifty variations are enough," Darren said. "Also write your Satan story on a bunch of benches in a particular park."

"That's true! Satan's role in this mess needs a special note."

"Oh, boy, that's a lot of extra work you must do now for these benches alone," Reza said.

"Well, can you help me with this bench project, especially for making sure it's done properly when I'm dead?" I asked Reza.

"Maybe… I like to help if I can…," Reza replied.

"Great! Will you kindly execute my will, too?" I asked Reza, as Darren went to the washroom.

"It's a big chore, but I'm also afraid of your daughters trying to kill me anytime I administer one of your tricky wishes."

"Actually, I'm afraid they might seduce and soften you to get their inheritance faster."

"You think I'm loose and easy around women like Darren?"

"I'll tell him what you just said," I said as Darren returned.

"Tell me what?" Darren asked.

"Should I tell him?" I asked Reza.

"I don't care… That's the truth and he's caused me enough torture for years," Reza replied.

"I'm glad to have friends like you, almost as crazy as I am."

"At least you have a creative passion and willpower to follow it, plus a chance for solitude," Darren said pensively and rather solemnly. "I need a big push and time myself to start painting."

"Having a big family has its drawbacks, ha?" I asked with an ironic satisfaction. "There're always tough trade-offs in life, ha?"

"You're right. Mahtab and the kids keep me busy and happy so much these days to consider any new painting project."

"Is that right?" I asked sarcastically with envy.

"Yeah...," Darren replied with a sigh. "This is a big dilemma I must sort out eventually, somehow, I hope!"

Yeah…! It sounded like a huge dilemma to me, too. But, we must wait for my next novel to see if he succeeds! I mused, while wrestling with some rowdy thoughts for a few seconds.

Hiding my cynicism about life, family, and hope from people has been exhausting and tough, while I have tried to stay grateful as a part of Darren's curious circle. I hope he never gets tired of his family, their serenity lasts forever, and nobody jinxes him the way I was cursed a lifetime. Still, witnessing his family mixing so naturally compared with mine, which is totally disintegrated and contacts me never, makes it difficult not to be cynical and a little envious, *only occasionally*! I am a lonely, selfish human, after all, with lots of goodwill and love for Darren's family. Ironically and luckily, my subtle envy mainly triggers the notion of good things happening to me, too, although the prospect feels slim.

"So, your writings are progressing nicely, ha?" Reza asked me to break the sudden silence and pensive mood.

"Yes. In fact, I think nobody can be a great writer without long solitude. I could've not finished anything useful, otherwise."

"Yeah, keep at it to stay healthy, too. It'll be a big catastrophe to die before finishing your will and mausoleum, not to mention your literary masterpieces!" Darren said.

"Do you have anything ready to read?" Reza asked.

"No… Maybe in a few months," I replied.

"I can hardly wait to read this *Final Plan* of yours," Reza said.

"I know I've nagged a lot recently about family issues, but I like to clarify something important," I said seriously.

"What's that?" Reza asked.

"That I'm not proud of my spite contrary to my words tonight and in my writings. In fact, I'm embarrassed and disgusted by it."

"You are?" Darren asked with surprise.

"Yes, when my logic and emotions clash they cause pain."

"We thought you were enjoying all these plots and plans."

"I'm not. Reprisal against people you love hurts. In fact, I've been so mad at my spiteful plans I have felt obliged to analyse and write about this issue to calm my psyche. Now I think I must even develop a theory around the whole thing."

"A theory for your spite?" Reza asked.

"Yes, I must analyse my psyche and justify my feelings and plans together. How can I do what I must do? I'm in limbo."

"Wow… You've now really confused me, too," Darren said.

"You see, it's both necessary and hard to reconcile my urge for retribution with my supposedly selfless love for my kids."

"Can you elaborate?" Darren asked.

"Most parents, like me, are naturally selfless towards our kids, but spite and reprisal reflect selfishness, which some of us also try to replace with selflessness to reach enlightenment," I replied.

"So, spite ruins both your goals of remaining a selfless parent and an enlightened individual," Darren said.

"Yes... But reprisal against tyranny might be justified as well, mostly as a principle, besides offering a psychological relief."

"Absolutely...! Your retribution sounds a matter of principle to me, too," Darren said mockingly.

"Still, spite and selflessness crash and bother my psyche," I said. "I wonder if I'm just boosting my selfishness at the cost of selflessness and enlightenment."

"Your dilemma is also bizarre," Darren said.

"How?" I asked.

"Spite chokes our logic and virtues no matter how much you try to justify it, but confusing a supposedly spiritual man's zeal for selflessness is a weird, embarrassing twist," Darren replied.

"It seems you should give up one of them, T.J.," Reza added.

"No, I'm still hoping to build a theory to justify reprisal when our selfless love for our kids faces such high disappointment and evil?" I said. "I think I can and must build this theory, although don't know how yet."

"I don't think you can mix these two conflicting urges," Reza said and Darren nodded. "You must choose, T.J."

"I disagree... My patient, reflective approach is by itself a promising clue about this possibility! I can't give up selflessness and modesty, but must justify reprisal against evil as a principle or an art for self-expression and self-preservation," I said giddily.

"Still, T.J., building such a theory feels ludicrous, no matter how creative or sneaky you try to be," Reza said seriously.

"Why? Don't you trust my genius?" I asked jokily and we laughed, while our dispute's seriousness felt amusing, too.

"Despite your renowned genius, trying to push spite into your selflessness and enlightenment regimen would sound hypocritical and foolish even if you can invent a theory," Reza replied.

"Well, it's got to be done as a matter of life and death! Or else I can't look into the mirror every day and live with myself," I said solemnly. Of course, I had my own doubts about the chance of effecting this tough marriage just for building a theory, although the foundation for this research seemed realistic.

"Let me ask a hypothetical question, then," Reza said.

"Okay…?"

"What if you can't build your alleged theory and must choose? Will you sacrifice many years of efforts to build your spirit and selflessness just for pursuing your spiteful Final Plan during the last years of your life?"

"Let's hope it doesn't come to that... But if it does, I'm afraid I must choose reprisal. At least that's how I feel these days."

"Good for you, that's what I'd do as well," Darren said.

"But I'm still hopeful to build my theory in time before being forced to ruin a decade of self-cleansing," I replied with a giggle.

"Well, good luck. You may reach a new height of insanity or enlightenment," Reza said with a sign of resignation. "But hoping to mix spite, science, and spirituality sounds ridiculous to me, on top of risking your chance of going to heaven."

"We'll see… But you guys can help me build this theory a bit faster… Will you help?" I asked.

"We can discuss it further in our next meeting if we're giving up smoking joint after tonight," Darren said.

"Don't you want to wait until I die to quit?" I asked giddily.

"Not if Feri says you'll live too long…," Reza said. "Besides, we're talking more nonsense anytime we smoke. Let's close this chapter in our lives now." We nodded agreeably.

"Yeah, we must now focus on our kids," Darren said sternly.

"I wonder how you guys can think without Marijuana after all these years...," I said teasingly. "But at least remember the two main bases of spite theory."

"What're they?" Darren asked.

"First, I think my spite has a logical limit and is necessary as a principle, compared with most people's urge to break someone's heart deliberately merely for personal satisfaction beyond what's justified as a principle. Second, reprisal against Devil's daughter and grandkids might be a holy war, in fact, rather than a sin."

"In that case, who are we to stop you?" Reza said teasingly.

"Actually, I often wonder if even Devil is as evil as Feri, let alone a so-called human allegedly capable of using her brain to distinguish bad from good for her own sake at least, maybe by learning some basic ethics."

"Are your kids also as bad as Feri?" Darren asked mockingly.

"Sadly, yes! It seems they know it, too, which is amazing."

"They've admitted it?"

"I was shocked once when Rose stated bluntly, 'I know what kind of a devil I am.' I couldn't say whether she was sorry and sad about it or only trying to scare and warn me."

"Gosh, T.J.… Are you kidding us?" Reza asked.

"No, I'm not... By the way, I'm also working on a few other revolutionary theories that support the upcoming spite theory."

"What other revolutionary theories?" Reza asked mockingly.

"It seems that parents' selfless love is in itself the least useful type of affection."

"Why?"

"The more I've loved my daughters and told them so openly, so unlike most Persian parents, the less they've cared for me, and actually hated me more. Is that weird or what?" I said with pain.

They burst into laughter and Reza said, "Yeah, that sounds like a strong theory. You'd probably have a better chance proving this one than the one for reconciling spite and selflessness."

"Still, I feel sad, instead of satisfied, for what I should do to my kids purely for principle," I said with tears in my eyes.

"Maybe you should've given them more money instead of selfless love," Darren said with laughter.

"In fact, I did that too, but they just became more demanding and showed more apathy. Generosity is also useless," I replied.

"That's another good theory in itself, then," Reza said.

"Yes, let's file this theory, too. Then again, my family seems so drastically abnormal... I gave them lots of love, money, and ultimatums, and none of them work on those brainless people."

"Still count your blessings, T.J.," Darren said.

"On what ground?" I asked.

"On the ground that at least your family hasn't tried to kill you yet, like it happens frequently nowadays," Darren replied.

"We can't be sure yet, and I shouldn't put down my guards. Still, it's sad and painful to live like this with an incomplete spite theory and pretend to be thankful as well," I replied with angst. "But your point brings another theory to my mind."

"Still another theory?" Reza asked with a chuckle.

"Yes, it's in relation to Feri's theory that I'd either kill myself or die from loneliness if they ignored and loathed me."

"Do you think your family wants you dead just out of hatred or only for getting your money?" Reza asked.

"Both... Her theory holds water, too, in general," I said.

"But not in your case?"

"No. Sadly, the more wicked they've become and want me dead, the keener I've felt to live longer merely for enjoying their frustration," I said. "Although maximizing my health with so much exercise and diet is taking a lot of my time and mind, too, not to mention my grudge against being per se."

"Gosh, T.J., you've developed a million theories around your marital life, besides pissing all over Feri's theory," Reza said.

"Yeah, T.J., we can safely say that you're the biggest family philosopher that ever existed," Darren said.

"And the testiest," I replied. "But Socrates started this whole shenanigan over two millenniums ago!"

"Will you at least leave poor Socrates alone... out of your sad life and stories?" Reza said wittily and we laughed.

"How are the kids and the rest of the family, Darren," I asked.

"Boys are growing up and Nazi enjoys playing with them."

"So everything is great?" I asked stupidly, though I had luckily at least stopped my loose mouth in time from adding "still."

"Oh, yes," Darren replied. "It's just an incredible experience watching my sons grow up—my rising Persian Suns."

www.ingramcontent.com/pod-product-compliance
Lightning Source LLC
LaVergne TN
LVHW010626110826
845149LV00014B/2787

* 9 7 8 1 9 8 8 3 5 1 1 5 5 *